MW00762652

The Crusade
Against Darkness

The Crusade Against Darkness

John DeFilippis

The Crusade Against Darkness
Copyright © 2014 John DeFilippis
Published by Crossroad Press

All rights reserved. No part of this book may be reproduced (except
for inclusion in reviews), disseminated or utilized in any form or
by any means, electronic or mechanical, including photocopying,
recording, or in any information storage and retrieval system, or
the Internet/World Wide Web without written permission from the
author or publisher.

Printed in the United States of America

The Crusade Against Darknessn
John DeFilippis

1. Title 2. Author 3. Fiction

ISBN 978-1-941408-11-7

Part I

Chapter One

As Solitus galloped toward Mavinor's West Gate, a myriad of thoughts raced through his mind. Given his conversation with Bovillus about the young scribe's research findings, he was now certain that Gobius was dead. Still he held out hope that Silex and the rest of the royal guards had survived, even if the rescue attempt failed. The entire situation begged the question of who was now in charge in Mavinor. Had Pachaias assumed power? Did Sicarius seize the throne by force? Or was someone else chosen to rule? And of course Solitus could not stop thinking about Cedrus, the cousin with whom he shared a special bond. He prayed to The Author that Cedrus and Minstro had not walked into a trap when they returned to Mavinor, and that they were still alive as well.

When he came within a hundred yards or so of the city walls, Solitus slowed his pace. He could see that the guards at the gate were now aware of his presence, and he didn't want to alarm them in any way. So he coaxed his mount until the horse had settled into a leisurely walk, and raised both of his hands to show that he was unarmed. The guards came out toward him flashing their swords,

1

and as he looked up at the watchtower he could now see the shadowy figure of an archer with his bow drawn.

"Who goes there?" one of the guards yelled out.

"Solitus of Mavinor," Solitus responded.

"Solitus?" the other guard said. "You are the cousin of Tonitrus and Cedrus, are you not?"

"Yes," Solitus answered.

"And the one who was recently offered a chance to run through the gauntlet in order to earn a place in Mavinor's army, along with your sister. Is that right?" the guard asked.

"Yes, that is right," Solitus said. "I am the one you speak of."

"Hand over any weapons you are carrying," the other guard said imperiously. "You'll be coming with us to the palace so that King Cidivus can decide what to do with you."

Solitus was completely shocked when he heard that Cidivus was now King of Mavinor. He tried to conceal this from the guards and willingly handed over his sword.

"Where are you coming from?" the guard asked.

"I was taken to Xamnon at the orders of King Gobius," Solitus responded. "I didn't want to go, but I was forced to leave Mavinor against my will. Now I have escaped and returned home, because I know this is where I truly belong."

"Do you?" the other guard asked. "Your beloved king is dead, along with all of his royal guards who foolishly tried to rescue him from his fate, including your dear cousins. Now a new reign has begun, and you say you want to be part of it?"

Solitus was heartbroken when he heard about the deaths of Cedrus and Tonitrus. He wondered who was responsible—who it was that dealt the lethal blow to each one of them—and promised himself right then and there that he would avenge their deaths. But again he did everything he could to hide his feelings, and somehow managed to wear a plain expression on his face. Anything less would heighten their suspicions and cause them to question his sincerity in joining the new regime. "Yes," he finally said. "I do."

"You do realize that he might have you killed as well, don't you?" the guard said. "In the end, you might suffer the same fate as your king, your cousins, and your friends."

"I will take my chances," Solitus responded. "I am a non-believer now, and I am ready to join your ranks. That is why I left Xamnon and have come back to Mavinor. I want to serve the new king any way that I can. Surely he'd rather have me in his service than carry out my execution. He is too wise to allow my talents to go to waste."

"We'll see about that," the guard said as he cuffed Solitus' wrists. Then he grabbed the young man forcefully by the arm and began escorting him through the gate.

At the Praetorium, the tribunes convened after Aramus had called an emergency meeting. They were none too pleased about coming together at this late hour, but the rules of the Tribunal allowed for any one of them to call a meeting at any time, day or night, so long as there was an urgent matter to discuss.

"Why do you call us together at this hour?" Pachaias asked Aramus.

"There is something very important that you all need to be made aware of," Aramus replied. "It has enormous ramifications for our code of law and the way it is implemented."

"Whatever are you talking about?" Theophilus asked.

"Do you all know what Cidivus has done on his very first day as King of Mavinor?" Aramus asked.

"No," Pontius responded. "Tell us."

"Shortly after his coronation earlier today, he had Sicarius send out his men to arrest the priests and the scribes," Aramus said. "They are being held in the dungeon. How can he possibly do that? They have done nothing wrong."

"How do you know they have done nothing wrong?" Pachaias asked. He pretended that he was completely unaware of the arrests.

"What could they have possibly done?" Aramus asked. "They are peaceful men who have devoted their lives to doing the work of The Author. The arrests are completely unjustifiable, and we as a Tribunal are obligated to intervene and inform the king that he must obey the law. Is that not why you condemned Gobius to death? You claimed he had taken the law into his own hands, so how is this situation any different?"

"It is not any different, not as far as I can see," Annus said.

"Exactly," Aramus said. "We need to act. Pachaias, as Chair it is your duty to set a course of action."

"My action will be to find out why they were arrested, but not at this hour," Pachaias said. "I will speak with the king tomorrow. As you know he is hosting a celebration in the Great Hall, so I'm sure that I can find some time to speak with him alone."

"That is not all," Aramus said. "They also exiled Tarmin and his men without first bringing them before the Tribunal. That is just as egregious as what they have done to the priests and the scribes!"

"Surely they would not have exiled them without bringing them before us first?" Theophilus said.

"But they did," Aramus said. "That is why we need to step in and re-establish our authority. If we do not set the boundaries now, then chaos will reign and the law will quickly become irrelevant. We have to rein them in."

"I will look into that matter as well," Pachaias said. "Once I have the information on why those men were exiled—if indeed that turns out to be the case—I will share it with the rest of you."

"If you find that Cidivus has taken the law into his own hands, then you will have him arrested, won't you?" Aramus asked. He was trying to paint Pachaias into a corner, knowing that the Chair of the Tribunal could not allow Cidivus to get away with the same crime that sealed Gobius' fate.

"Of course," Pachaias finally said. "I will conduct my own investigation and return to you with the facts. But now it is getting late, and we have had a very long day. Let us retire to our quarters and get some rest. I will see you all at the celebration tomorrow."

"Not all of us," Aramus said. "I don't believe I'll be seeing you until we meet to correct the numerous injustices that have already occurred on the first day of Cidivus' reign!" With that he stormed out of the room and went back to his estate. The others sat silently and watched him go.

At the palace, Cidivus was concluding his first day as King of Mavinor by attending to one final piece of business. He was engaged in an intense conversation with Albertus, the head of the Academy, over proposed changes to the education of Mavinor's youth. Albertus had been summoned unexpectedly and had no idea what he was in for when he entered the throne room. Little did he know that the king intended to revise the Academy's curriculum according to his own personal beliefs, and to jettison decades of tradition by forcing Albertus to remove all references to The Author and religious faith from the Academy's course of studies.

"You do understand what I mean, don't you, Albertus?" Cidivus asked.

"I understand," Albertus answered. "But I do not agree."

"It matters not whether you agree," Cidivus said. "All that matters is that you obey. You will obey, won't you?"

Albertus was slow to answer, and it was clear that any response he gave would be said begrudgingly. "Yes, sire," he finally uttered.

"Good," Cidivus said. "I knew you'd see things my way. As of tomorrow, The Author is to be removed from all discussion in the classrooms at the Academy. Any mention of that name will result in harsh discipline for the one who says it. Remember that I will have my people monitoring the classrooms, Albertus. I'd hate for them to report that my orders were not being carried out. It would be a shame, especially for the one whose responsibility it is to implement them. You do understand what I mean, don't you?"

"Of course, sire," Albertus replied in a somber tone.

"Very good," Cidivus said. "Then tomorrow begins a new age in the education of Mavinor's youth. No more shall they hear nonsensical lectures about an imaginary being in the sky who listens to their prayers. They will learn to rely on themselves rather than wait for an invisible deity to come to their aid, and this can only make our kingdom stronger." Cidivus smiled and laughed before walking down from his throne and placing his hand on Albertus' shoulder. "Thank you for your cooperation, Albertus," the king said. "You are now dismissed."

Albertus left the throne room with his head hung low, deeply saddened by the fact that education in Mavinor would no longer include mention of The Author and The Scrolls. Without instruction in faith and morals, he wondered what might become of Mavinor's next generation. As he departed, three guards entered and asked to speak with the king.

"What is it you want?" Cidivus asked them. "It is late, and I am ready for bed."

"We just wanted you to know, sire, that there is no one to be found at the whore's residence. It looks as though everyone has left."

"Where could they have gone?" Cidivus asked. "I want a guard watching that house day and night. If there is any sign of her, then bring her to me immediately!"

"Yes, sire," the guard responded.

One of the other guards then called out to the king as he prepared to leave the throne room. "Sire?" he reluctantly spoke in a meek voice.

"What?" Cidivus asked as he turned around, visibly annoyed.

"The torture chamber is ready, as you requested."

Cidivus smiled. "Good," he said. "We will put it to use first thing in the morning. Have the scribes brought there at first light and wait for me to arrive. That gives me something else to look forward to for tomorrow." Cidivus laughed haughtily as he left them and went to his quarters.

On their way out, the guards ran into the soldier who was

escorting Solitus to the throne room. "Who do we have here?" one of them asked.

"It is Solitus, cousin to Tonitrus and Cedrus," replied the guard from the West Gate. "He has returned to Mavinor, and claims to have undergone a conversion. He wants to join the new regime, and wishes to speak with the king."

"The king has retired for the night," one of the other guards answered. "You'll have to lock him in the dungeon. I'm sure King Cidivus will want to see him tomorrow morning."

"Lucky for you," the guard said to Solitus as he turned him back down the hallway. "At least you know that you will get to live one more day."

Solitus was brought down to the dungeon and led through the corridors. As the prisoners looked out through the small apertures in the doors to their cells, Solitus recognized many of the faces he saw. He walked right past the cell of Legentis, and then those of the other scribes. He saw the priests—Albus, Pretus, and Tauronis—all being held in separate chambers. He wondered what they could have possibly done to warrant being imprisoned.

When they reached the end of the hallway, Solitus was thrown into a very small cell, and the door was abruptly shut behind him. "Sleep well," the guard said contemptuously. Solitus looked back out through the door into the corridor. He wondered if indeed Cidivus would sentence him to death without giving him an opportunity to show his allegiance. The uncertainty caused him a great deal of fear and anxiety. Still even those emotions were dwarfed by his anger over his cousins' deaths. As he heard the guards leave the dungeon, he went back to lie on the cold stone floor. Solitus knew there would be no sleep this night. He had to find a way to stay alive and do what he could to save Mavinor, no matter what the cost. But just as importantly, he had to find out who was responsible for the deaths of his cousins and make them pay for what they did.

In the Eastern Woodlands, well north of Urmina, the ground shook from every single step taken by Hexula. The Beast plodded along as she slowly made her way to the kingdom she intended to destroy, plowing through trees and sending animals scurrying in every direction to avoid her path. Her approach was so deliberate that a good five seconds or so elapsed between her steps. Though she had no concerns about the damage she was causing to the forest—both to the trees and to the homes of its many inhabitants—the sluggish pace at which she moved enabled the animals to escape her wrath. Rabbits, deer, and squirrels alike were able to evade her and avoid being crushed under the weight of her gigantic claws, or the force from her monstrous tail as it undulated with each stride.

As Hexula advanced, she did so with only one purpose in mind. The Beast's goal was complete annihilation of the three kingdoms, beginning with Urmina. Her intentions were to completely tear down the infrastructure of the cities, to kill all of their citizens, and to leave not a single trace of life behind. No stone would go unturned and no life would be spared as she went about her business, and it mattered not to her whether the lives she took were innocent, defenseless human beings. She would stomp a man to death in a heartbeat, or thrash an entire home full of children with her spiked tail. She would breathe fire through a public square where vendors were simply trying to make a living and patrons were out buying food and clothing for their families. The Beast had no mercy, no compassion, and no remorse. There was no way to reason with her, no way to plead with her, and no way to convince her that what she was doing was evil, vicious, and vile.

The people of Urmina did not realize what they were in for, especially given the way their king had insulated them from the rest of the world. There was no information circulating in their kingdom with regard to the events in Mavinor, not even those concerning Gobius' death and Cidivus' coronation. They did not know about the claims that Gobius was the savior, The Author's one and only son.

Though they had felt the ground shake when he was killed and saw the drastic changes in the weather conditions, they were not aware that it could all be attributed to that one catastrophic event. They had no idea of the great evil that had been unleashed on the world, nor did they realize that a significant portion of that evil was now headed their way. In the end, they would have their isolationist ruler to thank for that, and unfortunately for them, the end was drawing near.

Out in the sea, Cedrus and Minstro had all but given up hope. Their lives were now held in the balance by a giant sea monster, whose tentacles clenched them in a vice-like grip, allowing no chance of escape. They knew it was only a matter of time until the creature devoured them, and there wasn't anything they could do to stop it. At this point, neither of them believed that the raven would ever return with the help it promised. The bird was the only one that knew of their predicament, and thus the only one in any kind of a position to assist them. But clearly its quest for help had been impeded by something, and now the raven would be too late to save them even if it did manage to return with the Legans.

Then something inexplicable happened. It was so unexpected—so unforeseeable and fortuitous—that neither Cedrus nor Minstro knew how to react. The monster suddenly let them go, releasing them in the open sea and leaving them to the mercy of the currents. As they began to tread water to stay afloat, they called out to each other simultaneously. The sky was dark now, too dark for them to see as they battled to survive the waves that tossed them about. But they continued to shout out in the hope that they could follow each other's voice and come together. In the end it worked, as both men ultimately joined hands and gave one another the semblance of an embrace. They were so worn down physically, mentally, and emotionally that all they could think to do was look to each other for comfort and consolation.

Then something caught Minstro's eye, and he gently pushed Cedrus away. "Cedrus, look!" he said. As both men stared toward the southwest, a light began to flicker in the darkness. Once lit, they could plainly see that it was a torch high up on the bow of a ship. They estimated that the ship was no more than two hundred yards away from them, so they began to swim in that direction.

"Come on, Cedrus!" Minstro yelled. "We can do it. We are going to be rescued after all!" His voice was full of confidence and conviction, and he hoped that it would raise the spirits of his weary companion, who was still grieving heavily over the many losses he had suffered.

Soon other torches were lit along the sides of the ship, and another one at the stern. They were now able to plainly see the outline of the vessel, and after examining its shape, size, dual masts, and the figurehead protruding from the bow, they realized that it was one of Mavinor's ships. Unbeknownst to them, it was the ship that brought Tarmin and his men to Patmos, now on its return trip home. "Over here!" they screamed in the darkness, hoping that someone would hear their cries for help. But when they realized they were too far away to be heard, they kept their arms and legs churning and continued to fight the tide as they swam closer and closer to the bow of the ship.

Then suddenly, both Cedrus and Minstro felt a powerful force propel them from under the water. It was as if something swam underneath them and shot a stream of water to the surface, thrusting them upward almost to the point where their bodies were hovering above the sea. A low rumbling sound was heard—a subterranean hum—that went through them like daggers of ice. "What was that?" Cedrus asked Minstro.

"No, not again," Minstro answered as he looked toward the ship.

In the circle of light surrounding the torch on the bow, they could clearly see a tentacle rise up out of the water. Once perpendicular to the surface, it thrashed against the hull of the ship and damaged several wooden planks. Cedrus and Minstro heard the sounding of a shofar echo off the raging sea, and soon they saw several men standing on the deck looking down at the water. As the tentacles rose up again, a flurry of arrows and spears shot through the air and down toward the creature attacking the vessel from beneath the surface. Cedrus and Minstro now realized that the monster had probably let them go in order to pursue the ship.

"Swim back!" Cedrus yelled to Minstro. "We might be hit by a stray arrow or spear."

Both men were very frustrated, but were left with no choice other than to retreat from the vessel they were counting on to save them. With a full-scale battle raging between the ship's crew and the sea monster, they couldn't afford to get themselves caught in between. All they could do was swim a safe distance away and watch to see who would prevail.

As they turned their backs to the action and swam for their lives, the air was filled with the sounds of the battle. Cedrus and Minstro heard the whistling of arrows streaming from the deck of the ship. They heard the splashing sounds of projectiles that misfired and landed in the sea. They also thought they heard the monster itself screech in pain from underneath the water as it continued to absorb blow after blow. Once they believed they were far enough away, they stopped and turned back to watch the rest of the conflict unfold.

It was evident that the creature was being weakened by the many direct hits it suffered. As the arrows and spears being hurled toward Tentaclus penetrated its skin, the sea monster drew back its tentacles and disappeared in a boiling maelstrom. Soon there was dead silence in the air, and the water grew calm. It was as if something had drawn a carpet over the waves, spreading it serenely until it was perfectly smooth. Believing it was now safe, Cedrus and Minstro began swimming toward the ship once again.

This time they came within twenty yards of the side where the crew had been firing weapons at the creature. They called out as loudly as they could, putting every last ounce of strength they had left into their voices. Cedrus thought about splashing around in the water to draw their attention, but then realized that it would be a mistake. He didn't want to risk drawing the monster back to the surface, nor did he want the men to think the splashing was coming from the creature. If they believed it had returned to launch another attack, Cedrus could easily find himself impaled by a spear hurled from the deck.

Finally, it became evident that one of the crew members heard them. He held out a torch in their direction, hoping to catch sight of the endangered castaways. Cedrus and Minstro continued to swim and call out in the darkness. They stopped to tread water and waved their hands in the air, with Cedrus flaunting his brother's shield in the hope it would reflect the torchlight and make it easier for them to be spotted. After a few minutes, the soldiers from Mavinor saw them and began making preparations for the rescue. They started assembling ropes and boathooks, and as Cedrus and Minstro got wind of what was happening, it began to sink in that they were finally going to be saved.

The light was much brighter now as there were several others standing on the deck holding torches, making it easier for Cedrus and Minstro to see what was going on. They saw the men tying knots in the rope, presumably to form loops that they would be able to wrap around their bodies after the rope was thrown into the water. It didn't take long for the soldiers to finish their work, and then one of the men on the ship called out to Cedrus and Minstro.

"We are going to cast the ropes in your direction," he said. "Put the loop around your body and tighten the knot so we can begin pulling you in. When you're close enough to reach the boathooks we're extending from the deck, grab them as well. Between the rope and the boathooks, we should be able to drag you out of the water and safely onto the ship."

The torches were held out and over the ropes as they were cast into the sea. This enabled Cedrus and Minstro to gauge where they were and find them quickly despite the darkness that surrounded them. When they had inserted their bodies into the loops and tightened the knots, they yelled out to their rescuers that it was alright to start hauling them in.

Once the tugging started, Cedrus and Minstro churned their legs in the water to help accelerate the rescue and take some of the strain off the men who were laboring to pull them to safety. But as they came closer and looked directly up at the light emanating from the torches, they saw something horrifying. The silhouette of several huge tentacles crept up from the opposite side of the ship and began to envelope the crew members. "No!" Cedrus yelled to them. "Look out behind you!"

It was too late. There were four tentacles that rose up from under the ship on the far side. They wrapped themselves tightly around the hull and came up onto the deck. In the blink of an eye, three others rose up on the near side, just a short distance from where Cedrus and Minstro were located, and wrapped themselves around as well. Once the creature had the ship within its grasp, it dallied devilishly with the doomed craft. The monster churned the water and shook the vessel in its vengeful wake, sending men tumbling overboard. None of them were able to mount another attack, as it was impossible to remain in position long enough to do so. Most of them lost their weapons and hung on to the gunwales for dear life. The men were forced to let go of the ropes, and the waves that formed from the rocking of the ship pushed Cedrus and Minstro further and further away.

Then in what was either a strategic move or just a show of strength, Tentaclus rolled the ship over until it was completely upside down, sending a huge wall of water toward Cedrus and Minstro. The two men managed to lock hands and stay together, even as they were pummeled by the massive wave that crashed over them and swept them a good distance away from the ship. When they rose back to the surface and looked out, they couldn't see a thing. The ship was lost and gone, blotted in the dark due to the torches having been extinguished after the vessel was flipped over. All they heard were the frantic cries for help from the men who had been tossed overboard. They bravely began to swim toward the ship again, hoping that they could unite with those who had survived. But the closer they got, the fainter the cries became. It wasn't that the men were losing their voices. Cedrus and Minstro came to realize that with each passing minute, more and more of them were being pulled under by Tentaclus. By the time they reached the vicinity of where the wreck had taken place, the last voice faded away. They called out, holding out hope that some of their fellow countrymen had survived. But there was no one left.

As they heard something rise up out of the water, they dreaded the thought of Tentaclus capturing them once again. Thus they were forced to retreat, and as they did they heard the creature's long tentacles lashing up against the hull of the ship and smashing it to smithereens. It wasn't enough for Tentaclus to kill every man on board. The unpitying monster had to continue the destruction, to finish what it had started by obliterating the remnants of the vessel. It was intent on annihilating each separate plank of which the craft was made until there was nothing left. When the creature was finally satisfied with what it had accomplished, it retreated back to the depths of the sea, leaving a mass of floating debris behind at the surface.

As the pounding stopped and silence permeated the air, Cedrus and Minstro began swimming toward the wreckage. Eventually they were able to latch on to one of the wooden masts, and for once they didn't have to tread water to stay afloat. They used the ropes they had around them to tie themselves to the mast. Though it had been broken off from the deck of the ship, the rigging was intact and the sails were still attached. Cedrus continued to wear his brother's helm and held Tonitrus' sword in his belt, but he tied the shield down on the mast by threading some rope through its handle. Then he and Minstro sprawled themselves out over the spars and used their hands as a pillow, resting their tired bodies just above the surface of the water. Though they fought to stay awake and remain vigilant lest Tentaclus returned, it wasn't long before they succumbed to the extreme fatigue that had overtaken them and fell fast asleep while adrift in the water.

Chapter Two

As she lay in her bed in one of guest rooms at Xamnon's royal palace, Magdala had a difficult time falling asleep. The terrible events of the previous day had taken a huge toll on her emotionally, and left her completely exhausted. But she couldn't stop thinking, as the thoughts of whether or not Gobius had been saved raced through her mind and tormented her. She was haunted to no end by the possibility that he lost his life in order to save her, and believed she could never live with herself if that was indeed what had happened. Finally she managed to fight off the dreadful images of her king being stoned to death, and was able to go to sleep. But it didn't take long for her mind to become active again, and quickly she became caught up in a vivid dream that she would not soon forget.

In her dream, Magdala is back in Mavinor standing alone outside in the open air. There is no one around her for as far as her eyes can see, and her hair blows steadily in the wind so that she is continuously forced to brush it aside from her face. There is a chill in the air, and when she looks down at herself, she realizes that she is not at all dressed for the weather. She is barefoot and wearing nothing but a chemise, so she looks around to see where the rest of her clothes might be. But she sees no shoes or stockings, no gown or robe. As the cold air raises bumps on her skin, she is forced to cross her arms and clutch them tight against her body. She shivers, and her teeth begin to chatter. Then she hears a voice calling to her, and immediately she turns around. But once again there is no one to be seen.

As the voice continues to call her name, she realizes that it is coming from somewhere ahead of where she is standing. So she begins to walk, still crossing her arms and bringing them up against her body in an effort to keep warm. The further she goes the louder the voice becomes, but there is still no one in sight. It is as if the person calling out to her is invisible. She even looks up toward the sky, but sees nothing except for a blanket of dark clouds that have completely cut off the sunlight. As she continues to advance, the surroundings become more and more familiar to her. She begins to slow her steps, and as she ponders it for just a minute, Magdala realizes that she is walking along the Via Mortis. The voice continues to call to her, and the closer she gets to it the more desperate it sounds.

Finally she reaches the end of the Via Mortis and finds herself at the Place of the Skull. The voice is still calling, and at this point she can only surmise that it is coming from beyond the edge of the slope that leads down the skull-shaped hill. She slowly walks toward the edge and peers down, only to see King Gobius holding on for dear life. He is on the verge of falling down the hill, and the only thing keeping him from doing so is a slightly elevated ledge above the right eye of the skull. He has grasped hold of it with his right hand, but he cannot pull himself up. He lunges toward Magdala with his left hand and begs for her help.

Magdala doesn't even give it a second thought. She takes two steps down the slope and stretches out toward him. But her arms are not long enough to reach him. He pleads with her to come closer, so she inches down even further. The rocky soil scrapes the soles of her feet, but Magdala ignores the discomfort. When she finally descends far enough and manages to touch his outstretched hand, Gobius loses his grip and falls down the hill. Magdala watches in horror as he tumbles down to the bottom, and when he lands his body just lies there motionless. "He is dead," Magdala tells herself. "My Lord is dead."

Then Magdala hears another voice coming from the top of the hill. "The king is dead! The king is dead!" the voice says. "Who killed him?" another voice asks. "The prostitute," the voice says. "It was the prostitute who murdered the king!"

"No!" Magdala calls out. "I did not kill him, I tried to save him."

"You killed him!" yells the voice yet again. This causes Magdala to fall to the ground crying. As she begins to feel herself sliding down the hill, she quickly stands and begins walking back up. When she arrives at the top, she looks around and sees a throng of people. They stare at her intently as she takes a step toward them, and soon she realizes that they are taking notice of the scantily manner in which she is dressed. They all begin to chant in unison, "Who killed Gobius? The prostitute killed Gobius! Who killed Gobius? The prostitute killed Gobius!" They repeat it over and over and over again.

Magdala begs them to stop, but they ignore her supplication. The chanting becomes so loud that Magdala is forced to cover her ears. She drops to her knees sobbing and lowers her head toward the ground. As it grows even louder, she curls herself up in a fetal position, puts her hands behind her head, and brings her forearms up against her ears as tightly as possible. But nothing seems to help. She cannot escape the unending chants of the crowd, and even her intense sobbing is not enough to drown out the sounds as they completely overwhelm her.

Then unexpectedly the chanting stops. Magdala places her hands on the ground and raises her head to look at those around her. She notices that all of them are now holding stones. She quickly rises to her feet and scans the crowd from one side to the other, hoping to see a familiar face. Finally her eyes meet those of Cedrus. "Cedrus!" she calls to him. "Help me!"

Cedrus gazes toward her, but his face wears a cold expression. Soon he directs his icy glare toward the ground, as if he is pondering what he should do. Magdala looks his way, hoping that he will answer her plea and come to her rescue. But instead he turns away and walks in the opposite direction. "No!" Magdala screams. "Cedrus!"

Pachaias then steps forward from the crowd and approaches Magdala. As he comes upon her, he says, "It is time to pay for your crimes." Then he raises his hand and gives her a backhand slap across the face. Magdala falls to the ground and rubs her cheek to ease the pain. Still she somehow finds the strength to rise to her feet again, and when she does, Magdala sees that all the people surrounding her have raised their stones and are getting ready to throw them at her. She is helpless to do anything about it, and simply falls back to the ground. "Let the one without sin cast the first stone," Pachaias calls out as he backs away from her. Magdala remembers the words as those of her Lord, and hopes they will save her from this cruel fate. But the people do not hesitate as they step forward and hurl their stones at her. Magdala accepts that she is going to die, but just as she curls up into a fetal position again to shield herself from the assault…

She woke in a cold sweat. Magdala picked her head up from the pillow and frantically looked around the room, then let out a deep breath when she saw that no one was there. As her head hit the pillow again, she found herself wide awake and unable to sleep. Magdala couldn't help but think the worst following her nightmare, and now believed that Gobius was gone, and that she alone was responsible for his death.

The raven continued to wait patiently for Apteris, though it was now beginning to worry that he might not return. It was tempted to fly out to sea to check on Cedrus and Minstro, but it knew Apteris to be honorable and one to always keep his word. So the bird continued to wait near the bushes where Apteris had promised to meet it, hoping that he would arrive soon.

When Apteris had initially said good-bye to Chaelim and Volara after they declined to join him in his self-appointed mission, he knew in his heart that he couldn't win the battle by himself. He began to think of what he could possibly do to convince them to stand and fight with him. Then suddenly he remembered the words of Gobius when the future king talked the Legans into leading his men out of the Labyrinth of Secrets. This impelled him to return and make one last attempt, believing that he could win them over just as Gobius had won over Orius. Chaelim and Volara were surprised when they saw him come back, and stared at Apteris intently as he landed alongside them.

"I thought you were going to the natural world to help a raven in fighting some sort of conspiracy involving Orius," Chaelim said sarcastically. "Why have you returned so soon?"

"I wanted to speak with both of you again and give each of you one last chance to join me," Apteris said.

"We are not going anywhere," Chaelim said. "We already told you that."

"But I have something more to say," Apteris replied. "I thought about it after I left both of you behind, and I wanted to bring it to your attention."

"What is it?" Volara asked.

"Remember when the men from Mavinor got lost in the Labyrinth of Secrets in their quest for the Medallion? They asked for our help, but Orius denied them at first. The one called Gobius then pointed out that the unicorn was with them, and that she would die with them if they were unable to find their way out. Since the unicorn was the last of her kind, it would mean the extinction of those wondrous creatures that The Author created."

"Of course we remember," Volara said. "Did we not discuss this recently? I was the one who implored Orius to intervene, even though it meant breaking the rules."

"Exactly," Apteris answered. "It was Gobius who imparted these words of wisdom, 'Were we created for the well-being of the law, or was the law handed down for the well-being of all creation?' "

"Yes, I do recall that," Volara said.

"What exactly are you trying to say, Apteris?" asked Chaelim.

"If we made an exception back then and broke the law to save the unicorn, then what is stopping us now from breaking the law in order to save the entire world?" Apteris asked them.

"I never agreed with Orius' decision," Chaelim said. "Only I kept quiet about it because you know that I have too much respect for him as our leader, and will always defer to him in these matters."

"But you, Volara, agreed with him," Apteris said. "As you said before, you were the one who urged him to intervene. Why then would you not feel that way now?" Volara did not immediately respond to his question.

"This is different," Chaelim said.

"How so?" Apteris asked, his voice fiery and intense. "How is it different, Chaelim? If anything, this situation is graver than the other. I can see no justifiable reason to sit back and watch the world burn. If the two of you are willing to do that, then you are failing to fulfill what you were created to do. For know that if you don't help me save the world, then soon there will be nothing in nature left to defend. Our roles will be irrelevant, and the creatures we have always protected will wallow in despair as they cry out for our help. If that help never comes, then wouldn't we have betrayed them? Wouldn't we have turned our backs on them? Wouldn't we have betrayed our very roles as they were assigned to us? And finally, wouldn't we be turning our backs on The Author Himself? If we do, then we will have contributed to the destruction of the world by not acting. We will be complicit in the plot that has been formulated, and will have facilitated its completion. Can you really stand by and watch as our friends struggle against a force that they cannot possibly defeat on their own? I will not do so. I will not watch the world burn. I'd rather risk losing my immortality and go to the grave knowing that I tried to save the world than remain here in this realm while it is consumed by evil. But if that is your choice, then so be it. Go ahead and follow the rules as they were once written, rules that were predicated on trust and service, and did not account for the outward betrayal and malicious acts that have recently occurred. Stay here and save yourselves while those in the world suffer and die. My conscience will never allow me to do such a thing. If all those whom we have been called to protect are destined to die from the evil that has been unleashed, then I will either save them from that fate or die as one of them. For me, there are no other options. Good-bye, my friends."

With that, Apteris turned his back and prepared to leave the Legans' realm. But before he set out, a voice called out to him from behind. "Wait!" Volara said. She looked carefully at Chaelim, and then stared back at Apteris. "I am coming with you," she said. Chaelim looked on in disbelief as Volara left to accompany Apteris back to the natural world, and soon he found himself standing all alone in the Legans' realm as he watched them go.

As morning broke in Xamnon, the sun was still nowhere to be seen. The dark clouds remained, and though it didn't rain, it perpetually appeared as if a storm was going to hit. The light was completely cut off, making it feel more like nightfall than daybreak.

After stopping by Solitus' room, Arcala came into the dining room where Henricus and Bovillus were having breakfast. "Where is my brother?" she asked.

"Did you check his quarters?" Henricus answered.

"Yes, but he is not there," said Arcala. "I would have expected him to be at the breakfast table if he was not in his room."

Bovillus finished chewing his food and braced himself to lie to Arcala, as Solitus had asked him to do before he left for Mavinor. He was a terrible liar, but he was ready to try his best to convince Arcala that her brother was out training somewhere on the palace grounds.

"He claimed that he is getting a little rusty with his sword," Bovillus said. "Thus he told me that he was going outside to conduct some drills and exercises."

"So early in the morning?" Arcala said. "That's odd for him. Where did he go?"

"That I cannot answer," Bovillus replied. "He did not say where he was going."

"I'm sure he is somewhere on our grounds," Henricus said. "Sit down and eat, Arcala. You can go out and look for him afterward."

"Very well," she said.

"Where is Magdala?" Henricus asked.

"I do not know," Bovillus said. "Perhaps I should go and check on her."

"Please do," Henricus answered. Bovillus swallowed one last spoonful of soup before excusing himself from the table.

"How are you this morning?" Henricus asked Arcala.

"Still quite anxious," Arcala replied. "You should be as well, given the condition of your king."

"I am," Henricus replied after pausing for just a moment, "though I try not to show it."

"You do a fine job," Arcala said. "I understand that you have to be a pillar of strength for this kingdom as your king's life hangs in the balance. Any sign of weakness shown by you will only work its way down to everyone else."

"So then you do understand," Henricus said.

"Of course," answered Arcala.

"Perhaps later on you and I could train together," Henricus said, "for I could use a partner. I cannot sit by the king's bedside every hour of every day. As long as I stay on the palace grounds, they can quickly reach me if I am needed."

Arcala did not answer immediately. She looked straight into Henricus' eyes and tried to read him as best she could. "If I didn't know any better, then I'd say you are making overtures," she said.

"Is that so?" Henricus asked. "Well someone at this table clearly thinks quite highly of herself."

"Am I wrong?" Arcala asked.

"Meet me outside at the back of the castle in one hour," Henricus said as he finished his breakfast. He rose from his chair and prepared to walk out of the room, never directly addressing her question.

"Now what kind of man leaves a lady alone at the table?" Arcala asked.

"I think you're more than capable of handling eating alone," Henricus said as he winked and went to check on King Antiugus.

Cidivus had ordered Talmik to bring him an extravagant breakfast consisting of meat, fish, bread, and ale. The king then proceeded to gorge himself as Talmik watched in disgust, eating as though he had been fasting for days. After he finished, Cidivus asked the guards if Legentis and the other scribes had been brought to the torture chamber as per his instructions the night before. When they confirmed that the orders were carried out, Cidivus had them accompany him to the dungeon, where he found the scribes lined up against the wall of the chamber.

"Good morning, gentlemen," Cidivus said. "I hope you're enjoying your stay." No one uttered a response to his derisive taunt. "Today I am feeling quite generous. After all, I am hosting a celebration in the Great Hall this afternoon to honor my coronation as King of Mavinor. It is sure to be a momentous occasion, and dare I say a historic event. Thus I am going to give you all one more chance to tell me where the tome is hidden. I want to know what has happened to the material that has been recovered from The Scrolls, and I want to know now!"

"We have already told you that we do not know," Legentis replied. "Cantos must have hidden it somewhere without telling us. We cannot provide you with the information you seek."

"Very well then," Cidivus said. "Guards, bring Legentis to the rack."

"No!" the other scribes cried out as Legentis was dragged to the center of the chamber. There was a machine there with a rectangular wooden frame, and the frame had a roller on each end. Legentis tried hard to resist, but they beat him with a club until he finally gave in. Then they manacled his wrists to one roller, and his feet to the other. There was a handle and ratchet attached to the top roller, and Cidivus walked right up to it as he stared down at Legentis.

"One last chance," Cidivus said. "Where is the tome?"

"I do not know," Legentis replied, "and even if I did, I would not tell you!"

Cidivus began to turn the handle to increase the tension on the chains. Then he slowly turned the rollers at each end, stretching Legentis' body by pulling it in opposite directions. At first, it wasn't so bad. Legentis felt the tightness in his muscles evaporate as his arms and legs were increasingly stretched. But once his limbs were elongated to their maximum points, the pain began to set in. Cidivus mercilessly turned the rollers little by little as he watched Legentis suffer, until finally the scribe experienced dislocations to all four of his limbs. Legentis screamed in excruciating pain as he felt his body being torn apart while his fellow scribes winced in horror.

Then Cidivus did something that could have been perceived as merciful. He stopped turning the rollers, and left Legentis in position on the wooden frame. The scribes breathed a sigh of relief, but quickly became anxious again when Cidivus gave further instructions to his guards. "Bring me the pokers," he said.

There was a fire burning in the corner of the chamber, and one of the guards went over to it and retrieved two pokers. They had been heated on one end, so Cidivus grabbed them by the opposite end when they were brought to him. Then he looked back toward Legentis while wearing a smug grin. At this point, it was obvious that the king had not been showing mercy and compassion when he stopped stretching the scribe on the rack. He was merely setting him up for the second phase of the torture session.

"It's about to get a lot warmer in here for you," Cidivus said. He began using the pokers to touch Legentis on various parts of his body, causing burns all over his arms, legs, and torso. Legentis howled in pain over and over again, and the scribes began to weep for their friend as they turned away, unable to watch and helpless to come to his aid.

"I wonder," Cidivus then said, "which part of the body is most valuable to a scribe? Wait, I know." Cidivus stared directly into the eyes of Legentis and smiled.

"No!" Legentis said. "NOOOOOO!" The scribe's pleas went unanswered as Cidivus took the pokers and jabbed them right into Legentis' eyes. The pain was unbearable, and Legentis' screams were deafening as Cidivus blinded him with the hot pokers.

At this point, a guard from another part of the dungeon ran into the chamber and asked to speak with the king. "What is it?" Cidivus asked. "Do you not see that I am busy?"

The guard proceeded to explain how Solitus had given himself up the night before and claimed to have a conversion. "He wants to join us," the guard said. "I brought him to the throne room last night, but you had already retired for the night."

"How interesting," Cidivus said. "Bring him here at once!"

While Cerastes crawled through the Tenebrae, he felt the ground pulsate ever so slightly as Hexula continued to march toward Urmina. The serpent was far enough away from her that he did not experience any violent tremors, but her steps were so heavy that he could still sense them as he slithered along. He even saw several flocks of birds and other animals fleeing from the direction she was heading.

As Cerastes prepared to enter the clearing where he and Orius always met, he heard a voice call to him immediately after he slipped out from behind the trees.

"You're late," the voice said.

Cerastes was caught off guard. "I am sorry," he said. "You startled me. I still have to get used to your new voice, not to mention your new appearance as well, Orius."

"Have you already forgotten that Orius is no more?" the voice said.

"Again, I am sorry," Cerastes replied. "Please forgive me, Malgyron."

As Cerastes came deeper into the clearing, he saw the dark form of Malgyron seated on one of the tree stumps. "Do you know where I have come from?" Malgyron asked.

"Where?" said Cerastes.

"The Northern Mountains," Malgyron said. "The Deliverers of Darkness are there, waiting to hunt the one who carries the Medallion. They have risen up from the Fire Below, just as the ancient prophecies predicted they would. However, it appears something interesting has occurred."

"What is it?" Cerastes asked.

"The Medallion has either been lost or hidden," Malgyron answered. "Their leader senses that whoever was bearing it has become separated from the sacred object. But wherever it is, it is completely concealed, so well in fact that he cannot even sense where it might be."

"Could it be that Gobius' disciple, the one to whom he has entrusted the Medallion, has been killed, and that the Medallion has been lost forever?" Cerastes asked.

"It is possible," Malgyron said. "Or as I said, he may have hidden it somewhere in the hope that no one would find it. Either way, I need your spies to continue doing their work. Find out everything you can. I want to know where that Medallion is, for I will need it eventually to present to the traitor. I have instructed the Deliverers to remain where they are, until they either sense the Medallion once again or we discover where it is being hidden."

"Perhaps it will never be found," Cerastes said.

"Maybe," Malgyron answered. "But until I have it in my hands and place it around the neck of the traitor, I will not be satisfied. It would trouble me to know that it's out there, for as long as it remains in the world, The Author's grace remains as well. Its power must be extinguished."

"I understand," Cerastes said. "I will tell my spies to listen very attentively and bring back any information they have, however miniscule it may be. Even the smallest clue could lead us in the right direction."

"Good," Malgyron said. "Send for me immediately if you come up with any leads. The Deliverers of Darkness are awaiting my instructions, and I will want to dispatch them as soon as we find out where the Medallion is located. I'll be back shortly. Right now I am going to monitor the Beast's progress."

"I can feel her steps, and I see how the creatures of the forest have been fleeing as she makes her way through the Eastern Woodlands," Cerastes said.

"Yes," Malgyron stated. "It's too bad for the people of Urmina that they will not have that same luxury. Their thick walls will keep them confined as she destroys their kingdom, and every single one of them shall die."

Cedrus and Minstro finally awakened after sleeping for several hours on the mainmast that served as their makeshift raft. Neither man felt rested despite the slumber, partly because they were still exhausted from the events of the previous two days, and partly because of their uncomfortable sleeping arrangements. As they looked up at the drear and ominous sky, they feared that a fierce storm might strike at any minute. If it did, then they were doomed. They would have virtually no chance of surviving a tempest out in the open sea. As it was, they were barely kept afloat by the rigging of a shattered mast that they clung to with every ounce of their being. The two men continually scanned the area around them for any more ships that might be sailing by, hoping against hope that they would be rescued before suffering any further misfortune.

The silence out in the water was eerie, but in some ways it calmed them. Neither man said anything about the shipwreck, or the sea monster that caused it. They prayed that the creature would not return, and that help would arrive soon. Then as the silence reached its peak, it was suddenly broken by a screeching cry from above. When Cedrus and Minstro looked up, they saw the outlines of three winged figures in the sky descending toward them. As the obscure forms drew closer, they realized that it was two of the Legans being led by the raven. Both men were moved by the sight, believing that they were finally going to be spared from a watery grave.

The raven perched itself on the mast and called to them. "See!" it squawked. "I brought help. Told you I'd find it."

"You did indeed, my friend," Minstro said as he and Cedrus untied themselves from the mast. "Thank you."

As Apteris and Volara hovered above them, Apteris asked how they were doing. Minstro saw that Cedrus was unusually quiet and perhaps in somewhat of a daze, so he answered for them. "We are alive," Minstro said. "That's more than we thought we'd be able to say after all we've been through."

"Where would you like us to take you?" Volara asked.

"Xamnon," Minstro responded. "We need to regroup and come up with a plan of some sort."

As he finished his words and cast away the rope that had fastened him to the makeshift raft, Minstro was suddenly yanked from the mast and dragged under the water by an unseen force. The same happened to Cedrus just seconds afterward, and the raven immediately left its perch and flew up toward Apteris and Volara. "What has happened?" Volara asked.

When Cedrus and Minstro both resurfaced, they could be seen wriggling within the clutches of the tentacles that now clasped them tightly and squeezed them to the point that they were gasping for breath. They did all they could to free themselves, but neither one could get the creature to release him. "Help them!" yelled the raven.

Apteris dove in first, attempting to free Cedrus. Volara went to save Minstro, but as both Legans closed in, two more tentacles rose up out of the water and lashed out toward them like huge whips. Volara ducked out of the way at the last minute, but Apteris was struck so hard that he fell headlong into the sea. He was even submerged for a few seconds, causing Volara to worry about whether he too had been captured.

Then the sea's surface became disturbed, almost as if a maelstrom was about to form. The water foamed and bubbled as Apteris burst through and soared into the air again. Volara rejoiced at the sight, but the momentary distraction cost her as a tentacle rose up and snatched her right out of the air. It held her arms at her sides, making it impossible for Volara to fight back and leaving Apteris as their last hope. He saw what had happened and drew not one but two swords as he courageously plummeted from the sky like a streak of lightning.

When the sea monster raised another one of its tentacles to attack Apteris, the Legan swung with all his might and slashed it from one side to the other. The creature pulled its injured tentacle back under the water as Apteris focused on saving Volara first. He tried to cut through the tentacle that had her in its grip, but Tentaclus skillfully dodged the swing. Apteris realized that though the monster's body was under the water, its vision was sharp enough that it could actually see beyond the sea's surface. He tried to free her again, but failed in his attempt. Then another tentacle rose up out of the water from directly underneath Apteris. It slithered around him as he fought with all his might to slip away. But its grasp was too strong, and soon Apteris found himself in the same predicament as the others.

All four of them were now being held in the clutches of the monster, while the raven helplessly looked on. The bird cried as loudly as it could to summon help, but there was none to be found. As it circled the air above them, it gazed downward and uncharacteristically began to despair. Even the resolute raven started to wonder if this was the end, and whether the world would now have any hope of escape from the Age of Darkness.

Chapter Three

As the guards brought Solitus into the torture chamber, he immediately took notice of the emotional state of the scribes as they cowered against the wall. They were visibly distressed, and when he looked toward the center of the room, he quickly understood why.

"Solitus," Cidivus said, "I'm so glad you have returned. I have something I'd like to show you."

The guard brought Solitus closer so he could get a good look at Legentis. The sight made him sick to his stomach, causing him to turn away. "Look!" Cidivus said emphatically. When Solitus turned back, he saw the badly burnt, elongated body of the scribe laid out on the rack, looking as though it had just been torn apart and baked in an oven. He could see the agonizing pain in Legentis' face, but what particularly horrified him was the sight of his eyes being burnt out. Solitus just couldn't bear to watch the man suffer so terribly.

"What is wrong?" Cidivus asked. "You did say that you were one of us now, didn't you? Did you not tell my guards that you wished to join us in ushering in a new age for Mavinor? Surely you'll want to be part of our plan to finally set things right, won't you?"

Solitus didn't answer at first. Then after realizing that he had little choice but to respond if he wanted to fool them into believing that he had switched sides, he looked directly at Cidivus. "Yes, of course I do," he said.

"Good," Cidivus replied. "Then perhaps you'd like to finish this. Show me that you really mean to join us and that you are not trying to infiltrate my regime as a spy for the believers."

"What would you like for me to do?" Solitus asked.

"Guards!" Cidivus said. "Take the scribe off the rack and place his head on the block. Then bring me the sword."

The guards untied Legentis and carried him to where a wooden block was located in another part of the chamber. He couldn't walk because his legs were dislocated from the torture on the rack, and his arms hung limp at his sides. They placed his head on the block as another guard brought Cidivus the sword he requested. Then the king motioned for Solitus to follow him over to the block.

"Here," Cidivus said. "Show me your loyalty, Solitus. Take this sword and behead the scribe."

At first, Solitus didn't budge. He carefully considered his response, for though he obviously did not want to execute Legentis, he also needed to convince Cidivus that he was on his side now. "No," he finally said. "I did not return to Mavinor to sever the heads off your prisoners. That role is better left to an executioner. I am here to fight for the new regime and restore glory to Mavinor. I want to protect our kingdom from the believers who have come to rule in Xamnon, for I felt like a traitor as I was accepted at their palace as an honored guest. I can give you some valuable information about what is going on within their kingdom, especially as it pertains to King Antiugus. But I will not have this man's blood on my hands."

Cidivus looked dissatisfied at first, but then he smiled. "So be it," he said. "I will do the honors myself." He walked up to the block and addressed the scribe. "Any last words, Legentis?" he asked.

"Go ahead," Legentis said. "Kill me. I am already dead, as you have taken that which is most valuable to me. Without my eyes, I can no longer continue doing the work The Author has called me to do. But I tell you this, Cidivus. The Author will triumph, even as you persecute those who follow Him and His ways. In the end, you cannot win."

"Oh, but I will," Cidivus answered as he brought down the sword and beheaded Legentis. His fellow scribes cried out as the sword fell, after which they heard the gruesome *thump* of their friend's head hitting the stone floor. "Hopefully that will change your minds about telling me where the tome is being hidden," Cidivus said to them. After handing the sword back to his guard, he ordered that the scribes be returned to their cells. He also asked that Sicarius, Tarsus, and Grodus be summoned to the throne room. "Come with me," he said to Solitus. "I have plans for you."

Solitus looked sadly upon Legentis' headless corpse, wishing he could have saved him. But in his heart he knew there was nothing he could have done. As Cidivus arrived at the door and looked back, Solitus turned and went to accompany him out of the dungeon.

The kingdom of Urmina kept a small military outpost roughly a mile north of the North Gate. It consisted of a square-shaped, three-story watchtower constructed of stone and wooden planks. The stone formed the foundation for the tower and comprised the entire first floor. The top two floors were made mostly of wood, with a small window on each of the four sides of the second floor and much larger openings on each side of the third floor. It was on the third floor that the watchmen kept vigil, and there was a small barracks alongside the tower which had sleeping quarters for no more than five men. Usually two guards manned the tower while the other three slept, ate, or conducted drills. They rotated shifts, and were generally relieved by another group of five soldiers after serving at the outpost for three days.

As Hexula drew closer to Urmina, the guards began to feel the ground move beneath them. It was a slight vibration at first, and although they sensed it, the feeling wasn't strong enough for any of the men to raise concern. They feared their fellow guards might perceive them as mad if they claimed to feel a pulse from underneath the ground, especially if the others felt nothing at all. So they kept it to themselves until the throbbing became more powerful and it was clear that something out of the ordinary was happening. "What was that?" one of the guards finally asked.

"It sounds as if something is approaching, something massive," another guard answered.

All of them went up to the watchtower to see if they could get a glimpse of whatever it was that may have been coming toward the outpost. As they looked into the distance, all they could see were trees falling to either side. Something was plowing through the forest, knocking aside anything that obstructed its path like a gigantic boulder rolling down a mountain. "What could it be?" one of them asked.

At that time, some troops showed up to relieve the others of their guard duty. Thus there were now ten men at the outpost. They too felt the tremors, and as one of the guards left the watchtower, they asked him what was going on.

"We don't know," he said. "Something is approaching, but we cannot see what it is. What we do know is that it is powerful enough to hammer the trees of the forest to the ground. I'm going to retrieve some weapons and bring them up to the watchtower. Those in the tower will be armed with crossbows, others with spears and swords. Have you brought arms with you?"

"Yes, we have," replied the soldier.

"Good," the guard said. "Then assume a position, and prepare for anything."

Once everyone was armed, they stationed three archers in the watchtower. The window facing north on the third floor was large enough for two men to fire arrows through. Since the window on the second floor was much smaller, only one archer was placed there. The others took up positions to the right and left of the tower, armed with spears and swords, save for one young bowman named Arcus. Since he was the junior man among the four archers, he was forced to stand outside the tower with the others.

As they stood guard—ready to defend their territory against whatever was coming their way—the ground shook more violently with each resounding BOOM. Their anxiety grew as the thing drew closer, causing their brows to become coated with sweat and bumps to rise up on their skin. When the last of the trees began to fall, they experienced chills as they waited for the unseen force to emerge from the forest. Finally when the Beast came into view, they very nearly dropped their weapons and ran.

The archers in the watchtower rained arrows down upon the Beast, but they bounced off her impenetrable scales and fell harmlessly to the ground. Six men then surged forward from the two sides of the tower and hurled their spears. All of them were on target, and each one of the forged iron tips found their way to the monster's breast. But again they failed to pierce the Beast, who now seemed indestructible. The soldiers called back to Arcus and told him to flee, urging him to bring word of the dreaded dragon back to Urmina. As Arcus mounted, the Beast quickly turned and lashed out with her tail, destroying the watchtower with one single blow and killing the troops inside.

The men on the ground somehow managed to avoid the cascading debris from the watchtower and ran to their horses, hoping to escape Hexula's fury. But just after they mounted, the Beast roared and breathed fire so hot that it consumed them instantly. All were smoldered, leaving Arcus as the only one to evade the monster's wrath. He looked back at his fallen comrades and paused for just a moment, then spurred his horse to full speed in an effort to outrun the Beast. If the Beast had one weakness, it was that she moved very slowly. She knew that she could not catch the one who escaped, so she simply finished the task at hand by stomping on the barracks until there was nothing left but a pile of rubble. Then she let out another roar—one that could deafen men, fell trees, and split stone— before continuing her march toward Urmina. From a distance, Malgyron watched her, smiling broadly and feeling his strength increase as the Beast began her assault on the three kingdoms.

As Bovillus went to check on Magdala, he knocked on her door and called out to her. "Magdala," he said, "are you there?"

At first there was no response. He tried again, and as he placed his ear against the door, he could have sworn that he heard her sobbing. It was a muffled sound, as if she was crying while holding a pillow to her face. Again he knocked and called out. "Magdala, I can hear you crying. Whatever is wrong? Please open the door; we are worried about you."

After another minute elapsed, Bovillus heard her getting out of bed and walking toward the door. The knob turned and the door was opened, but only a crack. Magdala had unlocked it and walked away, going back over to the window while holding a pillow in her hands. Bovillus stepped in and closed the door behind him.

"Magdala," he said. "Please tell me what is wrong. I only want to help."

"I don't see how you can help me," Magdala replied. "I have greatly sinned, and my sin caused a great man to die. I know it now, because I saw it in a dream. He is gone, Bovillus. The people of Mavinor have executed our savior and the one and only son of The Author. And it has all happened because of me. How can I ever forgive myself? How can I even go on living? The world would have been better off if I had never been born."

"No, Magdala," Bovillus answered. "You must not say such things. Moreover I can help you, because I can tell you with certainty that you are wrong in your assumptions."

"How am I wrong?" Magdala said.

"You did not cause the death of King Gobius," Bovillus said. "All of us did."

"All of us?" Magdala said, incredulous. "What do you mean by 'all of us?' You certainly had nothing to do with his death. The good people of Xamnon had nothing to do with it. And obviously Silex and the rest of the royal guards had nothing to do with it. After all they tried to save him, didn't they?"

"Yes, they did," Bovillus said. "But like you and I and everyone else in the world, they are all sinners. Great men that they are, they are still sinners."

"What does that have to do with anything?" Magdala asked.

"I have been making great progress on The Scrolls," Bovillus replied. "I recently uncovered a good deal of material concerning the son's death, and why it had to happen. You are right. Gobius is dead, for everything I have found confirms it. But he is not dead because of you. He didn't just sacrifice his life for you, Magdala. He sacrificed his life for all of us. I can even quote the exact passage I found. It goes as follows.

" 'When The Author's son has made the supreme sacrifice, know that the sacrifice was not made for one, but for many. For just as it is not the fault of one that he died, nor is the redemption that comes from his death for just one. Rather it is all of mankind that is responsible for his death, and all of mankind is redeemed through his sacrifice. The son will have given his life for the world in order to save its people from their sins. Woe unto those sinners who do not repent and do not believe, but blessed are those who do repent and do believe. Their reward shall be great, and the son will continue to watch over them, even after he dies.'

"Don't you see, Magdala? It is almost arrogant for you to claim responsibility for his death, because you would be saying that his sacrifice was for you and you alone. I believe that you are indeed the 'one' of whom The Scrolls speak, the one who is not at fault for the son's death. But you must believe it yourself. You must accept it in your own heart and realize that he gave his life for all of us, because all of us needed his redemption. Forgive yourself, Magdala, just as he forgave you."

Magdala was speechless. Her tears stopped flowing, and she turned away from the window to look directly at Bovillus. "Is it really true?" she asked.

"Come," Bovillus said, "let me show you. But first have something to eat. Then I will allow you to read what I have recovered, and you can see for yourself that you are not to blame for the son's death." Magdala placed her pillow on the bed and went downstairs with Bovillus to the dining room. For the first time since she and Gobius were sentenced at the Praetorium, she felt as if the burden of her guilt had been somewhat eased.

As Cidivus took his seat on the throne, Solitus stood at the base of the steps looking up at him. Sicarius, Tarsus, and Grodus then entered the room, as did Talmik, who came and stood by Cidivus' throne.

"Good morning, gentlemen," Cidivus said. "I wanted to show you who has come back to Mavinor. Surely you remember him, don't you?"

As Sicarius, Tarsus, and Grodus looked at Solitus, Grodus immediately spoke out. "Yes, I remember him," he said. "I could have killed him in the battle between Xamnon and Mavinor, but I went after the woman instead."

"He'd have been killed trying to make it through my gauntlet," Sicarius said, "if not for his cousins. Of course, we don't have to worry about them anymore, do we?"

"Very true, Sicarius," Cidivus said. "You do know, Solitus, that your king is now dead, as are all of his royal guards, including Tonitrus and Cedrus."

"So I have heard," Solitus said. He did his best to hide his emotions.

"Cedrus was the last to go," Cidivus said. "I wanted to fight him, but like a coward he ran away with the dwarf and rowed a faering out into the sea. There is no way they could have survived in such a small boat, especially given the conditions of the water over the last two days. They are dead, Solitus. All I am waiting on now is for their bodies to wash ashore. Then I will do what I intended to do with Cedrus. His body will be lowered into a cauldron of boiling oil. In fact, in order to prove your loyalty I believe I will have you lower the body yourself, Solitus. But first, we have to find it. And so I am appointing you in charge of that task. Every morning, beginning today, you will lead some troops to the sea and scour the shoreline for your cousin's corpse. When you find it, you will bring it to me so we can properly dispose of it. If you do that, then you will have convinced me that you are now one of us."

"What do you mean by saying that he will 'lead some troops'?" Sicarius said. "He is not a soldier of Mavinor. I never accepted him into my army, and I have no intention of doing so."

"Who said that he should be a soldier?" Cidivus replied. "For the time being, he is but one of my minions. Still, I want Solitus to lead the search for Cedrus' body. I think it is a fitting role for him. But first, Sicarius, maybe you should take him back to your office and show him your prized possession. Then he can go to the shoreline with the troops you assign to begin the search."

"That I can do," Sicarius said. "I'm sure he will very much enjoy the experience." Solitus looked at the general suspiciously but kept quiet.

"Grodus," Cidivus said, "I want you to begin destruction of the temples today. You have your men ready, don't you?"

"Yes, sire," Grodus replied.

"Good," Cidivus said. "Have them transport the battering rams and begin demolition. Bring torches as well to burn the interior. By tomorrow I want to see the temples razed to the ground."

"We will do our best, sire," Grodus answered.

"You are all dismissed," Cidivus said. "But be sure to come back to the palace later this afternoon. You don't want to miss our grand celebration in the Great Hall. I take it everything is ready, Talmik?"

"Of course, sire," Talmik said. "Everything has been prepared according to your specifications."

As they left, Talmik eyed Solitus cautiously, wondering if he really was looking to join the ranks of Cidivus and Sicarius, or if he came back to Mavinor with other intentions in mind.

As Tentaclus held Cedrus, Minstro, Apteris, and Volara in its grasp, the monster began to surface. Up to this point, neither Cedrus nor Minstro had seen what the thing looked like. It had only revealed its long tentacles, keeping its face and body hidden beneath the sea. As it rose, the four of them gazed down directly into its humongous eyes. The sea monster had the largest eyes that any of them had ever seen. Its head was bulbous and elongated, brownish in color with dark green circles scattered throughout. Directly beneath its head—where the tentacles came to meet in the center—was a huge, gaping mouth filled with rows of razor-sharp teeth. They anxiously stared down into the cavern-like orifice, fearing that it would be their final destination before death.

Apparently Tentaclus decided that Apteris would be the first one to go. It began lowering him toward its mouth, slowly curling its tentacle so that it could devour its prey. Apteris closed his eyes, unable to watch as he began his descent toward the huge, horrifying cavity. He could hear the crashing of the waves grow louder as the creature pulled him in closer, until finally he realized that he was only a short distance above the sea's surface. As he opened his eyes, Apteris saw the monster's mouth yawn like an open tomb. He knew now that all hope was gone, so he finally accepted his fate and prepared himself for imminent death.

Then he suddenly felt a gust of air whoosh by him from behind, as if a windstorm had just kicked up. The monster unexpectedly released him, and Apteris wasted no time in flapping his wings and getting as far away from it as possible. At first he thought the squall must have frightened the creature. But in reality its tentacle had been sliced clean through, and the portion that was cut away fell lifelessly into the sea. As Apteris looked up into the sky, he saw Chaelim shooting through the air. The monster squealed loudly and lashed out at Chaelim with a tentacle, but the Legan was able to dodge it. Then Chaelim dove toward Volara flashing his weapons, and as another tentacle came toward him, he spun and brought one of his swords around in a glittering arc. Again the blade sliced right through, enabling Chaelim to continue toward Volara and save her as well. He thrust his sword hard into the tentacle that held her, forcing the creature to release its grip. Now the Legans were free, and they quickly formed a plan to rescue Cedrus and Minstro.

As Tentaclus reared back, it lifted its tentacles high into the air, holding its last two captives a frightening distance above the sea. Chaelim motioned for Volara to fly beneath him, and as he attacked and slashed the tentacle gripping Minstro, the thing let go of him. Minstro screamed as he plunged from a dizzying height, hurtling toward the sea with no way to break his fall. But Volara flew in underneath and caught him in mid-air before he could crash into the raging surf.

While his fellow Legans were busy rescuing Minstro, Apteris was fighting his own battle to save Cedrus. After Tentaclus reached up and grabbed Apteris' foot, he thrust his sword right into and through the tentacle. Then he spun away—withdrawing the weapon in the process—and streaked toward Cedrus. When Apteris saw Chaelim hovering below, he rushed headlong into the space where Cedrus was being held and cut the beast's tentacle with both blades, slicing a portion of it away. Cedrus fell through the air as Minstro had, but was snagged by Chaelim just in time right above the surface of the water.

Now badly injured, Tentaclus elected to retreat back to the sea's murky depths, disappearing almost as quickly as it had emerged amid a huge mountain of foam. Apteris let out a breath he wasn't even aware he held, and then turned toward Chaelim. "How in The Author's name did you manage to find us?" he asked

"A dove led me here," Chaelim answered, "that one." He motioned with his head toward the east, and they saw a dove flying away in the opposite direction.

"Thank you," Apteris said. "We are all in debt to you."

"No, Apteris," Chaelim replied. "I am the one who is in debt to you."

"What do we do now?" Volara asked, happy to see her two fellow Legans seemingly patch up their differences.

"Xamnon!" the raven squawked as it flew back in among them. "Now we go to Xamnon!" With that they set out for Xamnon, with Volara carrying Minstro, Chaelim transporting Cedrus, and the raven and Apteris leading the way.

Chapter Four

Arcus raced toward Urmina, and when the guards at the North Gate spotted him, they immediately knew that something was wrong. He was one of the soldiers who had just left a short while before to relieve the guards at the outpost, so it was odd that he would be returning so soon and at such a frantic pace. They watched carefully as he approached, and Arcus wasted no time in sounding the alarm once he came within earshot of the watchtower.

"To arms! To arms!" Arcus shouted as he arrived at the gate. "Sound the shofars, round up the troops, and prepare for battle! Something dreadful is heading this way!"

"What is it?" one of the guards asked.

"A monster," he answered. "It is a fire-breathing dragon, and it has destroyed our outpost and killed all our men. I was the only one to escape."

"Come now," another guard said, "a fire-breathing dragon?"

"Yes!" exclaimed Arcus.

"Arcus, you are always forboding gloom and doom," yet another guard said. "Why should we believe you now? This tale sounds more like a bedtime story for children than anything else." The others laughed at his statement.

"You do not believe me?" Arcus said. "But you must, or our kingdom will be destroyed." When Arcus plainly saw that they would not accept his words as truth, he directed his mount to where Gladius, the general of Urmina's army, was standing just fifty yards inside the North Gate. He immediately raced toward him, and the thundering hoofbeats quickly caught the general's attention.

"General!" Arcus yelled. "General, you must round up the troops. Something terrible is heading this way. It killed all of our men at the outpost, and I had no hope of defeating it myself. Thus I have returned to warn you so you can plan your strategy for turning it back. It is a fierce beast—a fire-breathing dragon—and it appears bent on total destruction."

"Come now, boy," Gladius said. "Do you really expect me to believe such a thing? After all the years I have fought, all the roads I have traveled, and all the battles I have won, no one knows the perils of the world more than me. I can tell you that fire-breathing dragons are not among them."

As Gladius finished rebuking Arcus, they began to feel the ground beneath them move. They looked into each other's eyes, and then back toward the gate. Even the skeptical guards were now scurrying about with perplexed looks on their faces, wondering what could possibly be happening.

"Can you feel the tremors now?" Arcus said. "That is the Beast, slowly plodding toward our city walls. It aims to eradicate us. You must believe me. I saw what it did, and I saw how our spears and arrows were practically useless against it. We have to do something, General, but I honestly don't know what."

"We can start by lining up the archers," Gladius said, now showing faith in Arcus' claims. "I want them armed with yew bows and placed all along the walls at the North Gate, a hundred of them at least. This monster may have been able to withstand an attack from our men at the outpost, but let's see how it handles a flurry of hundreds of arrows flying in from all sides. I want the catapults loaded, and every guard summoned from the East and West Gates. By the time it arrives, we will be ready."

Gladius then dispatched Arcus to the palace in order to notify King Bardus of the coming storm. As he left, there was a whirlwind of activity at the North Gate. Archers filled their quivers with arrows, packing them in tightly. Soldiers loaded heavy stones onto the catapults. Men sharpened the tips of their spears, donned their armor, and drew their swords. There was no doubt that they would be equipped for the battle with the Beast when it finally arrived. They only hoped that their preparations would be sufficient to help them stave off the attack.

Grodus rode out to make his rounds and ensure that destruction of the temples was proceeding as planned. The battering rams had all been transported to their locations, and were now in place to begin the process of demolition. The plan was to first set fire to the interior of the structures, reducing whatever woodwork there was to ashes. They would start with the inner sanctum and work their way out to the chambers and furnishings beyond the sanctuary. Once the interior was consumed, the fire would be put out and the demolition of the outside could commence by swinging the battering ram. The ram would then be rotated around the structure until every wall had been knocked down.

At one of the three locations, a large crowd gathered while the fire inside the temple raged. When Grodus arrived, they surrounded him and began questioning him about what was going on.

"Why are you destroying our temple?" a woman called out. "I do not understand."

"I am working under the orders of King Cidivus," Grodus responded.

"Then why has the king issued such an order?" another man

asked. "We heard just this morning that our priest was arrested and imprisoned, and word around the city is that the same thing is being done at the other temples."

"It is time for Mavinor to realize the truth," Grodus replied. "The king realizes it. The general of your armies realizes it. The Chair of the Tribunal realizes it as well. There is no 'Author.' You people spend your time worshipping a being that doesn't even exist when you can spend it doing something for your kingdom instead. You rely on an imaginary entity to come to your assistance and save you, when you should rely on your government, your military, and yourselves. It is time for Mavinor to move forward. Stop looking back at the mistakes of your ancestors. They were ignorant and foolish, but our society today is far more sophisticated, and superior to them in every way. Trust me, the day will come when you will thank us for what we are doing."

"But shouldn't each and every one of us have the freedom to choose what we want to believe, and whether or not we want to worship?" asked a young man. "Why would you take that right away from us?"

"Sometimes sheep need a shepherd to show them the right path," Grodus replied. "We are doing all of you a favor, not a disservice."

"That's awfully arrogant of you," another man said. "I will not allow you to tear down my temple. I have worshipped here with my family for many years, and I refuse to stand by and watch while you take the battering ram to it."

"And just how do you plan to stop us?" Grodus asked haughtily.

There was no response, so Grodus walked right past him while wearing a wry smile on his face. He went to talk with the soldiers assigned to the task of demolition in order to find out how things were progressing. Grodus peeked inside the temple and saw that everything was incinerated, so he ordered his men to extinguish the fire and bring the battering ram into place.

As they prepared to swing the great ram and land the first direct hit on the outside wall of the temple, someone stepped in between the machine and its intended target. When Grodus was made aware of it, he turned and saw that it was the same man who had challenged him earlier, saying that he would refuse to stand by and watch as his temple is razed to the ground.

"What are we to do?" one of the soldiers asked Grodus.

"You already know what to do," Grodus replied. "Knock down that wall. If you have to go through him to do it, then so be it. It will be a message to anyone else who is tempted to interfere. Somehow I don't think they'll be standing in line to obstruct us when they see his body splattered against the stone."

With that, the soldiers prepared to swing the ram while several other people watched. They began to urge the man to step aside, screaming as loudly as they could. "They're going to kill you!" they yelled. "Get out of the way! You cannot stop them."

The man refused to stand down. He held his ground, firmly believing that they would not dare try to tear down the wall as long as he remained in front of it. He stood tall and proud, his arms folded across his chest and his eyes staring straight ahead at the soldiers who were preparing to swing the ram. When Grodus saw that they were still hesitant to move ahead with the demolition, he called out to them.

"Ram it down," Grodus shouted, "or I will do it myself!"

The men reacted quickly when they heard the imperious tone of Grodus' voice. They reared the ram back and swung it forward mightily. The man never moved, and as the battering ram struck, it thrust him backward against the wall. He was crushed to death under its great weight, and the people who were watching could have sworn that they heard the cracking sound of his bones breaking when he was flattened against the stone wall. As his body slid downward and lied in a crumpled heap at the base of the wall, Grodus ordered his men to remove it and proceed with the task at hand. "Knock down every one of these walls!" he commanded. "When I return later, I want to see the entire temple torn to the ground. And if anyone else should get in the way, treat them the same as this one," he said while pointing down at the man's lifeless body. With that, he went to check on the demolition at the other temples before returning to the palace to celebrate Cidivus' coronation in the Great Hall.

Sicarius and Tarsus led Solitus and some other soldiers back to the general's office. As they strode up to the entrance, Solitus could clearly see a stake in the ground just outside. The top of the stake was covered by a burlap satchel, leaving him to wonder what was being hidden underneath.

"I have something to show you, Solitus," Sicarius said. He smiled toward the others as he walked up to the stake and untied the satchel. "Tell me, gentlemen, do you think he'll enjoy the surprise?"

There were some snickers among the men standing behind Solitus. Solitus didn't know what Sicarius had in store, so he prepared himself for anything. He watched Sicarius as he finished untying the satchel and placed his hand on top of the stake. When the general quickly flicked his wrist upward and removed the satchel, Solitus found himself staring straight into the eyes of his cousin. For the first time, he learned that Tonitrus had been decapitated.

"Do you like my new decoration?" Sicarius asked Solitus. "I did the honors myself, and keep the satchel tied over it to make sure the flies stay away. I'd hate for them to ruin my prized possession."

Solitus was extremely emotional, but he had to hide his feelings. Inside he was fighting a battle unlike any he'd ever fought. Part of him wanted to fall to his knees and weep before the stake to mourn his fallen hero. Another part of him wanted to grab a sword and cut the head off Sicarius to avenge his cousin. But he couldn't allow himself to give in to either urge. He managed to stand there stone-faced before the head of Tonitrus, and quickly turned to the others. "We'd better get going," he said. "The king wants us back in time for the celebration, and we have a lot of searching to do along the shoreline."

"Yes, please go," Sicarius said. "Perhaps you'll find his brother so we can give him his final resting place as well. It would make a fitting gift for the king as he prepares to celebrate his rule."

Solitus stormed off, leading five soldiers down to the coastline. He walked well ahead of them, not trusting anyone to see his face. His eyes became teary as he imagined what it must have been like for his cousin in his last moment as the sword came down on him. But it didn't take long for his feelings of sorrow and grief to be overtaken by anger and rage, and he swore that he would not allow them to get away with what they did to Tonitrus.

When they arrived at the shoreline, Solitus split the group up into two teams of three. He sent three of them west toward Xamnon to scour the beach, while the other two went east toward Urmina with him. They walked hundreds of yards along the coast, even looking behind rocks to see if anything had washed up. But there was no sign of any bodies or articles of clothing that Cedrus or Minstro might have been wearing. Solitus dreaded the thought of finding his cousin's body. He didn't even know what he would do if he did discover it. He certainly wasn't going to allow Cidivus the satisfaction of watching it burnt in a vat of boiling oil. But what would he do with it? Where would he take it? At this point, he was even beginning to wonder whether he made the right decision by coming back to Mavinor.

When they came to a part of the shore that was particularly rocky, Solitus asked the two men who were with him to explore the area among the rocks and see what they could find. He decided that he would travel the rest of the way alone until he reached the boundary between Mavinor and Urmina. As he walked along the sand and stared up into the dark sky, his mood became more somber. He wondered if there was any hope at all of saving Mavinor, and couldn't help but think that his homeland had reached the point of no return.

As his mind wandered, the reverie was broken by the sounds of a fish floundering around in the surf along the beach. Solitus wondered why it had washed ashore, and walked over to help it back into the sea. When he came up to where the fish was lying and gazed down at it, he immediately noticed that it bore an uncanny resemblance to King Gobius' insignia. The shape and size of its body, its eye, its fins, and even the direction in which it was facing all matched perfectly with the fish that was depicted on Gobius' breastplate and shield. As he looked closer, Solitus saw something hanging from the fish's mouth. He reached down and picked up the fish, which didn't offer him any resistance at all. As he pulled it upward from the sand, he saw that the object hanging from its mouth was actually a gold chain.

Instinctively he grabbed the chain and gently tugged at it. The fish opened its mouth wider and wider as Solitus continued to extract the chain from its body. Just as Solitus thought he would succeed in the task of plucking the object from the fish, something blocked its path. The creature then opened its mouth even wider, wider than Solitus would have ever thought possible. This allowed the chain to be pulled freely once again, and as Solitus drew it out, he saw a golden medallion attached to it. But it wasn't just any medallion. Solitus noticed right away that it looked exactly like the Medallion of Mavinor. He had seen it when Cedrus showed it to him right before they left for Xamnon. Now he was looking down at the image of a unicorn, the same image he admired when he examined the Medallion previously. When he turned it over and saw the image of The Scrolls, he got a chill down his spine as he realized that what he was holding in his hands was without question the Medallion of Mavinor.

The fish began squirming once the Medallion was removed from its mouth, so Solitus released it back into the water. It circled back once and splashed its tail above the surface before swimming out to sea. As Solitus watched it go and clutched the Medallion tightly, a loud voice called out to him.

"Have you found anything?" the voice said.

Solitus quickly realized that it was one of Sicarius' soldiers. "No," he yelled out, "how about you?"

"We have found nothing," the man said.

"Very well," Solitus replied. "Let us head back and see if the others had better luck than we did." He hid the Medallion in his pouch as he turned to walk back toward them, and as he strode along the beach he looked out toward the horizon. Though it was dark and ominous, he began to feel a strong assurance regarding Cedrus' fate. Something inside told him that his cousin was still alive. It was a force he could not name and could not comprehend, but it was strong and impossible to ignore. It buoyed his spirits as he prepared to return to the castle, and he started to think about what he could do to reverse the tragic turn of events in Mavinor. Strengthened by his newfound resolve, he made up his mind that he would not give up on his homeland…not now, not ever.

Chapter Five

As Henricus prepared to meet Arcala outside for drills, he heard someone clamoring down the hallway. After going to investigate, he realized that it was coming from the room where Bovillus was doing his work on The Scrolls. The closer he came to the room, the more evident it was that Arcala was doing the shouting. Henricus walked in to find poor Bovillus cowering at his desk as Arcala stood over him. She was pointing her finger toward his face and screaming incessantly, all while Magdala stayed a safe distance away.

"Where is he?" Arcala kept asking him. "You have lied to me! I know my brother all too well. He never trains first thing in the morning. I have searched the palace grounds twice over, and he is nowhere to be found. Now tell me the truth, Bovillus, or you will be quite sorry you didn't!"

"Wait!" Henricus said. "Whatever are you doing, Arcala?"

"Bovillus has lied to me," she said. "My brother did not go out on the grounds to train. He went somewhere else. He went back to Mavinor, didn't he? Tell me, Bovillus. Where did he go?" She unsheathed her sword and held the flat of the blade up to Bovillus' neck as she finished her question.

"Stop this, Arcala!" Henricus said as he went over and grabbed the blade. He pushed it back and away from Bovillus, whose facial expression was now one of sheer terror.

"I want to know the truth," Arcala said. "You can forget about our drills, Henricus. I am not doing anything until I find out where my brother is."

"Then I will tell you," Bovillus finally said. "Solitus has indeed returned to Mavinor. Please do not hold any animosity toward me for telling the lie. He made me promise to do it for him. He wanted enough of a head start that no one would try to chase him and change his mind. I am sorry. But there was nothing I could do to talk him out of it."

"Don't worry, Bovillus," Henricus said. "This is not your fault. We all knew Solitus was planning to do it. Ultimately there was no way to stop him."

"You could have alerted your guards at the East Gate!" Arcala said. "You could have told them not to let him out of the city. Why didn't you?"

"What did you want me to do, keep him here as a prisoner?" Henricus said. "It is not my place to do such a thing. Solitus is a man—a young man—but a man nonetheless."

"He is not even twenty years old," Arcala replied. "There is no telling now what he has gotten himself into by going back home."

"I'm not sure what else I can say to you," Henricus answered. "What is done is done. Solitus has made his choice, and now we can only hope that the choice he made was the right one."

At that point, a guard came running into the room. "General," he said, "you are not going to believe this."

"What is it?" Henricus asked.

"We have visitors," replied the guard. "A talking raven, three winged creatures that appear human but are really not, a dwarf, and one of the men from Mavinor."

"One of the men from Mavinor? Who?" Arcala asked.

"The one named Cedrus," the guard answered. Arcala became ecstatic when she heard the news, while Magdala's eyes sparkled and her heart began beating rapidly.

"Bring them here at once," Henricus said.

When the guard brought Cedrus and the others to the room where Henricus, Arcala, Bovillus, and Magdala were waiting, all were mesmerized by the sight of the Legans as they entered. The raven accompanied Apteris, perched on his shoulder, while Chaelim and Volara walked in side by side. Minstro came in next, followed by Cedrus. Cedrus looked downtrodden, still wearing his brother's helm and carrying Tonitrus' sword and shield. He and Minstro were soaking wet from their time at sea, and they were exhausted. But as unattractive as Cedrus appeared, the sight of him did not stop Arcala from rushing over to embrace him. She was so elated to learn that her cousin was alive that she barely even noticed the Legans despite their striking presence.

"I am Henricus, General of Xamnon's armies," Henricus said. "Cedrus and Minstro I know, and I have even had the pleasure of meeting the raven. But who, may I ask, are all of you?" The Legans then introduced themselves one by one, and Henricus proceeded to introduce the others to them.

"How is King Antiugus?" Minstro asked.

"I am afraid he is not well," Henricus answered. "He is still in a deep sleep of some sort, barely clinging to life. I know not whether he will make it."

"I am sorry to hear that," Minstro said.

"What has happened, Cedrus?" Arcala asked, her attention focused entirely on the situation back home. "Please tell us."

Cedrus sat alone in a chair and placed his brother's gear on the floor beside him. He then bent over and buried his face in his hands, almost oblivious to the presence of the others. Minstro noticed that his friend was despondent and wasn't about to speak, so he took it upon himself to explain what had happened.

"The Mavinor you all knew is no more," Minstro said. "They have killed King Gobius. The rescue attempt failed, and Silex and the others were all killed as well. They have crowned Cidivus as their new king. When Cedrus and I returned, we were captured at the gate. The raven rescued us, but Cedrus was caught once again. I was lucky enough to hide under a water trough and ultimately find my way to where Cedrus was being held. Cidivus had planned to lower him into a cauldron of boiling oil, but we managed to escape. Our only hope at that point was to row out into the sea, where we endured continuous misery over the past few days. Without the raven bringing us food and the Legans saving us from a giant sea monster, we would not have survived."

Cedrus briefly raised his head and scanned the room. "Where is Solitus?" he then asked.

"He has gone back to Mavinor, looking for you and the others," Arcala replied. They could plainly hear the emotion in her voice as she grieved for those they lost and at the same time feared for her brother's life.

"No!" Cedrus said before once again burying his face in his hands.

"I am going back for him," Arcala said.

"But you cannot," answered Minstro. "It is not the same Mavinor that we left, Arcala. You will never get in through the gate, and even if you did, what could you possibly accomplish?"

"You can fly?" Arcala asked the Legans.

"Yes, we can," Chaelim answered.

"Then take me there," she said. "Take me back to Mavinor and drop me in an isolated place. I'll find my way to rescue my brother."

"He may not need to be rescued," Bovillus said. "What if he managed to fool Cidivus and convince him that he wants to be part of the new regime?"

"What if he did not?" Arcala asked.

"You cannot go alone," Henricus said. "We have to come up with a plan, and it has to be something more than one of the Legans dropping you over the city walls of Mavinor so you can seek out your brother."

"The Scrolls, The Scrolls," said the raven.

"What about them?" Henricus asked.

"Can they help?" the bird asked.

They all looked toward the center of the room where Bovillus was seated, surrounded by piles of paper at his desk. He was hesitant to say anything at first, but then he spoke when he realized that the entire group was looking right at him.

"I continue to make progress," Bovillus said. "There are many things I have learned, even during the short time I have been here in Xamnon. But I'm afraid that none of it is good."

"What is it?" Arcala then asked. "What is it you now know?"

"Please do not make me tell you," Bovillus pleaded.

"If there is anything you can share with us, Bovillus, then you must do so," Henricus said. "Even if the news is grim, we must all learn what we are dealing with or we will never be able to win the battle we now face."

"That's just it," Bovillus stated. "The battle may already be lost." He paused briefly, and then did as Henricus asked.

"In the material I have recovered from The Scrolls, it states that the death of The Author's one and only son will result in a great evil being released into the world. The ground will shake, the thunder will roar, the lightning will flash, and the darkness will cover the sky for all eternity. Should the people crown the one who betrayed the son as their next king, then the Age of Darkness will officially begin.

"First, the Beast will emerge from the Black Hollow. She will go to destroy the three kingdoms, crushing everyone and everything in her path. No life shall be spared, no matter how innocent. No structure shall be left standing, no matter how small. The Beast is bent on total destruction and will not cease until the last stone falls and the last life is taken. She is all but invincible, and virtually impossible to stop.

"Second, the Deliverers of Darkness shall rise from the Fire Below mounted on their great horses. Their leader, Bellicus, will come forth wearing red armor and bearing a sword so massive and so mighty that no one can stand against him. He will have his companions riding alongside him in their quest to plunge the world into eternal darkness. First there is Fames, clothed in black and riding a black warhorse. Then there are Pestis and Mortis, wearing gray and pale armor respectfully. They have come to seize the Medallion of Mavinor and forever neutralize its power, and ultimately they will go to the Mortuus Valley and claim their army, which will be known as the 'Army of Lost Souls.' It will consist of the souls of all those who died refusing to believe in The Author and accept His ways. Those who never renounced evil will be resurrected and united with the four horsemen, who will lead them to their ultimate destiny, which is to serve the King of Darkness." Cedrus' heart pounded as Bovillus spoke of the Deliverers of Darkness. He clearly remembered the visions he had, and now he knew that they were more than just a figment of his imagination.

"Finally," Bovillus said, "the King of Darkness will come to rule. He is the one who orchestrated the betrayal of The Author's only son. He is the one who ushered in the Age of Darkness, and whose actions freed the Beast and the four horsemen. Ultimately they will bow to him, as he is the one who released them from the prisons that held them all these years. He will look to rid the world of The Author's grace once and for all by extinguishing the power of the Medallion, and come to rule for all eternity. If he should succeed in gaining immortality, then he may even challenge The Author Himself."

There was dead silence in the room when Bovillus finished speaking. As the young scribe looked around at them, he saw nothing but blank stares and expressions of despair on their faces. Finally Apteris broke the silence, his voice conveying an unmistakable tone of urgency.

"How then do we stop it?" he asked. "Surely there is a way. You cannot tell me that we are helpless to stand by and watch as the world we once knew disappears forever."

"I wish I could answer that question," Bovillus said. "But I have found nothing that offers any solutions to our problem. That is why I cannot help but think that it is too late."

"It is never too late!" Apteris said defiantly. "There must be a way; we cannot give up."

"I'm afraid that it is too late," Cedrus said as he stood from his chair. "I must tell you something. Before I left Mavinor, King Gobius presented me with the Medallion. He said that it was his will and The Author's will that I have it. But when Minstro and I were attacked at sea by the monster, I lost the Medallion. I watched helplessly as it sank to the bottom of the sea after the chain slid off the blade of my sword. It is lost forever." He walked across the room and out onto a small balcony carrying his brother's helm, staring out into space as he passed by the others. The raven flew outside and landed on the rail next to him, trying its best to offer encouragement.

"Must believe," it said. "Without hope, we have nothing."

"I have lost the Medallion," Cedrus said. "I lost my king. I lost my best friends, and I have lost my one brother. How then can I not lose hope?" The raven bowed its head in sadness as Cedrus turned away. Magdala walked over to the door leading to the balcony and very nearly stepped out. Then she realized that Cedrus probably wanted nothing to do with her, so she turned and left the room. The others looked around at each other, perplexed, anxious, and unsure of what to do next.

Arcus galloped through Urmina's streets on his way to the palace. Because the air was chilly, most of the people were indoors, leaving him ample room to speed through the city unimpeded. When he arrived, he raced up the stairs and rushed into the throne room to speak with King Bardus. The king sat comfortably in his seat, examining his fingernails and almost looking disinterested as Arcus ran toward him. "King Bardus!" he yelled.

"What is it?" the king asked in a tone that indicated he was annoyed. Bardus was a short man with a neatly trimmed beard and a golden crown on his head that was laden with all kinds of precious stones. He wore a magnificent purple robe and had two servants attending to him, one on each side of his throne. As small as he was in stature, the grandeur of his regal attire and stately chair of royalty gave him a commanding presence.

"There is a great evil approaching," Arcus said. "It is a monster, a dragon that destroyed our outpost and killed all of our men who were stationed there. I was the only one to return, and now I have come back to warn our people."

"Even if I am to believe your tall tale, how does this concern me?" Bardus asked.

Arcus was stunned by the king's response. "Sire," he said, "does this not concern all of us?"

"Have you told the general?" Bardus asked.

"Of course, sire," Arcus replied. "He is mobilizing the troops at the North Gate as we speak."

"Then you have done well," Bardus said. "This is his concern, not mine. Tell me, am I the one who formulates and implements military strategy, or is that the task of a general?"

"It is his task, sire," Arcus answered after a brief lapse.

"You are right, young man," Bardus said. "Perhaps then you learned something new today. I am a king, and in my role as king I am above such matters. Let the general deal with the dragon. I will concern myself with more noble affairs."

Arcus was disillusioned, but he could say nothing more. As he excused himself and left the throne room, he heard King Bardus call to one of his servants. "Bring me more wine," he said, "and tell me if my lunch is ready to be served. I am starving." Once Arcus fully realized that the king was more concerned about a lavish meal than the welfare of his kingdom, he took it upon himself to go out and warn the people of the coming danger.

As he streaked through the streets of Urmina on horseback, Arcus bellowed instructions for its residents to batten down the hatches. They peeked out their windows to see what the commotion was all about, but most of them just looked at Arcus quizzically and dismissed his plea. They thought the young man had gotten too worked up over something and was prematurely sounding the alarm, something he was known to do. Arcus did all he could to spread the word of Hexula's approach, but when he realized the people would not believe him, he went off to join his fellow troops at the North Gate as they prepared to defend their city.

Chapter Six

By the time Arcus arrived at the North Gate of Urmina, the tremors were far more intense than what they had been. At least a hundred archers—just as the general had demanded—stood atop the city walls on each side of the watchtower. The walls of Urmina were thicker than those of Mavinor or Xamnon, and allowed for men to stand and move freely along their top portions. The archers already had their bows and arrows in hand, ready to aim and fire at a moment's notice. The same could be said for the catapults, which were all cranked back with the cogs in place and the stones loaded. The gate was secured, and several other mounted warriors—their ranks a brilliant wash of blue and gold—stood just inside armed with swords, spears, maces, and battle axes. The tension in the air was so thick that it could have been cut with a dagger, and the drear sky only served to heighten the sense of fear and anxiety as the Beast drew ever closer to Urmina.

Finally the guards in the watchtower got a clear view of Hexula on the horizon, marching slowly but steadily in their direction. They called down to their general, who began to mobilize his troops. One of the lieutenants came up to him and made a suggestion, and Gladius couldn't decide whether it was extremely courageous or exceptionally mindless.

"Let me lead some of our men out to meet it," the lieutenant said. "Why remain within our walls and wait for it to attack us? Let us go and launch an assault against it before it even comes within striking distance of our city."

"I'm not sure that's a wise tactic," Gladius replied. "I'd rather we wait until it comes within range of our catapults and archers. Once we observe how it reacts to being besieged with arrows and boulders, we can make a better determination of how we should execute our strategy. For now, let's see if the attack we launch from behind our walls causes it to retreat."

"If it doesn't," the lieutenant responded, "then I'm riding through the gate to go and confront it, and I'm bringing my men with me."

"We'll see about that," the general said.

With every step that Hexula took, the troops looking out from atop the walls marveled more and more at her great size. From a distance the Beast hadn't seemed so fearful and formidable. But as they were able to make out some of her features—such as her thickly muscled legs and frightening yellowish eyes—the terror within them grew. The roar of the Beast's terrible approach grew louder, and once Gladius discerned that the creature had come within range of their catapults, he signaled to his men to prepare to fire. Hexula was marching in a straight line toward the North Gate, so they angled the catapults toward the center and waited patiently for the general's order. "Fire!" he finally yelled out.

All at once, the stones were launched from the catapults and flew over the walls toward the Beast. The whistling noise of the hurtling boulders filled the air like the sounds from a mighty gust of wind. Hexula heard the stones approaching and immediately caught sight of them. Somehow she managed to turn to the side as they came upon her, and swung out her tail so that she smacked one of the boulders back toward Urmina. It flew at a downward trajectory towards the North Gate, and landed just a few feet in front before bouncing and crashing right through it. It happened so fast that the men in the watchtower couldn't give adequate notice to the soldiers standing behind the gate, and as the stone smashed through, it killed a few of them instantly.

Two boulders that had been launched from the other side were smoldered to ashes before they even reached their target. The Beast drew her breath and let out a stream of fire that scorched them in mid-air, achieving something no one would have thought possible without witnessing it firsthand. Another boulder that had been launched from the same side as the one she swatted away landed harmlessly and bounced off her enormous body. Having successfully countered the attack, Hexula turned to face Urmina head-on and began to march once again.

Despite what she managed to do to the North Gate, Gladius ordered his men to reload the catapults. He also gave the signal for the archers to prepare for their assault, and in unison the expert marksmen drew their bow strings back to their ears and aimed the tips of their arrows toward the Beast. They looked for a chink in her armor, a spot where she might be more vulnerable to an attack. Some of them aimed at her eyes in an attempt to blind her, while others thought they'd have a better chance of piercing her neck or breast.

When Gladius gave the command, the barrage of arrows shot toward the Beast and rained down on her. But fire leaped from her jaws and obliterated the ones that flew directly from the area closest to the watchtower. Kindled by her burning breath, the horde of arrows was reduced to ashes and crumbled to the ground. The others that were shot more at an angle further away from the watchtower bombarded Hexula's body from both sides. But they snapped and rattled on her impenetrable scales, bouncing off her skin as if they had collided with stone walls rather than the flesh of an animal.

Gladius looked on nervously as he watched the arrows fall

harmlessly to the ground, and turned to the troops manning the catapults. "Prepare to fire!" he said to them. Then he turned back toward the archers. "Don't let up! We will fight the dragon to the last arrow if we have to! Fire away!"

Another hail of arrows was launched toward the Beast, but again the attack was futile. No arrow hurt or hindered her more than the insects of the forest. Still they kept firing in accordance with their general's command, refusing to go down without a fight.

Soldiers manned the catapults as per Gladius' orders and hurled another array of stones at the dragon. But just like the last assault, it backfired on them. This time she swung out her tail and belted not one but two stones back over the city walls. They landed where several troops had been stationed, and many of the general's best men were crushed under the weight of the boulders.

At this point, the lieutenant pleaded with the general to let him lead some of the troops outside to confront the Beast. The monster was using their tactics against them, and if the arrows shot from a distance couldn't inflict any damage, perhaps several spears launched at short range might tear through her skin.

"Are you mad?" Gladius asked. "Did you not see how easily it smote the stones with its fiery breath? The same will happen to you if you run out to meet it."

"But we must try," the lieutenant replied. "We have our armor and shields to protect us. You can no longer justify waiting behind our walls until the dragon comes to us. Look at what it has done. Let me lead some men out to attack it. I believe we can stop it."

In Gladius' eyes, it was nothing less than a suicide mission. "No," he finally said. "You must not do it."

The lieutenant quickly grew angry and turned toward the men who reported directly to him. "Our general has grown fearful of our enemy," he shouted. "He is now but a coward, and I can no longer follow his orders. Who will join me in protecting our homeland? Who will ride with me to confront the Beast?"

Most of them stood by the general, but there were at least twenty men who stepped forward to accompany the lieutenant on his charge through the gate. The aspiring hero led them out toward the Beast armed with spears. They rode together in a tight formation as they advanced, leaning over in the saddle and crouching behind their shields. When they finally came within range, the lieutenant signaled for his men to sit up straight, raise their spears and rear back in preparation of the throw. As he released his weapon the others followed suit, but the Beast did not even flinch. It was as if she perceived their stratagem with a malicious intelligence that could only be ascribed to her. Hexula did not attempt to dodge the attack or breathe fire toward the spears. Instead she stood still and waited for the projectiles to make contact with her body, this time looking to prove a point. They crashed against her neck and breast, and Hexula watched as they bounced off and landed at her feet. The lieutenant could have sworn that he heard the Beast emit a semblance of a susurrus laugh, right before she launched her head forward, opened her mouth, and let out a huge ball of fire that seemingly rolled toward her attackers. Urmina's troops were smoldered by the scorching flames, and soon the Beast was on the move again.

At this point, the general was in panic mode. For the first time in his long, decorated military career, he was actually terrified. He was torn between his duties of protecting the city and protecting his troops, for he now realized that his men did not stand a chance against the dragon. In an uncharacteristic move, Gladius called for his men to retreat. Arcus was stunned to hear the command, and immediately spoke out. "General," he said, "how can we allow the Beast to freely walk through our fortifications and lay waste to our city? We must stand and fight!"

"Stand down, soldier!" the general said. "That's an order!"

There was a huge lance lying on the ground a short distance away from where Gladius was mounted. He had anticipated that he might have to use it, so he quickly told two of his men to bring it to him.

It was stout, heavy, and easily fifteen feet in length. The iron tip was sharp enough to rip through any type of armor. As they handed it to him, Gladius gripped the lance behind the vamplate and again ordered them all to retreat. They were still quite hesitant to abandon him, but he insisted. "Go!" he said, his voice grim. "If I do not kill the Beast, then you are to escort as many people as you can to the sea and use our ships to escape. Save them, and save yourselves. This could well be my final order to you; heed and obey it!"

As much as they wanted to stay and fight alongside him to the death, the remaining troops respected him too much not to follow his orders. So the archers and cavaliers fell back, though they continued to watch to see what their general planned to do. The ground was now shaking violently as Hexula drew within fifty yards or so of the North Gate, and Gladius remained just inside the city walls as the last man standing to face off with her.

While the general looked out toward the encroaching dragon, he quickly developed a plan to surprise her. He backed his mount up so that the watchtower would block Hexula from seeing him. Since the gate was directly beneath the watchtower and the Beast's eyes were a good twenty feet off the ground, the general and his horse remained out of sight by staying in a position where the tower would obstruct Hexula's view. He knew that if he timed it right, he could spur his horse to extra speed and charge through the gate just as the dragon was arriving, all without her anticipating the attack. Gladius intended to thrust his lance through the breast of the Beast and kill her instantly, and he knew that if he did not succeed, then Urmina would be annihilated. Failure for him was not an option.

Patiently the general waited as Hexula plodded along, step by step by step. His mount stamped and snorted, eager to spring into action. He clutched the reins tight with his left hand, and tightened the muscles in his right arm and shoulder as he held the bulky lance at his side. Beads of sweat began to form on his forehead as he watched the Beast draw closer. His heart raced; his stomach churned. But Gladius managed to overcome the anxiety and focus single-mindedly on lancing the Beast and saving his kingdom. He fixed his eyes straight ahead, and when he saw Hexula reach a point where she was close enough to the city walls that he could drive through and launch his surprise attack, he spurred his restless mount and bolted for the gate.

The horse wasted no time in breaking into a full gallop, quickly picking up speed as it drove toward the Beast. Gladius leaned forward in the saddle, becoming one with his mount and holding the lance outward, almost parallel to the ground. Hexula was now at a point where her head was right in front of the watchtower, so her line of vision was completely blocked off. The general was fully confident that she was unaware of his approach, and the closer he got to her, the more he believed that he would slay her and save the day.

Hexula began to turn slightly, looking to thrash the walls with her tail and send them crumbling to the ground. But before she could fully pivot, the general and his mount burst through the gate and caught her by surprise. Urmina's would-be savior used every ounce of strength in the right side of his body to point the lance upward and drive it full throttle into the body of his unsuspecting prey. The sharp tip jabbed Hexula in a spot where Gladius thought her heart might be located. He felt something give, and for a moment he believed that he had accomplished what he set out to do. He thought the lance had pierced Hexula's skin and tore through her body, and that she would soon keel over and die just outside the gate.

But he was wrong. Though the force from the lance did push her scales inward, it never managed to penetrate the Beast. The lance actually came to a dead stop at that point, and if not for the vamplate, the general's hand would have slid all the way up the shaft. Instead he was thrown from the saddle as his mount kept running, and landed hard on the ground at Hexula's feet. The warhorse saw there was nothing it could do, so it quickly galloped away before the Beast could kill it. With several of Urmina's troops watching in horror from a safe distance away, Hexula gazed down at her stunned attacker. Gladius's face was grim, and a pale death glimmer lit up his eyes as the Beast reached down and grabbed the general in her mouth. She kept him there for a moment as she stared ahead at his men, making sure they could see her. Then she reared her head back and swallowed him whole. Once she ingested him, the Beast let out a thunderous roar and began focusing on demolishing the city walls.

Knowing there was nothing else they could do, the general's men ran hastily in the other direction and began calling for Urmina's residents to evacuate. They knocked on doors and windows. They pulled women and children from their homes and dragged them through the streets. Many resisted, not knowing what was going on and believing they were being forced to leave against their will. But many others knew that the army would only have their best interests in mind, and grabbed whatever they could before fleeing with the troops.

Urmina's army had one important factor in their favor as they evacuated everyone from the city: time. The Beast moved slowly to begin with, and she would have to labor to make it beyond the kingdom's fortifications. The height and thickness of the city walls made it impossible for her to step over them, and she was far too big to fit through the gate. So the Beast was forced to use herself as a battering ram in order to carve a path to enter Urmina. But in her haste to break through, she weakened the foundation of the watchtower and brought it crashing down to the ground. It created a mountain of rubble which only made her task that much more difficult, and bought Urmina's soldiers even more time as they ushered women and children to the shore and huddled them into the ships.

One of the troops made a beeline for the castle and warned the guards of the dragon's approach. They hastened to the throne room and informed King Bardus, but he was just as dismissive toward them as he was toward Arcus when he was first told about the Beast. Bardus sat at his table cutting his meat, never once raising his eyes toward them as he administered a harsh tongue lashing. "If our city is indeed being attacked, then I would expect our general to defend it. I have no intention of leaving, nor should you. Your role is to guard the palace and protect me from harm. Now I do not wish to be bothered with this any further. I have more important matters to attend to, and I tire of hearing dragon tales." He took a sip of wine to wash down his food as he dismissed them. "Now go and do what needs to be done!"

At the docks, Urmina's troops escorted the people onto the kingdom's three ships along with whatever supplies they were able to gather on such short notice. At one point, Arcus looked back inland and saw still more women and children fleeing from the danger. He knew that others were still holed up in their homes, possibly because they had been asleep or simply too frightened to leave. With a look of determination on his face, he told his fellow soldiers that he was mounting and going back to save those who were left behind.

"Are you mad?" one of them asked. "Did you not see what that thing did to us at the North Gate? We have no choice but to set sail as soon as we possibly can. There is no time to go back, Arcus. Those who decided to remain have chosen their own fate. You heard our general's orders; we must leave immediately!"

"I do not believe that Gladius would have set sail without making one last sweep of the city," Arcus said. "Look at them. Don't you see that there are women and children still lagging behind? I have to go back, for even if I save but one life, it will have been worth it."

"Suit yourself," the soldier said. "But know that we cannot and will not wait for you. We will be casting off the moment our ships are loaded, with or without you, Arcus."

"I understand," Arcus replied. "I will make it back in time."

Arcus' mount flashed through the kingdom even faster than it had before. He saw that there were others still collecting their belongings in anticipation of their looming voyage. Arcus urged them only to take what was absolutely necessary, and promptly corralled them into the streets. "Go!" he said. "Do not waste another moment, for the dragon is coming and intends to leave our city in ruins. Run to the shore and board the ships, for they will soon be setting sail!"

From where he stood, Arcus heard the Beast's thrashing of the walls at the North Gate. With each resonating BOOM, he knew that Hexula was one step closer to entering Urmina. But it didn't stop him from continuing up the city's main route and shouting to the homes that surrounded him on both sides, hoping that he could salvage even more lives from the Beast's wrath. When he finally reached a point where he could see the North Gate, Arcus noticed that the dragon was close to penetrating the fortifications. With one final sweep of her tail, Hexula brushed aside the last of the stones that blocked her path and slowly marched beyond the walls.

"She has made it through!" Arcus yelled. "Run! Run for your lives! To the shoreline, run!" He knew there was little he could do now but urge those who remained to flee as quickly as possible.

Amid shrieks and wailing and the shouts of men, the Beast approached and began setting the city ablaze. Where there was peace and tranquility just a short while before, there was now chaos and confusion. Joy turned to dread, comfort to mourning, and exultation to wailing as the Beast carved her path of destruction. Wooden beams burned, thatched roofs crumbled and crashed to the ground, and structures collapsed entirely as the Beast's fury blazed to its height. She withered every field and pasture, and killed all the people and animals that had stayed behind. As flames unquenchable burst high into the air, Arcus knew that his homeland would soon be razed to the ground and completely deserted.

The young warrior started riding toward the coastline, always making sure that he was out of reach of the Beast's fiery breath. But when Arcus was roughly halfway there, he heard a child crying and immediately halted his mount. As he pivoted and looked back, he saw a young boy out in the middle of the road. He must have just run out of his home after Arcus had already gone by. The child had clearly been abandoned, and it was only a matter of time before Hexula stomped on him or smote the little boy with the burning hot flames that shot from her mouth.

Arcus did not hesitate. In that one moment, he reached deep down and uncovered a boundless courage he didn't even realize he possessed. He spurred his horse in the boy's direction, riding straight toward the menacing jaws of the Beast, which were opened wide and spewing out fire in every direction. Arcus knew he didn't have much time; if he lost even one second during the rescue attempt, both he and the child would be doomed. By then the Beast would be close enough to reach them with her burning breath. But he refused to allow the threat to deter him and raced toward the boy, who was now standing and looking back at the Beast. Arcus leaned over in the saddle and canted to the right, lowering his arm as far as he could. As his mount came upon the child, Arcus grabbed him and hoisted him into the saddle in one fell swoop. Then he made a sharp turn and coaxed his mount in the opposite direction. The trained warhorse executed the move perfectly, not sliding even one inch as it pivoted back. Hexula opened her mouth wide and shot a stream of fire in Arcus' direction. He felt the heat upon his back, and for a moment he thought he might be singed by the encroaching flames. But the horse outran it, and as the flames subsided, Arcus' mount bolted forward as if it were shot from a catapult. Hexula now had no chance of catching them as they dashed to the shore.

When the sea came within sight, Arcus immediately noticed that two of the ships had already left the docks. There was one left, and from a distance Arcus could see them untying the ropes and raising the sails. He continued to incite his mount, and soon it turned into a race to see if they could make it in time before the last vessel set out. The horse took them across the sand and onto the dock, its hooves rattling like thunder along the wooden planks. "Brace yourself," Arcus said to the child he now held in the saddle. "Hold on, and hold on tight!"

The soldiers on the ship saw Arcus approaching and backed away. The ship was now roughly five feet from the shore, so they couldn't imagine what he had in mind. In fact, it wasn't until the horse reached the edge of the dock that they realized what he intended to do. For just when it looked as if the animal would careen off the wooden structure and fall into the water, the warhorse dove over the edge in a fluid leap and landed safely on the deck of the ship. Arcus quickly dismounted and handed the child over to the women who were on board. "Please tend to him," he said. Then he looked over and saw the soldier who had warned him about returning for one last sweep of the city. "See," Arcus said, "I told you I'd make it back in time."

As the troops on the last ship to leave port looked back, the Beast came into view. She was lumbering toward the shoreline, clearly unwilling to let them get away unscathed. "To the oars!" one of the soldiers shouted. "The Beast is coming for us!"

The men on board rushed to the oars and began plying them through the water with rippling swiftness. But they were working against the tide, and as slow as the Beast moved, it became evident that they would be unable to escape the range of her shooting flames once she got to the shore. Arcus realized this as well as anyone, so he left the oars and grabbed his bow. "Where are you going?" one of the men asked him.

Arcus didn't answer. He ran to the stern and climbed to its uppermost point, placing his left foot just above the sternpost. He took an arrow from his quiver and drew his bowstring back as far as possible, aiming toward the Beast. "What do you intend to do?" one of the soldiers asked. "Arrows are useless against the Beast. We saw that firsthand at the North Gate."

"I have an idea," Arcus said. "Whether or not it works is another story, but we have to try something to prevent the dragon from scorching our vessel and plunging us into the sea."

When Arcus went back a second time to evacuate the citizens, he made it a point to observe the Beast as she laid waste to the kingdom.

He noticed that whenever she breathed fire, she would first lower her head and flare her nostrils. He wondered what might happen if he could land an arrow in her mouth before the flames shot out. Would it have an effect on her? Could it thwart her attack?

As Hexula arrived at the water, she actually began to wade into it. The men from Urmina knew not whether she could swim, though they had assumed it was beyond her abilities to do so. When the Beast stopped at one point—apparently intimidated by the water's depth—it became obvious that she could go no further. But it was never her intent to swim toward them. She only wished to get as close to the ship as possible so she could reach it with a flurry of flames. Arcus eyed her carefully, waiting for the Beast to make her move.

Hexula almost seemed to be smiling as she looked out toward the vessel. She was fully confident of her ability to singe the wooden planks that made up the hull and bury her victims in a watery grave. Arcus looked straight into her yellowish eyes—the focus of a terrifying visage—and despite the fear they induced, he would not allow himself to be intimidated by the Beast. Arcus knew his arrow could well be the last hope for those on board, so he continued to focus on the countenance of the dragon. The window he had was small. Arcus needed pinpoint accuracy on his shot, and he had to time it perfectly. If he shot the arrow too soon, her mouth might not be open. If he fired too late, then the arrow would be consumed by the Beast's breath.

He trusted his instincts, and allowed himself to be guided by them. Finally Hexula lowered her head, and her nostrils began to flare. Arcus held the bow steady and fired the shot. His fellow troops watched as the arrow imbedded itself in the roof of her mouth just as it had opened, causing her to roar and throw her head to the side. She shook her head violently and lowered it to the surface of the water, pawing at her mouth and trying desperately to remove the arrow. The other men on the ship continued to row, and they managed to put more distance between themselves and the Beast with each passing second.

Finally Hexula stopped shimmying, though it was unknown to the ship's crew whether she was successful in dislodging the arrow. Without warning, she pointed her head back toward the vessel and lowered it again. This time she was quick to release the fire she previously failed to launch, and it darted across the sea toward the fleeing ship. The water turned golden as Hexula lit the surface of the sea aflame, but it fizzled out before reaching the craft, leaving behind a trail of vapor. Hexula let out a thunderous roar when she realized her prey had escaped, and those who were on board rejoiced, congratulating Arcus on his well-placed and perfectly timed shot.

But the celebration was short-lived, for the people of Urmina were now adrift at sea with no destination in mind. Their resources were limited, and it wouldn't be long before their supplies would have to be replenished. They certainly didn't want to sail into the ports of their enemies, believing that Mavinor and Xamnon would either sink their ships or take all of them as prisoners. Sadly they watched the smoke billow from the pile of debris they once called home, knowing they could never go back, and not knowing where they could now turn.

Part II

Chapter Seven

Before hosting the celebration of his coronation in the Great Hall, Cidivus held a brief meeting with his inner circle. He asked for Pachaias, Sicarius, Tarsus, and Grodus to rendezvous with him privately to discuss the affairs of the kingdom, and to see how plans were progressing.

"We have a bit of a problem that might need to be addressed," Pachaias said.

"What is it?" Cidivus asked.

"Aramus is inquiring about the exile of the believers, and trying to convince the other tribunes that the arrests of the priests and the scribes were unjustifiable," Pachaias answered.

"That doesn't sound like much of a problem to me," Cidivus said. "You have always had Annus, Pontius, and Theophilus under your thumb, Pachaias. I would expect that you can prevent Aramus from bringing them over to his side, and keep all future votes at four-to-one in our favor. You can do that, can't you?"

"Of course, sire," Pachaias said. "I just wanted you to be aware of it."

"What else should I be made aware of?" Cidivus asked.

"The destruction of the temples is progressing well," Grodus said. "This morning I visited all three sites, and watched as the interiors were burned and the walls rammed to the ground."

"Perfect," Cidivus said. "Was there any resistance?"

"In fact, there was," Grodus answered. "One man tried to stand in the way of the battering ram, but I made an example out of him."

"How so?" Tarsus asked.

"By crushing his body against the stone wall," Grodus replied. "What did you think I meant?"

"You could have simply dragged him out of the way, or arrested him," Tarsus said. "You didn't have to kill him."

"You did well, Grodus," Cidivus said, interrupting Tarsus and eyeing Sicarius' first lieutenant warily. "And what of The Author's Temple? When is that scheduled for demolition?"

"Tomorrow, sire," Grodus said. "But we have received word that a resistance is forming among some of the believers, and that they plan to surround The Author's Temple in order to protect it."

"Well, clearly you know what to do," Cidivus said.

"Yes, sire," Grodus replied. "I know what to do, and I very much look forward to doing it."

"Surely you're not going to kill all of them?" Tarsus said. "Why would you do such a thing? They are not looking for a fight. They are merely trying to protect their faith. Moreover, slaughtering them will only serve to incite hostility among the rest of our citizens, and create more problems for us down the road."

"Problems I believe we can solve," Cidivus said. "Do you agree, General?" he asked Sicarius.

"Yes," Sicarius replied. "Such matters are easily resolved. There can be no arguing with brute force. Submission is the lone option."

"I do not see why this is necessary," Tarsus insisted. "Don't you want the people to support the new regime? Don't you want them to embrace our philosophy? It is one thing to separate the powers of state and religion, and quite another to infringe upon their freedoms.

The believers have their rights, just like any other. What you're doing is in violation of the law."

"I am the law," Cidivus replied, "and the only rights people have are the ones that I am willing to give them. I am troubled by the contentious tone of your voice, Tarsus. Surely you do not intend to hinder our efforts, do you?"

"I do not mean to sound contentious, nor will I hinder your efforts," Tarsus replied. "I am merely stating my opinion and offering advice in the hope that you will listen."

"Your advice is appreciated, but in this case, rejected," Cidivus said. The king then turned to Grodus. "Grodus, by the end of tomorrow I expect a full report on the demolition of The Author's Temple, and I anticipate that I will be pleased with what I hear."

"I am certain you will," Grodus said.

"And what of my dear boy, Solitus?" Cidivus asked. "General, can you tell me where he is and whether he found anything along the shoreline?"

"I took him back to my office and showed him my prized possession," Sicarius said. "I think it's fair to say that he was unnerved by the sight, as he abruptly headed to the shore with the men I assigned him. But I know not whether they found anything. I would expect them to show up on time for today's festivities, and in fact I would not be surprised if they are waiting outside the Great Hall even as we speak."

"Then let us not keep them waiting," Cidivus said. "How fitting would it be to have Cedrus' corpse on display for my moment of triumph?" No one answered him, for they suspected it was just a rhetorical question the king asked to reinforce his growing reputation for sadistic spectacle. "Thank you, gentlemen," Cidivus said. "Now let us go to the feast."

Sure enough, Cidivus found Solitus waiting outside with Talmik when the meeting was over. He was extremely disappointed to hear about their fruitless search along the coast, but was quick to remind Solitus that this would be his daily routine until Cedrus' body washed ashore. Then he informed the young man that he had special plans for him, and that he would play a prominent role in the festivities at the Great Hall. "Not only will you be assisting Talmik in serving our guests," Cidivus said, "but you will also aid in setting the tone for my reign. I think you will like what I have in store for you. Talmik, show him the way."

Cidivus slapped Solitus on the back and watched him follow Talmik down the hall. The king's aide wore a look of exasperation on his face, though he was careful to hide it from all those who were present. Talmik was still unsure of Solitus' intentions, and knew that he couldn't bear to serve Cidivus much longer. He continued to communicate secretly with Aramus, telling the tribune about Legentis' death and the king's strong-arming of Albertus. Talmik hoped and prayed that they could find a way to dethrone Cidivus, but their options were few and far in between. Until a plan could be devised, the aide was left with no choice but to feign loyalty to Mavinor's new ruler and serve as a spy for the one good, honest man who still held power in the kingdom.

Guests began pouring in for the king's grand celebration. They filed through the antechamber into the Great Hall, where several long, glossy, wooden tables had been arranged. Most of the attendees were affluent members of society, patricians who had previously been part of Cidivus' social circle. Annus, Pontius, and Theophilus arrived together and sat at a table with Pachaias. Notably absent was Aramus, who had previously revealed that he had no intention of attending the event. Sicarius led Tarsus and Grodus into the Great Hall, along with several other officers in Mavinor's army. They reported in full gear, their armor having been polished to a fine sheen.

When everyone had arrived and all the guests were seated, Cidivus had his servants pour a glass of wine for each invitee. As the cups were being filled, the king asked Talmik if Solitus was ready, and when the aide confirmed that he was, Cidivus took his goblet and stood at the front of the room. He called for everyone's attention and began to speak, basking in his moment of glory and making as big a show of it as possible.

"Good afternoon, my friends," he said. "Today is a fine day, for it is a day that we celebrate a new era for Mavinor. My reign will return prosperity to our kingdom, and help us become the great power we once were. No more shall we appear weak in the eyes of our foes. No more shall we extend our hands in friendship to those who have persecuted us. No more shall we place our trust in a being that does not even exist. No more shall we fail to enforce the laws that have been handed down to us, or lighten the sentences administered by the Tribunal. We will not allow criminals to elude the punishment they deserve, and we will certainly not allow prostitutes to escape imprisonment, or death if it is warranted. The past year has been an aberration, but when all is said and done, it will be but a distant memory, erased from the minds of our citizens and wiped away from the annals of our history. Never again shall Gobius' name be associated with Mavinor, and soon his reign will be forgotten. Let us now celebrate this momentous occasion, and drink a toast to our promising future. Raise your glasses with me, my friends, as we usher in a new age, an age of abundance, glory, and victory for Mavinor, and a time that will forever be remembered in our kingdom's future chronicles." With that they drank, and afterwards gave the new king a rousing ovation that he reveled in. When the applause died down, Cidivus again grabbed their attention. "Now," he said, "I have something I want to show you." He signaled to Talmik that it was time for Solitus to come out.

As Solitus entered the Great Hall from an alcove off to the side, he displayed a black and silver military uniform that would become the new attire for Mavinor's army. The helm was silver with a black crest that was mounted longitudinally. Protecting the torso was a black breastplate bearing a silver insignia for those who may have earned it. On his hands, Solitus sported silver plate armor demi-gaunts, under which he wore black gloves made of padded leather. The leg armor consisted of silver greaves and black leather boots, and though it had an adverse effect on the soldier's mobility, the extra protection it afforded more than compensated for it.

"Behold," Cidivus said, "new military uniforms for a new era!" Again the crowd erupted in cheers as Cidivus unveiled his unique creation. "I hope you like them," he continued, "for I know that our general certainly approves of our army's redesigned image." Sicarius bore the semblance of a smile as the crowd looked over at him, but inside he was really stewing.

"And now," Cidivus said, "I should introduce to you the young man who was kind enough to pose for us this afternoon. You may remove your helm, boy." Solitus was irked at the way he was being utilized and addressed by Cidivus, but he played along and followed the king's directive.

"Do you all remember this youth?" Cidivus asked his guests. "He is Solitus, sister of Arcala and cousin to Tonitrus and Cedrus. He was a believer, and a loyal follower of King Gobius. Trained in the art of battle by Ignatus, he attempted to enter Mavinor's army, only to be deemed unsuited for it by our fine general. When the battle to reclaim Mavinor began, he fled to Xamnon unwillingly, or so he claims. But now he has returned to his homeland, a new man with a fresh outlook on life. He has seen the error of his ways, and is ready to join us as we bring our kingdom forward into a new age. In fact, he has volunteered to display his loyalty here today, in front of all of you. Isn't that right, Solitus?" Solitus stared at Cidivus in consternation, having not the slightest idea what he was talking about. Before he could even give it a second thought, two guards came up from behind and grabbed hold of his arms. They escorted him to where the king stood, and by pressing down on his shoulders they forced him to his knees at Cidivus' feet.

"There now," Cidivus said, "exactly where you belong. Now show us your loyalty. Prove that you have let go of your past ties, and that you are ready to join our ranks."

Solitus didn't budge, but at the same time he was afraid to fight back. He knew they would punish him if he offered any resistance, and that showing the slightest insubordination toward Cidivus could well seal his fate. So he remained there and allowed the king's ruffians to force his face to the ground until his mouth was inches away from Cidivus' boots.

"Go ahead," Cidivus said. "Show us why you returned to Mavinor. Show your devotion, and pay your king the homage he deserves." One of the guards twisted Solitus' arm so that he grunted in pain, and when his mouth opened wide they pushed it over the toe of Cidivus' boot. They pressed down even harder so that his tongue tasted the leather, and slid his head forward to leave a trail of saliva on the vamp.

"There you go," Cidivus said as he examined the boot. "You're a natural, boy." The guards pulled Solitus back to his feet and had him turn and face the crowd. "How about a round of applause for young Solitus, the newest member of my charmed circle?" Cidivus happily announced. The guests clapped uncomfortably as Solitus stood there red-faced and full of anger, his icy glare directed back in Cidivus' direction. "Now, let us eat!" Cidivus said. He ordered Talmik to have the servants bring out the food. Solitus was coerced into joining them, and he was forced to wait on the guests in full body armor. The king wanted to make sure he had a walking exhibit for the army's new uniforms, as he had every intention of bragging about them for the rest of the afternoon.

After all the food had been served, Solitus went off and hid in an alcove at the back of the Great Hall. He was both embarrassed and enraged over what Cidivus had done to him, but his resolve to turn the tide in Mavinor grew even stronger. He took the Medallion out of his pouch and examined it closely, peering down into the eyes of the unicorn emblazoned on the front. It practically put him in a trance, until a voice broke his reverie and startled him completely.

"How did you find it?" the voice asked. Solitus turned to see that it was Talmik standing alongside him.

"You must not tell anyone," Solitus said. "Please, Talmik, you must not reveal that I have recovered it."

"You have my word, Solitus," Talmik said. "I always wondered what happened to the Medallion. King Gobius often showed it to me, and even let me hold it from time to time. But how did you come to possess it?"

"Before his death, Gobius gave the Medallion to Cedrus," replied Solitus. "He told him that it was his will and the will of The Author that Cedrus have it. But when he escaped from Mavinor and rowed out to the sea, he must have lost it. For when I was exploring the shoreline this morning, I found a fish washed up on the beach. Looking down at it, the fish reminded me of Gobius' insignia. I saw a chain dangling from its mouth, and when I extracted the chain from its body, I saw that it was the Medallion of Mavinor."

"Incredible," Talmik said.

"Even more incredible is the fact that after I found it, I was overcome by a sense of assurance that Cedrus had survived," Solitus said. "He is alright, Talmik. I know it. Only I don't know where he is."

"That is encouraging to hear," Talmik said. "I only wish he would come back to Mavinor and help rid us of this tyrant."

"Then you do want to see him ousted," Solitus said. "I wondered whether or not I could trust you when I returned."

"And I wondered the same about you," Talmik said. "But now we both know that we can trust each other. I am sorry for the way he humiliated you in public."

"I'm alright," Solitus said. "In the end, I will have retribution. Any indignity I am forced to suffer in the interim is but a small price to pay. Are you willing to help me dispose of Cidivus?"

"Yes," Talmik answered. "In fact, I have been working with Aramus, telling him about all the terrible things that Cidivus has done since he claimed the throne. He is the only one with any kind of power or influence who can help us now. The rest are all aligned with Cidivus."

"What can we do?" Solitus asked. "What options have you and Aramus discussed?"

"At this point, the only idea that comes to mind is inciting a rebellion," Talmik answered. "If we can get the people on our side, then maybe we'll have a chance."

"I can assist you with that," Solitus said. "I also have the perfect candidate for leading it."

"Who?" Talmik asked.

"Ignatus," Solitus answered. "I will be going to his house tomorrow. I am sure he will join forces with us to save Mavinor."

"We can only hope," Talmik said.

"We cannot afford to lose hope, Talmik," Solitus said. "It is all we have now."

"I have not lost hope," Talmik said, "and clearly neither have you. We will work together, Solitus, and we will make things right again." The two men sealed their alliance with a handshake. Then they went back to their duties waiting on the guests, all to fool Cidivus into believing their loyalty and willingness to serve him were genuine.

Chapter Eight

While Cidivus and his devotees enjoyed themselves at the feast, Aramus remained at his estate and checked on Magdala's parents to make sure their health was improving. His servants tended to them dutifully, and though they missed their daughter, both of them were faring rather well. As Aramus sat at their bedside, one of his servants came into the room and announced that he had a guest.

"Who is it?" Aramus asked.

"Ignatus," the servant answered.

"By all means, show him in," Aramus said.

Aramus met Ignatus in one of the guest rooms where they sat down and discussed the events of the previous few days. Both men realized the situation in Mavinor had become dire, and they knew it had to be addressed sooner rather than later.

"Since Cidivus assumed power, he has been waging a war on our religious faith," Aramus said to Ignatus. "First, the believers in our army were exiled. Then the priests and the scribes were arrested for no valid reason. Today I learned that Albertus was forced to revise the curriculum at the Academy and remove all references to The

Author and The Scrolls. Just as Sicarius executed our good friend, Tonitrus, this morning Cidivus beheaded Legentis for refusing to tell him where the material recovered from The Scrolls is being hidden. He even had Grodus demolish the temples, and word is that they plan to raze The Author's Temple to the ground tomorrow."

"I cannot believe this is happening," Ignatus replied. "It is all so surreal. If only…"

"How many times do I have to tell you?" Aramus asked. "You must stop wallowing in self-pity, Ignatus. There is nothing you could have done to prevent this from happening. Even if you had accompanied Silex and the others on their ill-fated rescue mission, you only would have died along with them. Difficult as it may be, you have to move on."

"Then what are we to do?" Ignatus asked.

"The only thing I can do," Aramus said. "I am going to take my case to the people. I am the only one left with the platform to do so, and I plan to take full advantage of it. Soon the entire kingdom will hear about the atrocities that have taken place, and I am confident they will not stand for it. We are going to stir up a rebellion, Ignatus. It is the only way."

"A rebellion?" Ignatus replied, incredulous. "What are they going to do, fight Sicarius' troops with spades and sickles? They will all die, Aramus."

"Do you have a better idea?" Aramus asked, clearly agitated. "Tell me, Ignatus, what other alternatives do we have? Shall we stand by and watch as our faith is expunged from society? Shall we allow them to burn our temples to the ground and imprison our priests? Shall we sit back as the scribes are executed, leaving us no hope of ever fully recovering The Scrolls? Where will we worship? Who will lead us in prayer? What about our next generation? If they are not instructed in faith and morals at the Academy, then what will that mean for Mavinor's future? I am well aware that the odds of succeeding are long, but what else can we do at this point other than lead a revolt against Cidivus' regime?"

Ignatus did not answer. He could not even conceive of a way to respond to Aramus' reasoning, for the tribune was right. There were no other options. He simply stood up from his chair and walked across the room.

"I know you are deeply troubled, old friend," Aramus said to him. "I understand the pain you feel inside, the guilt over not doing everything you could to save Gobius. I can only imagine the grief you endured as you watched Silex and Ferox die on that battlefield. But it does us no good to dwell in the past. You must put it behind you. You have to let it go."

"Much easier said than done," Ignatus said.

Aramus told Ignatus that two petty thieves were being sentenced at the Praetorium the following day, and that he would seize the opportunity to address the people. "Will you be there?" Aramus asked. "This will be our moment, a time when we can gauge the reaction of the crowd to see if they might support an insurrection."

"I will be there," Ignatus said. "But I worry about the retaliation that Cidivus and Pachaias will direct toward you. You are risking your life, Aramus."

"Worry not about me," Aramus said. "Worry about our kingdom, and know that if I am executed for inspiring a revolution, it will have been worth it to reclaim our homeland and set Mavinor on the right path again."

"Very well," Ignatus said after pausing briefly. "I will see you tomorrow then. May The Author be with you."

"And also with you," Aramus said as he showed Ignatus out.

Back in Xamnon, Henricus saw to it that the city walls were well-fortified given the potential threat imposed by the Beast. He had no way of knowing if the prophecies of The Scrolls would prove to be accurate, but he wasn't going to take any chances. Thus all of the troops in the kingdom were mobilized and placed on high alert in preparation for a possible attack.

The Legans too were wary of the Beast's approach, but they didn't let it deter them in any way. They suspected that Orius might be hiding in the Tenebrae, so they went to search for him despite the chances of coming face-to-face with the Beast. The raven went with them, and they promised to return to Xamnon as soon as possible to share their findings.

Henricus made sure that Cedrus and Minstro got cleaned up after their long ordeal at sea. He had the royal servants prepare a hearty meal for them, and invited the others to the table as well. As the food was about to be served, they all took their seats and waited for Cedrus and Minstro.

When Minstro entered the dining room, he saw Henricus sitting at the head of the table. To his left was Arcala, and next to her was Magdala. Bovillus was seated on the opposite side, so Minstro went over and sat beside him. Shortly thereafter Cedrus entered, and when he noticed where Magdala was seated, he promptly turned away and went to the opposite side of the table. He didn't even look at her as he walked around and sat in the chair next to Minstro.

It was unusually quiet as they ate their meal. Part of it had to do with the fact that Cedrus and Minstro were starving, and gorged themselves without interruption, not even to take a breath between bites. But mostly it was the solemn mood that hung over them like a menacing array of storm clouds. Bovillus' discovery was nothing short of depressing, and they felt helpless to do anything about the fate of the world as the Age of Darkness commenced.

Then suddenly, Minstro stopped chewing his food even as a mouthful of vittles was ready to be swallowed. One by one they noticed that something was happening as his eyes lit up and he wiped the broth from his chin. Realizing that he'd be unable to speak with his mouth full, he quickly gobbled up the last bit of meat and took a sip of ale to wash it down.

"I have an idea," he then said. "I think I know how to get the answers that elude us."

"Are you sure?" Henricus said.

"Yes," Minstro replied. "There are people who can help us, and I know exactly where we can find them."

"Whoever are you talking about?" Cedrus asked.

"You know, Cedrus," Minstro answered, "for you have seen them yourself. They are the ones who helped us on our quest for the Medallion. Without their assistance, I am certain that we never would have succeeded."

"The Seers?" Cedrus said with a hint of skepticism.

"Yes," Minstro said. "We can go to the Northern Mountains and seek their help yet again. If anyone has the answers we so desperately need, it is them!"

"Who are these 'Seers'?" Arcala asked.

"When we arrived in the Northern Mountains during our quest for the Medallion, we lost our way," Minstro replied. "We arrived at a triple fork in the road, something that Cantos did not anticipate. He suggested we take the road all the way to the right, but it proved the wrong one. We entered a cave that we believed would lead to the labyrinth where the Medallion was hidden, only to come upon three ancient women who told us the labyrinth was located elsewhere in the mountain range. They were majestic in appearance, their voices authoritative and assuring. The Seers shared with us a set of three prophecies, which were cryptic and confusing at the time. But in the end those clues were crucial to helping us find the Medallion and escape the labyrinth. If we beseech them, I firmly believe they will not ignore our supplication. Rather I am convinced that they will share with us what they can—enigmatic as it may be— and that the information will only serve to help our cause."

"It sounds like it's worth pursuing," Henricus said.

"When can we go?" Arcala asked.

"As early as tomorrow morning," Minstro said. "The Legans should return by then, and we can ask them to bring us there."

"Do you remember where the Seers' cave is located?" Bovillus asked. "From what you've told us, it sounds as if the mountain passages formed a maze that was difficult to navigate."

"I think I can find the way," Minstro said. "Between Cedrus and me, our collective memories will lead us in the right direction."

"Speak for yourself," Cedrus said. His voice lacked conviction, and he still appeared to be very despondent.

"I will go with you," Arcala said. "But know that if we do not get the answers we need, then I will sneak into Mavinor myself to find my brother. There will be no stopping me."

"No one is holding you here," Henricus said. "You know that you are free to come and go as you please. As for me, I'm afraid that I do need to remain here in Xamnon, given Antiugus' condition. It only grows worse by the day."

"Understood," Arcala said. "Cedrus, you will go with us, won't you?"

The young warrior was slow to answer. They were trying to be patient with him, for they knew that he had suffered more calamity than any of them. Yet at the same time they needed his courage and fighting spirit, now more than they ever had. But it was nowhere to be found. Cedrus was lost in his malaise, just as the light was lost in the skies above the three kingdoms.

"I suppose I will," Cedrus finally said. He then finished eating and abruptly left the table, still without even casting an eye in Magdala's direction. The young woman sat there broken-hearted as she watched him go, and began to realize that she might never be able to mend their relationship.

When the Legans and the raven began searching for Orius, it didn't take long for them to uncover the destruction wrought by the Beast in the Eastern Woodlands. Trees lay along the forest floor by the hundreds, their trunks having been snapped like twigs. It deeply saddened them to see the land they once protected ravaged so terribly, and the urgency of the situation began to settle in, especially for

Chaelim and Volara, who had been hesitant to return to the natural world with Apteris.

They discussed among themselves whether they should follow the trail left by the Beast or continue searching for Orius. It was decided that they would split up, with Apteris and the raven following the Beast's path while Chaelim and Volara kept looking for their former leader. By now, Chaelim and Volara were completely convinced of Orius' treachery. The raven had explained everything to them regarding the conversations that took place between Cerastes and Orius, and the evil plan they hatched to have Gobius killed. They saw the darkness in the skies and the devastation to the forest. They had heard Bovillus' revelation regarding The Scrolls, and came to realize the truth, namely that Orius was indeed the one who aspired to be the King of Darkness.

Chaelim warned Apteris not to face off with the Beast alone, but Apteris made it clear that he would only intervene if there were still lives to be saved. In turn, Apteris asked Chaelim and Volara to be careful in their quest to find Orius. With the Surnia and the Colubri in league with him, it would be unwise to provoke him in any way. Both Legans assured Apteris that they would only make an appeal for him to relinquish his plans and bring light back to the world. If they failed to do so, then they would leave his presence immediately. They all agreed to meet at The Author's Garden—the birthplace of The Great Tree—before nightfall in order to assess the situation.

After Apteris and the raven left for Urmina, Chaelim and Volara flew west to explore the Tenebrae, where the forest's dark canopy of trees was still standing. They circled the area above, but saw nothing. There were no signs of life anywhere. It was as if all the creatures had disappeared into thin air, leaving nothing behind on the forest floor but withering plants and the scent of rotting moss. Little did they realize that the Surnia were concealing their dark bodies amidst the Tenebrae's thick foliage, and the Colubri had camouflaged themselves as they slinked through the underbrush. Both the serpents and giant owls became aware of the Legans' presence, and eyed them closely as they hovered above the treetops.

Eventually Chaelim and Volara dove from the sky into a clearing in order to conduct a ground search. From the shadows, another being had been watching them with lurid eyes, and began to slowly emerge once they both descended. When the Surnia and the Colubri became aware of what was happening, they started to close in on the Legans. Chaelim and Volara heard the rustling of leaves up in the trees, and sensed something stirring in the bushes all around them. They spun around and scanned the entire area. Their hearts began to race as they wondered who or what was surrounding them. As Cerastes finally came into view, they stared into his glittering eyes until an unfamiliar voice called out to them from behind. Chaelim and Volara turned almost in unison and beheld one of the ghastliest sights they had ever laid eyes upon.

Against the backdrop of an ominous sky, a grotesque creature deliberately approached them from behind the thicket. It was tall and muscular, with two thick, curved, pointed horns emerging from the top of its head. Its eyes were dark and dreary, and its ears pointed out to the side. Huge, webbed wings were attached to its back, and its smile revealed two rows of unsightly teeth. The creature almost looked as if it was swaggering as it walked across the clearing, and the smug grin on its hideous face only served to support that notion.

"Well if it isn't my old friends, Chaelim and Volara," the creature said. "How nice of you to come visit me."

"What are you?" Chaelim said, his tone conveying complete shock.

"Don't you remember me?" it said.

There was a long pause as Chaelim and Volara thoroughly examined this new apparition. It was Volara who then broke the silence. "Orius?" she said.

"Orius is who I used to be," the being said. "My name is now Malgyron, and that is how you are to address me from here on."

"But…how can it be?" Chaelim asked.

"Let's just say that I have undergone a transformation," Malgyron said. "The world has entered a new age, and with new beginnings come new appearances."

"From what we have seen since returning to the natural world, the appearance of this new age is not all that alluring," Volara said. "Have you not noticed the devastation in the Eastern Woodlands? So many trees have been killed, the animals have seemingly vanished, and all signs of life here are dwindling. The sky has been perpetually darkened, and we have been told that it can all be attributed to the murder of The Author's one and only son."

"Is that so?" Malgyron asked. "Who told you that?"

"It doesn't matter," Chaelim answered. "What matters is that a great evil has been unleashed, and all signs seem to indicate that it is you who have opened the gates and allowed this chaos to reign."

"So you blame me for all that has happened?" Malgyron said as he sat himself down on a tree stump. "Is that right?"

"We do," Volara replied.

"Then know that you are right," Malgyron answered in a haughty tone. "I am indeed the one who brought this all about, for it is time for me to take my rightful place. It is I who was born to rule. My time has come; the door has been opened. Soon the world will be a very different place, one that neither you nor anyone else will recognize. In due time, even The Author Himself will bow down to me."

"You are mad," Chaelim said.

"And you, my friends, are fools if you would rather spend the rest of your lives as servants when you can be served instead," replied Malgyron. "Trust me, it is better to reign in darkness than serve in the light. Now but one question remains, and that is whether or not you will decide to join me."

"Never!" Volara stated with conviction.

"Then I would suggest you return to your realm," Malgyron warned. "If you're not with me, then you're against me, and believe me when I say that you do not want to be against me." As he finished his statement, the Colubri began hissing and flashing their serrated teeth. Surnia descended from the trees and perched themselves on tree stumps, besieging the Legans on all sides. It was a menacing sight, and Chaelim and Volara quickly realized that to antagonize Malgyron even further would be a bad idea.

"You cannot defeat The Author and His grace," Chaelim said. "You are fighting a losing battle. In the end, you will have no one to blame but yourself for the fate you suffer." He looked over at Volara and motioned for her to follow him. Then he flapped his wings and soared into the air above the Tenebrae. Volara hesitated for just a moment as she looked into Malgyron's caliginous eyes, which reflected like dark mirrors. Then she too left the forest, following Chaelim as he flew toward The Author's Garden.

Cerastes let out a low hiss as he crawled further into the clearing and slithered up to where Malgyron was seated. "Do you think they will be foolish enough to interfere?" he asked.

"Time will tell what they plan to do," Malgyron said. "The Surnia will be shadowing them, and I'll know what their intentions are sooner rather than later. For now, there is no need to worry. The Beast has rolled through Urmina like a juggernaut, and will leave the kingdom in ruins. I feel myself growing stronger with each life that she takes and each structure she tears down. It is only a matter of time before I grow to be unstoppable, and the world and everything in it becomes mine. Just continue to have your spies monitor Mavinor and Xamnon. I want to know where that Medallion is hidden, for the Deliverers stand ready to retrieve it for me."

"I have had them watching things very closely," Cerastes said. "I'm sure they will have some answers for us shortly. You will be the first to know."

"Not to mention the first to purge the world of The Author's grace," Malgyron said as he let out an evil laugh.

Despite the havoc in Urmina, King Bardus remained deep inside the thick walls of his castle, enjoying his sumptuous meal while washing it down with goblets of wine. He was oblivious to what was happening outside, for his castle was somewhat isolated from the rest of the city. Although he did feel the tremors from the Beast's steps and had been made aware of the fact that several of Urmina's citizens were fleeing, it didn't faze him in the least. He took it for granted that his army would do what needed to be done in order to save the day, and that his palace guards would keep him from harm. But now all of Urmina's troops were either dead or boarded on the three ships that left port. The Beast was tearing through the kingdom like a scythe through a field of wheat, and there was nothing and no one left to stand in her way. As Bardus finished off the last of his food, the captain of his royal guard came running into the throne room.

"Your majesty, the situation has become dire," he said. "Our kingdom is crumbling, and it appears our army has failed to fight off the Beast. It is razing everything to the ground, and everywhere you look there is nothing but surging smoke and burning flames."

"Then do what you have to do to kill the dragon," the king replied.

"But sire," the captain said, "it appears to be indestructible. If our entire legion of men could not defeat it, then what can we possibly do?"

"You can do whatever needs to be done," Bardus said as a servant poured him yet another cup of wine.

The captain of the guard stormed out of the throne room without saying another word. He could see his efforts to sway the king were futile, so he decided to abandon the palace in order to save himself and the rest of the guards. But as he corralled his men and tried to exit, the Beast was right outside waiting. She breathed fire so hot that they were consumed instantly, and Hexula immediately began swiping the base of the palace with her tail. She lashed out at each stone as if she were wielding a humongous whip, and took the walls apart piece by piece.

Finally Bardus began to sense the gravity of the situation as his table started to wobble and his hand quivered just enough to cause the wine to spill from his goblet. His servants deserted him, leaving the king sitting in his stately wooden chair alone in the center of the throne room. He went to stand up, but the force from the Beast pounding against the palace brought him to his knees. Another resounding BOOM from the thrashing of her tail caused him to keel over and strike his head hard against the floor. Now in a daze, Bardus had virtually no chance of getting back to his feet as the palace shook more fiercely with each passing second.

The floors of the royal structure began to cave in, and the Beast salivated as she drew even closer to destroying it completely. In a last ditch attempt to save himself, Bardus crawled across the floor and grabbed the hem of his fur-trimmed robe, yanking it from the place where it hung. He wrapped himself tightly in the garment, hoping that it would provide a cushion if he should plummet to the floor below. When the throne room finally did collapse, Bardus braced himself and rolled up into a ball. Fortune smiled upon him as he landed safely on a couch below that was covered in a rich material, and the stones and debris fell all around him. At first he didn't realize how lucky he was. Then he peeked out through the robe and saw that he was lying in one of the royal guest rooms. The castle stopped shaking, and the rubble stopped raining down from above. Thinking his ingenuity had saved him from the Beast's wrath, he actually began laughing and stood from the couch, staring at the wreckage around him.

Then from out of nowhere, another thunderous BOOM rocked the castle and shattered the outside wall of the guest room where Bardus had landed. He fell flat on his back, and when he gathered his senses and looked up, the king found himself gazing into the frightening eyes of the Beast. The sight paralyzed him with fear and caused him to scream, but there was no one left to hear him. The foolish monarch had for so long isolated his kingdom from the rest of the world, and had even insulated himself from his people, the ones he was called to serve. He always believed that he was above those he ruled, but now that inflated sense of self had cost him dearly. For Bardus found himself alone in his confrontation with the Beast, and he watched helplessly as she lunged forward and snatched him up in her mouth. Her teeth impaled him and caused blood to drain out from all over his body. As the life was sapped from him slowly but surely, Urmina's soon-to-be former king began drifting in and out of consciousness. Just before taking his last breath, Hexula reared back and devoured his torn body, putting an official end to his reign.

Apteris and the raven arrived in Urmina shortly after Bardus was slaughtered. They could not believe the extent of the damage as they surveyed the area. It was far worse than what they had seen in the Eastern Woodlands, and there were no signs of life anywhere. Still Apteris searched through the piles of debris in the hope that some-one or something had survived. But as he and the raven went deeper into the city, they heard the roar of the Beast and saw her terrible stare for the first time. She lumbered toward them, and quickly the raven darted away.

"Apteris!" the raven shouted. "Apteris, run!"

"Not yet," Apteris replied. The Legan drew his two swords and prepared to face off with the Beast. But when she projected a huge stream of fire in his direction, he was forced to retreat. Apteris stopped in mid-air when he had reached a point where he was out of the Beast's range, but the raven called out to him again.

"It's gone, Apteris," the raven said. "Nothing left."

Apteris wanted to believe that there were survivors waiting to be rescued, but in his heart he knew otherwise. He also knew that he couldn't battle the Beast alone, so while something told him to stay and fight, he ultimately realized that there was nothing left in Urmina to fight for. So he fled the city with the raven, and looked back to see the Beast revert to tearing down the structures that were still standing. She seemed intent on crumbling every last stone to dust and smoldering every slab of wood to flickering ashes. All Apteris and the raven could do now was regroup with Chaelim and Volara in The Author's Garden and hope their companions had better news to share than they did.

When Apteris and the raven arrived there, they barely recognized The Author's Garden. It was a shell of its former self. Once a glimmering oasis filled with the vibrant colors of beautiful buds and blossoms, its dark and dreary aura now lent itself more to a graveyard. Apteris knew it could never be the same without The Great Tree, the humongous hardwood that once served as the springboard of life when The Author first created the world. He still felt that it was the death of The Great Tree that marked a turning point in the world, and its swift and sudden demise always heightened his suspicions. Now as he stood in the center of the garden, alongside the huge, jagged shell that had been the tree's base, he peered around at the pale, sickly foliage that conveyed a clear image of death, and it deeply saddened him.

"What did you find?" Chaelim asked, breaking the silence.

"Urmina has been destroyed," Apteris said. "There is nothing left. We saw the Beast, and I tried to confront it. But it was useless. The monster is huge, and its fiery breath is not something to be trifled with. Had there been anything left to salvage, I would have put forth a greater effort. But it appeared as if every living thing was either dead or gone. There were no signs of life anywhere, and like the trees of the forest, most of the surrounding structures had crashed to the ground. The Beast seemed determined to lay total waste to the city."

"Based on what Bovillus told us, it may be targeting Mavinor or Xamnon next," Volara said.

"All the more reason why we need to stop it," Apteris answered. "One thing I observed is that it moves quite slowly. Between its lack of speed and apparent intent to stay in Urmina until its task is completed, we can buy ourselves a little time. But when we meet with Cedrus and the others in Xamnon, we'll have to formulate some kind of a plan and get moving."

"And not just to address the Beast," Chaelim chimed in. "We also need to deal with our former leader."

"Did you locate Orius?" Apteris asked them.

"Yes," Volara said, "and no."

"Whatever do you mean?" asked Apteris.

"We found him, but he is not who he once was." Volara said. She became emotional and choked back tears as she continued to speak. "He has been transformed into a hideous creature as a result of the choices he has made. He told us his name is no longer Orius, and that he will now always be known as Malgyron. He was indeed the one who orchestrated the betrayal of The Author's son, and brought forth the great evil that now threatens the entire world. Malgyron said that he is tired of serving, and longs instead to be served as the King of Darkness."

"I told you," Apteris said. "I told you he betrayed us. I always knew something was awry, from the moment this glorious creation of The Author died unexpectedly." Apteris gestured toward The Great Tree as he made his point. "He was planning this for some time, to betray The Author and to leave us behind. There is no doubt in my mind."

"Looking back now, I'd have to say you're right," Chaelim said. "I was wrong all along, and for that I owe you an apology."

"No worries, old friend," Apteris said. "But tell me, what did you say to him?"

"We tried to get him to reverse course," Volara replied. "But it is clear that there is no turning back now. He is bent on ruling the world, and even talked about vanquishing The Author. He asked us to join him, but we refused. Malgyron then told us to go back to our realm and not interfere with his plan, inferring that there would be severe consequences if we did."

"How did you respond?" Apteris asked.

"I told him he was making a grave mistake, but left it at that," Chaelim said. "We were encircled by Surnia and Colubri, so a show-down with Malgyron was out of the question. We thought it best to leave his presence and live to fight another day."

"Then will you stand with me?" Apteris asked. "Despite the long odds we face, will you join me in this battle?"

"I am with you, my friend," Chaelim said. "I wouldn't have left our realm if I didn't intend to unite with you in this struggle. You have my word."

Apteris then looked toward Volara. "And I would not have went with you if I wasn't going to stand beside you right up to the end," she said. "We are in this together, along with all those who are imperiled by the Age of Darkness. There is nothing left for us to do but fight for the world we once knew."

Apteris scanned the area around The Author's Garden once again as he addressed them. "Know that we will win this war," he said. "I vow to one day return this garden to the beauty and grandeur it once possessed, to resurrect it and restore life here to its fullest." The intensity in his voice and the fire in his eyes were unmistakable, and it buoyed the spirits of his companions as they prepared for what would undoubtedly be the fight of their lives.

Chapter Nine

The next morning Solitus again led the search of the coastline for his cousin's body, but found nothing as he knew they would. He simply could not ignore the powerful feelings that overcame him when he discovered the Medallion, the feelings that convinced him that Cedrus was still alive. He only wondered when he might see him again, and whether they could come together to defeat the great evil that now resided in the world.

Knowing that two petty thieves were being sentenced that morning at the Praetorium, Solitus concocted a plan to steal Sicarius' prized possession. He discovered that both Sicarius and Tarsus were going to be there for the sentencing, so he dismissed the soldiers who were with him and immediately rode to Sicarius' office, where his cousin's head remained mounted on a stake and covered by a burlap satchel. He saw that no one was around, so he quickly removed the stake and carried it to the rear of the structure, ensuring that he wouldn't be seen. Solitus untied the satchel and turned the stake upside down, holding the top of the bag to make sure it didn't slide off. Then with Tonitrus' head lying on the ground, still covered by the satchel, he gripped the top of the burlap sack tight enough so that it wouldn't budge, yet not so tight that the stake could not be pulled free. Slowly he then began to withdraw the tip of the stake, and eventually he managed to take it out with the head still in the bag. Solitus discarded the stake and tied the satchel tight, then quickly mounted and rode off with Tonitrus' head in tow. He cajoled his horse toward the road that led to the home of his mentor, Ignatus, the man he hoped would lead them in the planned revolt against Cidivus' regime.

At the Praetorium, two young brothers named Dismus and Gestus were brought before the Tribunal for sentencing. Both were first-time offenders who had been caught stealing from the vendors in the town square, participating in a juvenile scheme to see which one of them could walk off with more items. The Tribunes knew it was a petty crime that called for a light sentence, and they prepared for what they thought would be a routine, run-of-the-mill trial.

But Aramus had other plans, for he fully intended to put his oratory skills to good use and give the speech of his life, all to inspire the people to rise up against Cidivus and his cronies. He knew that Pachaias was not going to take action, and that the other Tribunes would go along with the Chair no matter what the situation might call for. Aramus was fully unaware of Pachaias' plan and the deal he made with Orius. Pachaias still believed that he would be crowned king soon, and that as Cidivus dug a deeper hole for himself the door for his coronation would continue to open wider. He foolishly trusted Orius, believing the Legan had his best interests in mind and would intervene on his behalf to make his dream a reality. But Pachaias—just like King Cidivus—was merely a pawn in Malgyron's game. Even General Sicarius had been fooled into thinking that Orius would help him seize the throne at the appropriate time. They had all allowed themselves to be manipulated like children, and not a single one of them had a clue as to what the aspiring King of Darkness really had in mind.

As Dismus and Gestus were brought before the Tribunal, Pacha-ias began the proceedings. He asked the people what they believed the sentence should be, and everyone who spoke out seemed to agree that a couple of days in the dungeon would give them enough of a scare that neither boy would ever steal again. The boys' mother advo-cated for her sons, though conceding that what they did was wrong and acknowledging they should be punished for it. When no one else stepped forward to speak, Pachaias suggested to his fellow Tribunes that Dismus and Gestus be sentenced to three days in the dungeon. He also proposed that they be forced to provide free labor to the ven-dors they robbed until the debt was repaid. Annus, Theophilus, and Pontius readily agreed. When it came time for Aramus to vote, the elder statesman stood from his chair and advanced toward the top of the steps where Pachaias was still standing. He glared at the Chair of the Tribunal as he walked by him, and Pachaias immediately saw that Aramus was about to do something out of the ordinary. Aramus looked out at the people and made eye contact with Ignatus, who was standing in the middle of the crowd. He saw Sicarius and his men, clothed in their new silver and black uniforms. In his mind he ran through the words he wanted to say one last time, right before he called out in a loud voice that belied his small stature and olden appearance.

"Citizens of Mavinor," he bellowed, "I want to take this oppor-tunity to make you all aware of what is going on in our kingdom. You have seen the temples torn to the ground. You are cognizant of the fact that the priests and scribes were imprisoned, and for no valid reason. You were once told that the believers in Mavinor's army deserted us like cowards. But I tell you that they were exiled, forced to leave Mavinor without any semblance of a fair trial. Do you know that the head of the Academy, Albertus, was strong-armed into revis-ing the curriculum to omit all references to The Author, The Scrolls, and the deep faith that for so long has served as the foundation of our society? What will that mean for Mavinor's youth, and for the future of our kingdom? Where will our children learn the moral lessons required for them to grow into model citizens? The two youths standing before us today stand trial for a crime that is more reflective of tomfoolery than malicious intent. But I tell you that if we go down the dangerous path being hewed out by the new regime, then the acts committed by Dismus and Gestus will pale in comparison to those carried out by our next generation of young men and women.

"Cidivus' barbaric approach to ruling has already manifested itself. For one of the scribes, a good man named Legentis who had devoted his entire life to serving The Author and the people of Mavinor, was executed yesterday after being tortured repeatedly. Again, this happened without a fair trial. He was placed on the rack and stretched until his body became broken. He was burned all over his body, and blinded with hot pokers. His only crime was not revealing where the material our scribes have recovered from The Scrolls is being kept. Our new king aims to destroy it, to wipe out all the gains we have made after the many years of tireless effort to recover those sacred documents. Legentis swore that he did not know where the material was hidden, but that didn't stop Cidivus from mercilessly beheading him. It is only a matter of time before he does the same to the other scribes.

"You must know that Cidivus' real intentions are not to separate religion from government. He is actually aiming to eradicate the believers, to cleanse our society of what he believes to be a scourge upon it, when in reality it is our faith that serves as the foundation for all we are and all we do. Our faith is the moral fabric that holds our kingdom together, just as wool serves to bind a quilt. Without the fabric, the quilt falls apart, and the same will happen to our kingdom if we lose our sense of faith and morals.

"My fellow citizens, you must join with me if you wish to prevent Mavinor from suffering this tragic fate. You must rise up and not allow this tyrannical regime to take away our freedom. You must fight back before it is too late, before the underpinning of our society is transformed into something we will neither recognize nor wish to have. Unless you want to stand by and watch as Mavinor marches down the road to perdition, you must come together and prevent this implosion from taking place. For if it does, there may be no going back. The Mavinor we always knew will be gone forever, taken from us just as cruel death seizes the last breath from our mortal bodies.

"I will stand with my fellow tribunes in approving the sentence for these young men, but I do not stand with them in all other matters related to the kingdom. For they have aligned themselves with Cidivus' administration, leaving me as the lone steward of the people to speak out and appeal for your intercession. The power is in your hands, and now you must decide whether or not you wish to wield it. Should you choose not to act, you will be forced to watch as Mavinor collapses in on itself, leaving your children without a future and our kingdom without hope of ever being restored to the greatness it once knew. But if you decide to intercede, then you still might be able to salvage what is left. The choice is clear, and I only hope you will make that choice, that you will all rise up and fight for Mavinor, for you are the only hope we have left."

As he finished, Aramus turned away very slowly and stared directly into the eyes of Pachaias, who wasted no time in addressing him.

"You have made a grave mistake, old friend," Pachaias said, low enough so that only Aramus could hear him.

"But you, old friend, have made an even graver mistake," Aramus replied. He then walked back to his marble chair as Pachaias continued to eye him, while the crowd stood in stunned silence. They neither cheered nor scoffed at Aramus' speech, making it all but impossible for anyone to read their thoughts.

Finally Pachaias ended the lull by announcing that the sentence for Dismus and Gestus was approved by a 5-0 vote of the Tribunal. Sicarius, Tarsus, and their men then led the thieves away to the palace, where King Cidivus would have the final say on their punishment. As the crowd dispersed, Ignatus looked closely at those who walked by him. Cyrenus, the man who had carried Gobius to the Place of the Skull when he wasn't able to walk the last few steps, was among them. So was Rovenica, who had wiped Gobius' face with her veil as he walked the Via Mortis. Ignatus watched intently as an old man with a cane dragged himself along, surrounded by a throng of people. It was Jobus, the man who was arguably Gobius' biggest detractor while he was king. Jobus was the one who had persuaded the people to walk out on Gobius' speech in The Author's Temple when the former king asked them to embrace Xamnon as an ally. He was also the man who hurled the final stone at Gobius' execution, the one that toppled Gobius over the hill at the Place of the Skull as he fell to his death. Jobus' pensive demeanor indicated that he was at least considering what Aramus had entreated the citizens to do. But Ignatus still had strong doubts that a rebellion could ever succeed, and wanted no part of it. He looked up at Aramus, and the two locked stares for a moment before the old soldier turned and left the Praetorium.

As Grodus led his men to The Author's Temple with their battering ram in tow, from a distance he could see that a large group of people had surrounded the huge structure. The Author's Temple was a sight to behold, standing 50 feet high and measuring 180 feet long by 90 feet wide. It was built with vast quantities of cedar and huge blocks of the choicest stone quarried. Grodus knew that demolishing The Author's Temple would be an arduous task in and of itself, thus he wasn't in the mood for dealing with anyone or anything that might obstruct the process. But he was well prepared for this, having previously heard rumors that a faction of believers would not allow their prime place of worship to be torn down. Grodus remembered his conversation with Cidivus, and he had every intention of doing what both of them had agreed needed to be done.

"You all know that you should not be here," Grodus said to them as he approached on his huge warhorse. "Surely you heard about what happened to the man who tried to stand in our way yesterday. I would hate for any of you to suffer the same fate."

"As would we," a woman shouted. "But we cannot let you do this. Please understand that this is the only place of worship we have left. If you tear it to the ground, then where will we go to pray? Where will our liturgies be held?"

"There is no longer any need for prayer and liturgies," Grodus replied. "When will you fools begin to understand? This is why we have to take this step for you, because you are not wise enough to take it yourselves. Perhaps one day it will register in your dull minds, but until then we will do what we can to lead you to that point."

"How can you speak with such arrogance?" a young man asked. "Who are you to say that our minds are too dull to understand? Perhaps it is you and the king who do not understand."

His statement angered Grodus, who was quickly running out of patience and had no time to debate them. "Ignite the torches," he told his men. "Prepare to set fire to the interior."

The people overheard him and quickly realized that their emotional appeal would have no effect on the troops. Thus they were left with no choice but to pack themselves in tight at the front of the temple, blocking the entrance. They had no weapons, for their intention was never to fight against Grodus and his men. From the start, all they wanted was for their voices to be heard. They hoped they could convince them to relent in their demolition of The Author's Temple, but now it was quite clear that their request would fall on deaf ears.

As the soldiers lit their torches, they looked toward Grodus almost as if to ask how they should handle the situation. The big brute sensed that his men were seeking direction, so he called for those who did not have torches to draw their weapons and come with him. Several troops dismounted and unsheathed their swords, then walked with their leader toward the entrance to the temple.

As they strode up to where the crowd was standing, Grodus issued one last warning. "I tell you," he said, "that all of you shall die if you don't return to your homes. I am not asking you to step away from the door to the temple; I am telling you to do so. Soldiers who fail to heed orders must be prepared to suffer the consequences of their actions. The same can be said for civilians, and in this case, the consequences of your actions will be quite grave."

"How can you make such threats?" one woman shouted. "Look at us." She grabbed the hands of two children and gently pulled them until they were standing directly in front of her. "Do you really intend to hurt these children? Will you really slaughter us? We have no weapons. We did not come here to fight. We are peaceful people who seek a place to go and worship with our families. That is all we ask of you, that you allow The Author's Temple to remain standing and allow us to practice our faith."

"No such allowance will be granted," Grodus replied. He walked up to the people who were standing at the front of the crowd and grabbed a woman forcibly by the hair. Then he dragged her to the ground and held the handle of his mace to her neck for all to see. A man came running forth in an apparent attempt to save her, claiming to be her husband.

"Take your hands off my wife," he said as he grasped Grodus' left wrist and tried to coerce him into releasing the woman's hair. But Grodus pushed the handle of his mace forward into the man's stomach, causing him to double over in pain. He then shoved him to the ground and corralled his wife again, this time clutching her hair even more tightly than before.

The man recovered quickly and jumped back to his feet. He charged Grodus at full speed, this time looking to take the big man out. But Grodus laughed as he swiped him backhanded across the face with his mace, gashing him with one of the spikes. As the man fell to the ground, several others rushed to his aid. His wife began to scream and tried hard to wrest herself free of Grodus' vice-like grip, but her efforts were all in vain. Seemingly left with no other alternative, she thrust her leg upward and kicked Grodus in the groin, causing him to release her. Then she went over to check on her husband as he lied motionless on the ground.

Now down on one knee and grimacing in pain, Grodus went into a fit of rage. He jumped up and stormed the people with his mace, swinging wildly and taking out several of them at once. "Kill them!" he shouted to his troops. "Kill them all!"

The other soldiers came forward and began cutting down the civilians with their swords. One by one, the crowd of believers began to diminish as they were killed off by Mavinor's merciless military. Soon there was but a group of children left who huddled together and cowered in fear up against the wall of the temple. They had just watched their parents die, and many of them were crying. The only survivor left among the adults was the woman who Grodus had initially seized from the crowd. She sat by her husband as he took his last breath, and then rushed in front of the children to protect them.

"No!" she screamed. "I will not let you kill them!" She urged the children to run away, and though they hesitated at first, they eventually followed her command. When she turned back toward the troops, she saw Grodus standing over her.

"You bastard!" she said to him. "You killed my husband, and my friends. Do you really believe you will get away with these evil acts? Do you not realize that in the end there will be justice, and that you will receive retribution for what you have done?"

Grodus ridiculed her as he stared down into her eyes with a wry smile. "And who, may I ask, will deliver such retribution? The Author? The non-existent being that you senselessly worship?"

"He does exist," the woman replied, "and He will grant me the justice I seek."

Grodus yanked her by the hair again and brought her closer, then caressed her cheek with one of the spikes on his mace. "My dear, dear woman," he said. "How pretty you are. If only you were as bright as you are beautiful, then you would be a welcome addition to my stable."

"Only in your dreams," she said. "Let me go, murderer! Let me go!" She twisted violently and clawed at Grodus' arms in an effort to escape. He finally released her, but as she got up to run away she suddenly felt an excruciating pain in her back and fell face-first to the ground. Grodus stood over her still holding the handle of his mace, gazing down at one of its sharp spikes that he had imbedded in her back. She turned her head and looked up, then managed to discern what had happened. The woman howled as Grodus pulled the mace free. He examined the blood dripping from the spike and circled around her prone body until he was standing directly over her head. Her tears flowed incessantly as she lay at his feet, while Grodus peered down at his victim and made one final statement.

"I hope," he said, "that you find your 'Author' waiting for you on the other side. But something tells me that you're going to be bitterly disappointed." He then finished her off with one last blow and watched her suffer in her death throes before breathing her last.

"Burn the inside of the temple until there is nothing left!" Grodus ordered his men. "Bring the battering ram to the base of the wall on the east side, and prepare to begin demolition once the sanctuary and outlying areas have been incinerated. I want The Author's Temple to be a mere footnote in the annals of history by the end of today."

Before the Legans returned to Xamnon early that morning, they had briefly stopped in Urmina again to monitor the Beast. Upon doing so, they found her fast asleep in the center of the city. The havoc she wrought had taken a toll on her, and though Apteris suggested they launch an attack on her while she was slumbering, Chaelim and Volara talked him out of it. "Waking her will be a mistake," Chaelim said. "The Scrolls said she is all but invincible."

"There must be a way to defeat her," Apteris said.

"If there is, then we will find it," Volara said. "For now, let her sleep. For it will buy us even more time to convene with our friends and formulate a plan." Volara's advice was enough to convince

Apteris to leave Urmina and accompany them back to Xamnon.

When they arrived, Minstro explained the plan he proposed at dinner the night before. Immediately the Legans agreed to travel with them to the Northern Mountains and seek the help of the Seers of Fate, believing it to be their best chance of obtaining the answers they so badly needed. In turn, the Legans described what they had witnessed in Urmina and in the Tenebrae. News of the Beast's savagery and the emergence of Malgyron deeply troubled the others, and all of them now recognized that the fate of the world could well rest with the answers the Seers could provide them. "Let us go," Apteris said. "We cannot afford to lose any more time."

They took off from Xamnon and flew over the western end of the Tenebrae toward the Northern Mountains. Cedrus rode with Chaelim, while Minstro and Arcala were carried by Apteris and Volara, respectively. The raven accompanied them as well as they crossed over the woodlands, through the Mortuus Valley, and into the Northern Mountains. As they soared above the mountain paths, a sea of fire shooting flames high into the air was clearly visible even from afar. Immediately the Legans flew toward it and landed at its edge just behind a small stone wall.

"What is this place?" Minstro asked. "It wasn't here during our quest. I surely would have remembered it."

"I have seen it before," Cedrus said. He recalled his visions of the four horsemen, and quickly turned and ran down the mountain path.

"Cedrus, where are you going?" Arcala asked.

They all followed after him, and he stopped at a pile of stones roughly two-hundred feet down the trail. After surveying the mound of debris, he looked back toward Minstro. "Do you recognize this?" Cedrus asked.

Minstro paused for a moment, and then his eyes opened wide and gleamed like silver. "Yes," he said. "This is the entrance to the Labyrinth of Secrets."

"This is where you entered to search for the Medallion?" Arcala asked.

"And where we exited," Cedrus answered. "That is, all but for three of us."

Cedrus went back up the path and stood at the wall yet again. Staring down into the abyss, he felt the sweltering heat of the flames below as they coated his brow with sweat. He remembered feeling the same intense heat in his vision, and the appearance of everything from the path to the wall to the crevasse matched perfectly with what he saw when he blacked out on those two previous occasions. The only thing missing was the frightening cavaliers, the same ones described impeccably by Bovillus in the passages he recovered from The Scrolls. He could only wonder where they were, and if indeed they had risen from that deep chasm as he saw in his vision.

The others were now huddled around him as he continued to stare down into the seemingly bottomless pit. It almost looked as if Cedrus was in a trance, and Minstro began to worry about his friend. Cedrus' countenance was strikingly similar to what Minstro saw when his companion lost consciousness right before experiencing his previous visions. "No, tell me it is not happening again," Minstro said.

"No," Cedrus replied. "I am awake. But something doesn't feel right."

"What is it?" Arcala asked.

Before he could answer, the raven began screeching wildly. Apteris immediately looked up and drew his swords. "What is it, friend?" he asked.

"Trouble!" the raven shouted. "Trouble! We're not alone!"

They all turned around and looked back toward the passage. Now standing before them were four mounted warriors, all of whom gave the appearance of ghosts rather than men. The color of their armor matched that of their horses, and each one bore a terrifying weapon. Their faces were concealed by dark visors, and they could not have been more menacing in appearance.

"It is them," Cedrus said.

"The Deliverers of Darkness," Minstro said, "just as Bovillus described them."

"And just as they appeared in my visions," Cedrus replied.

"Something tells me they're not here to exchange greetings," Apteris said. "Arm yourselves now!" They all drew their weapons at once, and waited for their new adversaries to make the first move.

Chapter Ten

Quickly the Legans took up strategic positions and provided cover to Cedrus, Arcala, and Minstro. They eyed the horsemen carefully, and saw that they were beginning to spread out and advance toward them. The Deliverers of Darkness were looking to encircle their prey and block off the lone escape route, trapping them up against the wall. The Legans did not have time to attempt to fly off with their companions. If they sheathed their swords and went to hoist the others into the air, the Deliverers would most certainly charge and possibly reach them before they could get away. They saw no other option at this point but to stand and fight.

The cavalier in dark gray armor had a bow drawn, and Chaelim was watching him more closely than the others. Since the fighters in red, black, and pale armor all carried swords, they would need to draw closer in order to mount an attack. But the archer could fire his arrow at any time and take one of them out. It was difficult to gauge the horsemen because their faces were shielded by the visors, making it impossible to read their eyes and anticipate when they intended to strike. So rather than focus on the demeanor of the bowman, Chaelim concentrated on the tip of the arrow that pointed in his direction.

Finally, the gray attacker released his bow and let the arrow fly. Chaelim saw it all the way, and wasted no time in striking it aside with his sword. But as the arrow was fired, the other cavaliers charged and immediately began to engage their foes.

Volara faced off with Mortis, who rode high atop his pale horse and swung his sword with great precision. Volara used her ability to fly to her advantage, at one point standing with her back against the wall but then quickly darting directly over Mortis and hovering behind him. With a mighty swing she was able to knock him from the saddle, but when she shot downward to finish him off, he managed to roll out of the way. He rose to his feet as Volara drew her blade free of the soil, and soon the two were squaring off face-to-face on the rocky ground.

Chaelim was ambushed by Fames, the demon in black armor who wielded a double-edged sword. The Legan was initially forced back on his heels, but like Volara, his ability to fly gave him a decided advantage over the horse and rider. Chaelim shot up toward the sky and dove quickly at Fames, spinning in the air as he brought both swords around in a glittering arc. The horseman held up his shield and clutched it tightly, but the force of the impact was too much for him. He was forced to let go of the reins and tumbled to the ground, leaving him in a vulnerable position. But as Chaelim descended, Fames parried Chaelim's sword away and quickly got back to his feet. Now they too were engaged and rattled their swords against each other in a furious clash of wills.

Apteris inherited the unenviable task of facing Bellicus. The leader of the Deliverers of Darkness effortlessly waved his enormous sword through the air, almost as if it were but a wand in the hands of a warlock. Apteris was forced to keep his distance due to the sword's length, and while his wings helped him stay far enough away as he streaked through the air, the sheer size of the sword made it extraordinarily difficult to launch any kind of an attack against Bellicus. He remained mounted atop his reddish horse, his armor looking as though it were running with blood. Apteris just tried to keep him at bay and prevent him from going after the others, all the while keeping an eye on Chaelim and Volara as they fought for their lives.

Pestis drew an arrow from his quiver and looked to get off another shot. He was aiming not at the Legans, but at Cedrus, Arcala, and Minstro, all of whom stood shoulder-to-shoulder back against the wall. But as he pulled back his bow and prepared to let the arrow fly, it was snatched away by the talons of the raven. The bird dropped it to the ground and began flying into the face of the archer. Although he was protected by the visor, it bothered him enough that he continuously tried to wave the raven away as it kept coming back at him.

As the conflict raged on, Volara and Chaelim began to get the best of their adversaries, neither of whom could fight the Legans off long enough to remount. The guardians of nature finally plunged their swords into the bodies of Mortis and Fames. Thinking they were finished, the Legans went to join Apteris and help him in his battle with Bellicus.

But Mortis and Fames were far from deceased. As Cedrus, Arcala, and Minstro watched in horror, both of them rose to their feet as if they weren't even wounded. Mortis went to join Bellicus in fighting off the Legans, while Fames came right at Cedrus, who quickly stepped forward and told Arcala and Minstro to run.

Cedrus knew he was overmatched, but his courage didn't waver as he began fighting for his very life. He kept his legs firmly anchored and his shoulders taut as he stood up to the strikes of the black demon. He didn't have any room to maneuver behind him, so if he let Fames drive him back, he would risk falling over the wall and plummeting into the pit of fire. As Fames aimed high at one point, Cedrus ducked and rolled in the opposite direction, thus getting away from the wall and putting himself in a more advantageous position.

Minstro hurled a dagger at Fames, but he smacked it aside with his shield, even as he continued to duel Cedrus. Cedrus expertly coordinated the fight so that he and Fames found their original locations reversed. Now it was the horseman who found himself with his back against the wall, and Cedrus who was in position to attack and drive him over and down into the abyss.

In a venturesome maneuver, Arcala jumped onto the top of the wall and began creeping toward Fames. She hoped to sneak up from behind and thrust her weapon into his back, but the plan quickly went awry. For Fames caught sight of her, and as Cedrus lunged at him, Fames parried away the young warrior's sword and knocked him nearly unconscious to the ground. Then the dark rider spun around and swept his sword across in a wide arc toward the top of the wall. Arcala saw the blade coming at her feet and nimbly jumped over it, managing to keep her balance as she landed back on the ledge.

As Fames whiffed on his attempt, he lifted his sword high into the air in one fluid motion and came at Arcala with a thundering overhead swing. Seeing that there would be no way to avoid it other than by skittering aside, Arcala spun and shuffled over to her left. Her right foot slipped off the ledge and down toward the flames, and for a moment Minstro thought she was a goner. But she somehow kept her left foot planted and pulled her right foot back up. Minstro then took a run at Fames, but he swatted the little man aside like a mosquito as he swung his shield and thrashed Minstro's undersized body.

Now Fames had Arcala cornered, as she stood on the ledge just a few feet from a high stone crag at the end of the wall. He positioned himself directly in front of her and swung his sword in a huge arc from left to right. Behind Arcala was the crevasse, in front of her the demon, to her right was his blade flying toward her waist at maximum speed, and to her left was the crag. In what was the most terrifying moment of her life—one in which she literally stood on the verge of death—she somehow had the presence of mind to execute an amazing acrobatic move that saved her life. Arcala took two quick steps toward the crag and leapt as high as she possibly could. Then she planted her right foot against it and vaulted herself into the air, performing a reverse somersault as she jumped back over Fames' sword and landed with both feet on the ledge.

Fames' swing was so powerful that his sword penetrated the stone that Arcala had used to launch herself backward. Its blade became stuck, and Arcala immediately sensed an opening. Just as he tried to pull it free, she pounced down from the wall and rammed her sword into the cavalier's side. "You should have stayed in the pit," she said to him, before withdrawing her weapon and focusing her attention back toward the others.

But again, the piercing of the rider's body seemingly had no effect. For after briefly dropping to his knees, he rose back to his feet and yanked his blade free of the crag. Cedrus and Minstro, who had now come to, were in total disbelief, and it became clear that their only option was to retreat. So Arcala ran with them back to the trail, and they called out for their friends to follow.

The Legans were fighting a fierce battle and had Bellicus and Mortis surrounded. Apteris and Volara managed to back them up against the wall, giving Chaelim an opening. But as he was about to move in and strike, Chaelim heard a familiar murmuring sound. It was soft but clear, and when he turned his head toward a large boulder just fifteen feet away, he spotted a dove. "Could it be?" he thought. "Could this be the same dove that originally led me to the sea monster, and helped me rescue the others?" The bird continued to coo without ceasing, making it impossible to ignore.

"What do you suppose it wants?" Arcala asked.

"It wants us to follow him," Chaelim yelled out. "Start running up the trail, we'll come get you."

Fames saw them trying to get away and mounted his horse. But before he could chase them, Chaelim rushed at him and caused the horse to rear and flash its hooves. Then he called to the others and exhorted them to flee. "Follow me!" he shouted.

Knowing their weapons were useless against the Deliverers of

Darkness, Apteris and Volara launched one last offensive from above just to keep Bellicus and Mortis at bay a little longer. Then without hesitation, they sped away in the opposite direction and sheathed their swords while still in the air. The raven followed as they scooped up the others and soared toward the mountain peaks—led by the dove—where the four horsemen had no chance of reaching them. Pestis did fire one last arrow after finally retrieving his bow, but it fell short as the Legans disappeared beyond the ridge high above the Fire Below.

On his way back from the Praetorium, Ignatus encountered two of Sicarius' men, both clothed in the army's new black and silver uniforms. He didn't look closely at their faces, but as he walked past them he heard a very familiar voice call out.

"Ignatus," the voice said. "Remember me?"

When Ignatus looked back toward the soldier, he immediately recognized that it was Nefarius, the one who had searched his home when Sicarius' troops came looking for Silex and the rest of the royal guards. "Yes, I remember you," he said.

"What do you think of Mavinor's new ruler?" Nefarius asked. "Surely you have an opinion."

"I do," Ignatus replied. "But it's not one I wish to share."

Nefarius laughed and marched right up to where Ignatus was standing. He scrutinized Ignatus from head to toe before turning back toward his comrade. "You know," he said, "I am willing to wager that Ignatus could never serve in Mavinor's new army. Granted he is now but a broken old man, his skills having been severely diminished by age. But even in his prime, I don't know that he would have been worthy of donning the silver and black."

"In my prime, I was ten times the soldier you ever could hope to be!" Ignatus retorted.

Nefarius laughed again. "Careful there, old fellow," he said. "You wouldn't want to instigate anything, now would you?"

"I believe you're the one doing the instigating," Ignatus said.

"I think you'd be best advised to keep walking," Nefarius said as he placed his hand on the hilt of his sword, which was still in its scabbard.

Ignatus looked at the other soldier, who was now sporting a smug grin, and then turned his back on Nefarius. As he walked away, it was impossible not to hear the gales of laughter that filled the air. But he didn't look back. Ignatus kept going until he reached his home, reflecting on the incident as he turned the knob to open his door.

When he walked in, he was startled by the appearance of someone sitting at the table, just below where his shield hung from the wall. But he felt a sense of relief when he realized that the intruder was none other than Solitus.

"Solitus," Ignatus said, "what are you doing here?" He locked the door behind him and came over to sit at the table.

"I'm sorry," Solitus said. "I had to let myself in, for if I had waited for you outside I might have been spotted."

"I wasn't talking about my house," Ignatus said. "I was talking about Mavinor. Why have you come back?"

"How could I not come back?" Solitus replied, his tone indicating that he was surprised by Ignatus' question. "This is my home."

"It is not the same place that you left behind," Ignatus stated. "A lot has changed in just a short span of time. It is not safe for you here."

"But I had to come back," Solitus said. "When Cedrus and Minstro took us to Xamnon, they immediately returned to help Silex and the others rescue Gobius. I now know that Gobius was killed and the rescue attempt failed, and that my dear cousin was forced to flee in a faering. But I didn't know that at the time, so I returned hoping that I could be of assistance."

"It is too late," Ignatus said. "The war has been lost."

"You must not think that way," Solitus said. "Even now when the situation appears hopeless, we cannot give up. Something tells me that Cedrus is still alive, and I have found out that Aramus intends to spark a rebellion. You can lead the people to take their kingdom back from the tyrants who have seized power, Ignatus. You are the right man for the task. It may be our only chance."

"I have already had this conversation with Aramus," Ignatus answered. "Only a fool would believe that farmers and laborers stand a chance of winning a war against Sicarius' army. I am too old now to lead them, and too wise to think that an uprising under these circumstances could ever be successful. Our best fighters are gone now, Solitus. As you know, Silex, Ferox, Tonitrus, Pugius, Og, and Sceptrus are all dead. Tarmin and the rest of the believers in Mavinor's army have been exiled. There is no one left. It's over. There is nothing left for me to do but finish writing my spiritual exercises."

"How can you possibly admit defeat?" Solitus asked in a fiery tone of voice. "What kind of soldier are you? Did you not tell me during the course of my training, 'Once a soldier, always a soldier.'? Where is your courage? Where is your valor? Where is the fighting spirit that once led you to amass more honors at arms than anyone in the history of the kingdom? Have you really given up on your homeland? Are you ready to watch it burn under the rule of Cidivus, and see everything you've fought for your entire life crumble to the ground in a heap of ashes? Is that what you want, Ignatus?"

"Of course it is not what I want," replied Ignatus. "But what you, I, or anyone else may want at this point is irrelevant. Our kingdom has already crumbled, so what point is there to continue holding the dust in our hands, hoping to somehow put it all back together?"

Solitus saw the look of defeat in his mentor's eyes and the despair in the scarred and weathered lines on his face. He could not remember a time when Ignatus looked so feeble and helpless. He realized now there was nothing he could say or do to inspire him. "Tell me," Solitus said, "where is Tonitrus' body?"

"I'm afraid his body was cremated, as were the others," Ignatus said. "Cidivus had their corpses burned as a final insult, though

Aramus managed to collect their ashes in urns and place them in the mausoleum that Gobius had built."

"In this satchel," Solitus said as he picked up the burlap bag from the floor, "is my cousin's head. Sicarius was keeping it on a stake outside his office, and called it his 'prized possession.' This morning I stole it, and I wish to unite it with Tonitrus' body."

"No one saw you take it?" Ignatus asked.

"No, I am certain," Solitus said. "Even if they did, I couldn't honestly care less at this point. Let them come after me. I am going to kill Sicarius anyway. I am going to cut off his head, just as that coward beheaded my helpless cousin. You'll see, Ignatus. I will have my revenge."

"It will only get you killed as well," Ignatus said.

"One of us still believes this kingdom is worth dying for," Solitus answered.

Ignatus stared down at the bag and then looked up at Solitus. "I will have Aramus' servants burn it and place the ashes in Tonitrus' urn," Ignatus said.

Solitus said nothing in reply as he placed the satchel down on the table. He slumped his shoulders and walked toward the front door, looking back just for one moment before he unlocked it. It was as if he had something more to say, but couldn't bring himself to utter the words. Solitus opened the door and took one step outside before finally realizing that he had to convey one last thought before he left. Thus he turned back toward Ignatus and looked him in the eye as he addressed him. "You are not the same man who served as my mentor and trained me to be the fighter I am today, and I know now that you never will be."

Ignatus remained seated as the door closed, pondering Solitus' words heavily. Then he rose from his chair, stared out the window, and watched Solitus go. But just as Ignatus began to turn away and revisit his spiritual exercises, he saw Solitus collapse to the ground. Without hesitating, he rushed out the front door to where the young man was lying. "Solitus! Solitus!" he shouted while holding him in his arms.

It took a minute or so, but Solitus finally came to. Ignatus helped him to his feet, and they locked stares one last time before Solitus turned away and started walking back toward the palace. Solitus didn't say a word, even refusing to tell Ignatus about what he saw...a powerful vision of four frightening figures mounted on huge war-horses, standing above a raging pit of fire and then beginning to ride down a mountain path.

Ignatus went back inside, and when he closed the door, a serpent slithered out from behind a barrel. It started slinking toward the North Gate, expertly camouflaging itself when necessary and avoiding the wandering eyes of passerby as it made its way back to the Tenebrae.

Chapter Eleven

The dove led the Legans up and around the side of a mountain to a cliff face that opened up into a jagged cavern door. The entranceway stood at least ten feet in height, and deep in the depths of the cave there appeared to be a flickering light.

"This is it," Cedrus and Minstro said almost simultaneously.

"Are you sure?" Apteris asked.

"Positive," Minstro answered. "I remember the appearance of the cliff, the doorway to the cavern, and the light burning inside. This is unquestionably where the Seers reside."

The dove perched itself on a rock just outside the entrance to the cave and started murmuring again. "Yes, little friend, we understand," Chaelim said as he approached it. "Let's go," he said to the others.

Chaelim walked in with the others following close behind. When they descended roughly fifty feet into the cavern, the pathway forked. The light was shining from the left, and it immediately brought back memories for Cedrus and Minstro.

"That way," Minstro pointed. "When we go to the left and turn the corner, they should be sitting right there. We will see them immediately."

One by one they rounded the corner and stepped into a circular chamber centered by a fire. There they encountered the Seers of Fate, appearing just as Minstro had described them. The Seers were seated in chairs of carved wood painted with gilt and encrusted with crystals and jewels, giving them a commanding presence. The women sat calmly and quietly until all had entered. Then the one seated in the center with whitish hair and sapphire eyes leaned forward—the very picture of a majestic goddess on a divine throne—and began to address them.

"Welcome Chaelim, Apteris, Volara, Cedrus, Arcala, and Minstro," she said. The raven squawked and swooped down, landing on Apteris' shoulder. "And you as well, dear raven," she said with a bright smile and a tinkle of laughter.

"How do they know who we are?" Arcala whispered to Cedrus and Minstro.

"We not only know who you are, Arcala," the woman said, "but what it is you seek. We know why you have come, and we know what you hope to find."

"Can you give it to us?" Apteris asked.

"We shall try," the woman responded. "Whatever The Author inspires us to tell you will be revealed. I only pray that it provides you with the answers you need. As you know, the world is now in mortal danger. They have killed The Author's one and only son, and crowned his traitor as king. This has led to the onset of the Age of Darkness, and the beginning of the end for all we hold dear. Let us see how we can help."

The three of them rose from their chairs and formed a small circle on the far side of the fire. Joining hands, they faced the heavens and slowly closed their eyes. The flames of the fire began to rise, lengthening the shadows in the cavern, while the dim light danced on the Seers' hair. As the seven of them looked across the chamber, the fire increasingly obscured their view, though the bright light shining forth from the flickering flames seemingly reflected off the Seers' glowing skin and provided a clear image to focus on. They stared in wonder as the one in the middle opened her eyes and began to speak.

"To combat the Age of Darkness, you must first slay the Beast, Hexula. She has risen from the Black Hollow, her fury unleashed on the world for its sins against The Author and his one and only son. The Beast aims to destroy the three kingdoms and take every life within her path of destruction. It is already too late for Urmina, and Xamnon will be the next to fall, followed by Mavinor. In order to kill the Beast, you must retrieve the Ivory Sabre from the Cavern of Trials. The Sabre must then be thrust through the heart of the Beast. Only he whose destiny it is to face the Beast can retrieve the Sabre, for it is a solitary task reserved for he who has already decided to go it alone in this struggle. But it is not assured that even he can obtain it, for just as gold is tested and purified by fire, he too must be tried before he is found worthy to wield the Ivory Sabre. If he succeeds in his mission, then he is the one destined to slay the Beast. But be warned that he will need assistance from two of his allies in order to accomplish the feat and save both Xamnon and Mavinor from destruction."

Her words hung in the air like smoke and then danced away, replaced by the crackling of the fire. She lowered her head until she faced the other two and, as if by some mental command, they took a step to the left, bringing the second woman around to face directly across the rising flames. Her voice then proceeded to ring out as the words came to her from above.

"Second, the Deliverers of Darkness have risen up from the Fire Below. Soon they will begin to ride, and will go to the Mortuus Valley to call upon their Army of Lost Souls. They too must be defeated. As they are horsemen, only the one whose horse is superior and who wears the Medallion of Mavinor can lead his men to victory over the Deliverers of Darkness and their legion of evil spirits. They aim to capture the Medallion and bring it to the King of Darkness, who will strip it of its power forever and thus remove The Author's grace from the world. Where they go, the Army of Lost Souls will follow."

As the sound of her voice died away, the Seers circled a final time so that the last of the three faced Chaelim and the others. Her eyes seemed to glow with a brilliant white light as she looked up and began to speak.

"Finally, the Evil One who aspires to be the King of Darkness must be stopped from presenting the Medallion to the traitor. The prophecies have stated that although the Medallion is devoid of power when it falls into the hands of those who do not believe, its power will be restored if those faithful to The Author should come to possess it again. There is only one way to eternally extinguish the power of the Medallion, and that is to place it over the neck of the traitor as he sits on the throne in Mavinor. For even if the Medallion should fall to the depths of the sea or the scorching flames of the Fire Below, its power will remain. Only by permanently uniting it with the traitor can The Author's gift to Mavinor be rendered useless.

"Though the traitor serves as ruler now, this is only temporary. The Evil One plans to rule for all eternity, and he will if he succeeds in vanquishing The Author's grace from our world. He will place the traitor on the throne and furnish him with the Medallion, then kill him once he has served his purpose. The Beast, having already been unleashed on Urmina and Xamnon, will then destroy Mavinor once and for all. She, along with the Deliverers of Darkness and their Army of Lost Souls, will serve the King of Darkness, who resurrected them from their graves.

"The Evil One has lost his immortality by virtue of his betrayal of The Author, but he grows stronger as darkness continues to engulf our world. The deeds of the traitor's brutal regime, the devastation wrought by the Beast, as well as the sinister acts performed by those aligned with the Evil One only serve to increase his might. The powers of good alone cannot defeat him, for he has become too strong.

In the end, one of you will have to go ahead of the others to face the Evil One and isolate him from the conflict, keeping him at bay until help can arrive. Otherwise he will lead his forces to victory and gain back his immortality through the powers of darkness, making him impossible to stop. The Evil One and his minions must somehow be defeated.

"Three virtually impossible tasks, yet all three must now be completed to avert the Age of Darkness and bring light back to Mavinor and the entire world."

Her words echoed briefly, and then the chamber fell to silence once more. The flames of the fire burned lower, and the three women released each other's hands. They seemed almost to shrink as they fell back and sat in their chairs. For a long moment no one spoke. Then Arcala stepped forward and broke the silence.

"What about my brother?" she asked. "Is he alright?"

"Your brother has chosen his path, and is on his way to fulfilling his destiny," the Seer seated in the middle answered. "There is nothing you can do to alter his fate, Arcala, and no assistance that you can provide him. He is on his own. That is all I can tell you."

Arcala stood there dumbfounded and frustrated at the same time because she did not get the definitive response she wanted. Minstro then stepped forward.

"I do not understand," Minstro said. "How can The Author let this happen? How did this all come about? What kind of deity would allow such evil to be freed and wreak havoc on us?"

"My dear Minstro," the Seer said, "you do not understand because you do not know the history of our world and how it came to be. You do not comprehend The Author and His ways, and how He has chosen to deal with His creation. Allow me to share it with you.

"In the beginning, there was The Author. He first created the sky, then the stars, and then our world. He created the land and the sea. He saw that it was good, and decided that He would breathe life into His creation. So He planted a tree that would become the springboard of life for our world. The tree grew to such a great height that its limbs touched the clouds. Its branches were alive with greenery, its foliage lush and vibrant.

"The Author saw that it was good, and He named it The Great Tree. He created a garden around The Great Tree, an array of flowers and plants that formed a sea of bright color and filled the surrounding air with its fragrant scent. Then He created animals to live in the garden, birds to fly in and around the boughs of The Great Tree and bees to pollinate the beautiful flowers.

"He saw that it was good, so he expanded life to other parts of our world. He created many trees, all different shapes and sizes, and rabbits and deer to wander through the forests. He created fish and all kinds of aquatic creatures to swim the waters of the sea. He created a menagerie of beasts, from the wriggling serpents to the ferocious bears to the magnificent unicorns. He even created a beast bigger than any other, a marvelous creature that He named Hexula. Then, when nature was complete, He assigned it a guardian and created Orius to fulfill that task. He bestowed on Orius the power to sense when nature was in trouble, and gave him license to intervene on its behalf. He also granted him immortality, ensuring that nature would always have someone to watch over it.

"When He saw how good nature was, The Author decided to take things a step further. He created man in His own image and likeness, and watched from afar as man built the kingdom of Mavinor. Mavinor would become the apple of The Author's eye, and would remain as such throughout the ages. The Author chose to reveal Himself to His creation by inspiring men to write about Him. Through divine inspiration, numerous scribes contributed to writing a set of holy documents that came to be known as The Scrolls. The Scrolls revealed the nature of The Author and His ways to the people He created, so that they could be called His own.

"But over time, men began to turn on one another. There was discord, even to the point that factions left Mavinor to form their own kingdoms. This is how Urmina and Xamnon came to be. Their sins led to war, famine, pestilence, and ultimately, death. It is man who brought these scourges upon himself and introduced death into the world through his actions. Through his misdeeds, man lost his immortality.

"The Author looked down on man with pity and longed to save His greatest creation, so He sent man the Four Guardians. The Author gave them immortality and the power to protect man from all evil. He created Fames to protect man from famine, Pestis to guard man from plague and disease, Bellicus to prevent war, and Mortis to protect man from death.

"Though in the beginning it was good, the Four Guardians ultimately betrayed The Author. They came to realize their great power and decided to use it for their own ends, bringing pain and suffering to man instead of shielding him from the evil that had come into the world. As a result they lost their immortality, and were transformed into demons so hideous that they donned visors to cover their faces. The Author presented man with a Medallion that would grant the one who bore it the power to defeat the Four Guardians. Mavinor's greatest warrior received the Medallion and was asked to lead a war against the Guardians. Despite suffering heavy losses, he ultimately defeated them with the help of the unicorns. Only one unicorn survived that battle, the one that would later take that same warrior to the Northern Mountains when he had to secret the Medallion away for one of Mavinor's future generations.

"The Author banished the souls of the Four Guardians to a place He called the Fire Below, where they would suffer from the flames for all eternity, their tongues perennially parched and the heat forever raising painful blisters on their scalded skin, which peeled off and grew back only to burn again. But through The Scrolls, He warned Mavinor to keep the Medallion and revealed that He would save them from their sins not by another fleet of guardians, but by sending His one and only son.

"Unfortunately, Hexula saw the actions of the Four Guardians and fell victim to the same temptation. She was the largest creature in the forest, beautiful and majestic. Hexula was at one time as gentle as she was gigantic, but that faded when she too realized that she could use her power to hurt others. Her sheer size and strength made her a queen among beasts, but when she misused her great gifts, she was transformed into a ghastly monster. Hexula became an unstoppable force, and went on a rampage as she aimed to destroy all of creation.

"The Author saw what was happening, and presented Mavinor with yet another sacred object in order to save the world from ruin. He gave Mavinor the Ivory Sabre, which was then passed on to the kingdom's greatest warrior. The Author put a mark on the underbelly of the Beast in order to make her vulnerable. By thrusting the Sabre through the center of the mark, one could slay the Beast and put an end to her wrath. The great warrior faced the Beast and defeated her, sending her deep into the abyss of the Black Hollow. Just as with the Medallion, The Author warned Mavinor to retain the Ivory Sabre and preserve it in case it was ever needed again.

"After the destruction caused by the Beast, nature's guardian, Orius, implored The Author for assistance in defending nature. The Author heard his plea and created three winged sentinels to help him in his task. Chaelim, Apteris, and Volara were thus born, and along with Orius would heretofore be known as the Legans. The Author granted his newest creations the same immortality he had bestowed upon Orius, but emphasized that Orius would be their unquestioned leader and nature's foremost guardian. Like the Four Guardians, the Legans would also lose their immortality if they used their gifts for anything other than what The Author had intended.

"As The Author prepared to send His one and only son, He continued to inspire the scribes to prophesy through The Scrolls so His people could anticipate the son's arrival. It was written that a great king would come into the world, a king first recognized through a vivid dream which the dreamer would then interpret as a vision. Though coming from a humble background, the future king would show wisdom beyond his years and great prowess in battle despite minimal training. He would succeed in a great quest, returning to Mavinor triumphant, and be named as heir to the throne. Once crowned, he would be a just ruler of and a loyal steward for the citizens of Mavinor. They would one day refer to him as the one who was chosen, the one and only son of The Author.

"But The Author was quick to warn them through The Scrolls that a great evil would be unleashed on the world if His son was rejected. For if His son should be betrayed by a member of his inner circle, and the people turn against him so that they execute him and crown the traitor as king, the world will be plunged into eternal darkness.

"For an act of such great evil would allow the Beast to surface once again to destroy the three kingdoms, and resurrect the Four Guardians, who would be known as the Deliverers of Darkness. Bellicus, their leader, would guide them to the Mortuus Valley to resurrect the souls of all those who rejected The Author and His ways, and claim those lost souls as an army to accompany them on their mission. That mission would be to seize the Medallion and strip it of its power, to bring about an end to the talisman that caused their destruction. Bellicus would possess the ability to sense the Medallion, even to get inside the head of he who bears it. They would not cease until their task is completed.

"Both the Beast and the Deliverers of Darkness, along with the Army of Lost Souls, would bow to the one who orchestrated the betrayal of the son and freed them from their respective prisons. Not the traitor himself, but the one who used the traitor as a pawn in his own plan to reign eternally. He is the one who would grow stronger as darkness envelopes the world, and the one who would ultimately aspire to possess the Medallion. Should he obtain it, he would do the one thing that can forever render it powerless, and that is to present it to the traitor. The first step in removing The Author's grace from the world is the betrayal and murder of His one and only son. The second is the crowning of the traitor as king. The third, and final step, is for the Medallion to be placed around the neck of the traitor. Once that happens, the world would be on its own, having completely turned its back on The Author.

"He who orchestrated the betrayal of the son would come to be known as the Evil One. Once the power of the Medallion is extinguished, he will murder the traitor and fulfill the prophecy, 'Woe unto the traitor, it will be better for him if he had never been born.' Then he will take his place as the King of Darkness and rule forever.

"These were the revelations contained in The Scrolls. But when Xamnon invaded Mavinor and destroyed every existing copy of those sacred documents, the people came to forget what had been revealed. King Monolos of Mavinor feared for his kingdom, and worried that Xamnon might even capture the Medallion and the Ivory Sabre. After experiencing a powerful vision, he placed Mavinor's two most valuable possessions in the hands of its greatest warrior, the same warrior who had defeated Hexula and the Four Guardians. The king asked him to take his best men and ride hard into the Northern Mountains, all to secret the items away for a time when Mavinor would need them again.

"The brave warrior, named Haggiselm, mounted the unicorn and led his men north through an array of obstacles and adventures. It is he who hid the Medallion in the Labyrinth of Secrets, and as he made his way back to Mavinor, The Author appeared to him in a dream and told him to take the Ivory Sabre deep into a mysterious cave, where it would be safe until the one destined to have the weapon came to claim it. The cave would come to be known as the Cavern of Trials, and those not destined to enter would experience all kinds of negative emotions if they ventured inside, ranging from awe to fear to sheer terror.

"Over time, the believers in Mavinor did all they could to recover the material in The Scrolls and live their lives in accordance with The

Author's precepts. But Xamnon and Urmina had already fallen away from the faith, and the people of Mavinor slowly but surely began to do the same. More and more people turned away from The Author, and they forgot His teachings. Thus when their savior finally arrived, they did not receive him properly. They resented his teachings, and ultimately turned against him. They murdered him, crowned his traitor as king, and brought this evil into the world. The Author did not cause this to happen. Rather it is man who brought this fate upon himself, and that is why it is man who must now reverse it. The unthinkable has happened, for the Age of Darkness is upon us, and you may well be our last hope. We have told you what needs to be done, now go and fulfill your destinies. May The Author be with you as you confront the evil that threatens our very existence."

There was dead silence in the chamber as the leader of the Seers finished speaking. The Legans looked at each other, wondering how they could possibly overcome such insurmountable odds and complete the formidable tasks that now lay before them. Minstro and Arcala were equally distressed, and as they looked back toward Cedrus, they saw that he was gone.

Chapter Twelve

Cedrus had begun to leave the cavern even before the leader of the Seers finished explaining the history of how the world began and how its people came to shun the light and embrace the darkness. He was tired, too tired to even think about how they might be able to save their world, let alone accomplish the Herculean tasks that were now required to stave off the Age of Darkness. As he held Tonitrus' sword in his hands, he gazed down at the insignia. He saw the red cross with the blade as its base, and wished that his brother were there to help them. "Brother," he said, "if only you were here. We cannot do this without you and the others." The sorrow in Cedrus' heart was so great that it almost crushed him, and he became despondent, believing now more than ever that the world could not be redeemed.

"Cedrus," a voice then called out from behind a nearby boulder, "your time has come."

It was a familiar voice, one that exuded calm and comforted Cedrus in his hour of need. As he turned, Cedrus could not believe what his eyes were seeing. For standing before him was none other than King Gobius of Mavinor.

"You must stop tormenting yourself," Gobius said. "The world needs you, now more than ever. There is no time to wallow in despair. You are to return to Xamnon and mobilize the forces of good. Mavinor must be liberated before it is too late. You have the capacity to save our kingdom, Cedrus. Despite what you're feeling, all hope is not lost."

"But my Lord, I have lost you, my brother, and the others," Cedrus responded as he turned his back and walked away. "I have lost the Medallion, which you entrusted to me. How then can there still be hope?"

"Do not let your heart be troubled, Cedrus," Gobius said. "I will ask The Author and He will send you a helper, so that he may abide with you forever."

"What about you, my Lord?" Cedrus asked, still standing with his back turned to Gobius. "Will you also remain with me?"

"Know that I am with you always and everywhere, even until the end of time," Gobius said in a soft tone that quieted Cedrus' fears and sustained him in his darkest hour.

Cedrus paused for a second, overcome with emotion. Then he turned back toward Gobius, only to see that he wasn't there. It was as if he had suddenly vanished, leaving nothing behind but the words he had spoken. Cedrus came to believe that his deep depression was now causing him to see and hear things that weren't real. "My Lord wasn't here with me," he thought. "It was all a hallucination." He sat down on a large rock, leaned over, and buried his face in his hands. Only when he heard the others exiting the cave did he uncover his eyes and look up.

"Cedrus, are you alright?" Arcala asked.

Cedrus did not respond. He rose to his feet and walked away, then stared down over the edge of the cliff, seemingly lost in his thoughts. Arcala began following him, a look of concern draped over her face. But Minstro placed his hand on her arm, and then shook his head as she turned toward him.

As they watched Cedrus from afar, the murmuring sound of the dove returned. Their feathered friend was back, and once it got their attention the bird took off and flew southwest, toward Xamnon.

"It's time to go," Chaelim said. "We can discuss the Seers' words after we return to Xamnon."

"There is one favor I need to ask," Minstro said. "Could one of you please take me to Mizar? I must speak with my people about what has happened, for they are surely unaware of the events that have led to this tragic state of affairs."

"I will take you," Apteris said.

"Thank you, Apteris," Minstro said.

Immediately they departed with the raven in tow. Arcala took one last glance at Cedrus before walking over to Volara, who took her in her arms and soared toward the dark clouds that hung overhead.

"Cedrus, it's time," Chaelim said.

Cedrus didn't react at first, but then he turned away from the cliff and left with Chaelim, who held him at his side as they flew through the sky above the mountain peaks.

After they left, one of the Surnia emerged from behind a boulder at the top of the path and eyed them from afar as they streaked back toward Xamnon.

As Malgyron and Cerastes met in the Tenebrae, one of the Surnia swooped down into the clearing where they were having an animated conversation. The giant owl was transporting a Colubri spy, which then unraveled itself from the Surnia's talon and dropped to the ground. The serpent slinked up to them and let out a low hiss before raising its head until its body was mostly erect.

"I have information to share with you both," it said.

"Do tell," Malgyron replied.

"The one called Solitus is trying to incite a revolt against Cidivus' regime, and asked Ignatus to lead them. But he refused. Now I believe Solitus may try to lead it himself, and Aramus, the tribune, is also using his influence to start an uprising."

"Well done," Malgyron said. "A visit with the king is long overdue for me. I shall pass this information along to him so he can crush the rebellion before it even takes shape. We must do everything we can to keep him in power until he has served his purpose, and then I will dispose of him and take my rightful place. All of you will join me, and you will be rewarded for your loyalty as we move forth to conquer the world. May darkness reign forever!"

Malgyron spread his wings and left the clearing as Cerastes flashed his razor-sharp teeth in the semblance of a smile and watched him go.

Cidivus waited patiently on his throne for Sicarius to bring Dismus and Gestus back to the palace. He knew the thieves would receive a light sentence for their petty crime, but he had other plans for them. This was an opportunity for the king to send a message and establish his authority, and he had every intention of making an example out of the young brothers. As he pondered what he might do, Cidivus' reverie was broken by Talmik, who informed the king that Grodus had come to give him an update on the demolition of The Author's Temple. "Send him in," Cidivus said.

From the moment Grodus walked into the throne room, Cidivus could read his body language. The brawny warrior was smiling broadly and swaggering as he crossed the room and arrived at the base of the stairs that led up to the throne. "I take it you have good news to report," Cidivus said.

"Of course, sire," Grodus answered. "As expected, my men and I encountered a crowd of believers surrounding the temple when we arrived. I gave them a stern warning, but they refused to back down. Thus we did what we had to do."

"Were there any survivors?" Cidivus asked.

"Only the children," Grodus answered. "The last woman remaining urged them to leave, right before I killed her."

Cidivus began to snicker as he heard the news. "And what about The Author's Temple itself?" he asked Grodus. "Have the flames engulfed it yet?"

"The fire burns as we speak," Grodus replied. "By tomorrow, it should be but a pile of rubble."

"Well done, Grodus," Cidivus said as he stood from his throne and began descending the stairs. "Somehow I always knew you were the right man for the job." He put his hand on Grodus' massive shoulder and grasped as much of it as he could. "I have big plans for you," he continued. "One day, you and Sicarius will lead our men to Xamnon and destroy their kingdom. I will issue an order that you and you alone have the pleasure of killing Antiugus. Once Xamnon has been obliterated, we can focus our attention elsewhere and branch out until we have conquered the entire world."

"When will this happen, sire?" Grodus asked. "I will lead a raid on Xamnon tomorrow if you wish."

"Not yet," Cidivus replied. "Right now we need to focus on what is inside Mavinor rather than what lies outside. Once we have formed the foundation for our new society, then we can begin to take that vision elsewhere and spread it throughout the whole world. It is only a matter of time before it all belongs to us, Grodus. We will help the world realize its full potential, as it becomes a world that learns to shun faith in the fictitious and embrace the reality that the only ones we can rely on are ourselves."

As Cidivus finished talking, he heard the marching of footsteps and the clanking of armor coming from just outside in the corridor. Sicarius and Tarsus then paraded in with their troops, escorting the chained brothers who were to be sentenced before the king. Pachaias was there too, as it was the Chair's responsibility to communicate the Tribunal's sentence before the king made his final decision. Also present was the mother of Dismus and Gestus, who was hoping for clemency but would be willing to accept the punishment handed down by the Tribunal.

"Your highness," Pachaias said, "these two brothers, Dismus and Gestus, were just sentenced at the Praetorium by the five members of our Tribunal. They are guilty of theft, and by a unanimous vote we have sentenced them to three days in the dungeon. Once they are freed, they will be required to labor for the vendors from whom they stole, right up until every last bit of their debt is repaid."

Cidivus gazed down at the youths with a cold stare that soon turned into a smug grin. "No need to worry about the labor requirement," Cidivus said. "I am going to release them from that portion of the sentence." The boys' mother smiled as her sons breathed a sigh of relief, but Pachaias looked on in dismay.

"But sire," he said, "we must have them repay their debt. Think of the vendors who cannot recoup what they lost since these criminals devoured the food they pilfered. It is only fair that they get some form of compensation."

"No need to worry, Pachaias, for they will be compensated," Cidivus replied. "But it will not be in the form of labor. Rather they will get to enjoy the spectacle as our boys, Dismus and Gestus, are executed tomorrow in the Praetorium."

"NO!!!!" cried the boys' mother.

"I must say, sire," Pachaias said, "that sounds a bit harsh even by my standards."

"Are you questioning my decision?" Cidivus retorted.

Pachaias carefully considered his words before answering. "Not at all, sire," he then said. "It is the king who has the final say in these matters, and your sentence will be carried out tomorrow, as you have directed."

"NO!!!!" the boys' mother continued to shout. She sobbed uncontrollably as she ran toward her sons, but Sicarius' men grabbed her arms and held her back. Dismus and Gestus were stunned and speechless, and two guards led them down to the dungeon as Sicarius and Tarsus watched them walk by. When Tarsus saw the frightened looks on the youths' faces, he immediately turned to Sicarius.

"How can he do this?" Tarsus asked his general. "Does he not know what might happen?"

"Whatever are you talking about?" Sicarius asked.

"The people will not stand for this," Tarsus said. "They will rebel. It is all but assured now. Why the need to sentence two juvenile thieves to death? I do not understand."

"Don't you see?" Sicarius asked. "The king is using them to send a message that he will not tolerate crime of any sort."

"A bit heavy-handed, don't you think?" Tarsus asked.

"One cannot be too heavy-handed," Sicarius answered, "especially when he has just risen to a position of power. The king needs to establish himself, to set the boundaries for his rule. I had to do the same when I first became General of Mavinor's armies, so I can relate to him."

"It would seem that Cidivus' boundaries allow little room to maneuver," Tarsus said.

"Tarsus, I cannot help but wonder what is going on with you," Sicarius said. "You have questioned the new regime on several matters, from imprisoning the scribes and the priests, to demolishing the temples, to attempting to locate and destroy what is left of The Scrolls. When the believers got in the way of our razing of the temples, you pushed to have them arrested rather than killed. You even seemed a bit hesitant when I had the believers in our army exiled, and I saw the squeamish look on your face when I mounted Tonitrus' head on a stake outside my office. Now you express doubt over the sentencing of these thieves, implying that their penalty is too harsh. Tell me then, where is the combativeness—the indubitable fighting spirit—that my right-hand man has always demonstrated?"

"The spirit to fight is more robust than ever," Tarsus replied. "The question isn't whether I have the will to fight, but what exactly it is I'm fighting for."

As Tarsus finished speaking, a guard ran into the throne room and came up to where Sicarius was standing. He was breathing heavily, but he still managed to get out his words.

"General," he said, "I'm afraid that something is missing."

"What is it?" Sicarius asked.

"Your prized possession," the soldier answered. "It's gone."

Sicarius' eyes filled with rage, but he kept the tone of his voice calm when he finally responded. "Find Solitus," the general said, "and bring him to me."

After the guard left, Sicarius and Tarsus went over to Cidivus, Pachaias, and Grodus, who were discussing Aramus' speech and its ramifications. The king found it interesting that their archenemy on the Tribunal was fully aware of everything that had happened and decided to take his case to the people. "I do believe I have a traitor in my midst," Cidivus said, "one who is telling Aramus things he should not know."

"Perhaps it is Talmik," Pachaias replied, "or maybe Solitus."

"Sooner or later I will find out," Cidivus said, "and they will receive retribution for what they have done."

"But in the meantime, what are we to do about Aramus' inflammatory remarks at the Praetorium earlier today?" Pachaias asked.

Cidivus laughed at the idea of a revolt, but then his tone became more serious as he outlined what he planned to do. "We will deal with this tomorrow, at the execution," Cidivus said. "Aramus will live to regret his words, though he won't live for long. It is time to swat the last fly and move forward without any further annoyances. After tomorrow, there will be no one left to stand in our way."

When the people of Mizar saw Apteris descending from the sky with their beloved Minstro, they stared in complete awe. Though the thirteen had shared stories with them about the Legans' existence when they passed through Mizar on the quest, none of them had ever seen one of The Author's winged guardians of nature. Now one was landing right in the middle of their village, and had even brought Mizar's favorite son with him.

Minstro acknowledged his fellow Mizarians as the crowd gathered around them. Word spread quickly that he had returned home, and people made their way into the streets hoping to at least catch a glimpse of him. It wasn't long before Minstro's two best friends in the Mizarian guard, Roki and Lexi, made their way through and stood in front of their longtime companion. "Roki, Lexi!" Minstro shouted as he embraced them.

"And what may I ask brings you back to Mizar?" Roki asked. "I thought you had moved on to bigger and better things in the outside world."

"I wish I could say that the purpose of my return is to recount our past deeds of mischief, and perhaps even add to those fond memories," Minstro said. "But truth be told, I'm afraid that there is a very grave matter that has arisen. I have come to speak with Orn and make him aware of it. I wish I could stay, but I will need to leave for Xamnon immediately and address the situation with my friends. It simply cannot wait."

"We understand," Lexi said, "though we wish we could come with you. We miss you, Minstro. Roki and I always look back to that fateful day when I came to alert you after the thirteen asked to enter our land. The three of us returned to the moat, and you made the decision to extend the bridge and let them cross over. If I had turned them away myself, then you'd still be with us. I suppose it was simply your destiny to leave Mizar, but it's never easy to lose a friend."

"You haven't lost me," Minstro said. "Look…I'm still here, and my heart will always be in Mizar. I know I don't visit as often as I should, but I promise to come back soon and spend some time with both of you."

"Promise?" Roki asked."

"Absolutely," replied Minstro. "But right now, I need to speak with Orn. Do you know where he is?"

"In his cottage," Lexi replied.

"Thank you, Lexi," Minstro said. "I'll see you—both of you—before I leave Mizar."

Minstro led Apteris and the raven to a quaint cottage in a secluded area of the village. It was situated next to a small hill and had two floors, with a stairway that led up the hill to the second floor. The porch and the entrance to the cottage were actually located on the second floor, and the doorway was no more than four feet high. As Apteris reached the top of the steps, he realized that he would not even fit under the roof that extended over the porch, let alone squeeze through the miniature passage that led inside. "You'd better wait here," Minstro said with a chuckle.

Minstro walked onto the porch and knocked on the door to the cottage. Several minutes passed without anyone answering, causing the raven to grow impatient. "Anyone home?" it shouted.

Minstro quickly looked back at Apteris and the bird. "Shhh… quiet," he said.

From inside Minstro could hear the clop of a cane against the wooden floor. It grew louder with each step, and soon the door opened and a short man with a silvery beard peeked outside. "Minstro?" he said.

"Yes, Orn," Minstro replied. "It is I."

Orn's eyes opened wide as he leaned outside and took Minstro in his arms. "It has been too long," he said.

"I know," Minstro replied. "May I come in? There is something important we need to discuss."

"By all means," Orn said.

Minstro wasted no time in telling Orn all about the events in Mavinor that led to the world being cloaked in darkness. He shared with him the story of Gobius' execution, how Mavinor's king had been sent by The Author to redeem mankind, and how Silex and the others were all killed when they tried to rescue him. Orn mourned for the loss of his friends as Minstro continued to explain the details of Gobius' betrayal and how it led to the Age of Darkness. The elder shrinked back in fear when Minstro told him about the Beast and the Deliverers of Darkness, and what now needed to be done in order to bring light back to the world. When he had finished, Orn looked exasperated and just sat there quietly in his chair, holding on to his cane.

"I am sorry to be the bearer of bad news," Minstro said. "But I had to let you know. You must be prepared for what is to come. Know that my friends and I will do our best to combat this evil."

"Come home, Minstro," Orn said. "Come home. Do not involve yourself in this conflict. For you had nothing to do with what happened to Gobius. None of it is your fault. Do you not see now why I kept all of you close to home when you were young? The world is a dangerous place, but we have managed to remove ourselves from the world, and thus eliminate the danger that comes with it. If you return to Mizar, you will share the peace that we enjoy. Why risk your life for this cause when you can come back to the life you once had?"

Minstro thought long and hard for a moment before answering. "I can't," he finally said. "I know it is difficult for you understand, but I cannot return to the life I once had because I am no longer the man I once was. When I left Mizar to join the quest, I saw some terrible things. I was captured by the Strya and nearly killed before the thirteen came to rescue me. I saw the ghastly Cyporsks in the Mortuus Valley, and fought yet another battle with the Strya in the Northern Mountains. I watched as two of our men were buried in a makeshift tomb, victims of the savages' vengeful wrath. I found myself all alone at one point when my comrades were captured in a giant spider's web, and for the first time I came to know what it felt like to experience the paralyzing fear of isolation and impending death. But I faced it head on and overcame the challenges.

"We lost another one of our men before we escaped the Labyrinth of Secrets, a man that we deeply respected and loved. Never before had I experienced such loss. Never had I felt such pain and grief.

As we began the journey home, I started to understand that I was a changed man. I had lost my innocence, Orn. I was no longer the young guard who was walled in and had not been permitted to experience the nature of evil. I didn't even know that evil truly existed, not until I joined the thirteen on their quest.

"Now, so much has happened even since I left Mizar. I have encountered evil on a level that so few men have had to face, having lost my king and my best friends. At one point I managed to sneak into a room in the dungeon where their bodies were being kept. Do you have any idea what it was like to look down upon their lifeless corpses, to see the countless stab wounds on Pugius' body? Not even the deaths of Thaddeus, Nomis, and Alphaeus could have prepared me for losing someone so close to me. Pugius wasn't just a mentor and a friend to me. He was my brother, and when they killed him, they killed part of me as well.

"Through it all I somehow managed to survive, even as the enemy pursued Cedrus and me all the way to the sea. We escaped in a faering, after which we endured the strain of hunger and fatigue, the danger of choppy waters, and the wrath of a giant sea monster. Ultimately we were rescued, but the happiness was short-lived when we found out the repercussions of Mavinor's misdeeds. Knowing what I know now, I could never return to the life I had in Mizar. I am in this fight, Orn, and this fight is in me. There is no turning back."

Orn looked Minstro in the eye and began nodding his head as he turned away. "Very well," he said. "Your path lies elsewhere then. To this day I wish you had never left, but I must respect your wishes. Go, Minstro, and do what you must do."

Minstro reached over and placed his hand on Orn's wrist. "You will see me again, Orn," he said. "I promise."

When Minstro exited the cottage, he saw Roki and Lexi standing beside Apteris and marveling at the creature's great height and mystical appearance. "Minstro!" Lexi said. "What happened?"

"I have explained everything to Orn, and he will soon explain it to all of you. But right now, dear friends, I'm afraid I must go."

"Can we come with you?" Roki asked.

"Better for you both to remain here," Minstro said. "They will need you to guard them against the evil that has risen, should it ever reach you. Trust me, we will meet again."

"You promised to return, and to spend some time with your old friends," Lexi said. "Don't forget that."

"I won't," Minstro said with a smile. He said good-bye to Lexi and Roki, and they watched as Apteris took him and sailed high over the moat that surrounded Mizar, with the raven flying alongside them.

Chapter Thirteen

As Ignatus sat at his table pondering his discussion with Solitus, there was a knock at the door. He thought the young man may have returned to speak with him, for Ignatus felt uneasy about how they had parted ways. He wondered what caused Solitus to collapse the way that he did, and why he walked away from him without saying a word. Ignatus was now quite worried about the youth, and he hoped their previous conversation wouldn't be the last time the two of them spoke.

When Ignatus answered the door, he saw that it was Aramus. The tribune was clearly agitated, and he walked in before Ignatus could even extend the invitation to do so. "What is wrong?" Ignatus asked.

"You are not going to believe what has happened," Aramus said.

"What now?" Ignatus asked.

"I just received word that Cidivus has sentenced Dismus and Gestus to death!"

Ignatus was horrified to hear the news. "What?" he uttered in total disbelief.

"Do you see what I mean?" Aramus said. "Do you understand

why I had to do what I did? This is nothing short of insanity. If this is how Cidivus plans to govern, then we may as well say farewell to our kingdom. Removing him from the throne by force is the only option we have left."

"But again, how can you possibly succeed in such a task?" Ignatus asked. "Cidivus has the backing of Sicarius' army, at least as far as I can tell. The people cannot win if they revolt against him. They will die, Aramus, every single one of them."

"Even if we do not act, we will die," Aramus replied. "Our faith will die, our morals will die, and our society, which has been built upon faith and morals as its foundation, will die. Better to die knowing we tried to save Mavinor, than to live regretting that we didn't. I am pushing for the revolt to take place tomorrow, before the boys can be executed. I have been in contact with Jobus, and right now it seems as if the majority of the people will support it. Sentencing Dismus and Gestus to death was the final straw."

"How do you intend to carry this out?" Ignatus asked.

"The plan is to storm the Praetorium and overwhelm Sicarius' men with sheer numbers," Aramus answered. "You know that the general only assigns a limited number of troops for trials and executions. If we can beat them back, then we can capture Cidivus and depose him."

"And what happens when the rest of Sicarius' men learn about the revolt? They will surely come after all of you, Aramus. What will you do then?" Ignatus asked.

"We will have Cidivus as a bargaining chip," Aramus replied. "I think we can negotiate with Sicarius, for I can't imagine the army will want to continue supporting a king who the people despise."

"It is too risky," Ignatus said.

"But it is a risk worth taking, because it is our last hope," Aramus said. "Will you help us, Ignatus?"

"Solitus came by to see me earlier," Ignatus said. "He spoke about the rebellion, and encouraged me to lead it. But my time has come and gone, Aramus. As you yourself told me, if I had accompanied Silex and the others to rescue Gobius, I only would have died as one of them. How is this situation any different?"

Aramus sat and pondered Ignatus' words for a moment. Then he nodded his head and turned away. "Perhaps you're right," he said. "I suppose the one difference is that the rescue mission was already in very capable hands. It was being executed by Mavinor's greatest warriors, and being led by Silex, arguably the most valiant of them all. It was just cruel fate that they walked right into a trap. In this situation, we do not have the greatest of warriors. We do not have a capable leader. There is a great void that needs to be filled, and Solitus thought you might be just the one, perhaps the only one in all of Mavinor, to fulfill that role. But obviously you feel otherwise, and if that is your final decision, then so be it." Aramus did not look back at Ignatus. He started walking toward the door and grabbed the knob before Ignatus called out to him.

"Aramus, wait," he said. He then picked up the satchel that contained Tonitrus' head. "Solitus gave this to me; it is the head of Tonitrus. Sicarius had mounted it on a stake and displayed it outside his office as a trophy of sorts. Solitus managed to steal it without being seen, and he wishes for it to be burned and for the ashes to be reunited with those of Tonitrus' body."

"I will have my servants tend to the matter," Aramus said as he accepted the bag from Ignatus. "Just recently I had the urns inscribed with the insignia for each of Gobius' men. I had marked them initially so that we would later be able to discern which was which. Thus we will be able to fill Tonitrus' urn with the rest of his ashes. I only wish they all hadn't died in vain. It saddens me to think that they risked their lives so bravely for Mavinor's future, yet that future for which they were willing to sacrifice themselves is now in jeopardy, and may disappear forever. Good-bye, Ignatus."

Aramus left and closed the door behind him while Ignatus sat and deeply reflected on the tribune's words. He processed them over and over in his mind, but he was no closer to joining the rebellion than before. He still saw it as a suicide mission with zero chance of success, and thought better than to die with his fellow countrymen in such a foolish undertaking.

Cidivus sat alone in a private courtyard on the interior grounds of the palace. He was sipping a goblet of wine and contemplating his rule, as well as the progress that had been made in expunging the believers. He ran through all of it in his mind, recalling with fondness Gobius' execution, the defeat of Silex and the royal guards, and the exile of the believers from Mavinor's army. He reveled in the fact that all of the temples in Mavinor had been destroyed, the priests and scribes imprisoned, and the Academy's curriculum revamped to exclude all references to religious faith. Cidivus was about to set a major precedent by executing two petty thieves whose lives meant nothing to him, and send an undeniable message to the people of Mavinor that he was now in charge. This was his kingdom, where he would set his own rules, and they would have no choice but to follow them unless they wished for death. All he needed now was to find where The Scrolls were being hidden, capture Magdala—who he wanted as his own personal servant—and recover Cedrus' body. He had enjoyed torturing and killing Legentis, and was looking forward to doing the same to the other scribes if they didn't tell him what he wanted to know. Once the foundation for his reign in Mavinor had been laid, he would look to crush his foes, beginning with Xamnon, and spread his philosophy of governance throughout the world. In his mind he was unstoppable, and he truly believed that his vision for the world was inevitable.

As he stood from his chair and began walking back inside the palace, a voice called out from behind one of the fig trees. When Cidivus turned to see who it was, his eyes met the hideous form of Malgyron, who immediately sensed the king's fear.

"Do not be alarmed," Malgyron said. "It is I, he who helped you ascend to the throne."

"It cannot be you," Cidivus said, his eyes wide and his voice filled with trepidation.

"But it is," Malgyron said. "I know my appearance has changed, but inside I am still the same being who assisted you in righting the wrongs in Mavinor. I continue to watch out for you, as you well know, with the help of my spies. That is one of the reasons I have come. There is something you must know."

"What is it?" Cidivus asked, still appearing frightened.

"The one called Solitus is trying to stir up a rebellion against you, along with Aramus, the tribune," Malgyron warned. "I have been told that he asked a man named Ignatus to lead the revolt, but he refused. Thus I believe that Solitus himself will lead it, and that it will take place as soon as tomorrow."

Cidivus smiled. "I suspected young Solitus might have been looking for revenge when he came back to Mavinor," he said. "I wanted to believe him when he said that he wished to be part of my regime, but in the meantime—until I was convinced that was the case—I planned to use him for menial tasks such as serving guests at my dinner parties and searching the shoreline for his cousin's corpse. It is quite unfortunate that I will now have to execute him. I knew about Aramus, as the old fool had the audacity to openly encourage an uprising in a speech at the Praetorium. Tomorrow he will be arrested, and now Solitus will be arrested along with him. It will be the perfect complement to the beheading of Dismus and Gestus, for not only will I send the people a message that crimes of any kind will not be tolerated, but also that any threat of a rebellion will be met with swift and severe action, and the dissidents will be wiped out completely."

"You are as decisive a leader as I have ever encountered, Cidivus," Malgyron said. "I knew you were the right choice for Mavinor's throne, and I am happy that I was able to facilitate your coronation as king. Just make sure you have enough troops on hand for the execution tomorrow, in case the rebels attempt to rescue the criminals through their planned insurrection."

"I will get word to the general immediately," Cidivus replied. "We will be ready for them. It won't be the first time I set a trap for an ill-fated rescue mission."

Malgyron smiled at Cidivus' reference to the snare they laid for Silex and the rest of Gobius' royal guards. "I am sure this one will be just as successful," he then said.

"I would like to say that they will live to regret their decision," Cidivus replied, "but unfortunately I can't, since most of them, if not all, will die."

Malgyron emitted a manic laugh as he envisioned the massacre taking place. "Good," he said. "Tomorrow you shall forever establish your rule, Cidivus. Once this is over, no one will ever challenge you again."

"Can you tell me anything about Xamnon?" Cidivus asked. "Now that I know Solitus returned here as a spy, I wonder if they are plotting something against me."

"If they are foolish enough to launch an attack against you, then you will have advance notice and can set a trap for them as well," Malgyron said. "For my spies always have their eyes and ears open, in Xamnon as well as Mavinor. Right now you are wise to focus on rectifying the situation here in your kingdom, but I will let you know if an external threat arises. You may want to make a habit of visiting this courtyard each evening, even if just for a few minutes. It is the perfect location for us to meet."

"I will do just that," Cidivus said.

"Good. Then perhaps I will see you tomorrow, and you can tell me all about your victory. Be well, King Cidivus," Malgyron said.

Cidivus watched Malgyron fly off and returned inside, feeling more assured than ever that his kingship was safe. But as he got closer to the throne room, he heard loud shouting and what sounded like someone pounding on his wooden table. When he entered, he saw that General Sicarius was in a fit of rage and directing his anger toward Solitus.

"Where is it?" Sicarius said. "I know that you took it! Where did you hide it?"

"Whatever is wrong?" Cidivus asked as he sat in his throne with Talmik looking on.

Solitus rushed up the stairs and stood beside Cidivus. "Sire, he is accusing me of something I didn't do. I give you my word that I was only fulfilling your orders."

Cidivus looked back at Sicarius to hear his side of the story. "My prized possession is missing," Sicarius said, "and I intend to recover it by any means necessary."

"You mean someone took it from where it was displayed, right in front of your office?" Cidivus said in disbelief. "That is quite a brazen act, and one not too many men are capable of carrying out."

"Clearly it was Solitus who stole it," the general said. He unsheathed his sword and began walking toward the throne. "I want it back, NOW!"

Solitus again appealed to Cidivus. He had to think quickly if he wanted to avoid Sicarius' wrath, so he immediately concocted a bold lie. "Sire, I saw something at the shore today," he said. "I would swear it was Cedrus' tunic out floating amongst the waves, but I could not reach it. The tide was going out, but I wanted to come back and tell you as soon as I could. With your permission, I'd like to return there and see if it has washed up. If his tunic has come ashore, then his body cannot be too far behind."

Cidivus' eyes opened wide as he heard the news. "Interesting," he said. "Yes, I think I would like for you to return and see what you find."

"But not before he returns my prized possession," Sicarius said.

"I do not have it!" Solitus yelled. "Sire, you must believe me. I had no time to do that which the general is accusing me of doing. I was too busy at the shore trying to retrieve the tunic. You can check the quarters you have assigned me if you want. I swear I did not take it."

"I believe you," Cidivus said. "Now do not waste another moment.

Go and bring me Cedrus' body, for the cauldron is patiently awaiting its arrival."

"Yes, sire," Solitus said as Talmik looked on.

Solitus walked by Sicarius—whose face bore a stern expression—and left the throne room. As he exited, Sicarius turned back toward Cidivus. "I want my prized possession back," Sicarius said.

"I'm sure you will recover it, General," replied Cidivus. "For now, let him complete the task I have assigned him. Tomorrow he shall realize that I have special plans for him, which will be announced to all at the Praetorium when Dismus and Gestus are executed. You'll be in attendance, and soon you too shall see what I mean." With that, Cidivus went back to his quarters, leaving Sicarius behind staring in consternation and Talmik wondering what type of "special plans" Cidivus had in mind for Solitus.

When Minstro, Apteris, and the raven arrived back in Xamnon, they found Volara, Arcala, and Chaelim in the main guest room explaining the Seers' advice to Henricus and the others. Cedrus was sitting in the corner, almost looking disinterested.

"So that is what they told you," Henricus said. "Where then do we begin?"

"I wish I could answer that question," Minstro said. "We need the Ivory Sabre to defeat the Beast, but it is hidden in a place called the Cavern of Trials. The Seers told us that only the one destined to have it can possibly retrieve it. But we don't even know where the cavern is, let alone have someone go in and find where the Sabre is hidden."

"Could Solitus be the one destined for it?" Arcala said. "The Seers said that the one who will enter the Cavern of Trials is the one who has already decided to go it alone in this struggle."

"It may well be," Minstro said. "Arcala, I think you have deciphered the Seers' riddle!"

"Then we must return to Mavinor and help my brother," Arcala said.

"No," Apteris cut in. "You heard the Seers. There is nothing we can do to assist him, and no way to change his fate. He is on his own. We need to focus our attention elsewhere."

"Where then do we go, and what do we do?" Arcala asked Apteris, clearly irritated at his response to her.

"It all seems tied to the Medallion," Chaelim said. "The Seers said we will need it to defeat the Deliverers of Darkness. That is probably why our weapons seemingly had no effect on them. The Medallion is also the key to Malgyron's plan. He aims to strip it of its power and remove The Author's grace from the world. Malgyron must do so if he is going to claim his place as the King of Darkness."

Cedrus, who seemed like he was oblivious to the entire conversation, suddenly rose to his feet and yelled across the room at them. "Don't you understand?" he said. "That is why the war is already over. I had the Medallion in my possession, but lost it to the depths of the sea. There is no way to get it back, not unless one of you wants to swim to the bottom and look for it. It is gone—gone forever—and it is entirely my fault."

"You are being hard on yourself, dear friend," Minstro said. "I would hardly say it's your fault given the fact that we suffered a vicious attack by the tentacles of the sea monster."

"Even if you say it wasn't my fault, the Medallion is nonetheless gone," Cedrus said. "Now we have no way to stop the Deliverers of Darkness from claiming their army, and no way to defeat them once they do. From my standpoint, the situation is hopeless. The people of Mavinor chose their fate, and now that fate has been sealed. For me, there is nothing left to do but get as far away from this world as possible."

"What do you mean?" Arcala asked.

"I am leaving," Cedrus said. "I made my decision when we were up in the Northern Mountains. I have suffered enough pain and endured enough grief. I do not need more of the same."

"Wherever will you go?" Henricus asked.

"Anywhere but here," Cedrus said. "I will go to a place far from the three kingdoms. Perhaps I'll pass through the woods to the northwest and travel all the way to the marshlands. No one will find me there."

"No, Cedrus, you cannot abandon us," Arcala said, her voice tinged with shock.

"I am not abandoning the world," Cedrus said. "It is the world that has abandoned us through its treachery. I no longer want any part of it."

The room fell to dead silence as Cedrus finished his words. Henricus then asked the others if he could have a moment alone with Cedrus, and they promptly left and closed the door behind them.

"I cannot even begin to tell you how grave your mistake will be if you leave," Henricus said.

"Then again, you cannot even begin to understand what I have endured," Cedrus said. "It is not your kingdom that has been lost, your king who was executed, your friends and your one brother who were murdered."

"That is why I asked them to leave," Henricus said. "I do understand, more than you realize. But I did not wish to have everyone hear what I am about to tell you. When I was a child, my parents were murdered. Their only crime was their faith, but Xamnon had grown increasingly intolerant of religion and began to execute those who believed. I was orphaned, and held a deep-seated hatred for those in power throughout my childhood. I wanted to run away, and at one point I did. I absconded into the woods with everything I could possibly carry, and began walking aimlessly to get as far from Xamnon—and from my pain—as possible. But I soon learned that you cannot run away from your grief. Wherever you go, it goes with you. So I returned to Xamnon and vowed instead that I would rise to power one day and change the kingdom from within. I joined the army and aided an underground faction of believers in their efforts to live out their faith in a society that condemned it. I spent many years walking a fine line between advancing our cause and remaining a loyal soldier, knowing that I would be executed if my superiors ever discovered who I really was. I prayed to The Author day and night that Xamnon would change, and that my parents did not die in vain. I hoped I could help bring about the change needed to ensure that no one ever suffered the same fate as my mother and father. Finally that day arrived, and it all happened because one great man, King Gobius, came here to broker peace. You know how the rest of the story unfolded, and now I realize more than ever what a terrible mistake it would have been to abandon my homeland all those years ago, when the situation seemed all but hopeless."

Cedrus listened attentively to Henricus' words, but they did little to change how he felt inside. He was too far gone now, well past the point where anyone could possibly convince him that he was choosing the wrong path. He briefly pondered what Henricus said and then turned to face him.

"This is different," Cedrus said. "I am not going to debate which one of us has suffered the greater loss, but I can say this. Losing your parents did not bring about the beginning of the end for the three kingdoms. The deaths of my king, my friends, and my brother have done just that, and we cannot reverse it. I lost the one item that could have aided our cause, the Medallion that Gobius trusted to me. I cannot understand now why it was his will and the will of The Author that I have it, because I was not able to preserve it. I was the wrong choice, and now it has cost us dearly. It is over, Henricus. All that is left is for the Beast to destroy Xamnon and Mavinor, the Deliverers of Darkness to claim their army, and the Evil One to be crowned as the King of Darkness. The light is gone and shall never return to our world, just as I am going and shall never return to the three kingdoms."

Cedrus turned to leave the room, and Henricus shouted at him as he exited through the door. "You cannot run from your troubles, Cedrus," he said. "They will find you wherever you may go." As

Cedrus walked out and went up the stairs to his guest quarters, the others came back into the room.

"What happened?" Minstro asked. "Did you convince him to stay?"

"No," Henricus answered. "I'm afraid not. He has made up his mind; there is no changing it. We will have to make do without him."

"No!" Arcala shouted. "My cousin cannot and will not abandon us." She turned and ran upstairs, presumably to go after Cedrus. The others stayed put, and shortly thereafter they heard Arcala scolding Cedrus as he came back down the stairs.

"You cannot go!" she exclaimed. "What about Solitus? Are you going to leave him behind? You must help me find him."

"I'm sorry," Cedrus said. "But I must go. I can no longer be part of this, Arcala. Good-bye, dear cousin."

Arcala stopped following him, finally realizing that her efforts were futile. She watched him go, and then came back into the room and began denouncing Cedrus for his decision to leave.

"I am speechless," she said. "How can my cousin, a man I always looked up to as a brave warrior and loyal servant in the royal guard, leave us behind and give up this fight? How can he abandon us when we need him most?"

"He is not himself," Minstro answered. "Trust me when I say that Cedrus is not in his right state of mind. His judgment has been clouded by the terrible sorrow and guilt he feels in the recesses of his heart. I don't know whether he can ever be the same man again. All that is left for us to do is pray for him."

Arcala hung her head and left the room. Magdala walked out on the balcony and looked out from the palace. She saw Cedrus walking with his belongings in tow, his back turned to her and his long brown hair blowing in the breeze. She watched him go until he disappeared far off in the distance, all the while shedding tears that fell like raindrops over the edge of the balcony to the garden below. In her heart, something told her that she would never see her one true love ever again, and that she would be forced to live with that regret for the rest of her life.

As Solitus sat on the beach peering down at the Medallion, he wondered if the people would listen to Aramus and rise up against Cidivus. He was still extremely disappointed in Ignatus, but he knew he had to move on. There was no time to waste on anyone, and he was determined to do what needed to be done, even if he had to lead the revolt himself.

Just when he placed the Medallion back in his pouch, the silence in the air was broken by several loud voices, and as Solitus looked up he caught sight of Sicarius' men approaching the shoreline and scanning the surrounding area. Quickly he went and hid among the rocks, for he believed that Sicarius had sent them to capture him and bring him back to the general for questioning. He found a tight, secure spot where his slender frame allowed him to squeeze in and shield himself from the soldiers' sight. The troops passed right by him, and as he watched them walk along the shore and continue their search, he realized that the palace would be the safest place for him. So he waited until the soldiers were a safe distance away and decided to make a run for it.

When he arrived back at the throne room, he informed Cidivus that Cedrus' body had still not washed ashore. The king didn't seem as disappointed this time around, which caught Solitus off-guard. He sensed something odd was going on, but he just played along.

"Very well," Cidivus said with a broad smile. "You can resume the search tomorrow morning. Now if you'll excuse me, I have a busy day tomorrow and wish to turn in early."

"Yes, sire," Solitus replied.

As Cidivus and Talmik left, Talmik motioned for Solitus to wait. The aide escorted the king to his quarters and made sure he had everything he needed before rushing back to the throne room to speak with Solitus.

"I just received a message from Aramus," Talmik said. "The revolt is going to take place at the Praetorium tomorrow. The death sentence for Dismus and Gestus led the people to their breaking point, so they are now ready to take action. They plan to arrive shortly after the brothers are ushered to the Praetorium and save them from execution. Then they will depose Cidivus and force Pachaias to appoint a new king."

"I will be there," Solitus said. "I am supposed to search the coast in the morning, but I will sneak away and join the others at the Praetorium. Will you be there as well?"

"Yes, of course," Talmik said. "I cannot carry a sword with me, for that will certainly heighten suspicion. But I plan to hide a dagger in my belt. I will fight for the cause right alongside the rest of you."

"May The Author be with us, Talmik," Solitus said.

"He will," Talmik said. "We will succeed, Solitus. I have no doubts in my mind."

"I only hope and pray that you are right," Solitus said, "for if we fail, then Mavinor may be lost forever."

Part III

Chapter Fourteen

Cedrus' departure only served to make the mood in Xamnon more dismal than it had already been. What promised to be a titanic struggle became an even more formidable task now that the man who was arguably their best fighter had abandoned the cause. The Beast served as a constant worry for them, so Henricus made sure that his kingdom—especially the northeast corner where they expected the Beast might approach— was well fortified. The Legans again left to scout the Beast, promising to return and bring Henricus the latest details on her whereabouts.

In the meantime, Bovillus combed through potential material for The Scrolls in an attempt to find information on the Cavern of Trials or anything else that might be of help to them. He was essentially their only hope of discovering where the cavern was located. Arcala was still intent on going to Mavinor, but Minstro talked her out of it, given the Seers' words about how they would be unable to change Solitus' fate no matter what they did. Begrudgingly she retired for the night, as did Magdala, who simply could not stop thinking about Cedrus and wept behind closed doors over his departure. Minstro did his best to assist Bovillus, while Henricus went off to sit by Antiugus' bedside. As Xamnon's general sat there and looked down upon his king, little did he know that Antiugus' mind had become active once again, and that he was experiencing something deep and powerful even as he lay still on his feather bed.

Antiugus opens his eyes to find himself lying in his bed, only his bed is not situated in Xamnon's palace. It has been moved to an unfamiliar place, where the air is chill and the surrounding area is enveloped by a dense fog. As he sets his feet on the ground, Antiugus finds the soil to be rocky, and though he is not wearing shoes he decides to set out and explore his surroundings. The fog makes it difficult to see, so he walks very carefully, one foot in front of the other, keeping both his eyes and ears open. He walks for what seems like miles, and finds nothing that might indicate where he is. Antiugus is totally lost, and begins to wonder if he will ever find his way back home.

Then suddenly up ahead, a light begins to shine. It is exceptionally bright—even in the thick fog—and its aura lends a mysterious sense of comfort to the king. Antiugus is drawn to it, as if a force is pulling him in, and finds the lure of the light impossible to resist. He shields his eyes and begins to walk toward it, just as slowly and cautiously as he had been walking since getting out of bed. When he is almost there, he suddenly feels a sharp pain in his lower right leg. It quickly becomes so excruciating that it paralyzes him, forcing him to fall to the ground. As he looks down to examine the injury, he sees that there is a bite mark of some sort near his ankle. He tries to stand, but finds that he is now unable to do so. Despite being lame, Antiugus refuses to allow his condition to keep him from approaching the light. So he summons every ounce of strength and uses his arms to crawl along the ground, sliding over patches of scrub and roots that scrape his skin. It takes a while, but eventually he gets there, and finds himself lying just a few feet behind the light source, which he sees is now a man in a dazzling white robe.

He lies there motionless, in awe of the sight before him, and actually finds himself afraid to come any closer. Something inside tells him that this man, whoever he is, is so majestic in appearance that no one is worthy of seeing his face. So he stays put, suffering greatly from the pain in his leg and desperately trying not to scream in agony. He hides his face, partly to shield his eyes from the glow emanating from the man's garment and partly to cover his mouth as he grunts in pain. The throbbing in his leg becomes so severe that Antiugus comes to believe that he will die from the bite he suffered, and wonders what might happen to his kingdom without him there to lead.

Then suddenly Antiugus feels a gentle touch in the area where the bite mark is located. The touch is followed by a sensation unlike any other, a soothing feeling that makes him believe that all his afflictions are evaporating. When the person who touched him lets go of his leg, Antiugus realizes that his pain is gone. His leg is no longer numb, and he is able to stand. When he rises to his feet and looks before him, he sees the man in the white robe, only the light shining from his robe has dimmed. He looks into his eyes and sees something familiar in his face. "I know this man," Antiugus says to himself.

As he ponders it for just a minute, Antiugus realizes that he is looking into the bright eyes of King Gobius of Mavinor. He is speechless before him as he realizes that it was Gobius who healed his leg. He doesn't know why, but Antiugus drops to his knees and bows before him in the most natural of gestures, and addresses him as he has never addressed anyone before. "My Lord," Antiugus says.

"Rise, Antiugus," Gobius says, "and come with me."

Antiugus does as Gobius commands and follows him as he walks to the edge of a cliff. He now realizes that he is up on a high mountain, and that the fog around him is not a fog at all, but the clouds rolling through the heavens. As they look down, they see a massive fire blazing high into the sky.

"Whatever is that, my Lord?" Antiugus asks. "What could be burning so terribly?"

As Antiugus looks over at Gobius, he sees tears streaming down his face. "It is my kingdom," Gobius says. "Mavinor is burning, and there is little time left to save it."

"What can I do?" Antiugus asks. "Tell me, my Lord. I will do whatever you ask of me."

"Please liberate my people, Antiugus," Gobius says. "Free them from the chains that now bind them. Lead your army there and extinguish the flames that have engulfed Mavinor. You are my only hope."

"You have my word," Antiugus says. "I will free your people, my Lord, and I will save your kingdom from destruction."

Gobius looks at Antiugus and smiles. Then he begins walking away until he stands in the midst of a large, hazy cloud. The light from his robe begins to shine brightly again, and increases in intensity until it nearly blinds Antiugus. As he squints and looks as closely as he can in Gobius' direction, Antiugus sees the cloud rise and take Gobius with it. "My Lord, don't leave me here," Antiugus pleads.

"I will never leave you, friend," Gobius says. "I am with you always."

Then in an instant he is gone. Gobius disappears into the mist, melting away as if he had somehow been absorbed into it and become one with the air that surrounded him. Antiugus looks down again and sees the fire raging in Mavinor. He remembers his promise to Gobius, and he has every intention of keeping it. So he runs back in the other direction, back toward where his bed was sitting in the open air. When he arrives there, he finds the bed exactly as he had left it. For some reason he feels tired, and decides to rest before journeying back to Xamnon. So he lays himself down on the mattress and closes his eyes, hoping to get some sleep before setting out on his quest to save the people of Mavinor. His eyelids grow heavy and soon he is slumbering peacefully in the night air, dreaming pleasant dreams and recalling with fondness his encounter with King Gobius. As the dream ends and he opens his eyes...

Antiugus found himself back in the palace, in his quarters with Henricus seated beside his bed. As Henricus peered down at him, he seemed almost in disbelief that Antiugus' eyes had opened. "Sire?" he said in a dubious tone.

"It is I," Antiugus replied. He quickly sat up and threw the blankets off to the side, much to Henricus' chagrin. The general was worried that his king might overexert himself, so he gently tried to nudge him back down toward the mattress. But it was no use. "I want to see something," Antiugus stated as he pushed Henricus away.

When Antiugus pulled up his robe and examined his lower right leg, he saw that the wound he had incurred from Cerastes' bite was gone. When Henricus noticed it, he expressed complete and utter shock.

"It's gone," Henricus said. "But how is it possible? The serpent left a huge bite mark on your leg. I do not understand."

"I understand," Antiugus said as he got up and walked over to the window. "I understand perfectly."

Henricus was in awe and could hardly think of what to say. "Sire, perhaps you'd like something to eat? You must be quite hungry."

"How long was I asleep?" Antiugus asked.

"Several days, though it seemed more like months, especially given the turn of events that occurred during that span," Henricus replied.

"Then I have a lot to catch up on," Antiugus said. "Let's talk, Henricus."

"It is almost morning," Henricus replied. "I'll have the servants bring you your breakfast, and I will gladly tell you about all that happened while you were ill. But prepare yourself, for the news will not be pleasant to hear."

"I am already prepared," Antiugus said, "more so than you can possibly imagine."

Shortly after morning broke in Mavinor, Cidivus had Talmik bring him an extravagant breakfast, which he quickly wolfed down as he prepared to have Dismus and Gestus escorted to the Praetorium for their execution. He was seated in the throne room finishing his meal when Solitus came to inform him that he was leaving for the shore to search for Cedrus' body. But Cidivus suddenly and unexpectedly stopped him and called for two of his guards.

"Not today," Cidivus said to Solitus.

"What do you mean?" Solitus said, dumbfounded.

"You'll be coming with us, Solitus," Cidivus said. "I have something special in store for you." With that the guards came and cuffed the young man's wrists while Talmik looked on helplessly. Solitus was disillusioned as they led him away, and he glared back at Cidivus, who was now smiling.

"Are you coming with me, Talmik?" Cidivus asked.

"Of course, sire," Talmik replied, visibly jarred by Solitus' arrest.

"Isn't it a shame that young Solitus was planning to betray me?" Cidivus asked as he stood from the table and looked his aide in the eye. "You don't know of any other traitors in our midst, do you, Talmik?"

Talmik paused briefly before answering. "No, sire, but if I should find out, then you'll be the first to know."

"Very good," Cidivus said in a deliberate tone. "I knew I could trust you, Talmik. There are already enough heads about to roll. I really don't think we need another. Now prepare my mount. I'll be out shortly." Talmik began to sense that Cidivus was on to him, but he did as he was told and began to think about how he could possibly aid Solitus.

Cidivus and Talmik rode to the Praetorium, and when they arrived they saw that General Sicarius was waiting for them at the front gate.

"Did you receive word from the messenger I sent?" Cidivus said.

"I did," Sicarius said. "We are ready for them."

"Excellent," Cidivus said. "Let's go, Talmik."

Talmik now began to piece things together and started to realize what was happening as he and Cidivus entered through the gate. When Cidivus had told Sicarius the previous day that he had special plans for Solitus, those plans were to have him arrested. Somehow he had discovered that Solitus was a spy, and it seemed that Cidivus was now aware that the people would be launching their revolt this morning. Usually the king had Talmik dispatch his messengers, but this time Cidivus had taken it upon himself to send an envoy to Sicarius. That told Talmik that Cidivus no longer trusted him, and perhaps the king now knew that his aide was spying on him as well. Would Talmik thus be the next one to be removed? He suddenly felt tremendous fear and anxiety, both for his fate and the fate of the citizens who planned to rebel. But it was too late for him to do anything. The people were already preparing to march unwittingly to the Praetorium like sheep to a slaughter. They were walking right into a trap, and Talmik had no way to warn them.

Talmik and Cidivus rode in and through the square to where the tribunes were seated. As Cidivus dismounted, Pachaias came over to him and ushered him to a place where they would be out of earshot of the others. "What is going on?" Pachaias asked. "I couldn't help but notice the flurry of activity among Sicarius' men."

"You'll see," Cidivus said. "Just have a seat and enjoy the spectacle. Trust me when I say that you will not be disappointed."

Talmik looked up at Aramus and tried to make eye contact with him. But he couldn't send him any signals since the other tribunes were seated alongside him and thus also had Talmik in their sights. He felt more frustrated than he could ever remember, for a great tragedy was about to unfold, and though he knew it was coming he was helpless to stop it.

"Come, Talmik," Cidivus then said as he walked up behind him and placed a hand on his shoulder.

As Cidivus, Talmik, and Pachaias climbed the stairs, a crowd of people showed up at the front gate of the Praetorium. They were armed with pitchforks, sickles, spades, and sledgehammers. The mob was ready to take out the armed guards, but Sicarius' men simply stepped aside and let them through. The people were somewhat surprised at the lack of resistance, but they walked into the Praetorium and began parading into the square. The throng of revolutionaries was clearly visible to Cidivus and the tribunes, and immediately Pachaias, Annus, Theophilus, and Pontius rose from their chairs. Aramus was the only one who remained seated.

"They have taken Aramus' words to heart," Pachaias said. "I cannot believe they are doing this."

Cidivus stared haughtily at them, and then quickly pivoted and marched over to where Aramus was sitting. He stood over the long-serving tribune and bent down so they were at eye level. Cidivus then grabbed the arms of Aramus' chair as he addressed him.

"You old fool!" he said. "Do you really believe a revolt against me will be successful? I want you to look out at those people, at each and every one of them, because most of them will die today! Their blood will be on your hands, Aramus, as will the blood of the young man I bring before you in chains. I will have you arrested as well, but not before you watch the massacre unfold and mourn over their deaths, knowing that you are the one who led them to their graves."

When the crowd came to where Dismus' and Gestus' heads now rested on wooden blocks, they surrounded the youths in an effort to keep them from being executed. The throng consisted of men, women, and children, and even included many of Cidivus' friends who had attended his coronation celebration. They too now saw how absolute power had corrupted the man they once knew. Jobus stepped forward from the group, walking slowly with his cane until he reached a point where he could look up and address the king.

"Cidivus," Jobus said, "your coronation, which we celebrated just a short time ago, has already become the greatest travesty in Mavinor's history. When we deposed Gobius, we wanted change. We were slow to forgive Xamnon, and tired of hearing the king's preaching about love and forgiveness. Once we became aware of his leniency toward the prostitute, we reacted out of anger and urged for him to be executed. We realize now what a terrible mistake we made, for we allowed our emotions to get the best of us and caused an innocent man to die. We were told by Cantos that he was the savior sent to us, the one and only son of The Author. But we refused to believe. Instead we murdered him, and now we have seen the evil we brought upon ourselves and the entire world by doing so.

"We heard the thunder roar when Gobius died at the bottom of that hill. We saw the lightning flash across the sky, and the dark clouds roll in. We felt the ground shake beneath our feet, so much so that we could barely stand as the world seemingly rocked back and forth. A chill came and darkness set in, even though the winter had not yet arrived. We have not seen the sun nor felt its warmth since Gobius' death, and we have come to realize that we may never see the light of day again. When we crowned you as our king, we believed we were taking our kingdom in the right direction. But we were fools. Now we have seen you for who you really are. You are a merciless tyrant, drunk on power and intolerant of opposing points of view. You have no regard for the welfare of your people, only for your own. You have exiled men without a fair trial, imprisoned the priests and scribes without just cause, destroyed the temples, and even murdered those who implored you to stop the destruction. Now you aim to execute two young boys for a childish prank, all to set an example for how you intend to rule us with an iron fist. Well know that we will not stand for it. Though we can't go back to the past and undo what we've done, we can take action in the present and alter our future. That is what we plan to do, Cidivus, and that is why your reign ends today!"

Cidivus stepped forward and scanned the crowd, and then looked Jobus right in the eye. "You say you 'were' fools?" he said."I say that you ARE fools, all of you! The believers in Mavinor's army were cowards who deserted you. Their faith was a sign of their weakness, and I wanted to make sure such weakness never plagued our kingdom again. That is why I have demolished the temples, imprisoned the scribes and priests, changed the curriculum at the Academy, and continued to educate those who believe in the imaginary 'Author.'

Our kingdom can never become all it is meant to be as long as we are held back by the restraints of religious faith. Since there are still many in Mavinor who do not understand this truth, I have been forced to take the unusual step of implementing it for them.

"You pathetic worms once clamored for a real leader, one stronger than Gobius who would lead our kingdom back to prosperity. Now that you have been given what you asked for, you fail to appreciate it? Such failure will unfortunately lead to your ruin, as dissidents in my kingdom will not be tolerated. Prepare for your demise, Jobus, for now you shall die." Cidivus then looked toward Sicarius. "General, it is time," he said.

At that moment, only Sicarius, Tarsus, Grodus, and a couple of other guards were present. But as Sicarius bellowed in the direction of the Praetorium's private entrance off to the side, dozens of armed troops stormed through, and among them were two soldiers escorting Solitus. They brought him to the base of the stairs where Cidivus could plainly see him, his wrists chained as the guards forced him to his knees.

"Look what we have here," Cidivus said. "A mutinous youth, a traitor who I actually thought had my best interests in mind. Today he was going to join your little insurrection, but I'm afraid I could not allow it. Now he too will be sentenced to death, and those of you who I allow to survive today's bloodbath will be here tomorrow to witness his execution, which will be far more slow and painful than that of Dismus and Gestus." Cidivus then looked back at Aramus and smiled.

"You see what you've done," Cidivus said to Aramus. "I hope you are proud of the moving speech you gave yesterday."

As Sicarius fanned out his troops to surround the people, Ignatus came running through the crowd. He had seen the angry mob marching through town, and realized that Aramus' plan was now in motion. Ignatus went up to Jobus and tried to talk him into abandoning the revolt, but it was of no use. They had all made up their minds, and it was far too late to turn back now.

By the same token, Tarsus tried to convince Sicarius not to proceed with the slaughter. "Look at them," Tarsus said. "They are farmers, laborers, merchants, vendors…not to mention fathers, brothers, and sons. I will not let you kill them."

"Try and stop me, Tarsus," Sicarius said as he drew his sword. "I tire of your newfound empathy for these malcontents. There is no way of dealing with rebellions other than to squash them."

"We will not let you execute the youths!" Jobus shouted. "Nor will we allow Cidivus to remain king. We will fight for our kingdom until death."

"Then may your wish be granted," Cidivus said. He scowled and looked toward Sicarius, then nodded. Sicarius looked to his left and yelled, "Fire!" In an instant an arrow came whistling out of the legion of soldiers and imbedded itself in the heart of the old man. Jobus dropped his cane and immediately fell to the ground, where Cyrenus came over to help him.

"It is too late for me," Jobus said. "You were right all along, Cyrenus, from the time you helped King Gobius as he struggled to walk the Via Mortis. If only we had followed your example and came to his aid, rather than carried out his execution. I am guilty of an enormous crime committed against our kingdom, far guiltier than any of the others, for it was I who cast the final stone and delivered the death blow to our savior. May The Author forgive my dreadful sin and have mercy on me." With that, he expired.

"Get them!" Cyrenus yelled. "Fight! Fight for Mavinor!"

The crowd wielded their sickles and pitchforks and ran toward Sicarius' troops. Both Ignatus and Tarsus stood back from their respective sides and watched in horror as the conflict began. The people were slain in droves as they squared off with Sicarius' well-trained warriors, clearly no match for the military's might. Grodus swung his mace viciously and felled several men all by himself, and Sicarius joined in the killing as he hacked and slashed at all those who ran at him, cutting them down easily.

Cidivus began to smile and laugh as the mob's numbers dwindled, and when it became all but apparent that the revolt had been quelled, he stepped forward and began to speak, just as Sicarius had disarmed Cyrenus.

"Well done, General!" Cidivus shouted. "It would seem as though this little uprising of yours was a bad idea, don't you think?" Cidivus asked as he looked at Cyrenus.

"Let a curse be upon you!" Cyrenus said. "May you die a thousand deaths for your sins against us!"

Cidivus seemed more amused than offended at his words, and then looked toward Sicarius, who now held Cyrenus on the ground with his hands behind his back. "You know what to do, General," Cidivus said. The king then raised his right thumb in the air and slowly pointed it toward the ground. Sicarius wasted no time in plunging his sword into Cyrenus' back, causing the young man to fall forward and twitch as he breathed his last. Rovenica stood back and watched as Cyrenus was murdered, and then rushed forward with tears in her eyes to mourn over his body.

"Now then," Cidivus said as he turned toward Aramus, "I do hope you're happy with the fruits of your efforts. Congratulations, Aramus, on getting them killed. I am sure they are all quite grateful. Now for inciting that pathetic rebellion, I'm afraid that we will have to take you into custody as well. Guards!" With that, two guards rushed up the steps and cuffed Aramus' wrists before yanking him from his seat.

"No!" Solitus yelled out. Cidivus remained at the top of the stairs and addressed the remaining people in the crowd, all of whom were now being restrained by Sicarius' men.

"Isn't it a shame," Cidivus said, "how some people don't recognize greatness when they see it? Why is it that they don't appreciate majesty and splendor, even when it resides in their midst? Today, as a result of that failure, you saw dozens of people needlessly slaughtered, a veteran tribune arrested and removed from his position of power, and a promising youth sentenced to death. Do you not see the error of your ways?"

No one responded. Cidivus looked out into the crowd and saw Sicarius' men now in total control of the mob, holding the last of the survivors down on their knees with their hands behind their backs. He also caught sight of Ignatus, who now found himself standing in the center of it all and feeling completely out of place.

"There," Cidivus said. "There is a man you should all aspire to be like. Mavinor's once proud champion, Ignatus, was the only one among you smart enough not to join in this foolish undertaking. I have it on good authority that the boy, Solitus, asked him to lead your feeble cause, only to be turned down. Ignatus, I congratulate you on your wisdom, for it has saved you." Ignatus stared down at the ground almost sheepishly as Cidivus finished his statement.

"Now let's not forget why we are here, shall we?" Cidivus asked. "If you would all kindly direct your attention to the blocks where the heads of Dismus and Gestus lie, we can commence with our festivities."

"NO!!!" the boys' mother screamed. She had been standing beside her sons the entire time, even as the fighting raged on. But she was quickly corralled by Sicarius' men and ushered away as the executioners walked over to the blocks.

"Now," Cidivus shouted imperiously, "off with their heads!"

At that command the swords fell on both of them, and their heads rolled along the cobblestone as their mother collapsed to the ground in agony. Tarsus watched from a distance, grieving for the boys and their mother. His heart was filled with sorrow over the fact that he had been helpless to stop the bloodshed, and as he turned away from the carnage he mourned for all those who lost their lives. Tarsus immediately left the Praetorium through the same private gate that the troops had used to enter, and he managed to do so without being seen.

"I will allow the rest of you to live," Cidivus said, "for tomorrow all of you will come back to witness the executions of Solitus and

Aramus. Trust me when I say that I will be saving the best for last. Guards, take the prisoners back to the palace. Bring both of them to the throne room; I will be there shortly."

Talmik looked on in total dismay. He still had the dagger in his belt, but had been helpless to do anything with it. Now that the revolt had been crushed and Aramus and Solitus arrested, he suddenly felt all alone. After serving so faithfully during the reigns of two of Mavinor's noblest monarchs, Onestus and Gobius, he never could have imagined that he would find himself in this situation. Despite the epic failure in overthrowing Cidivus, Talmik could never bring himself to serve this king as dutifully as he had served Onestus and Gobius. He loathed him, now more so than ever. Though Talmik had always been a timid soul who was not given to fighting, he realized that desperate times called for desperate measures. The royal aide reached down by his side and felt the dagger hidden beneath his tunic, and as he gripped the hilt he knew that there was only one thing left for him to do. Though it would ultimately cost him his life, he had to use his proximity to the king to his advantage and assassinate Cidivus when the opportunity presented itself. Even if he couldn't save Aramus and Solitus, he had to at least rid Mavinor of its evil ruler.

Ignatus stood in the center of the square, staring solemnly at Solitus and Aramus as they were led away. They looked toward him briefly before turning their backs, and he began to feel an enormous sense of guilt, very similar to what he felt when he declined to join Silex and the others on their rescue mission. As he sadly looked away, he heard a familiar voice call out to him, the same one he had just heard the day before.

"Good for you, Ignatus," the voice said. Ignatus turned to see Nefarius looking right at him. "You were wise to decline the boy's request. It would have been a shame if we had to imprison you as well. I'd prefer to keep you on the outside, for you provide me with an ample source for amusement whenever I run into you." Nefarius' companions laughed as they heard his statement.

Ignatus stormed by them and walked through the square, leaving the Praetorium and marching toward his home with a sense of purpose that he had not felt in a very long time.

Cedrus had been wandering aimlessly ever since he entered the forest just beyond the northwest corner of Xamnon. He refused to slow his steps or stop even for a brief rest, as he wanted to distance himself from his past as quickly as possible. He traveled light, carrying only his brother's gear—Tonitrus' helm, shield, and sword—and a bag packed with his bedroll, a couple of filled waterskins, and enough food for a day or two. He had no idea whether he'd be able to find food and water in the forest, for he hadn't even given it any thought when he set out. His only goal was to ease the great pain he felt, the pain that overwhelmed him and seemingly tore the heart out of his chest. It was the sum total of all the losses he had suffered that finally brought him to the end of his rope.

As he walked briskly along the forest floor, he began to wonder if anyone else had ever suffered as greatly as he had. "I can't imagine," he said to himself, "that anyone else has ever lost his king, his best friends, and his dear brother in one fell swoop, along with the love of his life—who broke off their engagement to become a prostitute—and of course the Medallion, the one item that was needed to help save the world, which The Author's only son had entrusted to him." Cedrus convinced himself that only he had ever endured such torment and misery. He was sure of it, and it made him feel more alone than he had ever felt in his entire life. The loneliness only served to bring his spirits down further, if that were even possible at this point. He continued to long for his brother, for Gobius, and for Silex and the others. His trek through the forest brought back memories of the quest, and he found himself looking up at various points to see if he might spot the catapults, including the one he had loaded. But there was nothing to be seen. Cedrus recalled Henricus' words, yet he continued to defy them. He truly believed that he could outrun the pain, and that he could somehow leave it all behind if he traveled far and fast enough.

When he came into a clearing, he looked up at the sky and took notice of the dark clouds hovering overhead. He knew that neither he nor anyone else would ever see the light again, at least not in this world. Cedrus began telling himself that somewhere out there was another world, one where the light would resurface, and where he could earn himself a fresh start. It was the only thing that brought him any comfort, and he focused on it almost single-mindedly.

Cedrus finally began to tire, and not knowing how soon he might find another clearing, he elected to stop and have a quick meal before catching up on some sleep. He ate half a loaf of bread and two pieces of fruit that he had brought with him from Xamnon, and washed it down with the full volume of one of his waterskins, thus leaving him only one more for the remainder of his trip.

He then took out his bedroll and prepared it, but he did not lie down. His mind could not stop racing, as thoughts of his brother continued to haunt him. Cedrus wondered what it was like for Tonitrus in those last moments as Sicarius' sword came down on him. What was it like to be decapitated? Had he felt any pain, or did death come so quickly when one's head was cut off that he would not feel a thing? He was looking for ways to ease his state of depression, so Cedrus led himself to believe that Tonitrus' death was painless and that he had not suffered much at the hands of Sicarius. He held his brother's sword in his hand and gazed down at the red cross emblazoned on it. Though he did not know where he was going, in his mind part of his brother was going with him, and that somehow made it less daunting. Cedrus stared out into the clearing—toward the trees and the land beyond— all the while hoping that somewhere down that lonely path lied the answer he was looking for, the solution to his problems that would take away the pain and give him promise for the future. If no such thing existed, then he concluded that he would be left with only one alternative—to take his own life and end the anguish once and for all.

Chapter Fifteen

The morning after Cedrus had walked out on them, Bovillus continued to work at his desk, though he found it more difficult than ever to concentrate. Arcala simply stood and stared out the window, as if she was waiting for Cedrus to return. Minstro knew better than to hold such expectations, for he realized that his friend had lost himself and that nothing short of a miracle would ever bring him back. Still he prayed for that miracle, and urged the others to do the same. Magdala went straight to her room after finishing breakfast. She implored The Author to help the love of her life find peace of mind during his search, and to ease his pain from the heartbreak he had experienced. "Please, dear Author," she prayed, "bring him back to us." Magdala did not ask that Cedrus find it in his heart to forgive her and take her back. She only wanted for him to return safely, and to regain his courage so he could move on with his life and fulfill his destiny, whatever it might be. When she finished praying, she went downstairs to join the others, hoping against hope that Cedrus would return and that her prayer might be answered.

None of them knew that Antiugus had awakened, and that he

and Henricus had been meeting behind closed doors all morning to discuss the turn of events in Mavinor, the onset of the Age of Darkness, Bovillus' discoveries regarding The Scrolls, and the advice they received from the Seers of Fate. As they all sat in silence in their respective corners of the room, their reverie was broken when Antiugus stormed in on them.

"King Antiugus?" Minstro said. "It is you!"

"I have awakened, my friends," Antiugus said. Henricus came in and introduced the king to the others, and while they were getting acquainted, a guard escorted the Legans into the room.

"Well here they are, right on cue," Henricus said as he turned to Chaelim, Apteris, and Volara. "Friends, meet Antiugus, the King of Xamnon."

"Hello," Antiugus said to them. "Henricus has told me all about you. I must say it's also nice to see our old friend, the raven. If not for him, we would not have known about the terrible plot they hatched against Gobius."

"Welcome back, your majesty," the raven said as it bowed toward the king.

"You do know," Arcala said to Antiugus, "that the rescue attempt failed, and that all were killed except for my cousin, Cedrus, who has now abandoned us."

"I do," Antiugus said. "Henricus has told me everything, and I am now fully aware of where things stand and how dire the present situation has become. That is why I wanted to speak with you, for I have a plan of action."

"What is it?" Arcala asked.

"We will march on Mavinor and liberate her people," Antiugus replied. "While I slept and teetered on the brink of death, I had a vision of King Gobius. He healed me, and asked me to fight for his kingdom, which was engulfed in flames. I saw the tears flow from his eyes as he sadly looked down upon Mavinor from high up on a mountain peak, and I promised him that I would do as he asked.

Soon after the vision I awakened, and promptly discovered that my wound had healed." He showed everyone his lower right leg, which now bore no trace of even the slightest scar. "Then Henricus told me about everything that happened while I was asleep, and I immediately knew what I had to do. Today we will prepare, but tomorrow we will march."

Henricus then turned toward the Legans and asked about Hexula's location. They reported that she was still asleep in Urmina, seemingly exhausted from her rampage. "We only watched her from a distance, not wanting to get too close and awaken her," Apteris said.

"We have to plan this out carefully," Henricus said. "Sire, I understand that you are intent on saving Mavinor, but remember that the Seers predicted that the Beast would attack Xamnon next. We cannot leave our kingdom unprotected."

"We will continue to monitor the Beast," Apteris said. "We have every intention of doing so, and will keep you abreast of her location."

"But I need you for another task," Antiugus said. "When Henricus told me about you, I realized that we could use you to go ahead and scout Mavinor's defenses. It may even be possible for you to take out the guards at the West Gate and let us through when we arrive. We will have the element of a surprise attack in our favor, and it will greatly increase our chances of success."

"We can do that for you," Chaelim said.

"Then what about the Beast?" Volara asked.

"I will go," the raven said. "I will watch the Beast."

"But it is too dangerous, my friend," Apteris said. "You cannot go it alone."

"Not afraid," said the raven. "Will do what you need me to do."

"You are brave, dear raven, as brave as any man that has ever served under me," Antiugus said. He then turned to the others. "We will leave troops behind to man the guard towers and watch over the city. I think we can get away with using a smaller legion to launch an attack, as long as we have the Legans' assistance and the element of surprise in our favor. But we must begin our preparations immediately. Henricus, assemble our men in the Great Hall and start briefing them. I will come down shortly. Minstro, will you be riding with us?"

"Of course, sire," Minstro said.

"Then go with Henricus," Antiugus said. "You'll need to be on the same page as the rest of our men."

"And what about me?" Arcala asked.

"Sorry, young lady, but I do not permit women in our ranks," Antiugus said. "Now let's get moving." Arcala looked on in disbelief as the king left the room. Henricus started to walk out with Minstro, but Arcala grabbed his attention.

"You really don't think you're going without me, do you?" she asked.

"Well then why don't you come with us," Henricus said. "At the very least, it will be entertaining when the king sees you sitting amongst our men." He smiled as he left, and Arcala reached for her sword and followed after him.

Cidivus returned to the palace, accompanied by Talmik and the tribunes. Pachaias and the others were curious to see what fate would befall Aramus, so they came to witness the sentencing firsthand. When they arrived, they saw that Sicarius and Grodus already had Aramus and Solitus waiting in the throne room. Aramus was standing at the base of the steps leading up to the throne with his hands cuffed, while Solitus was hunched over a short distance away with Sicarius standing right in front of him. As they entered, they heard the general's loud voice echo throughout the room.

"Where is it?" Sicarius shouted at Solitus. When the young man did not answer, Sicarius slapped him hard across the face, causing him to nearly fall over. Grodus grabbed him and held him up so that the general could look him in the eye and ask him yet again. "Where is it?" When Solitus refused to respond, Sicarius struck him again.

"What is going on?" Cidivus asked.

"I am conducting an interrogation," Sicarius said.

"Stop for the time being," Cidivus said. "I want to address my two former friends, and reveal what the future holds in store for them."

Cidivus took his seat on the throne while Talmik came up and stood beside him. The tribunes positioned themselves off to the left, where they would be able to see Aramus' face as Cidivus handed down his sentence. They also had a clear view of Solitus, and they now noticed the bruises and welts on his face from the beating Sicarius had given him.

"So," Cidivus said, "you both wanted a rebellion, did you? I hope you're happy now that your wish was granted and several of Mavinor's fine citizens were led to their deaths. I was not surprised by your treachery, Aramus. I always knew you'd never support my coronation, and that sooner or later you'd turn on me. You've always been a thorn in Pachaias' side, haven't you? Well I think it's time for that thorn to be removed permanently, but not yet. Oh no, not yet.

"For first I want you to witness the pain you have caused. It is not enough for me that you saw the carnage at the Praetorium earlier today. I want you to suffer slowly, painfully, while you watch a young man die. For this young man was foolish enough to follow your advice. He betrayed me, and in the end it will cost him his life. It's such a shame too, because I had high hopes for him.

"You do know that, Solitus, don't you? You do know that I had big plans for you when you returned to Mavinor. How I wanted to believe that you were sincere, and that your loyalty to me was true. I know I first assigned you menial tasks, all to give you a chance to prove your worth and your allegiance. But I was ready to award you a much greater role once you earned it. I honestly believed that you could become my right-hand man, one that I could trust with my own life. But it was not to be. You disappointed me, my friend. Now you are no longer of use to me, even to serve my guests and lick my boots. All that is left is for me to watch you die a painful death, and enjoy every second as the life is slowly sapped from your torn and tattered body.

"For tomorrow, Solitus, you will be tied to a post at the Praetorium. Sicarius and his men will round up the people and bring them to the square, and they will have no choice but to watch as a group of archers is lined up before you. One by one they will fire their bows, sinking arrow after arrow into your bound body. You will bleed until every drop of life seeps out from your flesh, and by the time it's over, you will resemble a sea urchin as the shafts of the arrows appear as needles protruding from your torso."

"But before he dies," Sicarius said, "I want to know where my prized possession is. The time for him to tell me is now."

"I took it," Aramus said. "I am the one who removed Tonitrus' head from the stake outside your office." Sicarius looked toward Aramus in surprise as he finished speaking.

Solitus was still in pain from when Sicarius struck him earlier, but neither the likelihood of another blow nor the death sentence he just received stopped him from displaying a defiant demeanor toward the general. "It's gone, and you can never recover it," Solitus said. "It was not Aramus who stole your prized possession. I am indeed the one who took it, and I disposed of it in a way that honors the memory of Mavinor's greatest swordsman, the one who once beat you handily in a duel in front of your own men. You do remember that, don't you, General? I suppose that's why you had to execute him in such cowardly fashion, because you never could have faced him man-to-man. Truth is you were never as handy with the sword as he was, were you?"

Sicarius' fury reached its height as he stepped forward and belted Solitus in the jaw with a closed fist. The young man dropped to the floor and lied there with blood oozing from his mouth. Sicarius quickly grabbed hold of him and pulled him to his feet. Before anyone else could even say a word or make a movement of any kind, Sicarius hit him again and knocked him flat on his back. The second blow actually caused the Medallion to fall from Solitus' pouch and onto the floor. Sicarius then went to pick him up a third time, but paused when a voice rang out.

"ENOUGH!" Cidivus roared. It drew the general's attention for a moment, but as Cidivus started descending the stairs, Sicarius turned away and made like he was going to pummel Solitus yet again. He reared back his fist in preparation of the strike, but a hand quickly grasped his wrist and kept him from thrusting it forward.

"I said, 'ENOUGH!' " Cidivus barked as he pushed Sicarius' wrist back down to his side.

Sicarius was surprised that Cidivus had spoken to him so imperiously, and even more shocked that he had laid his hands on the general of Mavinor's armies. He almost reacted sharply to the king's brazen manner, but then opted to placate him instead. "Yes, your highness," he stated in a sarcastic tone.

Cidivus eyed Sicarius warily before gazing down at the floor. "Now what do we have here?" he asked.

Cidivus walked over to where the Medallion was lying next to Solitus. One of the guards picked it up and showed it to him, and as he examined it he realized that it was the Medallion of Mavinor.

"So," Cidivus said, "the Medallion rears its head once again. Solitus, I can only surmise that you found it along the shoreline. Is that right?" Solitus did not answer.

Cidivus continued. "Of course you did; you must have. It is the only place you could have possibly obtained it. Isn't it interesting how the talisman that everyone worships is such a curse to those who bear it? Think about it for a second. First Gobius is stoned to death by the citizens of Mavinor. Then Cedrus, to whom Gobius had given the Medallion, meets his demise at sea shortly thereafter. Finally, when young Solitus recovers the Medallion along Mavinor's coast, he promptly receives a death sentence for participating in a failed rebellion. It would seem to me that it is better to avoid the Medallion than come to obtain it. But unfortunately it is too late for you, Solitus. The curse has come upon you, and now, just as your cousin did before you, you will wear the Medallion as you go to your grave." Cidivus then placed the Medallion around Solitus' neck. "Take him away, along with Aramus," Cidivus said, "and put them both in the dungeon."

Sicarius stood and watched as Solitus and Aramus were led out of the throne room. The general wore an angry expression on his face, but then exchanged it for a wry smile. He turned to Cidivus, but didn't say a word to him before taking his leave. Grodus stood by awkwardly, watching Sicarius leave and then looking back toward Cidivus before deciding to follow after the general. Talmik began to reach for his dagger after the soldiers left the room, but had to withdraw his hand when Cidivus suddenly turned around. "I do believe I'll need to keep Solitus away from Sicarius until tomorrow," the king said. "I'd be disappointed if the general got to him before my plan is carried out." With that he walked out into the corridor, leaving Talmik behind alone with his thoughts.

As Cidivus exited, a serpent watched from a dark corner of the throne room, near the trap door. It had heard the entire conversation and witnessed everything, yet managed to slip back out through the crevice around the trap door without being noticed by anyone.

When Ignatus returned to his home, he walked solemnly through his front door and had a seat at the table. From the time that Solitus and Aramus were led away by Sicarius' men, he had been overcome with the same feeling he had when he saw Silex and Ferox give their lives during the failed rescue mission. Somehow he knew that his participation would not have made a difference, yet it did nothing to diminish the extreme feelings of guilt that overwhelmed him. He was all alone now. Silex, Ferox, Tonitrus, and the other royal guards who tried to save Gobius were dead. Tarmin and the rest of the believers in Mavinor's army had been exiled. Aramus was imprisoned, and his death sentence was all but imminent. The young man who he had trained to be a warrior—who so bravely returned to Mavinor in the hope of liberating it from Cidivus' rule—had also been arrested, and would be executed the next day in the Praetorium. There was no one left in Mavinor for Ignatus to turn to. As he stared down at his spiritual exercises and began thumbing through them, he came to realize that they afforded him little consolation. He had just finished them earlier that morning, after working on them for the past two years, since he officially retired from the military. He had promised The Author that he would lay down his sword, and devote himself to a higher purpose.

But something inside now told him that he failed to recognize the urgency of the events that had unfolded in Mavinor. Ignatus ran through all of it in his mind, and wondered how he could have made such a terrible mistake. As a veteran soldier, he knew that life was filled with intervals of both war and peace. The trick was in determining when it was time to bear arms, and when it was time to lay them down. No just man wanted to wage war; war was ugly, savage, and brutal. But sometimes it was a necessity, and the best leaders were the ones who could recognize when war was truly the last resort for achieving peace.

Now Ignatus felt as though he had failed his friends. He had experienced guilt when Silex and Ferox died, yet tried to deny it when Aramus assured him that he could not have saved them. But now the guilt had returned and was even worse than it was before, for he realized that if ever there was a time to fight, this was it. Despite the long odds, Aramus and Solitus were right in saying that the revolt was necessary. It was their last hope, and Ignatus had missed the opportunity to lead them and assist in the battle to save Mavinor.

Glumly Ignatus closed his book of spiritual exercises and laid it aside. He remembered the days of fighting as a young warrior among Mavinor's ranks, flashing his sword with unmatched speed and precision on the battlefield. He stared up at the wall just above his table, where his shield hung from a hook, displaying his insignia of the sunburst with a cross and three swords in a semi-circle. He looked upon the letters the shield bore, "IHS," which stood for "Ignatus Heroicus Sanctus," translated from Mavinor's ancient language as "the venerable and heroic Ignatus." He remembered what those words meant to him, and how he had always strived to live up to them. Now for the first time in his life, he believed that he had fallen short. He knew that he could never live with himself for failing to maintain the standard he bore through his insignia, and Solitus' claim that he was no longer the man he once was haunted him to no end. As a look of intensity came over his face, Ignatus stood from his chair. Then he walked over to the wall where his shield hung proudly for all to see. Ignatus stepped up to his shield, closely examined the insignia, and forcefully yanked it down from the hooks that held it in place.

When Tarsus had exited the Praetorium through the private gateway, he began walking down an isolated path and pondering the recent events in Mavinor. He realized now more than ever that he did not fit in with the current regime, and that he disagreed wholeheartedly with their philosophy. He still could not believe that Dismus and Gestus had been executed for such a petty crime, and he could not escape the sound of their mother's wailing, which still reverberated in his ears. He could not understand why they had slaughtered so many of Mavinor's citizens, and why they felt such a need to eradicate religion from society.

Tarsus thought back to the role he played in overthrowing Gobius and setting the trap for his royal guards, which ultimately led to their deaths. The pain and guilt began to overwhelm him, and for the first time in his life, Tarsus started to question the road he had taken. He was blinded by his loyalty to Sicarius all these years, and now it had cost him dearly. As he peered down at his new black and silver uniform, he realized how much he despised all that it stood for. He wanted to dispose of it, and put this entire episode behind him. But he couldn't. Life as a soldier in Mavinor was all he knew, and as much as he wanted out, there was nowhere else to turn.

Suddenly as he turned a corner, a bright light suddenly flashed around him. It stunned him completely, for the sky above Mavinor was still dark, and there was no sign of the sunlight ever returning. But the light that shone was so resplendent and so powerful that it actually blinded him temporarily and brought him to his knees. As he fell to the ground, he heard a voice calling, "Tarsus, Tarsus, why do you persecute me?"

"Who are you?" Tarsus replied.

"I am Gobius, whom you have persecuted," the voice said. "I need your help to bring light back to the world, Tarsus. You must save Solitus from execution and bring him to the Cavern of Trials in the Tenebrae. He will know the way, but you must do everything to ensure he makes it safely inside the cavern. Then you are to ride north to the Mortuus Valley, where you will find your destiny. Now go and do what you must do!"

As the voice faded away, so did the light. Tarsus was still blinded, but slowly he regained his sight and rose back to his feet. As he looked up, he saw a dove flying away. Part of him wanted to believe that he was seeing and hearing things that weren't real, but in his heart he knew otherwise. The voice was unquestionably that of Gobius, and the light he saw was undeniably present. He realized that he now had a new sense of purpose, and was being granted a second chance to right the many wrongs he had committed. The awe of the experience gave him chills, but it also lifted his spirits to a level they had never risen to before. As he gathered his thoughts, he decided to report immediately to Sicarius' office lest the general become suspicious. From there, he would develop a plan to rescue Solitus and flee from Mavinor.

Chapter Sixteen

When Antiugus came down to the Great Hall, there were roughly two hundred troops assembled there. Henricus greeted him and immediately turned things over to Xamnon's king, who wasted no time in taking the lead and addressing his men.

"As the general has already informed you, tomorrow we will march on Mavinor," Antiugus said. "You're probably wondering why, so allow me to explain. By now you are certainly aware that King Gobius was betrayed and executed, and that the new regime in Mavinor is a far cry from the ruler who extended his hand and made peace with us for the first time in generations. But what you do not know is that King Gobius came to me in a dream, a dream that I immediately realized was nothing less than a vision. While I was on death's door, he came to me and healed my wound, allowing me to awaken and return to the throne. He only asked one thing in return, that I free his people from the tyrant who now oppresses them. Here, I want all of you to see the miracle that has taken place." Antiugus lifted his robe and showed them that the bite mark was gone, and that not a trace of it appeared on his skin. They were all amazed, and when their collective gasps had died down, the king continued his speech.

"I feel a moral obligation to do this, for Gobius was a great friend who not only spared my life, but even saved my soul. I owe this to him. We owe this to him. Most of you experienced the same vision I did during our failed assault on Mavinor. You saw the same images in the sky that I did, the images of the unicorn and of The Scrolls that appear on the Medallion. You certainly understand the power such visions have to alter our lives. Mine was certainly altered that day, and dare I say that this vision was even more intense and had more impact on my life than the last one."

"Your majesty," one of the soldiers called out, "we understand the obligation you feel in your heart, but remember that you are asking us to risk our lives for people whom we do not know. It is a sacrifice many of us may not be prepared to make."

"Your point is well taken, soldier," Antiugus responded, "but it will be a sacrifice worth making. For know that Mavinor is in turmoil, and soon that turmoil may reach us if we do not act. If the evil tyrant is imposing his will on the innocents in his own kingdom, then he will eventually be looking to impose that same will on the other kingdoms that surround Mavinor. That is what tyrants do. Sooner or later we will come face-to-face with this evil, so why wait for it to come to us, on its terms? Let us go and confront it on our own terms, and crush it before it can even begin to spread."

"What is your plan, your highness?" another soldier asked.

"We will set out tomorrow, but not before dispatching our secret weapons. For know that the Legans, nature's guardians, have united with us in this battle, and are prepared to go ahead and scout the enemy. Their ability to fly will enable them to breach Mavinor's walls and take out the guards before they can sound the shofars. We will not even need to transport a battering ram or catapults, for they can let us in through the gate when we arrive. With their help and the tremendous advantage of a surprise attack, there is no reason for our raid to be unsuccessful."

Silence filled the Great Hall after Antiugus finished speaking. As he glanced around the room at his men, he saw anxiety and uncertainty in the looks on their faces. It was clear that they weren't fully aligned with his cause, and it began to worry him. If his troops did not buy in to his plan, then the assault on Mavinor would be doomed from the start.

"I can see that you are still not in complete agreement with me," Antiugus said to his men. "We cannot succeed without full cooperation and cohesion among our ranks."

"They will cooperate, sire," Henricus said. "I will see to it myself."

"No, Henricus," Antiugus said. "You cannot force it. I want them to believe in this cause, to believe as surely as I do."

"We want to, sire," another soldier said. "But I don't see how we can. Our last attack on Mavinor failed miserably, and now we have no reason to invade them, for there is no imminent threat to our security. I understand what you're saying about the likelihood that they will attack us in the future, but the truth is you cannot know for sure. Why risk the lives of your men when it may turn out to be unnecessary?"

Again there was silence until someone in the back stood up and removed the helm from his head. The soldier threw the helm down, causing it to clank and clatter as it rolled around on the floor. When everyone looked over and saw the warrior's long brown hair sweep over her shoulders, they realized it was not a man, but Arcala. All of them were shocked to see that a woman had been in their midst the entire time.

"What are you doing here, young lady?" Antiugus said.

"What am I doing here?" Arcala replied. "What am I doing here? I will tell you what I am doing here. I am riding with you to Mavinor, for unlike the men in this army, I realize how urgent the situation is. Do you all not know of the great evil that has come into the world? Do you not see the darkness that has enveloped us? It is not just Mavinor we are fighting to reclaim, but the entire world as well. We are all endangered by the terrible events that have taken place, and Urmina has already been destroyed by a savage beast that is planning to target Xamnon next. Demons—once buried deep underground—have been released from their tombs to wreak havoc among us. I know because I have faced them, and I have plunged my sword into one of them, only to learn that it was useless against him. There is a being out there who has orchestrated this entire sequence of events, and he grows stronger as the evil engulfs our world. He is the one who plans to wipe us out and rule the world for all eternity. But his plan is dependent upon the traitor remaining on the throne in Mavinor, and that is why we must remove him. If we can, then there may still be hope. Time is short, and you'd be wise to open your eyes and see what your king and general have already recognized, namely that you have no choice now but to mount and ride if you want to save your kingdom. I know I will ride, even though your king resents the idea of a woman accompanying his troops. But I am not a member of Xamnon's ranks, and I am not bound by your rules. I will go to Mavinor, with or without all of you. Tomorrow, we will find out who among you is brave enough to join me, and who is too cowardly to stand up and fight for our world. Let the cowards stay home while the real men stay the course." With that Arcala picked her helm up from the floor and stormed out of the Great Hall. Henricus smiled as he watched her go, while Antiugus just stared at her in bewilderment.

"Gentlemen," Henricus said, "I will see you all tomorrow, when we prepare to ride." He nodded to Antiugus, and both of them exited the Great Hall as the troops slowly stood and saluted them.

Aramus and Solitus were brought to the dungeon, where they were placed in separate cells far apart from each other. Solitus, already battered and bruised from the beating he endured at the hands of Sicarius, was thrown down hard against the stone floor when they imprisoned him. The guard slammed the door shut, leaving Solitus lying there in a weakened, weary state.

Solitus could barely move. He crawled to the wall and managed to pull himself up enough so that he was sitting against it. His cheek was sore, his mouth still bleeding slightly. But far more painful than any injury Sicarius inflicted on him was the fact that his soul was now crushed. The insurrection failed miserably, as someone had apparently tipped Cidivus off and enabled him to set a trap. Aramus was imprisoned, Ignatus had given up, and Solitus himself was now going to be murdered in public the very next day, impaled by a barrage of arrows. It was over. It finally hit him that Mavinor would never be the same, and that the kingdom they once knew and had tried to salvage was gone forever, seized by a barbaric faction that would perpetually oppress the people it was supposed to serve. He closed his eyes, hoping to fall asleep and not wake up until the next day, for he didn't want to have to think about the atrocities any longer. But as he was on the verge of slumber, he suddenly heard a soft voice call out to him.

"Solitus," the voice said, "do not let your heart be troubled."

Solitus frantically looked around the cell, but he saw nothing. "Who are you?" he asked as he attempted to get to his feet and look out through the door into the hallway. Facing the wall, he managed to pull himself up so that he was now standing erect. But when he turned toward the door, he saw someone emerge from the dark corner of his cell. The shadowy figure was clearly a man, tall and slender with a purposeful gait. Somehow he exuded a calming presence that lent Solitus a sense of comfort in his moment of distress.

"Solitus," the man continued, "I need you."

"For what?" Solitus asked in a tone of disbelief.

"You are to go to the Cavern of Trials in the Tenebrae and retrieve the Ivory Sabre. When the opportunity to flee arises, take it. Ride into the Tenebrae along the main path, until you reach a small mountain on your right. You will see a trail lined with rounded stones leading to a dark doorway. That doorway is the entrance to the Cavern of Trials. It is there that your destiny lies, Solitus. Do not take any weapons with you when you enter the cavern, for they will not be necessary, and take neither water nor sustenance. No one may accompany you as you go inside, for it is your destiny and yours alone to recover the Ivory Sabre."

"Whatever will I encounter inside there?" Solitus asked.

"You will see," the man said.

"But how can I possibly escape?" Solitus asked. "Do you not see that I am being held in a dungeon? Do you not know that tomorrow they are going to execute me in the Praetorium? What hope do I have of surviving this?"

"You have the Medallion; wear it, for it will save your life and help you to escape Mavinor," the man said.

Solitus looked down at the Medallion as the man spoke, and then raised his eyes toward him. "But even if I manage to flee Mavinor and find the Ivory Sabre inside the cavern, then what am I to do with it?" Solitus said.

"Exit the cavern once you have retrieved the Sabre," the man said. "It will be needed to kill the Beast, for she has risen from the depths of the Black Hollow and has already destroyed Urmina. She must be stopped before she can do the same to Xamnon and Mavinor."

"Who are you?" Solitus asked again. He stepped closer, and once he saw the outline of the man's facial features, he realized that he was speaking with King Gobius. "My Lord!" he said.

"Remember my words, Solitus," Gobius said, "and know that I will be with you to the very end."

"Lord, if I may ask one thing, please tell me whether Cedrus is still alive. Please, Lord, tell me that he survived his ordeal at sea."

"He is alive," Gobius said. "Pray for him, Solitus, for he is in despair, and his assistance in this war is badly needed. Do not lose your faith, and never lose hope. May The Author be with you."

Solitus watched Gobius walk back toward the corner. The young man froze for a minute, and then went to follow him. But he was gone. It was as if he had walked right through the wall of the cell. Solitus gazed down at the Medallion again, and then grabbed hold of it, hoping that Gobius' promise would somehow be fulfilled.

When Tarsus entered Sicarius' office, he walked in on an intense conversation taking place between Grodus and the general. Sicarius looked up at his first lieutenant with a scowl and asked him where he had been.

"I needed to be alone for a while and gather my thoughts," Tarsus replied.

"And what exactly were those thoughts?" Sicarius asked as he stood up and walked toward Tarsus. "Tell me, have you betrayed us? Are you ready to abandon your duties as a soldier of Mavinor? Has your loyalty to me come to an end?" The tone of his voice was clearly meant to intimidate Tarsus.

"No, of course not, General," Tarsus answered.

"I do have another who can easily replace you, Tarsus," Sicarius said as he looked back toward Grodus.

"I understand your concern," Tarsus said. "But I have known no other life than that of a soldier, and I have served under no one all these years but you, General. I have been somewhat troubled by the decisions to massacre Mavinor's citizens, but truth be told I can never abandon you. If this is what you decide is best for our kingdom, then I will stand beside you, just as I have all these years."

Sicarius eyed Tarsus cautiously before responding. "Very good," he then said, "for tomorrow I will need your loyalty more than ever."

"Why is that, General?" Tarsus asked.

"Sit down," Sicarius said. When Tarsus was seated, Sicarius continued speaking. "Grodus and I were just discussing my issues with the arrogant charlatan who currently sits on our throne. I have decided that as of tomorrow, his reign is over."

"But what about Orius?" Tarsus asked. "Remember what he said to us when we encountered him at the shore."

"I do," Sicarius said. "But I've come to realize that he has deceived me as well. My men who brought the exiles to Patmos should have returned by now. The fact that they haven't come back tells me that something has gone terribly wrong, and I suspect that Orius has something to do with it. Remember how he threatened me by saying he would see to it that they would never return unless I complied with his request? Well we have complied, and where now are my men?"

"But you saw how powerful Orius was," Tarsus said. "The three of us together were no match for him."

"Do you think he is a match for all my troops?" Sicarius said. "I may well have lost some of my best men on that ship, but we have plenty more who are ready to stand and fight. I cannot see how Orius could possibly defeat us by himself, nor do I even fret about it at this point. For I have lost all patience with Cidivus, and the time has come to humble the conceited aristocrat once and for all. Tomorrow, just when he gives the order for my men to fire upon Solitus, the archers will lower their bows. I cannot wait to see the look on his face when his orders are refused and I inform him that his rule has come to an end. He has asked that we gather all the citizens into the Praetorium to watch his grand show, in which he will lay down the gauntlet once and for all by killing the last rebel in the most perverse of ways. But little does he know that what they will see is a commanding display of power from their general, one which results in the dethroning of Cidivus and the usurping of the throne."

"What do you intend to do with him?" Tarsus asked.

"I do not know yet," Sicarius said. "I may kill him right there, in front of the lowly people he despises and expected to conquer, or I may have him thrown in the dungeon and plan something else."

"And what about Solitus?" Tarsus asked.

"I think you already know that I have special plans for him," Sicarius said. "He will be tortured beyond the point that no one would have thought possible, for he took from me the trophy of all trophies. For that, he will pay an enormous price."

"If you wish, General, I will gladly usher Solitus back to the dungeon and have the torture chamber prepared for him," Tarsus said. "Once you decide what to do with Cidivus and come to the palace, everything will be ready for you. Just let me know what methods and instruments you plan to use."

"I like the sound of that, Tarsus," Sicarius said, "for I do not want to lose even one minute of time as I prepare him for what I have in store. I will let you know tomorrow how I want the chamber to be arranged."

"Yes, General," Tarsus replied.

"Grodus, you will be in charge of assembling the people in the square," Sicarius said. "Just make sure every home is searched and every man, woman, and child is brought to the Praetorium. You know what to do with those who offer too much resistance. Tarsus and I can handle the rest."

"Of course, General," Grodus said. "It will be my pleasure."

Tarsus left after being dismissed by Sicarius, and though he wished he could stop Grodus from killing even more innocent people, he had to focus on the task that Gobius had assigned to him. Thankfully Sicarius had gone along with his suggestion to bring Solitus to the palace. All he had to do was take the young man on his mount and bolt for the North Gate when the opportunity arose. He didn't know what lay ahead, or what kind of fate was waiting for him in the Mortuus Valley. But he placed his faith and trust in Gobius, and was ready to give all he had to ensure that Solitus made it out of Mavinor alive.

Once Tarsus was out of sight, a serpent emerged from its hiding spot just outside Sicarius' office and slithered toward a nearby pasture where one of the Surnia promptly snatched it up and began flying back to the Tenebrae.

Chapter Seventeen

From a distance, the raven watched Hexula sleep amidst the wreckage in Urmina. The smoke was still rising from the remnants she left behind, and there were no signs of life left in the kingdom. The Beast snored loudly as she slept, and the sounds of her heavy breathing echoed off the mounds of stone that surrounded her.

When the snoring finally stopped, it caught the raven's attention, and the bird watched very closely as the Beast slowly opened her eyes. She yawned as she rose to her feet and stretched her forelegs, exposing her gaping jaws and the huge, jagged teeth that resembled long rock spires hanging from the ceiling of a mountainous cavern. The Beast scanned the area around her before unexpectedly pivoting and walking toward the shoreline. As she trudged along, she used her spiked tail to brush aside rubble and sniffed through the areas she exposed. Slowly the raven began to realize that the Beast was searching for survivors. She was going to sweep every inch of Urmina and make sure every trace of life was snuffed out before she left for Xamnon. That could only work to their benefit, as it gave them even more time to launch the raid on Mavinor before having to worry about

Hexula. The raven flapped its wings gently and began to follow the Beast, advancing just a short distance at a time as it hid behind piles of debris to shield itself from Hexula's view.

Cerastes crept out from the dark woods of the Tenebrae to where Malgyron was standing in their usual meeting spot. He was listening attentively to one of the Surnia, which was perched on a nearby tree stump and screeching wildly. "Interesting," Malgyron said when the giant owl stopped its squawking.

"What is it?" Cerastes asked.

"It appears that the last of Gobius' royal guards, the one called Cedrus, and the dwarf from Mizar somehow managed to survive their ordeal," Malgyron said. "Moreover, the Legans are assisting them, and brought them to the Northern Mountains to seek advice from a group of women who possess the gift of prophecy, a trio known as the Seers of Fate."

"What are we going to do?" Cerastes asked.

"I will handle it personally, but all in due time," Malgyron said. "I warned them not to interfere; now they have sealed their own fate. Regardless of what the Seers may have told them, there is nothing they can do. It is far too late to save their precious world from the Age of Darkness, and from my inevitable reign as ruler of all. There is nothing left for them to do but die."

"I have some other news to share from our spies in Mavinor, news that you may find interesting," Cerastes said with a hiss.

"Tell me," Malgyron said.

"First, the Medallion has been found. The one called Solitus has come to possess it, and Cidivus plans to have him executed tomorrow."

"Then Bellicus must certainly sense it," Malgyron said. "I just came from the Northern Mountains, where I dispatched the Deliverers of Darkness. They have just begun riding to the Mortuus Valley to claim their army, but maybe I can save them the trouble of recovering the Medallion, now that I know who has found it."

"But a potential problem has arisen," Cerastes said. "Another spy has told me that the general intends to overthrow Cidivus."

Malgyron growled at Cerastes' statement. "When does he plan to do this?" Malgyron asked.

"Tomorrow morning," Cerastes replied. "It will happen just as Solitus is about to be executed. Only the general will not allow Cidivus to go through with it. Sicarius has a gripe with the boy, and wants to keep him alive so he can torture him."

"I will handle this situation as well," Malgyron said. "I knew from the start that the general could pose a problem, but now it is time to rid myself of that problem once and for all. It looks like I'll be making a guest appearance, one where I'll be able to save Cidivus' reign and obtain the Medallion all at once. General Sicarius has unwittingly made things even easier for me."

Cerastes hissed with delight when he heard Malgyron's plan, but Malgyron's intensity remained as he turned to ask the leader of the Colubri yet another question. "What about Xamnon?" he said. "Are there any plans being made there?"

"We have heard nothing yet," Cerastes said. "But as soon as I know something, I will alert you."

"Good," Malgyron said. "Despite appearances, everything is very much under control." He then turned to the Surnia. "We have business to attend to," he said. "Lead me to the cave of the Seers."

Cedrus slept soundly all alone in the forest, curling up in his bedroll in an attempt to keep warm. He thought he would have trouble falling asleep given how deeply his mind and heart were afflicted, but he dozed off as soon as his head hit the pillow. The sky grew darker, and soon the clearing where he had set up camp was cloaked in utter blackness.

The setting was so peaceful that one would have expected Cedrus to sleep throughout the night. But just after nightfall, he awoke suddenly in a state of alarm, as if something had shaken him to the core.

He didn't know why it happened, and as he looked around he saw nothing out of the ordinary. He listened carefully, but didn't hear a thing. There was no explanation for his arousal, for he hadn't even been dreaming.

Then he heard something. It was a rustle of leaves, and it seemed to be coming from the trees straight across the clearing. Cedrus stood and grabbed his brother's sword and shield, then began advancing toward the site of the disturbance. He was forced to rely on his other senses in the darkness, using his hearing and sense of smell to detect whether there was anyone or anything in the vicinity. The closer he got, the more deliberately he approached. But when he reached the end of the clearing, the sounds had long faded away. He couldn't go any further into the woods, for it was too dark and he didn't know what he might encounter while wandering through. Convinced that it was nothing more than a small animal scurrying about, Cedrus decided to return to his bedroll and go back to sleep.

But as he turned his back to walk away, the sounds started up again. It was the same rustling of leaves, and now it was further away, deep in amongst the trees. It was still too dark for him to consider going in there, so he remained in position, staring into the forest to see if anything might emerge. Nothing did, but as he looked off into the distance, he suddenly caught sight of a bright light. "Where is it coming from?" Cedrus asked himself. "What could possibly be giving off such bright light here in the middle of the woods?"

He was hesitant to go and search for the light source, but something was reaching out to him. It was as if an unseen force was pulling him in, and he found himself helplessly gravitating toward it. Whatever it was, its allurement was virtually irresistible. Almost unconsciously, Cedrus began meandering through the forest, darting around tree trunks as if he was remarkably familiar with the trail that wound between them. But consciously he was aware that he had never walked this way before. The territory was completely foreign to him, and he couldn't comprehend how he was able to find his way in the darkness.

But he kept following the path, and the closer he got to the source of the light, the more anxious he became. The trees around him appeared as blurred walls of shadow. The faster Cedrus moved, the slower they seemed to pass through his peripheral vision. It was as if time itself had stopped ticking, but he continued to churn his legs, fighting for traction and doing everything possible to reach the light source before it disappeared. It continued to emanate a luminous glow, and as he drew even closer something flashed that caused him to stop in his tracks. Cedrus covered his face with his hands, but then lowered them when the flash of light had subsided. The glow was much softer now, and that made it easier for him to approach. Soon Cedrus found himself in yet another clearing, and as he stared across he caught sight of what it was that had been glimmering with such splendor.

Standing in the center of the clearing was a majestic unicorn. It glanced at him—eyes deep and liquid—seemingly searching his soul. It lowered its head, cropped the grass, and then shivered. The gesture was so much like that of a regular horse that Cedrus almost forgot what he had just seen. Then it glanced up at him again, and slowly began coming toward him. As the unicorn approached, Cedrus stared in wonder at the long, spiraled horn protruding from its forehead. "Could it be?" he asked himself. "Could this be the creature that served as King Gobius' mount?"

The closer the unicorn came to him, the softer the aura of light around it shone. As its horn came within reach of Cedrus, he sheathed his sword and gently reached out to touch it, but then retracted for fear that the unicorn might not allow it. But much to his surprise the animal moved even closer, and nickered quietly as if it was saying hello. When it nickered yet again, Cedrus reached out and stroked its horn. He stared into its sentient eyes, and suddenly felt himself becoming one with the creature. Cedrus remembered what Gobius once told him about his relationship with the unicorn, how he believed he could communicate with her, and her with him.

He never believed that such a thing was possible, but now that he was alone with her he began to believe otherwise. Cedrus started to feel as though she was speaking to him, but it was as if his ears were too dull to hear what she was saying. He focused on her completely, and even closed his eyes in order to hone in on his auditory senses.

Finally he came to understand the message she wished to communicate. The unicorn was telling him that his family, friends, and the entire world needed him. Running away was not the answer, she said. He needed to take up the fight, and if he did, then she would fight alongside him. Together they could do what needed to be done to save the world from darkness, and bring the light back once and for all. But she couldn't do it without him. He had to believe in himself again, to believe that all things were possible with The Author, no matter how desperate they might seem. If he could reach deep down inside and somehow find his faith again, then they would be a formidable team, one that could lead the forces of good in the epic battle about to be waged.

Cedrus heard something lurking in the bushes nearby, and when he saw it walk into the aura of light still shining forth from the unicorn, he realized that it was Minstro's horse. He remembered how the horse galloped away when they were attacked by the guards at Mavinor's West Gate, and knew what it would mean for Minstro to be reunited with it. The horse walked toward them unafraid. It stopped and stood right beside the unicorn, displaying how it was totally at ease in their presence. Cedrus then found himself stroking the manes of both creatures, and as he looked upon them he continued to hear the voice of the unicorn in his head. "We must go to Xamnon," she said, "before it is too late."

Something in the unicorn's voice struck a chord with Cedrus. He didn't know if it was her mystical tone or simply the substance of what she said to him, but its effect was nothing short of miraculous. Cedrus found himself regaining his courage and his sense of urgency. He looked upon her and realized that he was no longer alone. He would have a partner as he rode into battle, an awe-inspiring creature that could intimidate the most formidable of foes. In his heart, he believed that Gobius had sent her to him, and that it was the savior's way of telling him to go back and fight for his homeland. It would be a cruel twist of fate for Cedrus to lead an attack against his own kingdom, but he knew it was the only way to save it. As the unicorn strode up beside Cedrus and seemingly prodded him to mount her, he climbed on her back and pointed her in the direction of the clearing where his bedroll was located. Without hesitating she began galloping through the forest, and Minstro's horse followed close behind.

Hexula moved methodically through Urmina in her search for survivors. The raven continued to follow from a distance, careful not to draw her attention but always making sure it had the Beast within its field of vision. At one point the raven landed just below the top of a mound of rubble, shielding its body but peeking out around the loose pieces of rock to see what Hexula was doing. When the Beast finished perusing yet another section of Urmina, she moved on toward the shoreline. But as the raven flapped its wings and went to pursue her, it jarred the rock it had been perched upon and knocked it loose from the pile. The disturbance was enough to cause the stone to tumble all the way to the bottom, and it rattled and crashed into several other pieces of debris on its downward path. The sounds immediately caught Hexula's attention, and as she looked back she breathed fire in the direction where the noise originated. The onslaught forced the raven to dart off to the side in order to avoid having its feathers singed by the flames, and though it managed to escape what would have been certain death, the Beast was now aware of the raven's presence and began to chase after it.

The raven flew back toward Urmina's North Gate at full speed, using its fluttering wings to propel itself swiftly through the air and outrun the dragon's pursuit. When it arrived at what remained of the North Gate, it suddenly realized the gravity of its misstep. By drawing the attention of the Beast, it was now in a precarious position. If it flew back toward Xamnon, the Beast might follow it and thus make it impossible for Antiugus to execute the raid on Mavinor. Its only other option was to draw the Beast north into the Eastern Woodlands. The raven would be taking a huge risk, especially if it came face-to-face with the Surnia, which were undoubtedly patrolling the surrounding areas for Malgyron. But it was not about to let the assault on Mavinor fail because it had unwittingly drawn the attention of the Beast, so it decided to sacrifice itself and fly north. It knew that it could use the Beast's bloodthirsty nature against her, as she would surely become obsessed with killing the raven before moving on to her next target. The courageous bird was careful to stay far enough away from Hexula that her flames could not reach it, but remained in her sight so she would continue to give chase. As night fell, the Beast exited Urmina and stalked the raven even as it fled into the forest. The raven did all it could to evade her, and only hoped it could stay alive long enough to keep the Beast occupied until Xamnon's forces invaded Mavinor.

When Talmik was certain that Cidivus was asleep, he tucked his dagger away and decided to carry out his plan. This would be his best opportunity to assassinate the king, for Cidivus would be helpless to resist him. Talmik wasn't sure what would happen when Pachaias and Sicarius found out that Cidivus was dead, but at this point he didn't care. Even if they somehow discovered that it was he who had murdered the king, he was willing to accept his fate. It wasn't in his nature to kill, and under normal circumstances his code of ethics would never allow him to commit such a heinous act. But now his moral judgment had been clouded by Cidivus' reign of terror. Somehow he believed that killing the king in cold blood could be justified by the many lives that would be saved by removing him from the throne.

Talmik walked down the hallway and turned the corner. He had his head down, for he was deep in thought as he contemplated the consequences of his decision. But as he looked up after taking a few steps down the corridor that led to the king's quarters, he unexpectedly saw two soldiers standing guard outside Cidivus' door. They were now looking directly at him, so it was too late to turn back. Doing so would only serve to heighten suspicion, so he immediately altered his facial expression and continued walking toward them.

"What is it you want?" one of the guards asked.

"I have come to check on the king," Talmik answered. "Tomorrow is a very important day, and he needs his rest. If he should need something to help him fall asleep, I will gladly retrieve it for him."

"The king seems to be sleeping soundly," the other guard whispered. "I don't believe any such thing will be needed."

"Very well," Talmik said, now speaking very softly so as not to wake Cidivus. "If he should need my services, then please come and get me."

"That we will," the other guard said in a tone that was almost expressive of doubt.

Talmik quickly turned and walked back down the hallway. Cidivus had never assigned guards to stand outside his door as he slept. Perhaps now that he was aware of Solitus' intentions to betray him, the king was being more cautious than ever before. To Talmik, it also confirmed his suspicion that Cidivus no longer trusted him. It was clear now that the royal aide would need to tread very carefully, and that his plan was going to be far more difficult to execute than he ever could have imagined.

Chapter Eighteen

The next morning Antiugus joined the others at the breakfast table in the palace. His men were preparing to march later that afternoon, and he was ready to lead them. The vision of Gobius still remained at the forefront of his mind, and in his heart he was ready to give his life for the mission that Gobius asked him to undertake. Antiugus had already confessed that Mavinor's former king saved his soul, but now Gobius had even restored his life, and the least Antiugus could do was to use this second chance to fulfill Gobius' request.

Before they even finished eating, one of the guards ran into the dining room. He was breathing heavily, and was barely able to enunciate his words. "Sire, you must come downstairs! You will not believe what you see."

Antiugus didn't hesitate. He wiped some food from his chin and promptly stood from his chair. As he accompanied the guard downstairs, Henricus followed behind, and Minstro and Arcala went with him. When they reached the front door to the palace and exited along with the guard, they could not believe the sight that was awaiting them.

Standing before them in all her majesty and splendor was the unicorn, with Cedrus mounted on top of her and Minstro's horse alongside them. "Cedrus!" Arcala and Minstro both yelled out at the same time.

As Cedrus dismounted, Arcala ran into his arms and held him tighter than she ever had. "I knew you would come back," she said.

"You have found him!" Minstro cried as he went up to his horse and stroked his mane. Then he too embraced Cedrus and welcomed him back.

"Wherever did you find such a wonderful creature?" Antiugus asked.

"In the woods to the northwest," Cedrus answered. "But I didn't find her. The truth is that she found me."

Henricus walked up to Cedrus and extended his hand, which Cedrus immediately grasped. "It's good to have you back, my friend," Henricus said.

"It's good to be back," said Cedrus.

As they admired the unicorn, something in her demeanor began to change. She started snorting and stamping her feet as if something was wrong. "What is it, girl?" Cedrus asked her.

The unicorn let out a loud whinny and started galloping toward the bushes that lined the front of the castle. The others immediately noticed something lurking behind them and drew their weapons. Whatever it was, the unicorn managed to cut it off before it could escape around the corner and forced it out into the open. As it slithered into plain sight, they saw that it was one of the Colubri.

"Be careful!" Antiugus shouted. "Their bites are extremely venomous, as I know all too well."

The serpent rose up until it was mostly erect, then flared out its hood and flashed its teeth. Cedrus eyed it carefully as he stood a safe distance away, extending his sword and preparing for it to strike. He began to circle it, drawing its attention away from the others and causing it to focus solely on him. Minstro had managed to sneak toward the bushes, and was now in a position where he was outside the creature's line of vision. He drew a dagger and eyed his target, quickly discerning that his best chance for spearing his prey would be to aim for the hood. As Cedrus approached the serpent, its hood flared out even further, and Minstro let the dagger fly. The blade sliced right through the body of the Colubri, just below the head. It fell to the ground and twitched momentarily before dying from the strike.

"So that is how they've managed to do it," Cedrus then said. "The Colubri have been spying on us all along."

"That must be how they learned of the rescue attempt and were able to set the trap," Minstro said.

"If they have been spying all along, then they must certainly be aware that Solitus was planning to return to Mavinor to fake allegiance to the new regime," Arcala said. "They might have set a trap for him as well!"

"He is alive, Arcala," Cedrus said. "Trust me, for I have sensed it."

"But how can you know?" Arcala said.

"Again, remember the Seers' words," Minstro said. "Solitus is on his way to fulfilling his destiny. He will be fine, Arcala. You must have faith."

"Easier said than done," Arcala replied.

"Given what we now know, we should march on Mavinor sooner rather than later," Antiugus said. "The last thing we need is for another one of these creatures to spy on us. Henricus, start preparing the troops."

"Yes, sire," Henricus said. "Cedrus, are you with us?"

"I am with you," Cedrus replied. "I will ride with you at the front of the formation and help you lead the troops into battle." The unicorn strode up beside him, and after taking a quick glance at her, Cedrus turned back toward the others. "With her menacing horn she will lead us," he said, "and together we will drive our forces to victory."

They were all elated to see that Cedrus had regained his sense of
self and was more determined than ever to fight for Mavinor and for
the rest of the world. As Cedrus looked in their direction, he couldn't
help but notice that Magdala was standing several feet behind them,
just outside the entrance to the palace. She too was smiling, though
he could have sworn that he saw tears in her eyes even as she turned
away and walked back inside.

Solitus had barely slept as he lied in his cell throughout the night.
He wanted to believe that his vision was real and not just some kind
of hallucination that had resulted from his state of anxiety. He knew
the time was quickly approaching when the guards would come to
lead him to where he would be executed. But as Solitus continued to
contemplate his fate, something overcame him and caused him to
black out, just as he had done outside Ignatus' home. Only this time
the feeling was much stronger, and before he knew it, Solitus found
himself in an altogether different place.

*As Solitus opens his eyes, he sees that he is now in a desolate loca-
tion with nothing in sight for miles. It is a valley of some sort where the
air is hot and dry, and Solitus is very thirsty. He begins searching for
water, but there is none to be found. He feels the extreme heat rising
from the ground beneath his feet, but he continues to tread forward
in a desperate search to quench his thirst. Just as he catches sight of a
small spring, he hears a thundering noise from off in the distance. The
ground begins to shake, and soon it trembles so violently that Solitus
loses his balance and falls over to the side. As he raises his head and
looks out toward the horizon, he sees four dark figures approaching
on horseback. "Who are they, and what are they looking for?" Solitus
asks himself.*

*Eventually the riders arrive and halt their mounts a short distance
away. Solitus now sees that one of the cavaliers wears dark gray armor
and carries a bow, another wears black armor and carries a double-
edged sword, yet another wears pale armor and wields a sword as well,*

and the last one—whom Solitus perceives to be their leader—wears blood-red armor and flashes the largest sword that Solitus has ever seen. It is he who dismounts and begins walking toward him. Solitus now feels helpless to escape their wrath. He simply stares in awe at the frightening horsemen, and hopes that they have not come to kill him.

When their leader comes within two steps of where Solitus is kneeling, he stops and stares down at Solitus' chest. At first Solitus doesn't understand why, but after he looks down, he sees that he is wearing the Medallion of Mavinor. Could it be that the ghostly cavalier is searching for the Medallion? "Why have you come?" Solitus asks. "Is this what you want?" he says as he holds the Medallion out toward his stalker.

The horseman reaches out to grab it, but instinctively Solitus pulls it back and begins slithering away. The palms of his hands are burnt by the scorching floor of the valley, so he rises to his feet and starts running. The cavalier doesn't run after him. He doesn't have to, because his horse rides up beside him so he can quickly mount and pursue Solitus. The other riders follow, and it doesn't take long for them to catch the youth and surround him.

Solitus looks around from one warrior to the next, wondering which one will approach him. Once again it is the horseman in red armor that steps down from his mount and comes forward. He reaches out, takes the Medallion in his hands, and tries to remove it. But it will not budge. It is as if the chain is somehow welded to Solitus' neck, so he steps back and unsheathes his sword. "No!" Solitus yells. His plea for mercy goes unanswered as the warrior swings his mighty sword through the air, but as Solitus closes his eyes in anticipation of his death...

He awoke to the sound of a key opening the door to his cell. It was Cidivus' guards. "Get up!" one of them yelled as he came over and grabbed Solitus by the arm. Solitus rose to his feet and began walking out of the cell and down the corridor. He was in a daze, and at one point he even muttered, "They're coming."

It was loud enough for the guards to hear, so they asked him,

"Who is coming?" When Solitus didn't answer, they mocked him. "Do you think someone is coming to save you?" one of the guards asked. The others laughed at the statement. "I'm sure that Gobius believed someone would come to rescue him too," the guard then said. "But we all know how that turned out, and the same fate will befall anyone who dares try to save you from execution." They ushered him up the stairs and out of the dungeon, and Solitus remained silent for the rest of the trip.

They fed Cedrus a hearty breakfast after his return to Xamnon. Antiugus conferred with the Legans and explained what they would need to do in order to facilitate the attack on Mavinor. He asked all of them to fly ahead of the troops and disarm the guards at the West Gate. If they could do so without allowing them to sound the shofars, then there would be no troops waiting for Xamnon's army when they arrived at the city walls. The Legans could then let them through the gate, and from there they planned to storm the castle. "We will be able to march at a much faster rate without hauling catapults and a battering ram," Antiugus said. "If we time everything right, then we can be inside Mavinor no more than an hour after we begin to ride."

Henricus was already dressed in full armor as he assembled his men outside the palace. Minstro and Arcala finished their preparations, and then said good-bye to Bovillus and Magdala. Shortly after they left, Cedrus entered the guest room where Bovillus was working diligently. Magdala stood outside on the balcony watching the commotion below as the legions of men lined up to march. Cedrus caught sight of her and stared, and when Bovillus noticed what was happening, he immediately stood from his chair and walked over to him.

"I hope you can find it in your heart to forgive her," Bovillus said, "just as King Gobius did." With that he left the room, and after Cedrus watched him go, he turned back and started walking toward the balcony.

He approached so quietly that Magdala was unable to hear the footfalls behind her. It wasn't until he came outside and stood just a few steps behind Magdala that she was able to sense his presence. She quickly turned around and gasped when she saw him standing there.

"Sorry that I startled you," Cedrus said.

Magdala tried to catch her breath. Her heart was now beating rapidly, and she wasn't even sure that she would be able to speak without stumbling over her words. She opened her mouth, but nothing came out. So she simply turned around and looked back over the edge of the balcony.

"You don't have to say anything," Cedrus said. "It is I who must do the talking, for I am the one who scorned you. I am the one who wanted nothing to do with you and refused to forgive you, even though our Lord asked me to do so."

Magdala finally overcame the lump in her throat and began to speak. "Cedrus, how can I ever blame you for the way you have treated me?" she said. "I am the one who shunned you, and I can never forget the sorrowful expression on your face when I returned your ring. It haunts me to this day, knowing that I committed such a grave sin that caused me to lose both the love of my life and my dear king. Just a few days ago, I thought of jumping to my death from this balcony, believing that I was the one who caused all of this to happen. If not for my crime, then King Gobius would not have had to forgive me, and he would not have been executed. But Bovillus has since shown me how The Scrolls have revealed that his death was destined to happen. He was sent by The Author to die for our sins, and only now do I know that I alone am not to blame for the darkness that has descended upon the world. But my sin still caused me to lose the only man I have ever loved, and for that I can never forgive myself."

"But you must," Cedrus said, "for I have forgiven you. I understand what you were going through, Magdala, how caring for your parents took such a toll on you emotionally. I know you were not in the right state of mind when you did what you did, now more than ever. You see, I was also not in my right state of mind when I left yesterday and began wandering through the forest. I too contemplated suicide as I sat alone in the woods, hoping that I could get far enough away from my troubles that I could leave them all behind. I was ready to take my brother's sword and drive it into my heart if need be, that is until the unicorn came and saved me. She helped me understand what I needed to do, and somehow in the recesses of my mind she was able to communicate with me, telling me that she would stand beside me every step of the way. So now I say to you, Magdala, that I will stand beside you every step of the way as well, if you can somehow forgive yourself and move beyond the past. If I have already forgiven you, then can you find the courage in your heart to move forward, just as I did when the unicorn came to me?"

Magdala's emotions began to shift as she turned around to face Cedrus. She stepped forward and reached out, stroking his cheek. He looked into her brown eyes and placed his arms around her as she uttered her response while choking back tears. "Yes!" she said. Then he kissed her deeply, rekindling memories of the love they once had for each other. Somehow he began to believe that they could find that love again and recapture the dream they once shared, the dream to spend the rest of their lives together. As they unlocked their lips and slowly backed away, Cedrus kept his eyes fixed on her and began speaking with conviction.

"I will be back for you," he said. "We will win this battle, and I will send for you when we reclaim our kingdom. I promise you, Magdala, that you will see me again, and that we will be together… always."

Magdala embraced him as they heard a voice calling from inside. "Cedrus?" the voice said.

Cedrus and Magdala immediately released their hold on each other. "I am here," Cedrus called out. When he walked back inside, he saw that it was Minstro who was summoning him.

"It is time, my friend," Minstro said.

"I will be down right away," Cedrus replied. "There is just one last thing I need to do." When Minstro saw that Magdala was present, he briefly acknowledged her and left their presence so that Cedrus and Magdala could share one last good-bye kiss.

Cedrus bore his brother's gear as he came outside and mounted the unicorn. He looked into her eyes and saw that she was ready, sensing an unmistakable fire in her soul. The light from that fire shone back at him like the rays of the sun reflecting off a mirror, and made him realize that he had forgotten what those rays looked like. He was more prepared than ever to do whatever needed to be done to bring the light back into the world.

"Are we ready?" Cedrus asked as he came up alongside Antiugus.

"Just about," Antiugus said. He continued to stare in wonder at the unicorn, unable to take his eyes off of her.

"Thank you, Cedrus," a voice from behind said. It was Minstro, who was ecstatic to be riding his own horse again. "You have no idea what it means to me to have him back. He was a gift from Pugius, and thus I feel as if the horse is somehow an extension of him."

"I know exactly what you mean," Cedrus said as he looked down upon his brother's sword and shield. "May the spirits of Pugius, Tonitrus and the rest of our fallen comrades be with us in our fight!"

"And of course," Arcala said as she rode up toward them, "may King Gobius be always with us in all that we do to combat the darkness."

"He will," Cedrus said. "I can say that with certainty." He didn't tell them about the vision he had in the Northern Mountains, which he now started to believe was real.

"They are ready," Henricus said to King Antiugus. "It is time to ride."

"We are ready as well," Apteris said as the Legans descended from above and joined them. "The raven is watching the Beast, and will come to warn us if she begins making her way to Xamnon. Given her slow pace, we should have enough time to execute the raid and fend her off if necessary."

"You know what to do," Antiugus said. "Just take out those guards and let us into the city when we arrive. We'll do the rest."

"But not on your own," Chaelim said. "Even after you impinge through the gate, we will be with you as you battle Sicarius' army."

"Good to know, my friends," Antiugus said.

As they prepared to head out, something ominous occurred. A loud noise rumbled down from the sky like a strong wind, and though one could have easily perceived it as a normal gale, something in the sound told them that it was much more than that. They looked around at each other—perplexed as to what was happening—and then drew their weapons. As they gazed up toward the treetops, they saw a dove flying out from amongst the foliage and heading in their direction.

They could only wonder if it was the same dove that had been intervening on their behalf, the one that led Chaelim to rescue them at sea and later took them to the cave of the Seers. All of them stared in complete awe as it came to hover just above them without even flapping its wings. Somehow the dove managed to levitate as it folded its wings across its breast and closed its eyes. Then slowly it began to spread its wings, which appeared to be much larger than they were before. The dove opened its eyes, and they glowed as if they had been set afire. All of them were entranced by its presence. They were unable to move, talk, or even think as flames began emanating from the dove and spread out around them. Tongues as of fire parted and came to rest on each of them, and when everyone had been touched by the mysterious flames, the dove suddenly flew away. Slowly they emerged from their trance and began looking all around them.

"What just happened?" Arcala asked.

"I don't know," Cedrus said. Although they were conscious during the experience, they were not conscious enough that they could adequately describe what had just occurred.

"It is time," Antiugus said. "Let us ride to Mavinor."

At that the Legans took off and flew ahead of them. As they spurred their mounts, Cedrus took one last look back at the palace. He stared up at the balcony of the guest room, and there he saw Magdala looking down at them. She waved good-bye, and Cedrus smiled and nodded toward her as he rode the unicorn up to the front of the formation, occupying a space right beside Henricus and King Antiugus.

Part IV

Chapter Nineteen

The Surnia led Malgyron to the cave where the Seers of Fate resided. Shortly after he entered, Malgyron saw the light flickering deep down in the cavern and began walking toward it. When he arrived in the chamber where the fire was burning, he saw the Seers seated on their chairs staring across at him as if they were expecting his presence.

"So this is where you have been all of these years," Malgyron said.

"Were you looking for us, Orius?" the Seer seated in the middle asked him.

"Orius is no more!" Malgyron said angrily.

"You cannot escape who you really are," she said. "Your nature may have changed because of your actions, but your origin can never be disputed. The Author gave you your name and endowed you with the powers you have when He created you. But you have turned against Him, and now your connection with nature has been severed, and you have lost your immortality."

"But I will get it back," Malgyron said. "I will regain my immortality when darkness prevails, and when The Author's grace has been removed from the world. There is no hope for man now. They have betrayed The Author's son and crowned his traitor as their king. It is only a matter of time before their existence is wiped away, discarded like the chaff from the wheat."

"So you say," said one of the other Seers as she stood from her chair, "but I have seen it differently. I have seen the return of the light, and man's triumph over you and the forces you have assembled."

"I'm afraid that you are misinterpreting what you see, woman," Malgyron said. "Urmina has already been destroyed, and soon the Beast will obliterate Xamnon as well. I know now where the Medallion is—who is carrying it—and after I conduct my business here, I intend to retrieve it. Thus I will be able to save the Deliverers of Darkness the trouble of seeking it out, and they can merely ride to the Mortuus Valley to call upon their Army of Lost Souls. They ride as we speak, and there is no one left to stop them. The people who remain have no way of fighting the Beast, and no way to defeat Bellicus' army once it rises. It is over, not just for all of them, but for you as well. You foolish women! With your power to prophesy, did you not foresee your own fate?"

"We have," the Seers said in unison. Then the one in the middle spoke yet again. "But we have fulfilled the role The Author assigned to us. We have shared His instructions with those who are called to follow them, and now it is all in their hands. You may be able to kill us, Orius, but you cannot escape your own fate. In the end, it is you who will be defeated."

Malgyron went into a fit of rage. He was infuriated by the bold manner in which the Seers predicted his demise, and in cold blood he drew his swords and flew across the rising flames toward where they were standing. One by one he murdered them, and when he was done he cast their bodies into the fire and watched as their corpses burned to ashes. "Let us now go to Mavinor," he said to the Surnia. "I have a surprise for my friend, General Sicarius."

Talmik entered the throne room with his dagger tucked neatly away in the belt underneath his tunic. He saw that Cidivus was already having breakfast, and that his guards were once again standing by him at the table. Now more than ever he knew that Cidivus was on to him. The fact that he didn't even wait for his aide to bring him his meal was a sign that Cidivus suspected that Talmik might poison him. "Good morning, sire," he said.

"Good morning, Talmik," Cidivus said as he finished chewing a piece of fish. "My guards tell me that you came to see me last night as I was sleeping."

"Yes, sire," Talmik said. "I wanted to check in and make sure you were asleep, for today is an important day for you. Knowing that you needed a good rest, I would have gladly brought you sleep tinctures had they been needed."

"That's awfully kind of you," Cidivus said almost sarcastically. "But of course you understand why I placed the guards outside my door, and why I instructed them not to let anyone in."

"Of course, sire," Talmik said after a short pause, staring at the guards.

"There is no joy in being betrayed," Cidivus said. "In fact, it is quite a mournful experience. I was just beginning to trust Solitus, so to discover that he planned to revolt against me was similar to losing a close friend to the throes of death. Now I have to be careful and watch my back lest others are out to do the same thing. But I cannot do that for myself, now can I? Thus my personal guards will be doing it for me."

"I see," Talmik replied.

"You will be coming to the Praetorium to witness the execution, won't you, Talmik?" Cidivus asked.

"Yes, sire," Talmik replied. "I was hoping to accompany you."

"You may do so," Cidivus said. "Just be sure to keep your distance. I'm afraid my guards will not be allowing anyone to ride too close to me. It is quite unfortunate that it needs to be this way, but again I know that you understand." Talmik nodded as he stepped back, and the king eyed him warily.

When Cidivus finished his meal, he instructed his guards to prepare to escort him to the Praetorium. "It is time," the king said. "It is time for Solitus to pay the ultimate price for his crime against me. I hope the people finally get the message I have been sending them." He then turned toward Talmik. "I'd hate for this to happen to anyone else."

Talmik was shaken by Cidivus' remark, but he nonetheless followed him and his guards as they left the throne room. The aide didn't know how he was going to assassinate Cidivus given the fact that he was being guarded closer than ever before, but he was determined to detect even the slightest opening that might allow him to stab the king through his heart. "I am going to kill him," Talmik said to himself. "I am going to kill him if it is the last thing I ever do."

There were three guards stationed in the watchtower at Mavinor's West Gate. They passed the time with idle chatter as they looked out from the parapet toward the open plain. All was calm, and the last thing they were expecting was an attack against their city. Most of the troops were out that morning with Grodus, rounding up the citizens and ushering them to the Praetorium so they could witness Cidivus' latest display of public perversion. They were quite unhappy that they would have to miss it, especially since they knew what their general had planned and wanted to be there when Cidivus was deposed.

As they talked amongst themselves, they suddenly heard a loud noise coming from the gate. It was as if someone or something had crashed into it, and quickly they went to the edge of the tower and looked below. But they saw nothing.

"How can it be that nothing is there?" one of the guards said. "We all heard the sound."

"Perhaps it was a gust of wind," one of the others said.

"Or perhaps," the third guard said, "it is coming from inside the gate, not outside of it." Slowly they turned back and began walking to the other side of the tower. But as they arrived at the edge and prepared to gaze down, a being rose up and attacked them. It was unlike anything they had ever seen before, and it didn't take long for the creature to knock all three of them to the floor. Two other beings then flew in, and quicker than they could have imagined the guards found themselves disarmed, gagged, and bound with rope. "Nice work," Chaelim said to Apteris and Volara as they finished tying up the last one.

"What should we do with them?" Apteris asked.

"Leave them up here," Volara said. "One of us will have to guard them and make sure they don't get away."

"Very well," Apteris said. "The one who guards them can also open the gate for the army when they arrive, while the other two will have to watch the surrounding area inside the city. We must keep an eye out for any troops that come to the watchtower. The last thing we need is for Antiugus and his men to have a company of soldiers waiting to greet them at the gate."

"Good plan," Chaelim said. "I'll hide up in those trees just outside the walls and watch the entire space north of the tower."

"I will cover the south side," Volara said.

"I guess that means I'll be waiting here for Antiugus and the others," Apteris said. "Be careful, you two."

"No worries, my friend," Chaelim said. "We'll be sure to hold off anyone who approaches until you can let Xamnon's army through the gate." With that he and Volara left, and as Apteris looked out into the distance he could now see the legion of troops on the horizon, advancing steadily and probably no more than a half-hour away from their destination.

When Cidivus arrived at the Praetorium, everything was arranged just as he had specified. Solitus was tied to a post where everyone would have a clear view of him. A short distance away stood five archers with crossbows, ready to fire at a moment's notice. Grodus and the troops had rounded up the citizens and escorted them against their will into the Praetorium to witness the execution. Standing at the base of the stairs leading up to where the tribunes were seated were Sicarius and Tarsus. They had Aramus with them, and the veteran magistrate's wrists were bound with iron cuffs. Cidivus stopped to greet him before ascending the stairs to begin the festivities.

"Glad to see that you were able to make it, Aramus," Cidivus said with a smirk. "I would have been saddened had you missed today's show."

"You merciless tyrant," Aramus said. "The Author will grant us retribution, and you will pay for what you have done to our people. You will pay dearly."

"Not as dearly as you," Cidivus said, "and certainly not as dearly as young Solitus. What a shame that your influence on him is what will ultimately cost him his life. I hope you don't feel too guilty about that."

Cidivus walked up the stairs—accompanied by his two guards—as Aramus scowled at him. Talmik followed behind, and as he passed Aramus he looked the tribune in the eye and nodded his head very subtly. Aramus began to wonder what Talmik had planned and hoped he wasn't going to attempt anything foolish.

When Cidivus arrived at the top of the steps, he was greeted by Pachaias. But Cidivus more or less brushed him aside, eager to begin the execution and watch Solitus die a slow, painful death.

"Good morning, citizens of Mavinor," he said. "I am glad that you are able to join us for this momentous occasion as we say goodbye to the two men who were instrumental in stirring the pathetic rebellion that failed miserably and cost several innocent people their lives. First, Solitus will die at the hands of the firing squad that General Sicarius has so graciously assembled for me. It will be a gradual process as the arrows pierce him one by one—deliberately and tortuously—until every ounce of blood seeps from his body and takes the last token of life with it. Then it will be Aramus' turn, the long-serving tribune who so senselessly turned against me. I would have thought a man of his stature to be wiser, but I suppose it's not the first time I have been bitterly disappointed, nor will it be the last."

"Enough!" Aramus yelled from the base of the stairs. "My fellow tribunes, do you not see what is happening? Did I not tell you that the Tribunal would become irrelevant if we did not take action? You sat and watched while Mavinor burned, refusing to take a stand out of fear of retribution. Now you have reaped what you have sown, for your status means nothing anymore. This king will set his own rules and govern his own way, apart from the laws that we swore to uphold. He has arrested people without just cause, exiled believers without a fair trial, razed the temples to the ground, and now—in the most brazen move of all—has taken it upon himself to execute citizens as he pleases, in ways that are not in accordance with our code of law. Yet you sit there and do nothing. I tell you that you are worthless, every one of you! You have disgraced the office you hold, and by virtue of not taking action you have consented to these despicable deeds and are just as guilty as those who have carried them out!"

"I'm sorry, Aramus," Cidivus said. "Perhaps I should have involved the Tribunal in this decision. Pachaias, maybe you'd like to take a vote."

Pachaias was taken by surprise, but nonetheless smiled as he stood from his chair and called for the tribunes to vote on the executions of Solitus and Aramus. One by one, Theophilus, Annus, and Pontius all voted "yes," and when it came to Pachaias, he expressed his agreement with them.

"Not surprisingly, we have another 4-1 vote," Pachaias said as he looked down at Aramus. "It looks as though the wheels of justice have turned against you yet again, my friend. I'm sure I speak for all members of the Tribunal when I say, 'Farewell!' "

Cidivus smiled broadly as Pachaias sat back in his chair. But when he turned to look back out at the crowd, he saw something that made his smile revert to a look of consternation. For marching on horseback across the square, in full armor, was none other than Ignatus.

Even from a distance anyone could see that the old warrior's helm and shield were polished to a fine sheen, and his leather gear shone with oil and care. All eyes turned to the man with the sunburst on his breastplate as he rode across the cobblestone, and immediately they wondered what he was planning to do.

"General, how is it that he enters the Praetorium bearing arms?" Cidivus yelled down to Sicarius. "Where are the guards?"

"I pulled them from their stations," Sicarius said. "There was no need for them since all the people had already been brought here. Besides, they wanted to witness today's exhibition."

"Well clearly you missed someone as you gathered them in," Cidivus said.

"No need to worry," Sicarius said. "Ignatus is an old man, well beyond his prime and easily handled by even the greenest of my troops." The general then signaled to his men, and they cut off Ignatus' path immediately, led by none other than Nefarius.

"Taking a stroll down memory lane, are we?" Nefarius said to Ignatus as his fellow soldiers had a good laugh at Ignatus' expense. "It's always nice to recall one's glory days, even if there is no chance of reliving them."

Ignatus kept his sword in its sheath and halted his mount. He stared across the crowd and saw Solitus tied to the post, and though he wasn't sure how he was going to save him, he knew that he had to come up with a plan quickly. Solitus caught sight of his mentor in full battle gear and wondered if indeed he had come on a rescue mission. But seeing that almost all of Sicarius' troops were present, he knew it was impossible and actually hoped that Ignatus would not try to save him. The same exact thought ran through Aramus' mind as he looked out at Ignatus, while Tarsus now wondered if there was anything he could do to prevent the old soldier from unwittingly rushing to Solitus' aid and getting killed in the process. But Tarsus was too far away to say anything to him, and could only watch as Nefarius and his men surrounded Ignatus.

Talmik could see everything unfolding from the top of the stairs as he stood just a short distance away from Cidivus and his guards. He reached in his belt for his dagger and unsheathed it, yet held it underneath his tunic where no one could see it. He gripped the hilt tightly and watched Cidivus closely, waiting for an opening to sneak in from behind and plunge the blade of the dagger into his back. Talmik knew that he would be killed shortly after the assassination, but that no longer mattered to him. Solitus and Aramus were already going to be killed, and he was willing to die as well so long as he took Cidivus to the grave with him.

Talmik was so quiet and still that he believed the guards were now oblivious to his presence. He was standing off to the side, just in front of the tribunes but a couple of steps behind Cidivus. Talmik knew that the tribunes would be unable to jump from their seats and stop him as he rushed forward, so his only concern was getting by the guard on Cidivus' right side. Since the king and both guards were standing directly beside each other, Talmik believed he could get by without being seen before stabbing Cidivus in the back. He placed the dagger into position beneath his tunic so he could quickly thrust it forward into his prey, and prepared to take action. Sweat began to bead on his brow as the moment drew closer, for Talmik had never killed anyone before. It was his gentle nature that led him into a life of royal service rather than military duty. But now he had to defy that nature and do something he never thought he would have to do. He grabbed his tunic with his left hand, ready to pull it aside so he could drive the dagger into Cidivus with his right. When he was in perfect position, Talmik prepared to rush the king and end his miserable reign once and for all. But before he could even take one step, Cidivus started marching ahead and down the stairs, his guards following closely behind. Now Talmik was in a quandary, seemingly left with no clear, unobstructed path to accomplish his task.

When Cidivus arrived at the base of the stairs, he called for the archers to load their crossbows and prepare to fire. Solitus wanted to believe what Gobius had said to him the night before, but the faith and trust he had in his vision was gone. Once he heard Cidivus' command, he gave up hope and accepted his fate. Solitus prayed to The Author that He would have mercy on his soul, and forgive him for his failure to save Mavinor. His heart raced as he closed his eyes, but he immediately opened them when he heard a loud whinny coming from the crowd.

It was Ignatus' horse looking to fight through Sicarius' men to get to Solitus. Ignatus did all he could to lead his mount forward, but his efforts were in vain. For as the horse flashed its hooves, a soldier rushed in from the side and landed a solid blow on Ignatus with a club, knocking him from the saddle. Quickly Nefarius dragged Ignatus back to his feet and held the cold steel of his sword up against Ignatus' throat. "Nice try, old fellow," Nefarius said. "Now you will watch as the spectacle we have prepared plays out before your very eyes."

Cidivus was relieved to see that Ignatus was now in custody, and haughtily began his sadistic show. "Tell me, do I have yet another candidate for execution this morning? Once again I am disappointed by an old man lacking the wisdom I thought he possessed, but your wish to join Solitus and Aramus in their punishment will be graciously granted, Ignatus. For now, you can watch as Solitus suffers the death that both you and Aramus will soon experience. One at a time now, archers, aim your bows and fire!"

Cidivus gleefully watched in anticipation of the arrows piercing Solitus' body. But none were fired. He was baffled at first, but then considered that the archers may not have heard his command. "Fire!" he yelled again. Still there was no reaction on their part.

Slowly Sicarius stepped forward, grinning at Cidivus as he walked by him and then calling out to the bowmen. "Lower your weapons," he said. Immediately the archers brought their crossbows down to their sides. Solitus, Aramus, Ignatus, Talmik, the tribunes, and everyone in the crowd all stared in wonder and tried to perceive what was happening. Cidivus looked on in disbelief and turned toward Sicarius. "General?" he said quizzically.

Grodus and Tarsus came out from the crowd and stood beside Sicarius. Mavinor's general, his face now bearing a cold expression, looked Cidivus in the eye and plainly stated what was happening. "Your reign is over. From this day forward, I will be running the affairs of the kingdom."

"You are betraying me?" Cidivus said, still in a state of shock. "And you, Grodus?"

"Yes, Grodus too," Sicarius replied. "You have no allies left, Cidivus. In fact, you had none to begin with, at least not in Mavinor."

"Guards!" Cidivus shouted to the men assigned to protect him. Without hesitation they pointed their spears toward Cidivus, each one poking him in the side with the forged iron tip. One of them reached into the king's scabbard and pulled out Cidivus' sword, gripping the handle and admiring the décor of the silver serpent coiled around it. Sicarius laughed as he watched Cidivus cower in fear.

"Did you really think the men I assigned to watch over you would be more loyal to you than to me?" the general asked. "You fool! I may agree with your style of governance, but you are the last one who should have risen to the throne. If not for a superior being threatening me with severe repercussions, I would have never allowed it to happen." As he spoke, Pachaias got a shiver down his spine, for he was now aware that Orius had spoken with Sicarius as well. He wondered if his own plan to assume the throne was now in jeopardy.

"What are you going to do with me?" Cidivus asked. One could easily hear the terror in his voice.

"Now that is a good question," Sicarius said. He then turned to the people. "Tell me, citizens of Mavinor, what would you like for me to do with your king? Imprison him? Exile him? Execute him? This is your chance to have revenge on the man who oppressed you from day one of his reign. What would you like to see become of him?"

No one said a word. The people already knew that their lives would be no better with Sicarius as their ruler, and they had reached the point where they had seen enough bloodshed. As much as they despised Cidivus, they could not bring themselves to advocate for his execution.

"No one wishes to speak?" Sicarius said in a tone of surprise. "Very well, then. I suppose the decision will be left up to me." Sicarius' face bore a wry smile as he looked upon Cidivus, who had now dropped to his knees and was begging the general for mercy. "Look at you," Sicarius said. "You once thought you were above all of us, given your privileged background and the fact that you were chosen to succeed Gobius. You treated us as your servants though we had no respect for you. You arrogantly altered my troops' uniforms to reflect the colors on your insignia. You took the law into your own hands and did as you pleased, never once consulting those around you. Yet now you kneel before me begging for your life, you pathetic worm! Know that your pleas will fall on deaf ears, for the time has come to put an end to your wretched life and enable our kingdom to move on from this debacle. I have a special surprise in store for you. I do hope you like it." Cidivus buried his face in his hands as he anticipated what they had in mind, and he prepared himself to die at the hands of Sicarius.

Chapter Twenty

The three guards who were restrained by the Legans at the watch-tower were lying side by side on the roof, their hands and feet bound with rope. The shofars were hanging from a hook attached to the far wall, and they were determined to get to them so they could warn Sicarius' troops of the impending invasion. Apteris stood near-by, keeping a close eye on them but also watching Xamnon's army approach so as to know when to open the gate. Though the Legans had disarmed the watchmen, one of the guards had a boot knife con-cealed that he managed to reach. He made sure that he was lying with his back to the wall—facing Apteris—as he curled his legs and reached down into the boot. Since his hands were tied behind his back, Apteris did not see what he was doing. The guard reached in just beneath the cuff and unsheathed the knife, then started sawing away with the blade to cut through the rope.

When he cut all the way through and his hands were free, he contemplated cutting the rope that bound his feet, but then realized it would be a mistake to do so. Surely Apteris would catch him in the act, and even if he didn't, the guard wasn't about to rise to his feet and challenge the Legan to a fight. So he waited instead, and soon he heard the pounding of hooves against the ground. It grew louder and louder until it was apparent that the army had arrived and was just outside the gate. At that point Apteris left the watchtower to open the gate, and the guard quickly cut his legs free and removed the gag from his mouth. Then he ran across the roof to retrieve the shofars, hoping to sound them in time before the Legans returned.

Sicarius had his men place a wooden block not far from where Cidivus had already been kneeling. He then had the guards on either side of Cidivus drag him up to the block and place his head there. Pachaias and the rest of the tribunes watched helplessly from atop the stairs. Solitus was still tied to the post, and Aramus remained handcuffed at the base of the stairs. Nefarius held Ignatus tightly within his clutches, while Tarsus and Grodus stood alongside Sicarius as he salivated at the chance to finally rid himself of Cidivus. Tarsus was torn on what he should do. Part of him wanted to save Cidivus' life, but he knew that if he tried, he would jeopardize the chance to rescue Solitus. Though he did not wish to witness another execution, he recalled the many misdeeds of Cidivus and knew that if anyone deserved to be beheaded, it was Mavinor's ruthless king. So he simply stood by and pretended to be in Sicarius' corner.

Sicarius drew his sword and slowly walked up to where Cidivus' head was lying on the block. He watched as beads of sweat dripped from Cidivus' forehead down to the ground, and reveled in the fact that the man he so vehemently despised was now completely at his mercy. But before he could even raise his sword, Sicarius' imminent victory was sucked from the moment in the updraft from great wings. As he looked up, he saw a terrifying figure quickly descending toward him, and before the general could even react the being was upon him. Whatever it was, it was accompanied by two giant owls— identical to the ones that pursued the raven at Gobius' sentencing— and as the winged creature landed, it shoved Sicarius to the ground and immediately drew two swords.

Everyone in the Praetorium shrank back in horror when they saw the hideous monster. Some of the troops fanned out in an effort to surround the thing, while Sicarius rose to his feet and stared in awe of his new foe, not knowing what it was or where it came from.

"Hello, Sicarius," it said. "You do remember me, don't you?"

Sicarius stood in stunned silence before realizing that it had to be Orius, the same being that had threatened him and warned him not to overthrow Cidivus.

"It cannot be you, Orius," Sicarius said.

Malgyron smiled and laughed as he stared back at Sicarius. "Do you really think you can defeat me, general?" he asked. "Did I not warn you against seizing the throne? I'm afraid you have made a terrible mistake."

"Archers, prepare to fire!" Sicarius shouted. The men who bore crossbows aimed them directly at Malgyron and waited for their general's command. Malgyron just looked back at them with an arrogant expression on his face. The bowmen then noticed that the Surnia were circling the air above them, and it made them more than a little nervous.

"You cannot win, Sicarius," Malgyron said. "I never wanted to kill you, but now it seems as though you have left me no choice. You had your chance, but you went back on your word."

"You told me you would allow my men to return safely from Patmos if I complied," Sicarius said. "But they never made it back to Mavinor. Now you will pay for what you have done to them."

"I know not what you're talking about," Malgyron said. "I had nothing to do with the disappearance of your men."

"And you expect me to believe that, do you?" Sicarius asked. "Archers, fire!"

At Sicarius' command, the Surnia swooped down and took out two of the soldiers before they could fire their bows. The other ones let their arrows fly, but Malgyron easily dodged them by soaring into the air. He then eyed Sicarius, who was back on his heels holding up his shield and brandishing his sword. Malgyron raised his swords and prepared to attack, but he froze when he heard the clarion call of the shofars coming from Mavinor's West Gate.

Everyone in the Praetorium suddenly found themselves in a state of alarm, and for a second nobody even moved. It was Sicarius who then broke the silence as he shouted orders to his men.

"To arms! To arms!" he yelled to his troops. "Mount your horses and ride to the West Gate!"

Pachaias and the rest of the tribunes hurried inside to escape the pandemonium. Sicarius assigned two men to stay and guard Solitus, and instructed the ones guarding Cidivus to remain with him. As he and Grodus mounted and began to ride, he took a quick glance to his right and noticed that Tarsus was not there. Immediately he halted his mount and turned back. "Tarsus!" he said.

His lieutenant was still standing in the same position, armed but not giving off the slightest impression that he would be joining the troops any time soon. He directed a cold stare toward Sicarius, and soon the general realized that his right-hand man was going to betray him after all. But he had no time to address the matter given the impending attack on the city, so he shot an icy glare back in Tarsus' direction before turning around and riding to the West Gate with Grodus.

Nefarius still held his sword up against Ignatus' throat, and as he prepared to leave with the others, he whispered in Ignatus' ear. "Time to say good-bye, old man," he said. But as he went to slit Ignatus' throat, the veteran fighter landed an elbow to Nefarius' gut and managed to reach up with his left hand and push the blade of his sword away. Then he retrieved his own sword and turned back toward Nefarius, who was still doubled over in pain.

"Perhaps you'd like to see what an old man is capable of," Ignatus said.

The challenge elicited a smug grin from Nefarius, who stood

upright and prepared to charge. He rushed forth and brought his sword around in a wide arc, but Ignatus was able to stand up to the strike. Nefarius continued to swing mightily—but somewhat wildly—at Ignatus, aiming to take him out with one blow. But his maneuvers were nothing the seasoned swordsman hadn't seen before, and time after time Ignatus either dodged them or parried Nefarius' sword away. Ignatus planned to use Nefarius' aggressive style against him, and knew that sooner or later he would have an opening to make his move.

Ignatus baited Nefarius time and again, waiting for one of his forceful swings to compromise his balance. At one point, the blades collided and both men exerted their strength to push the other away. Ignatus then pretended to be overpowered and fell back, lowering his sword in the process. He anticipated that Nefarius would try to cut him down with one mighty swing, and when his opponent launched his attack, Ignatus spun to his left and narrowly avoided Nefarius' attempt. Ignatus then brought his sword around in a vicious arc that caught Nefarius' blade from behind and drove it forward even faster. With a cry, the wielder released his weapon, which spun through the air and landed on the ground several feet away.

An archer who was looking on saw that Nefarius was in trouble, so he loaded his crossbow with an arrow from his quiver. Solitus saw it unfolding from where he was tied to the post and immediately shouted out. "No! Ignatus, look out!"

Ignatus didn't hear Solitus until it was too late, and would have surely been killed if not for Tarsus, who lunged forward and stabbed the archer in the back. He dropped his crossbow on the ground, and when the soldiers guarding Solitus saw what happened, they left their posts to confront Tarsus.

Malgyron was still in a state of confusion over everything that had happened. He didn't understand how Xamnon could have mounted an attack without him knowing about it in advance. It was obvious that the Colubri spies had failed in their mission, and now he had to find a way to address the problem. But first he decided to free Cidivus by killing the soldiers who were guarding him. He knocked the spears from their hands and thrust his swords through each of them with ease. Then he pulled Cidivus to his feet and looked over toward Solitus.

"That youth has the Medallion in his possession," Malgyron said. "Get it, and find a place to hide here in the Praetorium. I will be back for you. Right now I need to go and defend your kingdom."

"Thank you," Cidivus said as he watched Malgyron take off with the Surnia and fly toward the West Gate. He took his sword back from the guard who had disarmed him, then looked toward Solitus. Though he regretted that he would not get to see Solitus executed in the manner he had decreed, Cidivus was happy that he would at least get to deliver the lethal blow to the one who had betrayed him.

The guards who had gone after Tarsus were in utter disbelief. One of them cried out, "Traitor! How could you turn on us, Tarsus?"

Tarsus stared at them intently and answered. "The real traitors are Sicarius, Cidivus, and Pachaias. They are the ones who created their own code of law, and exceedingly punished those who didn't follow it to the letter. They took away our freedoms and slaughtered the innocent. Now the time for retribution has come, and I will do whatever I can to help bring it about!"

They charged him, one from each side. But the expert swordsman quickly turned the tables on them. For as they both aimed high, he ducked under their blows and did a forward somersault before bringing his blade around in a wide arc and slashing one of them across the leg. His victim immediately fell to the ground, allowing Tarsus to attack the other guard and make quick work of him. The other one rose to his feet and prepared to charge yet again as Tarsus braced himself for his opponent's foray.

Once the guards became occupied with Tarsus, Solitus was left tied against the post with no one to protect him. Cidivus slowly made his way toward the youth, planning to kill him and seize the Medallion. But as he drew closer, he suddenly heard footfalls behind him. At the last second he turned as Talmik attempted to stab him in the back with the dagger he had been concealing. Cidivus spun around and narrowly avoided the blade, then swung his sword to counter the attack. Talmik dodged the attempt and retreated, managing to draw Cidivus' attention away from Solitus as the king pursued his would-be assassin.

Solitus' earlier warning call to Ignatus—though intended to save his life—actually worked against him, for it distracted Ignatus long enough for Nefarius to reclaim his sword. Again Sicarius' loyal officer rushed Ignatus and tried to cut through him with his blade, but Ignatus would have none of it. This time he decided to match Nefarius blow for blow, and his strength and fighting spirit caught Nefarius off guard. Now it was Ignatus' nemesis who found himself on his heels, doing everything he possibly could to fend off Ignatus' attack. As he felt himself being backed into a corner, Nefarius waited for Ignatus to rear back for an offensive maneuver and then thrust his blade forward toward Ignatus' midsection. But Ignatus saw it coming all the way, and he managed to shift to the side and block Nefarius' blow with a downward swing. Then he quickly followed up with a horizontal cut that sliced through Nefarius' abdomen. Nefarius had no way to block it, and he immediately fell to the ground while holding his hands over the wound. As Ignatus stepped back and saw Nefarius gazing down at the blood seeping through his fingers, he couldn't help but utter a final statement to his tormentor. "Perhaps one can reclaim his glory days after all," he said, just before walking away.

Cidivus doggedly pursued Talmik but couldn't catch him. As he turned back, he saw that Nefarius was dead and watched as Tarsus executed a brilliant move to finish off his last opponent. Knowing they would look to set Solitus free, Cidivus started running toward the post where Solitus was bound. But Aramus was watching the whole time and anticipated what Cidivus was planning to do. "Ignatus! Tarsus!" he yelled. Both men heard him and immediately started running back.

When Cidivus realized he couldn't get there in time to strip Solitus of the Medallion, he noticed a crossbow lying on the ground a short distance away. It belonged to the archer who Tarsus killed, and it was already loaded with an arrow. Cidivus grabbed it and aimed toward Solitus, and though Aramus, Tarsus, and Ignatus were all converging, none of them could get there in time. Cidivus fired the arrow right through Solitus' body, then dropped the weapon and fled. Talmik, who was hiding behind a pillar, saw what had happened and started racing toward Solitus. He got there just as the others did, and they immediately untied him and laid him on the ground.

"No!" Aramus cried as he sat over the youth. "It is entirely my fault."

"No, Aramus," Ignatus said, a tear dripping from the corner of his eye. "It is I who am to blame for this."

Tarsus wasted no time in tending to Solitus' injury. He saw that the arrow had penetrated deeply, so he rolled Solitus over onto his side. "Brace yourself," he told him. Tarsus placed his left hand just behind Solitus' right shoulder and put the palm of his right hand at the tail end of the arrow. Then he used his strength to push the arrow through, which caused the head to come out the other side and fall to the ground. The others could barely watch, though they were all well aware it had to be done to ensure the arrowhead didn't become detached inside the body. If it did, then Solitus' death was all but imminent.

Tarsus removed the shaft from Solitus' torso and prepared to deal with the bleeding. He reached toward his belt and pulled out a small pouch filled with yarrow. Then he pulled Solitus' tunic aside to apply the herb and staunch the wounds on his back and midsection. But as he exposed the skin, he was stunned to see that there were no visible marks on his body. "It cannot be," Tarsus said. "I pushed the arrow through myself, so I know the entry and exit points must exist. But I do not see them."

"By The Author!" Aramus exclaimed.

Solitus sat up and saw how taken aback they all were. Then he took hold of the Medallion and raised it toward them. "This is what saved me," he said. "I am sure of it."

"But how is it possible?" Talmik said.

"While I was in the dungeon awaiting execution, I had a vision of our dear king. He came to me and said that the Medallion would save my life. Now I know what he meant."

"Incredible," Aramus said.

When Aramus spoke, Tarsus noticed that his wrists were still cuffed. He took out the key and began unshackling him. Aramus was completely stunned, first by the miracle he witnessed, and now by Tarsus' conversion.

"Tarsus, are you really one of us now?" Aramus asked.

"I am," Tarsus replied. "Like Solitus, I too had a vision of King Gobius. He told me what I must do, and I have every intention of fulfilling the task he gave me."

"What did he say?" Ignatus asked.

"He told me to lead Solitus to where he needs to go by any means necessary, and to continue riding north to the Mortuus Valley," Tarsus said.

"The place I must visit is called the Cavern of Trials," Solitus said. "King Gobius said that it lies to the north, and he gave me instructions on where to find it. Can you take me there, Tarsus?"

"I will," Tarsus said.

Ignatus was still somewhat hesitant to place his full trust in Sicarius' long-standing lieutenant, so he stepped in and volunteered to help. "I am going as well," he said. "Solitus rides with me."

Tarsus sensed the dubious tone in Ignatus' voice and willingly yielded to him. "Very well," he said.

"Where is Cidivus?" Aramus asked.

"He seems to have disappeared," Talmik said while scanning the Praetorium. "He is most likely hiding somewhere." As they took notice of the surrounding area, they couldn't get over how a place that was so filled with chaos and commotion just a short time earlier was now completely desolate. All of Sicarius' troops had gone to the West Gate, while the people scattered and most likely returned to their homes to hunker down.

"There is no time to look for Cidivus," Ignatus said. "We need to get going. Tarsus?"

Ignatus saw that Tarsus was no longer among them, and when he turned he saw the man walking toward a fire that was burning off to the side. The soldiers had lit the fire earlier to keep warm, for a sudden chill in the air had made this the coldest day since Gobius' death. They all watched as Tarsus walked up to the fire, removed his breastplate, and threw it into the flames. He did the same with the rest of his military uniform before walking back to the others and mounting his horse.

"Come," he then said. "We can stop at my home on our way to the North Gate and pick up some supplies. Anything we may need for our journey I can easily provide."

"Aramus and Talmik, what do you plan to do?" Ignatus asked.

"I am going to the West Gate to witness the battle," Aramus said.

"I'll take you there," Talmik said. He had a mount, and he quickly went to untie it.

"Very well," Ignatus replied. "I will see you again, my friend, though I can't say when."

"May The Author be with you, all of you," Aramus said.

Ignatus and Solitus rode out of the Praetorium accompanied by Tarsus, while Talmik transported Aramus to the West Gate to see how Mavinor's army was faring in its latest battle.

Chapter Twenty-One

The shofars had sounded just as Apteris opened the gate for Xamnon's army, and immediately Chaelim and Volara rushed to the watchtower. They subdued the guard who had broken free, but it was too little, too late. The element of surprise was gone now, and they realized that it was just a matter of time until Sicarius' army arrived. Antiugus, Henricus, and Cedrus led the troops in through the gate and began to position them in anticipation of the impending battle. Henricus strategically placed archers in the watchtower and in other hiding spots where they could quickly emerge and fire arrows at Sicarius' forces. Some ducked behind huge bales of hay that Mavinor's bowmen used as targets. Others took cover behind the piles of stones situated next to the catapults. The cavalry was arranged in a tight formation so that their shields could deflect the spears and arrows fired by Mavinor's ranks and not allow any projectiles to penetrate the columns. The Legans flew just outside the city walls, where they could peer out over the top and wait for just the right moment to strike Sicarius' army from above.

Soon the thundering sound of hoofbeats filled the air, and as they looked down the main road that ran through the kingdom, they could see General Sicarius leading his troops around the bend. Eventually the two armies came face-to-face, and after halting his men Sicarius advanced a few steps further in order to address King Antiugus.

"You fool," Sicarius said. "Do you not recall what happened the last time you led your men in through that gate? Now you don't even have your general to lead your troops, for he and his most loyal followers have defected to another army…mine!" At that Sicarius looked back toward Grodus, and for the first time Antiugus and Henricus came to learn of Grodus' treason.

"I have faith in the man who replaced him," Antiugus said. "I have faith in every last one of these men, but most of all, I have faith in The Author and his only son, King Gobius."

Sicarius laughed and scoffed at Antiugus' remarks. "The Author doesn't exist, and Gobius is dead," he haughtily declared. "Our former king isn't here to spare your life this time around, Antiugus. You will not make it back to Xamnon alive, for we will kill you and every last one of your troops."

At that point, Cedrus forged ahead through the crowd mounted atop the unicorn. His eyes met those of Sicarius, who now saw that Tonitrus' younger brother had somehow managed to survive following his escape from the boiling cauldron.

"You will pay for what you've done, Sicarius," Cedrus called out. "You will pay with your very life."

Sicarius smiled. "I am glad you came back, Cedrus," he said. "For now I can finish what I started."

With that, Mavinor's general raised his sword and turned to face his troops. "To victory!" he shouted.

But before he could even lead his men forward, Henricus yelled out, "Now!" Xamnon's archers then came forth from their respective hiding places and rained arrows down upon Sicarius' men, taking several of them out. Sicarius angrily called for his troops to charge before the next round could be fired, but it was then that the Legans came swooping down from the sky toward Mavinor's troops. They flashed their weapons and cut through the sea of silver and black, knocking mounted soldiers to the ground with ease. The surprise attacks allotted Xamnon's army a head start, and soon Antiugus, Henricus, and Cedrus led the others into battle.

Sicarius' men were at a tremendous disadvantage from the start. Even as they engaged Xamnon's ground forces, they were forced to watch out for the stealth assaults from above. One by one, Mavinor's fighters fell victim to the silent but deadly strikes launched by the Legans, and Sicarius began to worry as he continued to lose men at a rapid pace. He was already short-handed, for several of his best fighters had never made it back from Patmos, and perhaps more importantly, he was without his right-hand man. It didn't take long for Mavinor's general to realize that not having Tarsus there to help orchestrate the strategy on the battlefield was a major blow to his chances of winning.

But the tide began to turn when Apteris suddenly dropped from the sky as if he had been struck by a bolt of lightning. He landed face-first on the ground with a sickening thud, and for a moment Chaelim and Volara thought he had been pierced by a spear or arrow. But when they saw something in the air descending toward him, they quickly discerned what had happened.

It was Malgyron, who landed just a short distance away from Apteris and began walking toward him. The Legan regained his senses and looked up, meeting the eyes of his former leader for the first time since his betrayal. Apteris remembered the description given to him by Chaelim and Volara, and realized right away that the grotesque form approaching him was actually Orius.

"Orius," he said as he rose from the ground. "How could you do this?"

"On the contrary, Apteris," Malgyron said. "How could you be so foolish as to oppose me? I warned Chaelim and Volara, but you refused to listen. Now you have left me no choice but to dispose of you permanently." He drew his swords, but took a quick step back when Chaelim and Volara landed on each side of Apteris.

"But why?" Apteris asked. "I knew something was wrong when you allowed The Great Tree to die the way it did, but I still don't understand why you turned your back on us and brought this evil into the world."

"Haven't you come to realize that it was I who poisoned The Great Tree?" Malgyron said. "I didn't allow it to die, Apteris. I killed it. It was the first step in a plan that was executed to perfection, and a plan I intend to see to completion. No one will stand in my way, not even the three of you."

Apteris was enraged when he learned that Malgyron killed The Great Tree. "You killed it?" he said. "You killed The Great Tree? How could you do such a thing? How could you turn on the world you swore to protect?" His voice was almost shaking as the words came forth from his mouth, for he could not believe what his former leader had done.

"I am no longer interested in an eternal life of service," Malgyron said. "Why serve when you can be served? Why be ruled when you can rule? Don't you see, Apteris? You would be a fool to live out the rest of your life as a slave to The Author. Join forces with me instead. Chaelim and Volara were too stubborn to listen, but surely you know better."

Apteris' eyes were focused squarely on Malgyron, and as he opened his mouth to respond all that emerged was a blood-curdling scream. Without warning, he stormed Malgyron alone and began clashing swords with his archnemesis. Chaelim and Volara weren't even sure of what to do at first. They saw that Apteris wanted to kill Malgyron himself to avenge the death of The Great Tree, but at the same time they didn't think he could do it alone. They watched closely for an opening where they might be able to intervene, but soon they too were attacked unexpectedly. The Surnia that had accompanied

Malgyron swooped down on them from behind, and quickly their attention was drawn away from Apteris' battle with the Evil One.

From the moment the battle began, Cedrus coaxed the unicorn in Sicarius' direction. He knew he would not rest until he avenged his brother's death, and there was no way he was going to allow anyone else the pleasure of killing Mavinor's ruthless general. He wanted that satisfaction for himself, so he pursued Sicarius immediately after charging the enemy's front line. But several of Mavinor's troops obstructed his path, leaving Cedrus no choice but to engage them and use his mount's wickedly sharp horn to his advantage. The unicorn was quick to gore those who came too close, making it easy for Cedrus to finish them off with the blade of his sword.

Grodus had wasted no time in rushing to where Antiugus was mounted. He wanted revenge on his former king for removing him as General of Xamnon's armies, and was unwavering in his intent to kill both Antiugus and Henricus during the course of the battle. When Grodus confronted Antiugus and began doing battle with him, it quickly became apparent that the king was not strong enough to stand up to the blows from Grodus' mighty mace. Antiugus shielded himself again and again, but it was only a matter of time before he was knocked from the saddle and fell to the ground. When a direct hit caused Antiugus to cant over to the side, Grodus saw an opening and reared back, swinging his club in a huge arc and pounding the flaming heart emblazoned on Antiugus' shield. This caused Xamnon's king to lose his grip on the reins and fall off his mount, leaving him lying on the ground in a vulnerable state.

Grodus dismounted and went over to finish him off, glaring down at his prey with delightful anticipation. "I have been looking forward to this moment for some time, Antiugus," Grodus said. "Now you will realize the error of your ways and regret your decision to embrace The Author, albeit too late to save what is left of your life."

But as Grodus prepared to deal the death blow, he was distracted by a loud whinny and the sound of a soldier's boots landing against the ground. Turning to his right, he barely raised his shield in time to protect himself from the sword of Henricus, who attacked aggressively and relentlessly. At first he put Grodus back on his heels, having caught him completely off guard. But then the giant recovered by using his freakish strength to drive Henricus away and reverse the momentum.

Now it was Henricus who found himself in trouble, and though he was able to stand up to the blows from Grodus' mace, he had no way of getting close enough to mount an attack with his sword. Antiugus got back to his feet and charged Grodus from behind, but his attempt was futile. Somehow Grodus managed to use his shield to repel Antiugus even as he took one wild swing after another at Henricus. When Antiugus' sword made contact with Grodus' shield, the big man shoved as hard as he could toward Antiugus and knocked him to the ground again. Henricus continued to fight bravely, realizing his valor might well be the only thing standing between his king and the man who intended to kill him. Finally he took a furious stab at Grodus with his sword, but it was ill-timed and fell short of its intended target. This made it easy for Grodus to bat it away and send the weapon flying out of Henricus' hand. Then he flattened Henricus by stepping forward and driving his left elbow up and into his chin. Seeing that Xamnon's general was now incapacitated, Grodus smiled and walked toward Antiugus, who was still lying on the ground a short distance away.

Henricus thought his king was a goner. Even Antiugus prepared himself to die at Grodus' hands, but just as Grodus raised his mace overhead he was suddenly jumped from behind by one of Xamnon's troops. The soldier climbed on Grodus' back, reached up, and grabbed the crest of his helm. Then he somehow vaulted himself upward so that his legs came over Grodus' shoulders. In what could only be described as an amazing feat of strength and agility, the warrior then wrapped his legs around Grodus' head and swung him down to the ground. The acrobatic move actually caused Grodus to lose his helm, and as he landed he grabbed the soldier's legs and pushed them away. Quickly he rose to his feet, but as he looked across he saw that his opponent had already gotten back up and was ready to square off.

Grodus lunged forward with a powerful swing, but his foe ducked and rolled in the opposite direction before following up with a backhand slash that cut Grodus across his leg. He grunted in pain as he tried to regain his balance, but as he turned back around, his opponent's sword was already whirling toward him and caught him in his side. He grabbed the blade and pushed it away, then briefly examined the wound before rushing forth with a rage unlike anyone had ever seen. Though he again whiffed on his attempt with the mace, he managed to sidestep his opponent's encroaching sword and grab the arm of his attacker. Then he flung him to the ground and reached as far back with his mace as he possibly could. With both hands firmly gripping the handle, Grodus raised the weapon above his head and brought it downward in a powerful overhand swing. The force of the blow was so great that the spikes of the mace could have easily passed all the way through the body of their victim. But Grodus' target rolled away at the last second and eluded what would have been certain death.

At this point, Grodus' frustration had reached its peak. He was being led by his emotions rather than his wits, and it showed in every move that he attempted. He may as well have been a mindless beast swinging wildly and aimlessly in order to cause as much damage as possible with one single blow. Ultimately it cost him when his opponent dodged one of his ill-advised attacks, then rolled forward in a perfect somersault and thrust the sword upward, deep into his abdomen. Grodus dropped his mace and reached down toward the blade, but it had penetrated too far for him to push it back out. In an act of desperation, he reached toward the soldier's head and tried to break the neck of his foe. But the fighter slipped away and Grodus was left only with his slayer's helm in his hands as he fell to the ground and breathed his last.

From the moment Grodus removed the helm of his assailant, Antiugus and Henricus noticed the long brown hair flow down over the soldier's back in a burnished cascade. When they saw the face and realized it was Arcala who had defeated Grodus, they were stunned. Antiugus rose and walked over to her as if he was in some kind of trance. "Thank you," he said to her. "You saved my life."

"Come!" Arcala said. "We have a battle to win."

It took a while for Chaelim and Volara to finally rid themselves of the Surnia. The mobility and quickness of the vexatious creatures made it difficult to mount an attack against them, but ultimately the Legans were able to get close enough to plunge their swords through the giant owls' bodies. The victory couldn't come soon enough, for both Chaelim and Volara saw that their friend was struggling in his clash with Malgyron and was in dire need of their help.

From the moment that Apteris charged his foe, Malgyron dominated him in every aspect of their one-on-one fracas. Even the rush of anger Apteris experienced over the murder of The Great Tree wasn't enough for him to gain the upper hand, as his attacks were repelled again and again. The Legans' former leader was stronger than his opponent, and used that to his advantage on several occasions when he either shoved Apteris away or even drove him to the ground. There were numerous instances where Apteris barely escaped being impaled by Malgyron's swords, and even he began to doubt whether he could defeat the Evil One without help from the others.

Just as Chaelim and Volara arrived, they saw Apteris and Malgyron battling in the air with their swords locked together. Each was pushing as hard as he could to gain the advantage, and ultimately the edge went to Malgyron. Again he forced Apteris toward the ground, but this time he managed to land on top of him. With an evil grin, Malgyron raised his sword to finish him off, but quickly he sensed someone sneaking up on him from behind. He used his long, pointed tail as a whip and lashed out, striking Chaelim just before his sword came within reach of Malgyron's back. Volara used the opening to dart in from the side and caught Malgyron by surprise. At the last second he managed to use his sword to parry her blade away, but she swung out her legs and kicked him as hard as she could, knocking him off of Apteris.

Though Malgyron's strength had grown as evil spread throughout the world, he sensed that he was not yet powerful enough to take on all three of the Legans at once. He felt the tide in the battle turning in favor of Xamnon, and realized that he might have to concede defeat and flee Mavinor. The most important thing was to save Cidivus and preserve his life, for he knew it was only a matter of time before the Deliverers of Darkness claimed their army and the Beast destroyed the three kingdoms. In the end, Xamnon's forces would have no chance to save the world from the Age of Darkness. So for now he was willing to allow them their moment of glory, since he knew it would be short-lived.

Malgyron sheathed his swords and began flying away toward the Praetorium. Chaelim and Volara pursued, but Malgyron swiped two of Xamnon's soldiers from their saddles and soared high into the air with them. Then he dropped them from a great height, forcing the Legans to catch them before they slammed into the ground. By the time they lowered them gently back onto their mounts, Malgyron was gone. "Forget about him," Chaelim said. "Let's focus on doing what we have to do to liberate Mavinor." With that, the Legans sprung back into action and began decimating Sicarius' army.

After Arcala had killed Grodus, she went with Antiugus and Henricus to aid Cedrus and Minstro, who were extremely outnumbered after being swarmed by a wave of opponents. Though the length of the unicorn's horn and the daggers Minstro hurled with pinpoint accuracy had been keeping their attackers away, it was only a matter of time before one of Sicarius' men got close enough to launch an offen-

sive. When Xamnon's king and his general stormed the troops surrounding Cedrus and Minstro, it caused them to waver and break.
Chaos ensued as Arcala joined the fray, and the Legans swept down
to aid their friends. No longer encircled and overmatched by Mavinor's troops, Cedrus and Minstro rushed forward into the heart of
the battle.

The air was filled with the sounds of the rattling of swords and
the feral screams of dueling warhorses as the cavalries squared off.
Cedrus continuously got the best of his opponents, whether it was
by way of his flashing saber or the unicorn ramming her horn into
their adversaries. As more of Xamnon's forces came to assist them,
Mavinor's ranks increasingly vanished. Sicarius' men simply couldn't
withstand the onslaught. The Legans' quick strikes from above com-
bined with Xamnon's ground forces was too much for them to handle, and Cedrus and the others began to feel victory within their
grasp. When two of Mavinor's last men standing snuck up on Arcala
and Cedrus, Minstro thrust his hands forward like a blur of motion
and took them both out with his daggers. Soon they were scanning
the corpses littered across the battlefield to see who had survived.
Mavinor's warhorses had abandoned their riders, almost all of whom
had been killed. But as they looked across the bloodstained landscape
and saw one of Mavinor's soldiers rise with a sword in his hand, they
quickly realized that it was General Sicarius. His silver six-eyed spider insignia still shone forth from his black breastplate, and without
hesitation Cedrus spurred the unicorn to the head of the pack and
dismounted.

"Stay here," Cedrus told the others as he began walking in Sicarius' direction. "He's mine."

Chapter Twenty-Two

Cedrus slowly advanced toward Sicarius, his eyes staring directly into those of the man he longed to kill. The general was all alone now; there was no one left to come to his aid. Yet he didn't seem the least bit concerned about it. He looked more confident than anxious, as if he was relishing the opportunity to face Cedrus. Sicarius gripped the hilt of his sword more tightly as Cedrus came closer, and when he was roughly ten feet from where Sicarius stood, Cedrus stopped in his tracks.

"I told you this day would come," Cedrus said. "Do you remember? Do you recall how you and your king ridiculed me as I hung above the cauldron, after I swore my revenge upon you both for what you did to my brother? Well now, Sicarius, that day has come."

"Soon you will wish it hadn't," Sicarius replied. "I don't know how you escaped the wrath of the raging sea, but you would have been better off succumbing to its fury. For now, young Cedrus, your death will be much slower, and much more painful. You are not half the warrior your brother was, and without him here to defend you, you do not stand a chance against me."

"There was no one in all of Mavinor—save for Silex and some other members of the thirteen—who was half the fighter Tonitrus was," Cedrus said defiantly. "But know that he taught me well, and while I may not have his skills, his spirit lives on within me. His sword remains, and it will be the sword that cuts you down and sends you to your grave." Cedrus held out his brother's weapon so Sicarius could clearly see the insignia of the red cross emblazoned upon it.

"It is not the sword that wins the battle, but the one who wields it," retorted Sicarius. "Your brother's blade is of no use in your hands, Cedrus. You are unworthy of bearing Tonitrus' arms. He told me as much right before I executed him. Before the axe fell, he expressed to me how disappointed he was that you had abandoned him, and how all the lessons he taught you were in vain."

"You lie!" Cedrus yelled.

Sicarius laughed. "If I lie, then prove me wrong," the general said. "Show me that you're not a coward. Show me that the hopes your brother had for you can actually be fulfilled. Prove yourself, Cedrus."

Cedrus' stare became colder as he looked into Sicarius' eyes, but Sicarius was not the least bit intimidated. He continued to smirk and spoke haughtily yet again. "Your brother," he said, "squealed like a pig right before I severed his head. If only you could have heard the terror in his voice."

"Never!" Cedrus exclaimed. "Never would my brother show the slightest fear even in the face of imminent death. Again you lie, Sicarius!"

"I also must say that your brother's head served as an admirable addition to my office," Sicarius said. "Never before had such a fine ornament adorned my surroundings. I'm sure you would have greatly admired the sight."

At that, Cedrus lost control of his emotions. Sicarius was using the circumstances of Tonitrus' death to get into his head, and Cedrus fell right into the trap. He charged the general almost mindlessly, taking wild swings with the sword once wielded by his brother.

With both hands on the hilt, he reared back and swung as hard as he could in a wide arc, only to be blocked by Sicarius' blade time and again. Though he couldn't penetrate Sicarius' defense, Cedrus did not relent in his swings, and soon he felt himself tiring. Sicarius stayed on his heels and let the young warrior continue to attack him. He felt the blows become weaker, and sensed the emotional fatigue that was beginning to set in and sap Cedrus of his strength. It wasn't long before Sicarius heard Cedrus' breath laboring, and as his opponent dropped his sword lower with each desperate swing, the general made his move.

Sicarius reared back and pushed off with his right foot, shifting his weight forward as he brought his sword around in a vicious arc that knocked Cedrus to the ground as he tried to defend himself. The blow jarred the weapon from Cedrus' hands, and he juggled it in vain as he fell down on his right shoulder. He saw the sword lying a few feet away from him, and frantically reached out to grab it. But it was too far away. As he looked out of the corner of his eye, he caught sight of Sicarius charging and raising his sword over his head, clearly intent on bringing it down on him and ending his life.

When everyone had left the Praetorium, Cidivus came out of hiding and ran toward the administrative offices of the Tribunal. He quickly ascended the stairs and tried to enter the front door, but found it locked. He knocked over and over again, and even began to call out to those who were inside. "Pachaias, let me in!" Cidivus shouted. But there was no answer. Either the tribunes couldn't hear him or simply refused to open the door. Cidivus was enraged, and he pounded hard against the door with both fists before finally turning and racing back down the stairs.

As he considered what options he had left, Cidivus suddenly saw something streaking across the sky toward him. When he recognized that it was Malgyron, he felt a huge sense of relief. The aspiring King of Darkness slowly descended as he glided through the air, and after he landed on the ground a few feet away from Cidivus, he looked him in the eye and smiled. "Do you have it?" Malgyron asked him.

"Have what?" Cidivus asked.

"The Medallion," Malgyron answered.

"No," replied Cidivus. "I was unable to get to Solitus in time. The others protected him, and now they are gone."

"No!" Malgyron said.

"Why is it so important for you to have that cursed object?" Cidivus asked. "I had it in my possession before, but quickly rid myself of it. It only brings misfortune and calamity on those who bear it."

Malgyron was livid when he heard that Cidivus had previously held the Medallion but decided to relinquish it. His facial expression quickly changed, displaying the rage burning inside him. Cidivus noticed the sudden reversal in Malgyron's countenance and began to shrink back in fear. When he sensed Cidivus' discomfort, Malgyron eased up and smiled once again.

"No worries," he said. "There is someone else who can retrieve it for me. For now, the most important thing is to get you to safety."

"What about the battle?" Cidivus asked. "Who attacked us, and were we victorious?"

"It was Xamnon's army," Malgyron replied. "My spies failed me, and their surprise attack was successful. I'm afraid we have lost, and that the only option is to flee Mavinor."

"No!" Cidivus exclaimed. "I cannot leave behind the kingdom I was chosen to rule."

"Your reign is over, Cidivus," Malgyron said, "but only for the time being. Take comfort in the fact that although we have lost this battle, we will win the war. For an army will soon rise, an army far superior to any that can be assembled by man. It is that army that will lead us to final victory, and restore your rule. But for now, you will need to accompany me so I can bring you to a safe place. Once the army is ready and the war has been won, you can reclaim your throne."

"Thank you," Cidivus said. "I cannot thank you enough for all that you have done for me."

"My pleasure," Malgyron said. With that he took hold of Cidivus and carried him up into the air, through the clouds, and off toward the Northern Mountains.

When Tarsus, Ignatus, and Solitus left the Praetorium, they went straight to the home of Tarsus to gather some provisions for their journey north. They hastily packed food, water, and weapons into their saddlebags, along with other supplies such as a flint and linen embedded with wax in case an improvised torch was necessary. When they had assembled all that they could possibly carry, they galloped toward the North Gate with Tarsus mounted atop his black and Solitus riding with Ignatus.

By the time they left Tarsus' home, Malgyron and Cidivus had already departed Mavinor and were well on their way to the Northern Mountains. There was only one guard remaining at the North Gate, as all the others had raced off to join the battle after the shofars sounded.

"What are we to do about the guard?" Ignatus asked.

"Leave that to me," Tarsus said. "Just conceal your weapons and act as if you are my prisoners."

When they arrived at the gate, the guard was surprised to see Ignatus and Solitus accompanying Tarsus. But since he wasn't aware that Tarsus had turned against Sicarius, the seasoned lieutenant was able to trick him into thinking he was still on their side. While brandishing his bow, Tarsus informed the guard that the general had ordered him to transport the prisoners outside Mavinor.

"Sicarius has special plans for them," he said, "so he asked me to take them to a safe place and watch over them until the battle is over."

The guard noticed that Tarsus was not wearing his uniform, which made him a bit suspicious. But he was not about to question the general's second in command, so he opened the gate and watched Tarsus burst through with Ignatus and Solitus riding alongside him.

As they hastened along the main thoroughfare, Solitus instructed them to break off and take the interior road that led through the Tenebrae. "Are you sure?" Ignatus asked.

"Yes, I am sure," Solitus said. "This is the way that leads to the cavern."

Neither Tarsus nor Ignatus were eager to enter that dark, forbidden forest, but nor did they hesitate as they turned left and darted along the path. As they stared up at the huge canopy of trees hanging above their heads, it quickly became evident why the woods of the Tenebrae were so lurid and ominous. The foliage was so thick that sunlight could barely filter through. But now that the sun had seemingly disappeared forever, the area was even gloomier than usual, and for a moment Tarsus considered breaking out his torch. Then he thought better of it, realizing it might be needed for something more pressing during the course of the journey.

Soon the ground beneath them began to shake, and the horses became spooked. They stopped dead in their tracks and started neighing loudly, as their riders scanned the surrounding area to discern what was happening.

"What could it be?" Solitus asked.

"It almost feels as it did when Gobius was executed," Ignatus said. "Could the same thing be happening again?"

Just as Ignatus finished asking his question, a loud cry rained down from above. The three of them looked up into the trees, but it was virtually impossible to see anything. All they heard was the clamorous squawking of a bird and the rustling of leaves overhead. Finally they were able to make out two dark forms flying through the air, one much larger than the other. "Help! Help!" a distinct voice shrieked from up in the trees.

"That voice," Ignatus said. "I know it."

Again the voice cried out. "Help! Help!"

As they looked up, they saw the dark silhouette of the larger bird stretch out one of its limbs and clip the wings of the smaller bird, causing it to flutter and fall to the ground. Ignatus dismounted and ran to the spot where it landed. When he saw it up close, he realized that it was a raven, and recalled the voice as the one that tried to warn Mavinor's people against killing Gobius on that fateful day in the Praetorium. "Ignatus, look out!" Solitus yelled.

The raven's predator was plummeting toward the ground with its talons open, ready to snatch up the bird and presumably finish it off. But before it could fully descend, Tarsus fired an arrow through its throat and caused it to drop like a stone to the forest floor. "What happened?" Ignatus asked as he looked back toward the raven.

"The Surnia are out to kill me!" the bird cried out as it quickly gathered itself and recovered from the fall. "Thank you for saving me!"

The ground continued to shake even as the raven spoke, and they all heard a loud roar echoing through the forest. "What in the world is that?" Tarsus asked.

"The Beast is coming! The Beast is coming!" said the raven.

"What in The Author's name is happening?" Ignatus asked.

"The Age of Darkness is upon us!" exclaimed the raven. "The Beast has wiped out Urmina! The Beast must be stopped!"

"It is my destiny to face the Beast," Solitus said. "The one thing that can destroy her resides in that cavern. I must get to it."

"Go," Tarsus said. "Take Solitus to the cavern, Ignatus. I will do what I can to fend off the Beast and buy you the time you need."

"But it is suicide," Solitus replied.

"Here, take these," Tarsus said. He took food, water, and a sword from his saddlebag and presented it to Solitus.

"I'm afraid I cannot accept these items," Solitus said.

"Why not?" Tarsus asked in total disbelief.

"When Gobius came to me in the vision, he instructed me not to take food, water, or weapons into the cavern," Solitus said.

Tarsus continued to fumble through his bag. "What about this?"

he asked as he extended the flint and strip of linen embedded with wax toward Solitus. "I'm sure it will get very dark as you go deeper into the cavern. Take these, gather some twigs and wrap the linen around them. Then use the flint to light the torch."

"Thank you," Solitus said as he accepted the supplies from Tarsus.

Tarsus quickly packed everything back into his saddlebags as the Beast drew closer to them. "Go now," he said.

"The Beast breathes fire!" the raven warned. "Keep away or you will lose your life!"

Tarsus eyed the raven and then looked back toward Ignatus and Solitus. "Perhaps in losing my life I shall save it," he said as he dragged the reins on his mount and pulled the black in the opposite direction. They watched him ride back to cut off the Beast, hoping against hope that their new ally could survive the encounter.

"Let's go," Ignatus then said. He and Solitus began galloping down the path even as the ground beneath them quaked from every step the Beast took. The raven watched as they left, and then it soared up into the trees to get a glimpse of Tarsus' confrontation with Hexula.

Chapter Twenty-Three

When Cedrus looked up helplessly toward Sicarius' sword as the blade fell toward him, several thoughts raced through his head. Despite the short span of time it took for the general to launch his assault, it almost seemed to Cedrus as if the world had stopped. In his mind he recalled the many lessons his brother taught him during their training sessions, and how hard he worked to live up to Tonitrus' lofty standards. He even swore that he heard his brother's voice ringing in his ears, shouting instructions and scolding Cedrus when he didn't follow them perfectly. Then the tenor of Tonitrus' voice suddenly changed. It projected a sense of urgency and admonition, but in a tone that was both gentle and calm. "Roll, Cedrus, roll," it said.

Without hesitation, Cedrus rolled to his right and dodged Sicarius' blow. Then in one fluid motion he retrieved his sword and rose to his feet, entirely cognizant of his opponent's location. He spun around and brought his sword into a defensive stance, keeping his shoulders taut and his grip on the hilt as tight as possible. Cedrus positioned his blade just in time to thwart Sicarius' follow-up swing and parry his sword away. Then he went on the offensive again, rush-ing forward and keeping his strokes shorter than he did the first time. This enabled Cedrus to strike rapidly and repeatedly, keeping the general occupied and affording him no time to launch a coun-terattack.

It wasn't until Sicarius absorbed a direct hit on the flat of his blade that he was able to use his strength to push Cedrus and knock him off balance. He then took an uppercut swing toward his foe, attempting to decapitate him. Cedrus did his best to avoid the blow, but his lack of body control made it impossible. Though he succeeded in escap-ing certain death by pivoting his neck away from the encroaching sword, Sicarius sliced his right shoulder and arm as the blade swept across. Cedrus groaned as he fell back, holding his left hand tightly over the wounds. When he withdrew his hand, he gazed down at the palm and watched as the blood seeped through his fingers.

Now Sicarius had a decided advantage. Cedrus' injury made it far more difficult for him to wield his sword. The general attacked ruth-lessly, feeling his confidence grow as he watched Cedrus grimace in pain. He believed it was now only a matter of time until his sword dealt the final blow, the one that would bring him ultimate victory over the brothers who had been a thorn in his side for so long.

But Cedrus refused to give in. He ignored the agony of his suffer-ing and let out a loud grunt each time he brought his sword forward to block Sicarius' attempts. As his friends watched from a distance, they could see that Cedrus was giving it all he had, but wondered if it would be enough. Sicarius smelled blood and refused to let up as he continued to hammer away at Cedrus. He fully believed that sooner or later the young man would be forced to give in and succumb to his pain, giving the general the opening he needed to finish him off.

As Cedrus continued to fall back on his heels, once again he heard his brother's voice reverberating in his head. He remembered the unique strategies and masterful maneuvers that Tonitrus had taught him, and the many hours he had spent trying to learn them. Now more than ever before, he needed one of his brother's ploys in order to escape with his life, as he felt the strength in his right arm and shoulder quickly evaporating. The voice once again spoke calmly yet urgently, saying, "Beat him as I once did." At that moment, Cedrus recalled Tonitrus' duel with Sicarius, the one that took place after Solitus and Arcala had made it through the gauntlet. He remembered how easily Sicarius fell into the trap that Tonitrus had set, and decided that he would try to replicate his brother's success by using the same tactic.

Cedrus continued to cede ground in the fight. He kept his parries short, tight, and close to his body, allowing Sicarius to advance. He waited patiently for Sicarius to extend his sword all the way out from his body, and when he finally did, Cedrus made his move. He thrust his sword out and touched the inside of Sicarius' blade, as if to parry it away. Then he took a step closer to him, brought his sword up almost vertically and wrapped his blade around that of Sicarius. Cedrus pointed the tip down suddenly towards the outside of Sicarius' blade, slid the sword down and then jerked it in hard towards his body. The perfectly executed maneuver caused Sicarius' sword to fly out of his hand in the direction Cedrus pulled it and land several feet away.

But despite losing his weapon, the general refused to surrender. He quickly stepped forward and put his left arm around Cedrus' throat, then reached around and grabbed Cedrus' right wrist with his right hand. He squeezed as tightly as he could in both places, trying to choke Cedrus until he was unconscious and get him to release his weapon. But Cedrus countered by jabbing his left elbow into Sicarius' side, which forced the general to momentarily loosen his grip. This afforded Cedrus the chance to slip out of the chokehold and down toward the ground. He then reached up and grabbed Sicarius' left arm, and exerted all the strength he had left as he flipped him over his body. Sicarius became dazed after his head hit hard against the ground. When he finally came to, he looked up to see

Cedrus standing directly over him.

"Go ahead," Sicarius muttered. "Finish it."

Cedrus held the tip of his blade to Sicarius' chest, and looked aside just for a moment to see the general's sword lying several feet away. Then he looked into the eyes of Henricus, who came forward when he realized that Cedrus had won. Finally he gazed back down at Sicarius, expecting to see the agony of defeat in his facial expression. But he was shocked when he saw that his opponent was now smiling widely.

"You can't do it, can you?" Sicarius said. "Like the rest of the believers, you are too weak to do what needs to be done. Even after the way I slaughtered your brother and hung his head on a stick for all to see, you still can't go through with it."

Cedrus felt his blood boiling in his veins. His eyes were filled with fire, his heart replete with profound rage. Almost unconsciously he retracted his sword until his elbow was pulled as far back as it could go. The others saw the fury in his facial expression and immediately realized what was about to happen. "No!" Henricus shouted.

But it was too late. Cedrus thrust the blade forward into Sicarius' torso and penetrated deeply. Even as it pierced his internal organs, Sicarius smiled and began to let out an evil laugh, one that irked Cedrus to no end and caused his anger to grow even more. Cedrus then placed both hands on the bottom of the pommel and pushed down with all his strength, driving the blade all the way through. As the blood oozed downward from both sides of Sicarius' body, the man who had led Mavinor's armies for so long finally breathed his last. Cedrus' rage began to subside, and though he was happy to exact revenge on the man who had killed his brother, he didn't realize the extent of his actions until he looked over at Henricus and saw how disconcerted he was. For only then did Cedrus recall how Henricus had once spared his life on that same battlefield after he too had fallen to the ground and lost his sword. But rather than extend that same mercy to Sicarius, Cedrus gave in to his ire and killed the general in cold blood to exact the vengeance he so deeply craved. It wasn't until after the deed was done that Cedrus finally began to understand that killing Sicarius could never erase the pain he felt in losing his king, his best friends, and his one brother.

As Ignatus galloped through the Tenebrae with Solitus, he focused solely on getting the youth to the cavern by any means necessary. He didn't even notice the looming forms of the huge catapults off to the left, though Solitus saw them immediately and stared back at them even as they passed by. The young man did not know that they were once used by Xamnon in an assault on Mavinor, nor was he aware that the thirteen spun them around during the quest, and that his cousin actually loaded a stone onto one of them with the intention of firing it.

Eventually the ground to the right of the road began sloping upward. What had been flat forest on both sides gave way to rocky outcroppings as the road wound its way around a small mountain. To the left, the forest remained as thick and impenetrable as ever. On the right, they passed stone cliff walls that were peppered with batches of scrub and roots. Stones had rolled into the road over time, dropping from the heights above, but no one was there to clear them away. They picked their way through the rubble carefully before coming to a dead stop in the center of the road. At this point the cliffs were a good fifty yards removed from the main path. A trail lined with rounded stones led away from the road and ended at a dark, yawning doorway in the side of the mountain. There were carvings in the stone to either side, but there was no evidence that there'd ever been an actual door closing the entrance. It was difficult to tell whether the opening was natural and merely decorated by men who'd found it thus or if it had been cut and widened, shaped into something more.

"This is it," Solitus said. "This is the Cavern of Trials, just as Gobius described it." He dismounted and began walking down the path between the rounded stones.

"Solitus," Ignatus called out, "please let me accompany you."

"I can't," Solitus said. "King Gobius said that I must go alone."

"Then take my sword, and my shield," Ignatus said.

"No," Solitus said. "It is King Gobius' wish that I take neither weapons nor sustenance into the cavern. Difficult as it may be, I must have faith in him. I know that he would not lead me astray."

"So be it," Ignatus said. "But don't forget these." He held out the materials that Tarsus gave him for the torch. "You will almost certainly need a light to guide you as you navigate your way through."

Solitus rushed back and grabbed the flint and the linen, but then immediately placed them back down. "Wait," he said to Ignatus as he reached beneath his tunic and removed the Medallion from around his neck. "Take this."

"I can't," Ignatus replied. "It saved your life once, it may do so again."

"I have faith in King Gobius, that he will protect me," Solitus said. "Perhaps this will one day save your life, or that of the one you pass it onto. Everything I need to fulfill the task before me lies somewhere in that cavern. I am sure of it. Let the Medallion fall to he who might need it more than I will."

Ignatus reticently accepted the Medallion from Solitus and peered down at the image of the unicorn upon it. He was honored to be its bearer, and for a moment he was almost entranced by the object. But soon his reverie was broken by the screeching of the raven. The bird had returned to warn them that Tarsus was in trouble. "Help! Help!" it squawked.

Quickly Ignatus gathered himself and prepared to ride. "May The Author be with you, my son," he said to Solitus. "Remember always what I taught you, for I will never forget what you have taught me." With that he spurred his mount and began dashing back down the road toward Mavinor.

Solitus watched him go before gathering some twigs and wrapping them in the linen. Then he used the flint to bring his improvised torch to flickering life. "Good-bye," he said to the raven as he slowly entered through the doorway of the cavern.

"Good luck!" the raven said. Then it flapped its wings and darted through the air back to where Tarsus was battling the Beast.

From the moment Tarsus caught sight of Hexula, he was awed by her appearance. Despite his many courageous deeds in battle and all the honors at arms that he won throughout his illustrious career as a soldier of Mavinor, nothing could have possibly prepared him for this. Sicarius' former right-hand man drew his bow and fired an arrow from a hiding spot he discovered while waiting for the dragon. But his ambush was all for naught, as he watched the arrow bounce off the scales of the Beast and fall harmlessly to the ground. Hexula let out a roar as she scanned the area around her in an effort to locate her attacker. Tarsus tried to still his horse, hoping to go unnoticed so he could launch yet another stealth assault against the Beast. But the black became nervous and skittish, and without warning it let out a loud whinny that Hexula immediately heard. She lowered her head and flared her nostrils, and as Tarsus watched helplessly, she opened her mouth and breathed fire so hot that it consumed the trees instantly as it made its way toward him. Tarsus cruelly dragged the reins as he forced his mount in the opposite direction, and though he felt the heat of the encroaching flames on his back, he somehow managed to escape unscathed.

Still he realized that he had to do all he could to hold her back until Ignatus could safely bring Solitus to the cavern. Tarsus turned and fired yet another arrow at Hexula, only to see it bounce off her seemingly impenetrable scales yet again. Slowly but surely the Beast plodded along, her frightening yellowish eyes focused straight in Tarsus' direction. Not knowing what else to do, Tarsus crossed the road and galloped straight into the woods, hoping to lure the Beast away from the main path that led to the cavern. Though he knew that it might prove difficult for his warhorse to navigate its way through the low-lying branches, he had to at least make the attempt.

Onward the Beast marched, incinerating the imposing trees of the Tenebrae to ashes with her burning breath. Tarsus continuously looked back to make sure the Beast was still in pursuit. The black wound its way through the shadowed trails and scattered trees with eerie precision. There was no hesitation in the creature. Once in motion, it flowed like a river dancing over and around stones. But just before entering a clearing, Tarsus took one last glance back at the Beast and failed to see a low-lying limb around the bend. As his horse streaked past the last tree before the clearing, Tarsus was knocked from the saddle and fell to the ground in a stupor, the back of his head having collided with the limb.

The black looked back at its master, and quickly returned to where he was lying on the ground. But despite its cries, Tarsus did not budge. He shook his head as if trying to clear it from some sort of cobweb, but remained lying face downward. As the Beast drew nearer, the black was left with no choice but to break and run. Hexula eyed her prey from afar, and though she could have burnt Tarsus to a crisp with one breath, she opted to eat him whole instead, just as she had previously done with both Gladius and Bardus.

When Tarsus finally turned over, he looked up and knew that he was a goner. He stared directly into the gaping jaws of the Beast and saw her long, pointed teeth for the first time. Tarsus accepted his fate, realizing that the dragon's mouth would be his tomb, yet hoping that his death would not be in vain. For as long as Solitus made it safely to the cavern, then Tarsus could say that he did what Gobius had asked him to do.

But as Hexula began to lower her head toward Tarsus, she suddenly reared back and let out an ungodly scream that rocked the forest to its very foundation. Quickly she pivoted her head and gazed back at her tail, only to see it seemingly set afire. Unbeknownst to her, Ignatus had arrived just in time. The quick-witted warrior grabbed a branch on his way into the woods and lit it aflame with the fire that

Hexula had ignited. Then he managed to sneak up behind her and wedge it in between the spikes on her tail before fleeing the scene. The Beast continued to roar and began lashing her tail against the ground in an effort to dislodge the burning torch.

The distraction gave Tarsus the time he needed to escape what would have been the cruelest of fates. He was still a bit dazed, but managed to climb to his feet and began searching for his horse. Though there was no sight of the black anywhere, Tarsus suddenly heard the pounding of hooves coming from across the clearing. His eyes met a dark form emerging from the shadows of the trees, bolting out of the woods like a flash of lightning. When he looked back at the Beast, he saw that she was about to squelch the flames on her tail, and knew that she'd immediately come for him once the torch was extinguished.

Without hesitation Tarsus began running full speed to the west, across the clearing. The black was racing north toward the direction of the Cavern of Trials, and it didn't take long for him to ascertain the warhorse's plan. Though two, Tarsus and his mount acted as one. After all the years they spent together on the battlefield, it was as if they could communicate with each other, even from a distance.

Tarsus continued to churn his legs, and as he looked straight ahead he saw a row of tree stumps. The approach of the black now rivaled the roar of the Beast. Its hooves beating against the ground gave all the semblance of a wicked hailstorm raging through the forest. As Hexula successfully dislodged the torch from the spikes on her tail, she turned back to see Tarsus leap onto one of the tree stumps. He landed with his right foot and immediately pushed off and catapulted himself forward, just as the black was racing by. In that one moment, Tarsus knew that his very life depended on him executing the plan to perfection. He reached out and extended his arms as far as he could, grabbing hold of his mount as it flashed by. His body thrashed against that of the horse, but the black somehow managed to keep running at nearly full speed. He struggled to take hold of the reins and lift his left leg up and over the horse's back. At one point he nearly lost his grip and fell to the ground. But somehow he managed to hold on, even as the toe of his boot scraped against the dirt.

With every bit of strength his muscles could generate, Tarsus shifted to his right and pulled his left leg up and over to the far side of his mount, all while keeping his hold on the reins. As he heaved himself up into the saddle, the Beast shot a stream of fire across the clearing, withering every blade of grass and blackening the soil. But it wasn't enough to reach the brave soldier and his speeding mount, who escaped into the woods on the north end of the clearing. The Beast growled in frustration as it watched its flames fizzle out before reaching their intended target. Then it lunged forward and began chasing Tarsus once again.

Chapter Twenty-Four

As Cedrus and the others gazed down at Sicarius' body, the sound of hoofbeats clattering to a halt came up behind them. It was Talmik and Aramus, both of whom quickly dismounted when they saw Sicarius' bloody corpse on the battlefield.

"Author be praised," Aramus said, "for you have won the victory and rid us once and for all of the merciless man who planned to use military might to seize the throne. His reign may well have been more barbarous than that of Cidivus."

"Where is Cidivus?" Cedrus asked in an intense, deliberate tone.

"He ran and hid at the Praetorium shortly after the chaos began," Talmik responded. "We looked for him, but we couldn't find him."

"Don't worry," Cedrus said, "I will find him myself." With that, Cedrus stormed past Henricus and the others and mounted the unicorn.

"Where are you going?" Arcala shouted. "Someone needs to tend to your wounds."

Cedrus ignored her while wrapping a cloth around his upper arm and shoulder to form a tourniquet. Then he started galloping toward the Praetorium, spurring the splendid creature to extra speed almost immediately.

"We'd better follow him," Minstro said.

"That's a good idea," Aramus said. "I have a feeling he has no intention of letting Cidivus live."

"What about the raven?" Antiugus asked. "Shouldn't the bird have returned by now?"

"I certainly expected it would," Apteris said. "The fact that it has yet to turn up tells me that something unforeseen has occurred. I have to go and investigate."

"We will go with you," Chaelim and Volara said.

"Just be sure to come back as soon as possible and tell us what you find," Antiugus said.

"Don't worry," Apteris said. "We'll keep all of you informed. You have my word that one of us will return to Mavinor when there is news to report."

"Very well," Henricus said. "Now let's get going."

By the time Henricus, Antiugus, Arcala, and Minstro arrived inside the Praetorium, Cedrus had already searched the entire perimeter. He checked in alcoves and behind pillars, but Cidivus was nowhere to be seen. "Could he be inside the offices of the Tribunal?" Minstro asked.

Cedrus dismounted and ran up the stairs to the entrance of the Tribunal. When he found the door locked, he kicked it in and barged through with his sword drawn, ready for action. The others followed and aided in the search, and though they were unable to locate Cidivus, they did manage to discover Pachaias and the rest of the tribunes trembling in fear as they hid under a long table in one of the meeting rooms.

"Come out from under there!" Cedrus yelled imperiously.

One by one the tribunes crawled out from under the table and stood before them, with Pachaias being the last to emerge. "Where is he?" Cedrus asked.

"Who?" Pachaias said.

Cedrus wasted no time in rushing Pachaias and grabbing him by his magisterial robe. Then he flung him up against the wall and stared right into his eyes. "You know quite well who I am talking about!" Cedrus said. "Do not make me ask again!" Cedrus held the tip of his sword to Pachaias' throat to show how far he would go to get the answer to his question.

"If you are referring to Cidivus, then I swear that I am unaware of his whereabouts," Pachaias said. "When the trouble started, the four of us ran in and locked the door behind us. Sometime later, there was a series of heavy knocks on the door, followed by someone shouting. I think the voice was that of Cidivus, but I can't be sure. After a loud pounding against the door, the noise subsided, and I know not what happened to him after that."

Cedrus was livid that Cidivus had seemingly vanished, but he believed that Pachaias was telling the truth. He removed his sword from Pachaias' throat and placed it back into his scabbard. "Come with us," he then said.

"Where are we going?" Pachaias asked.

"To the palace," Cedrus said.

"Whatever for?" replied Pachaias.

"So the four of you can be put where you belong, in the dungeon," Cedrus said.

"You cannot place us in the dungeon!" Pachaias yelled. "We are the tribunes, the ones who are charged with upholding the law in our kingdom. You will never get away with this."

"I'm afraid there is no one left to stop me," Cedrus answered. "Sicarius is dead, and in fact his entire army has been wiped out. I'm afraid the end has now come, both for you and your friends."

Pachaias recalled how he had once uttered those same words to Cedrus after he was captured upon his return to Mavinor. With a look of dismay on his face, the Chair of the Tribunal allowed himself to be led away while his colleagues followed begrudgingly behind.

Eventually Tarsus was able to rediscover the road that wound through the Tenebrae. Once on it, his mount charged forward with reckless abandon, no longer inhibited by the tree trunks and low-lying limbs that blocked its path in the dense woods. But as he heard hoofbeats behind him, Tarsus turned and saw Ignatus following after him, also trying to outrun the Beast. He slowed his pace just for a few seconds to allow Ignatus to catch up.

"I'm glad I made it in time to help you escape," Ignatus said.

"Then it was you who torched the tail of the Beast," Tarsus said.

"It was the only thing I could think of doing," Ignatus replied. "Thank The Author it worked."

Both men looked back as they heard the roar of the Beast and the crackling of fire as she lit the forest ablaze. They knew now that their only option was to keep riding north. Though their mounts were considerably faster than Hexula, the Beast had one advantage over them. The road through the Tenebrae was meandering and circuitous, forcing Tarsus and Ignatus to move both east and west even as they traveled north. But the Beast carved out a path for herself through the trees that enabled her to progress in a straight line toward the Black Hollow. She knew her surroundings well, and realized that Tarsus and Ignatus would eventually run out of room and put themselves in a predicament. Hexula quickened her pace—moving a bit faster than she had during her approach to Urmina—and was extremely confident that she would be able to eventually capture and devour her prey.

Tarsus and Ignatus bolted through the Tenebrae at breakneck speed as they eluded the Beast. They traveled the same road the thirteen once had, but covered far more ground in a much shorter span of time. The thirteen had traveled very cautiously and stopped numerous times along the way, such as when they turned the catapults or explored the dark cavern. They also endured an attack by the Surnia and a tense confrontation with the Legans. But Ignatus and Tarsus were unimpeded as they passed through, and couldn't afford the same leisurely pace given the terror that was slowly creeping up behind them.

It took a long time, but eventually their tired mounts reached the Black Hollow, arriving at the makeshift bridge that had once been The Great Tree. The horses whinnied nervously as both Ignatus and Tarsus surveyed the area.

"What do we do now?" Tarsus asked.

Ignatus stepped forward cautiously to the lip of the hollow and peeked down into the abyss. "We're certainly not going down there," he said. "It's far too steep, and too dark at the bottom as well. We have no idea what might be down there."

"We could travel east or west along the hollow, but that would take us far from the main road," Tarsus said. "Even if we did manage to escape the Beast, we'd most likely find ourselves lost in the middle of nowhere."

As he finished speaking, the ground began to quake from Hexula's lumbering steps, and the two men promptly looked into each other's eyes. "We have no choice," Ignatus said. "Let's find our way up through these branches and cross the bridge. It may well be our only hope."

When Malgyron finally brought Cidivus to the Northern Mountains, he placed him near the stone wall overlooking the Fire Below. Cidivus was in awe of the sight, and Malgyron immediately noticed the fear in his eyes. As Cidivus turned, he found himself surrounded by the Colubri and the Surnia, all of whom had assembled there to meet their master. Cerastes slithered forward and let out a contemptuous hiss, after which Cidivus backed up against the wall, his facial expression filled with terror.

"Fear not, dear king," Malgyron said. "We are your friends, your allies in this war that has now begun. I know you are distressed over losing the battle to defend your throne. But as I told you, another army is rising. It is an army that will be invincible, and crush our enemies to dust beneath our feet. Though the battle has been lost, the war will be won. We need only be patient. In the meantime, it is imperative that we keep you safe. That is why I brought you here. We will prepare a dwelling place for you in a nearby cave, and the Surnia will bring you food and water when you need it. You have nothing to worry about. The day will come when you can reclaim your throne and be crowned king once again."

Though he wanted to feel secure, Cidivus couldn't help but be leery of his newfound allies. Something inside just told him that there was more to this story, and that Malgyron was holding back information. But he had no choice in the matter. He was stuck up in the mountains, with no horse and thus no means of finding his way back to Mavinor. Even if he did have a mode of transportation and returned to his homeland, he'd have no way of reclaiming his kingship on his own. Mavinor's army had been defeated, and with the people having rebelled against him, they would almost certainly execute him upon his return. Cidivus' only option was to trust Malgyron and hope that he really did have his best interests in mind. Thus he went along with what had been proposed, accompanying Cerastes as he slinked away to show him his new living quarters. Malgyron smiled as he watched him go, reveling in the fact that his plan was coming together, and that it was only a matter of time before he claimed his rightful place as the King of Darkness.

When Cedrus and the others returned to the palace, they brought the tribunes to the dungeon and locked them away. While walking through the corridors, they peeked in through the doors and realized that the scribes and priests had been imprisoned. Cedrus retrieved the keys to their respective cells from the hooks where they hung and released the prisoners, finally bringing about an end to their plight. "Let's get you cleaned up and fed," Cedrus said.

He brought them to where they could bathe and asked them to come upstairs after they were done. Then Cedrus led the others up to the throne room, where they found Aramus and Talmik waiting. "We need to talk," Cedrus said as he entered. "There is much to discuss."

"Not the least of which is the whereabouts of my brother," Arcala said. "Where is he?"

Aramus and Talmik looked into each other's eyes for a moment before Aramus began to speak. "He has left Mavinor," Aramus said. "Cidivus was going to execute him, but he was saved thanks to the efforts of Talmik, Ignatus, and Tarsus."

"Thank you, Talmik," Arcala said.

"It was the least I could do," Talmik replied.

"Did you say they were aided by Tarsus?" Cedrus asked, incredulous.

"Yes…Tarsus," Aramus said. "He has had a conversion, and is on our side now. He claims to have had a vision of Gobius, a vision in which the king assigned him tasks to complete."

Cedrus got chills when he heard that Tarsus also had a vision of Gobius. "Where did he and Ignatus go?" Cedrus asked.

"They accompanied Solitus on a journey to some kind of cavern," Aramus said. "Solitus told us that it is The Author's will that he enter this cavern to locate an object of great importance."

"The Cavern of Trials," Minstro said. "It is the Ivory Sabre that he seeks."

"In which direction did they ride?" Arcala asked.

"North, toward the Tenebrae," replied Aramus.

Only then did it occur to Cedrus that the Cavern of Trials was actually the cave that he, Nomis, and Cidivus had entered during the quest. He recalled how Tonitrus opposed the idea of him entering, and how his brother scolded him when he raced back out, clearly scared out of his wits. He then realized that the feelings of sheer terror that caused each of them to panic and exit the cave could be attributed to the fact that none of them were destined to be there. Only the one whose destiny it was to enter the cavern could do so, and that one was Solitus.

"Why were the priests and scribes imprisoned?" Cedrus then asked.

"Cidivus did all he could to eradicate our faith during his short reign," Aramus said. "He destroyed the temples, forced Albertus to remove all references to The Author and The Scrolls at the Academy, and even tortured and killed Legentis for refusing to tell him where Cantos kept the tome that contained all the material recovered from The Scrolls."

They all hung their heads in sadness when they heard the news. "Know that The Scrolls are at least safe," Cedrus said. "Cantos trusted the tome to Bovillus. He is in Xamnon working tirelessly to locate more material."

"Speaking of which, perhaps we should now send for him and Magdala," Arcala stated.

"I will send two of my men to Xamnon," Antiugus chimed in. "They will bring them both back to Mavinor."

"Thank you, Antiugus," Cedrus said.

"What of Tarmin and the believers in Mavinor's army?" Arcala asked. "I was looking out for him on the battlefield in the hope that he and his men would turn on Sicarius and side with us in the fight."

"They are all gone," Aramus said. "They were exiled, and I'm not even sure where Sicarius took them."

"No!" Arcala shouted in disgust.

"Is there anything else we should be aware of?" Cedrus asked.

"Just know that terrible things have happened since Cidivus claimed the throne," Aramus said. "He even executed two youths for pilfering food in the town square, and when the people rebelled and tried to stop the execution, he had Sicarius and his men slaughter most of them. It was I who incited the rebellion, for there were no other options. But a spy must have revealed that the insurrection was going to take place that morning, as our citizens walked right into a trap."

"Not a surprise," Minstro said. "We know how they did it."

"How?" Aramus asked.

"The Colubri," Minstro replied. "There were serpents sneaking in and out of both Mavinor and Xamnon, gathering information and sharing it with the other side. Had we not found and killed the one spying on us at Xamnon's palace, then Cidivus and Sicarius might well have known about our plan before we could execute it."

"Whatever has happened?" Talmik asked. "The skies have been perpetually darkened, the weather has grown cold, and now we have serpents spying on us and winged monsters dropping from the sky, even into the Praetorium."

"A winged monster came to the Praetorium?" Cedrus asked.

"Yes," Talmik said. "Sicarius betrayed Cidivus and was actually going to have him executed in the Praetorium, but a beast unlike anything we ever saw came to save him. It had horns on its head, wings, and a long, pointed tail, along with one of the most grotesque faces I have ever laid eyes upon."

"Malgyron," Minstro replied.

"So it was Malgyron who saved Cidivus," Cedrus said.

"It makes perfect sense," Henricus said. "Didn't Bovillus say that he needs the traitor in order to carry out his plan?"

"Yes, he did," Cedrus said. "Cidivus is but a pawn and doesn't even realize it."

"I wonder where he took him," Arcala asked.

"I don't know, but mark my words," Cedrus said, "I will find him!"

"What is this plan you speak of?" Aramus asked.

"Aramus and Talmik, I'm afraid that our entire world is in mortal danger," Cedrus said. He went on to explain to them Bovillus' findings, as well as the prophecies of the Seers of Fate. Both Aramus and Talmik immediately became very distraught when they heard how the fate of the world was now hanging in the balance.

There was a knock on the door, and when Talmik went over to open it he saw the priests and scribes standing before him. "Come in," he said.

"Talmik, give them something to eat," Cedrus called out from across the room. "They must be starving."

"Of course," Talmik replied. He then went to the palace kitchen to prepare a meal for them. As the priests and scribes were seated at the table, a guard entered from the corridor and escorted Volara into the room.

"Volara, did you see the Beast?" Cedrus asked.

"No," she replied. "There was no sign of the Beast or the raven in Urmina."

"Where could they have gone?" Minstro asked.

"Most likely the Tenebrae or the Eastern Woodlands," Volara answered. "Chaelim and Apteris split up to explore both areas. I wanted to come back and relay the information to you before going out to search myself."

"What if the Beast is already marching toward Xamnon?" Antiugus asked.

"No," Volara said. "I went out to examine the plain between Mavinor and Xamnon, and again there was no sign of her. You are all safe for now. Wait for the three of us to return before you formulate any other plans."

"Very well," Antiugus said. "We will be waiting right here."

With that Volara left them. Aramus then came up alongside Cedrus and told him about the miracle of Rovenica's veil. "You have to see it, Cedrus," Aramus said. "The image on the veil is a perfect reflection of King Gobius' face."

The tribune expected that Cedrus would be excited to hear the news, but his words did nothing to lift the young man's spirits. Cedrus just stood there staring into space, his eyes conveying the deep sadness he felt in his heart.

"Where were they buried?" Cedrus asked.

"I had Gobius interred in a tomb and placed it inside the mausoleum he built to honor Thaddeus, Nomis, and Alphaeus," Aramus answered. "The others were cremated by Cidivus, but I managed to collect their ashes into separate urns, all of which were later engraved with their insignia and placed on the altar in the mausoleum."

"Thank you," Cedrus said. He began leaving the room as the others looked on.

"Where are you going?" Minstro shouted.

"To the mausoleum," Cedrus replied. "But I must go alone. Please respect my wish."

No one budged as they watched him depart, understanding his need to privately mourn over the remains of his king, his friends, and his brother.

Chapter Twenty-Five

Tarsus and Ignatus stepped forward on their mounts and trotted over to the first large branch. They directed their horses to make a short leap and land on the huge limb, which they managed to do without too much difficulty. Then they scrambled up past another branch, then another and another. It took a while, but eventually they made it over the rim of the tree trunk and began to cross.

Hexula continued to plow through the forest in pursuit of her quarry. Trees fell to either side as the Beast cut her path, leaving nothing behind but wreckage and ruin. Though she was still far behind Tarsus and Ignatus, the pounding of the earth from every one of her steps shook the remnant of The Great Tree. This made the crossing far more difficult for both of them. Tarsus managed to calm the black and successfully guide it beyond the halfway point. But when he looked back, he saw Ignatus and his mount standing completely still.

"Ignatus, hurry!" Tarsus yelled.

Ignatus stared straight ahead, but he neither saw Tarsus nor heard his cries. All that he heard was the ear-splitting whinny of a frightening warhorse, and the only thing he saw was a vision of a cavalier wearing red armor, riding straight toward him as he unsheathed a massive sword.

Suddenly Ignatus finds himself in a valley of some sort, and no longer realizes that he is walking across the Black Hollow. When he turns to flee from the cavalier who is seemingly pursuing him, he quickly finds himself surrounded by three others, clothed in black, gray, and pale armor respectively. There is nowhere for him to run, and thus nothing to do but stand and fight.

Ignatus draws his sword and looks back toward the red horseman. He sees that he has now dismounted and is walking toward Ignatus. Ignatus drops down from the saddle as well, and then he grabs his shield, preparing to face off with his new adversary. The two of them circle one another for some time, feeling each other out and looking for a weakness that could possibly be exposed. Ignatus eyes the incredible length and breadth of his opponent's sword, and knows right away that he will be at a disadvantage. But his courage does not waver. Boldly Ignatus holds out his shield as the cavalier rears back and takes a mighty swing. Then just as the sword is about to crash against the sunburst emblazoned on Ignatus' shield...

Everything around him seemingly disappeared. Ignatus came to and found Tarsus right alongside him, holding his right arm and shaking him forcibly. "Ignatus, wake up!" Tarsus yelled.

Immediately Ignatus felt the bridge rocking back and forth, and heard the roar of the Beast's approach. Only then did he remember where he was, and as the fog cleared from his mind he nodded toward his companion. "Let's go!" he said.

The time lost due to Ignatus' sudden submersion into a hypnotic state allowed the Beast to gain ground. The quaking from her steps was now causing the bridge to rattle and roll, and it spooked the horses. Tarsus and Ignatus did what they could to still them and guide them the rest of the way. But just as they nearly made it all the way across, an errant breeze kicked up, and both men were almost pried from their saddles. Tarsus was forced to clutch the mane of his black when his left hand came off the reins, while Ignatus leaned forward and placed his arms around the neck of his mount. Somehow they were both able to hang on as the horses carried them beyond the final stretch, and as they finally reached the other side, they started examining the branches of the tree to find a way down from the bridge.

When the Beast finally came to the Black Hollow, she did something that neither Ignatus nor Tarsus could have anticipated. She stepped up onto the tree trunk with her gigantic claw and dug into the wood. Then she vaulted herself upward and managed to get her other foreleg onto the bridge, after which she tried to pull up the rest of her body. Hexula had trouble getting her hind legs all the way up, and as she scratched and clawed to get a grip on the trunk, it looked as if she might fall off. But just as it appeared that she would fail in her attempt, the Beast hauled her entire weight onto the bridge, causing it to shimmy back and forth. "I think that's our cue to flee," Tarsus said.

"This way!" Ignatus said.

Now that Hexula was crawling across the bridge, it trembled even more violently than it had as she approached it. Thus as the mounts of Tarsus and Ignatus cautiously descended through the branches, the vibrations caused the limbs to shift. On more than one occasion their hooves nearly slid off to the side, but the branches extended far enough from the limbs to form a railing of sorts, keeping the animals from careening off the edge.

Slowly Hexula crept across, placing one foot in front of the other. For a while it looked as though the huge tree trunk would hold and enable her to make it to the other side. But as she advanced further and further, the bridge struggled to support her weight. Her great width made it hard for Hexula to balance herself, and at one point she slipped as she stepped forward with her right foreleg. The leg fell off to the side, throwing off her balance and causing her body to cant to the right. Desperately she tried to hang on, even attempting to reach around with her left foreleg and grab hold of the trunk. But the circumference was too great, and soon she found herself hanging on by the tips of her claws as they dug into the bark of the tree.

When Ignatus and Tarsus realized what was happening, they spurred their mounts in an attempt to get off the bridge before it rolled over and crushed them under its weight. They were still a good fifteen feet off the ground, and it looked as if they weren't going to make it. "Jump!" Ignatus finally said.

"Have you gone mad?" Tarsus yelled back.

"It is our only chance," Ignatus replied. Given all the years he and his mount spent hacking out alone in the woods, navigating difficult terrain and leaping over all kinds of obstacles—from logs to ditches to water—Ignatus had full confidence in the animal. He applied firm pressure with his legs and loosened the reins. Then he cajoled the horse to a side of the limb where there were no branches that might obstruct the jump. Fearless, the mount dove forward in a fluid leap and landed safely on the ground below as Ignatus clutched the mane to keep from falling. "Your turn," he shouted back toward Tarsus.

Tarsus' black displayed an equal amount of courage as it too sprung downward and landed gracefully, somehow managing to plant its front legs firmly enough to support the rest of its body as the weight came crashing down. Now having safely crossed to the other side of the hollow, Tarsus and Ignatus gazed back into the terrifying eyes of the Beast. The dragon was struggling to hang on, sliding further and further down the side of the bridge. "We need to move before this entire tree trunk spins toward us," Ignatus said. "If we can't outrun it, then we'll either be squashed or swept out into the hollow."

"Neither is a favorable alternative," Tarsus remarked as they began to ride.

Sensing that she wasn't going to be able to pull herself back up, Hexula flared her nostrils and let out a torrent of fire toward the fleeing warriors. But Tarsus and Ignatus were too far out of reach, and the flames fell short as they barely reached the far side of the Black Hollow. With that the Beast slid off the bridge and fell deep down into the abyss, letting out a blood-curdling scream as she plunged to the bottom. When she finally landed at the base of the hollow, the earth quaked so fiercely that both Tarsus and Ignatus were nearly thrown from the saddle. Their mounts raucously brayed and flashed their hooves, as if they believed the world was about to end. But as the stillness returned, they were able to regain control and settle the horses down.

"I wonder if the dragon survived the fall," Ignatus said as he casually walked up toward the edge of the hollow and stared down.

"I don't know," Tarsus replied. "I only know that I need to keep riding north, toward the Mortuus Valley. That is where King Gobius directed me to go. I don't know what I will find there, but those were his instructions to me."

"I'm going with you," Ignatus said.

"Really?" Tarsus said, shocked at Ignatus' statement.

"Yes," Ignatus replied. "I must admit that I had my doubts when you claimed to be on our side now. But having seen the sacrifice you were willing to make in order for Solitus to safely reach the cavern, I know now that your loyalty is not in question. I can't allow you to go alone, Tarsus. Something inside is telling me that my fate is somehow intertwined with yours, and that I am destined to accompany you on your journey."

"It will be an honor, Ignatus," Tarsus said.

"Good, then let's get going," Ignatus said.

"There is just one thing I must ask you though," replied Tarsus. "What happened on the bridge? What caused you to stop halfway across, nearly costing us our lives in the process?"

"I don't know exactly what happened," Ignatus said. "But I'll gladly tell you about what I experienced as we journey north, together." With that they directed their mounts north, settling into a leisurely trot as they began to form a bond with one another.

From a distance, high up in a tree on the other side of the hollow, the raven witnessed everything. It sensed a peaceful stillness in the air as the tremors from the Beast's fall died down. For a moment, it almost felt like it did before the onset of the Age of Darkness. There was a certain calmness that had been missing for so long, and it soothed the creature right up until the silence was broken by the sound of Apteris' voice.

"There you are," Apteris said. "We have been looking all over for you. What in The Author's name has happened?"

"The Beast has fallen!" the raven answered.

"Where?" Apteris asked. "Into the Black Hollow?"

"Yes! Into the Black Hollow!" the raven shouted.

"Thank The Author," Apteris said as he peered down into the pit. He tried to spot her, but it was simply too dark to see anything. "I wonder if she is still alive."

"Don't know," the raven said.

"Come now, my friend. Let us return to Mavinor," Apteris replied.

Cedrus rode the unicorn to the mausoleum and stared beyond the gate at the entrance to the magnificent, marble structure. He was slow to dismount, and the unicorn quickly sensed it. She whickered softly, as if whispering something to him. Though he ignored her at first, she eventually got his attention. He realized now what she was doing. She could feel his grief, his enormous sense of loss over the death of the men he loved more than anyone else. The unicorn saw that he was almost afraid to enter, afraid to look upon their remains and acknowledge the fact that they were gone. She lowered her head and began to nuzzle his arm, almost trying to nudge him in the direction of the mausoleum. Finally Cedrus took a deep breath and started walking toward the gate.

After taking his first step, the sound of hoofbeats caught him off-guard and caused him to immediately turn around. From a distance Cedrus could see that Aramus was approaching on horseback, and he was none too pleased about it given his request for solitude.

"Why have you come?" Cedrus asked as Aramus arrived. "I told you that I needed some time alone."

"I understand," Aramus said. "But I forgot to give you the key to the mausoleum. After I placed the urns with the ashes of your brother and the others on the altar, I feared what might happen given the climate in our kingdom. So I had the door to the mausoleum secured, though from now on it should be safe to leave it open."

"I see," Cedrus said. He then extended his palm so that Aramus could give him the key. As he handed it over to him, Aramus couldn't help but notice Cedrus' somber demeanor.

"I know that you have suffered a greater loss than the rest of us, Cedrus," Aramus said. "But know that your kingdom needs you, now more than ever. Do not lose heart in this struggle."

"I won't," Cedrus said. "I almost did, but since then I have seen the light, all thanks to her." Cedrus turned and stroked the unicorn as he finished speaking.

"Good," Aramus said, "for while the battle to reclaim Mavinor is over, the crusade against darkness has just begun." With that he rode off and left Cedrus alone with his thoughts.

Cedrus turned back toward the mausoleum and reluctantly walked through the gate. When he strode up to the door, he paused for just a moment before inserting the key to open the lock. "What will it be like to look upon my king one last time?" he thought. "How will I react when I see the urns on the altar, especially the one that holds the ashes of my brother?" He hadn't experienced such loss since his parents died when he was a boy. Now all the emotions he felt on that fateful day when he and Tonitrus had buried their mother and father were being stirred up again. The closer he came to entering the mausoleum, the more it conjured up those memories, and the harder it was to move forward. But Cedrus finally gathered himself and managed to turn the key. When he heard the click of the lock opening, Cedrus grabbed the handle and paused one last time before slowly opening the door and walking into the mausoleum. From a distance, the unicorn watched as Cedrus disappeared inside and the door slowly shut behind him.

About the Author

John DeFilippis was born on March 9, 1970 in Bayonne, New Jersey. He grew up in the Greenville section of Jersey City, graduating from Our Lady of Mercy Grammar School in 1984. In 1988 he graduated from Saint Peter's Prep and went on to study at Rutgers College in New Brunswick, New Jersey. After earning his Bachelor of Science degree, Dr. DeFilippis attended the School of Theology at Seton Hall University for three years, from 1993 to 1996. During this time he earned his master's degree in theology and discerned a call to the Catholic priesthood. After ultimately deciding that he did not have a religious vocation, Dr. DeFilippis transitioned into the field of education. He taught for four years at both the elementary and secondary levels, and earned a second master's degree in educational administration. In 2000 Dr. DeFilippis made yet another transition, this time accepting an offer to become an academic administrator at Saint Peter's University in Jersey City. He would spend the next seven years there, and in 2007 he completed his Ph.D. in educational leadership at Seton Hall University. After finishing his doctoral degree, he accepted an offer to become a director in the Division of

Academic Affairs at New Jersey City University.

But through all the years of earning graduate degrees, teaching, and working in educational administration, Dr. DeFilippis never lost sight of his childhood dream. That dream was to become a published author. He loved writing, and he also loved fantasy stories as a child, especially those that contained courageous warriors, epic quests, and fierce monsters. Inspired by epic stories such as *The Hobbit*, *The Lord of the Rings*, and *Jason and the Argonauts*, Dr. DeFilippis began to use his free time to formulate ideas for his own series of fantasy novels. Over the course of several years, he developed detailed outlines and finally reached the point where he was ready to start writing. But balancing a full-time administrative position with part-time teaching and doctoral studies made it all but impossible to find the time. That all changed in July of 2010, when Dr. DeFilippis lost his job during the economic recession. Determined to turn a negative into a positive, he used his abundance of free time during his unemployment to focus on his novel. By April of 2011, the first draft of the book was complete. After having it edited for content, Dr. DeFilippis began marketing his novel to literary agents. But soon he discovered how cold, callous, and cut-throat the literary business could be. After enduring over 100 rejections, he refused to give up on his dream. Finally David Niall Wilson of Crossroad Press decided to take a chance on *The Quest of the Thirteen*, and in 2012 the dream was finally fulfilled.

Today, Dr. DeFilippis resides in Nutley, New Jersey. He is a devout conservative Catholic, and an avid supporter of religious freedom in an age of growing secularism. In his spare time, Dr. DeFilippis enjoys working out at the gym, watching sports (mainly his beloved New York Yankees, New York Giants, and Notre Dame Fighting Irish), fantasy football, taking walks in the park (especially when dealing with writer's block), going to the beach, and of course, writing. With the first three volumes in The Medallion of Mavinor series complete, Dr. DeFilippis has turned his attention to the fourth and final volume, to be titled *The Last of the Thirteen*. As the fate of the world hangs in the balance, the epic struggle between good and evil will finally reach its climax and be resolved once and for all.

Author's Website: www.drjohndefilippis.com
Author's e-mail: drjohnd@drjohndefilippis.com

Curious about other Crossroad Press books?
Stop by our site:
http://store.crossroadpress.com
We offer quality writing
in digital, audio, and print formats.

Enter the code FIRSTBOOK
to get 20% off your first order from our store!
Stop by today!

CPSIA information can be obtained at www.ICGtesting.com
Printed in the USA
BVOW01s0018200215

388397BV00001B/1/P